The Damascened Blade

Also by Barbara Cleverly

The Last Kashmiri Rose
Ragtime in Simla

THE DAMASCENED BLADE

Barbara Cleverly

CARROLL & GRAF PUBLISHERS
New York

Carroll & Graf Publishers
An imprint of Avalon Publishing Group, Inc.
245 West 17th Street
NY 10011-5300
www.carrollandgraf.com

First published in hardback in the UK by Constable,
an imprint of Constable & Robinson Ltd 2003

First published in the USA in hardback by Carroll & Graf 2004

Reprinted 2004

ISBN 0-7867-1333-X

Printed and bound in the EU

Library of Congress Cataloging-in-Publication Data
is available on file.

To the memory of Great Uncle
Brigadier Harold Richard Sandilands, DSO,
Légion d'honneur, Corona d'Italia,
5th (Northumberland) Fusiliers
1876–1961

General Officer Commanding, Peshawar District,
North-West Frontier Province, India
1927–32

Foreword

Coming to the end of this novel, in August 2001, I wondered how many readers would be familiar with the setting – the North-West Frontier Province of the Indian Empire – or even its neighbour, Afghanistan. How many had heard of its fiercely independent inhabitants, the Pathan? Sadly, after the events in New York and the subsequent tracking down of suspected terrorists to Afghanistan, our television screens are filled with stark images: bleak khaki hills, precipitous mountain passes, bearded and hawk-like faces shouting defiance, sinewy hands clutching Kalashnikovs, and with foreboding I read again Disraeli's judgement: 'The soil is barren and unproductive. The country is intersected by stupendous mountains where an army must be exposed to absolute annihilation. The people are proverbially faithless.'

And I fear that coming events may once again prove the truth of this. Alexander the Great, the Moghul emperors, the Sikhs, the British, the Russians have all left graves behind in these hills. Is it about to happen again? But then another quotation comes to mind. The Indian Viceroy, Lord Curzon, in 1904 said: 'No man who has read a page of Indian history will ever prophesy about the frontier.'

Prophesy? I wouldn't dare. But this story may well conjure up something of the character of the land and its people which seem to me to remain unchanged through the centuries.

B.C.

Chapter One

India, 1910

'This isn't human country! It was never meant that anyone should be here, stand, sit or walk here. This isn't country worth fighting for. Leave it to bake in the summer, freeze in the winter; leave it to bury its dead or not even to bury its dead – leave them to bleach away to nothing in the sun. What did Bismarck say? "Not worth the good bones of one Pomeranian grenadier." He was thinking of the Balkans or some other God-forsaken part of Europe but it's even more true of this part of India. The North-West bloody Frontier! Not worth the bones of a single gallant native Scout. Not worth the bones of a Sandhurst-trained British officer. *My* bones! A subaltern, who has – dammit – only been in this foul oven for two weeks.'

The serrated and crumbling mountains, grey with hideous old age, black with seams of basalt, were empty, sterile and useless. Empty? Not quite. In the middle distance a lonely signal flag was frantically wagging. All the watching officers turned their binoculars on this. Someone read it off. *Under attack. Carrying wounded. Three dead. Can you help?*

The Colonel turned to his second-in-command. 'Send this, Neil,' he said, '*Stand by to retreat on the Tit. Await my signal. Will cover you.*' He paused for a moment. With urgent speed the signal flag swished beside him in the hands of his second-in-command. 'Have they got that?' he asked anxiously.

'Yes, sir, they acknowledge.'

'Now send, *Abandon the dead*.' The signal flag swished again at his side. 'And add, *Don't abandon wounded*.'

Paddy Brownlow out there commanding the beleaguered patrol would know how to translate that – 'Bring them in if you can – shoot them if you can't.' Any British officer falling into the hands of the Afridi would, without question, be tortured to death. A process which would generally be extended to cover two full days especially if the women came down to join in the fun, and the same fate awaited any Hindu soldiery who might have the bad luck to fall into enemy hands.

'They acknowledge, sir.'

'In that case, Neil, send *Retreat* and open covering fire on the ridge . . . now!'

The three twin Lewis guns burst into a wild and deafening rattle of sound. Chips of stone began to fly and whine away from the ridge. Surely nothing could live in that?

The little temple, derisively designated 'the Tit' by the British, stood half-way between the relieving force and the retreating men. A swelling dome surmounted by a blunt pinnacle, it was aptly named. The Colonel was only reasonably confident. Out there were thirty men carrying wounded under fire, doubtless running short of water, exhausted by three days in action with half a mile of country to cover and only the fragile support of his advancing relief force. But at least they'd picked up his signal and the scrambling retreat had started. Had started according to a well-worn formula: a practised leap-frog, one unit to lay back and give covering fire while another passed back through them to lay back in its turn. Orderly. Safe. Well-tried.

The Colonel turned to Neil. 'Take over here, Neil, will you? I'm going in with the chaps. Just for once.' His eye lighted on the young subaltern standing by. 'You, Jock? Want to get a closer look at the Afridi? Come on then!'

At the double, the relieving force spread out across the naked hills under the cover of the three Lewis guns. Neil

10

watched them with agonized pride. This was where months of practice bore fruit. How many times had they in the familiar hills around the fort attacked, defended and retreated from various familiar features? Here, though, was grim reality.

The two forces met in the shadow of the Tit. Seamed and cracked, shattered indeed by a hundred baking summers and a hundred frozen winters, little of the Tit but its dome remained to suggest that this once had been the peaceful abode of God in these hills. What must once have been a placid statement now provided at least a sketchy shelter for the relieving force to combine with the desperate patrol.

After a little congratulatory back-slapping and sighs of relief as the two units mingled, a careful roll was called. 'Let's enter up the scoreboard,' said the Colonel. 'Let's make sure who's here and who isn't before we move. Hurry though. I don't want to stay here longer than necessary.'

The word came back to him – 'Four Scouts killed and five walking wounded if we get a move on. Jackie's badly hit but I think we can move him along between us.' And then after a long pause, 'Harry's missing.'

'Anyone know what happened to Harry?'

'Last I saw of him, he was strapping up Jackie's shoulder. He was supposed to be behind us. Oh, Lord! I know what happened to him, poor sod! Got cut off and had to come back up the black nullah. Had to climb a cliff face.'

'Anybody with him? You! Ahmad!' The Colonel switched easily to Pushtu and continued, 'Did you see what happened?'

It emerged that the three men who'd been with him had succeeded in negotiating the cliff face, one slightly wounded, one slashed across the face by a flying chip of stone. But Harry had been hit climbing the cliff and had fallen to its foot. He'd been shot through the shoulder and

11

one arm was useless. He'd broken his leg in two places falling down the cliff.

Harry had tried to move but he couldn't get his limbs to obey him. In his trouser pocket was a cyanide pill but he couldn't reach it. With years of experience of the frontier behind him he understood the situation in all its stark reality. If he was lucky he was within a few hours of death; if he was unlucky, within a few days. Uncomplicated, honourable and kind-hearted, Harry was well liked by all and loved by his men. The Pathan troopers he commanded were as uncomplicated as himself. They had no question at all as to what they should do. Slinging their rifles across their shoulders, they were already forming up to go straight back in and get him out but the Colonel took one further look at the terrain. Harry lay at the end of a narrow defile, thirty feet wide at the most at its base, overlooked on both sides by towering cliffs and by Afridi, each commanding a wide field of fire through which a rescuing force would need to pass. It was a lethal option.

'I'm going to have to give the order.'

He did.

'Leave it!' he said. 'Leave it! Prepare to fall back.'

Jock mopped his red face. His hands were shaking and his eyes unfocused with remembered terror at the mad forward dash. 'Bloody country!' He said it again to himself. 'Who wants the bloody place? And these people? Leave them, for Christ's sake, to kill each other as they always have and as soon as possible!'

He squinted up at the hills. Was he imagining it or had the enemy fire subsided? It was nearly dusk and the dark fell abruptly in these hills. Had they given up for the day and gone home to their tea? Not willing to answer back to the Lewis guns probably. He'd heard the Afridi, like all Pathan tribesmen, were clever tacticians, brave mountain fighters certainly – none braver – but they were careful and knew when to retreat. They had the skill to disappear into

12

the hills as silently as they had arrived. Save your men and bullets to fight another day was their policy. He listened hopefully. Yes, that's probably what they were doing. Getting out while the going was still good. It's what he would have done himself.

The men had fallen silent and were obeying the Colonel's command to prepare to withdraw back to the original position half a mile away, from where they could, under cover of darkness, make it back the five miles to their base at Fort Hamilton. Wounded were being tended, stretcher bearers were falling in.

The stillness was shattered by a thin and wavering scream. Rigid with fear, Jock said, 'For God's sake! What was that?' His fellow officers couldn't meet his eye. 'What the hell was that?' he asked again.

'That was Harry,' said one of them at last.

The scream was repeated again and again and again. The shrill note changed abruptly to a bubbling gurgle. The silent company went methodically about their business, flinging an occasional stony glance at their commander. But for Jock, disgusted terror and helplessness were turning to furious rage. He'd only met him short days ago but Harry had been kind to him from the moment of his arrival at the fort on attachment to the Scouts, welcoming, encouraging, joking and now in the throes of a hideous death. The subaltern was a Scotsman. He was, moreover, a hill man himself, a stalker by upbringing and, reared on tales of ancestral gallantry, he had considered himself a match for anyone. The cry – the despairing cry from the gathering darkness – was heard again and was now accompanied by shouts of laughter muffled by distance but ribald and derisive.

It was too much for Jock. He cast a calculating eye on the progress of the well-drilled movements around him then began to inch away and disappeared into the shadows. Fuelled with rage and hatred he set off into the hills, remembering the terrain which he had surveyed earlier in the day, marking down occasional remembered land-

13

marks, using the jagged country, exploiting skills acquired from a boyhood in the Trossachs. He advanced as fast as caution would let him towards the deadly defile at the bottom of which Harry lay agonizing, his screams now loud beyond bearing, even his sobs audible.

No one shot at him from the crags above. Could it be that they had all climbed down to watch the entertainment? Crouching behind a boulder he checked his pistol and felt the handle of the skian dhu that he wore, up till then as a gesture of bravado, in his sock, preparing for his assault. Red battle rage, the rage of his Pictish ancestors was burning in him, and his hands which in the race under fire to the Tit had been shaking and uncontrolled were now steady and purposeful. A creeping shadow amongst the shadows of the ravine, he inched his way forward until he had a view of the scene under a cliff overhang.

Two tall turbaned figures bent with relish over the body lying between them on the ground. Knives flashed in their hands and Harry groaned. Laughing, one of them strolled to a thorn bush and broke off a twig. Jock's stomach churned. He knew what they were doing. And he'd dismissed it as an old soldier's story told to frighten the new recruits. The death of a thousand cuts. With special Pathan refinements. Into each cut they were grinding grass and thorns. His sharp eyes swept the area with calculation. Only two men. Why only two? Why had these two been left behind the general retreat? Were they volunteers? Specialists? The night shift left in charge with orders to prolong the death until daylight when they could all muster and enjoy it?

He waited until they were absorbed in their handling and insertion of the thorns with the accompanying screams from their victim, timing his rush for the moment of greatest distraction. They didn't hear his soft footfall. The skian dhu caught one of them from behind in the heart ribs and the second looked up aghast to hear words he did not understand spat at him by a red-haired, white-faced devil. 'E'en do and spare not!' the Highlander hissed and he

14

plunged his dagger into the tribesman's neck. His severed throat spouting, the second fell across the body of his comrade.

'Harry! Harry! They're done for! It's me, Jock.'

He peered hopelessly down at the naked, shattered body. He was too late. But no. The eyes fluttered open and, he was certain, recognized him. Harry tried to speak but gurgled and choked as a rush of blood, black in the failing light, poured down his chin. They'd torn out his tongue and there was only one way he could get his message through to the horrified young face bending over him. He nodded and tried to smile with his eyes and then, unmistakable to Jock, came the message. The eyes slid down to Jock's gun and remained fixed there.

'Right. Right. I understand. Leave it to me. And, look here – if I get back, I'll say all the right things to those who need to hear them. No need to distress anyone.' He glanced at the broken, tortured body and added, 'I can imagine what you'd want me to say.'

The pain-glazed eyes looked up again at Jock's face and blinked in relief. Tearing a crucifix on a leather thong from around his neck, Jock thrust it into Harry's palm and closed his hand over it. 'Rest in peace, my friend,' said Jock and he put his Browning pistol to Harry's head.

There was one more thing his intense rage pushed him to do before he left the scene. Pulling up the baggy dirty shirt of the second man he'd killed he took his knife and, in a few swift strokes, he slashed letters into the dead flesh.

With infinite care and guile, Jock began to track his way back along the defile. He had gone perhaps fifty yards when his stretched senses sounded a warning. A glint of dying sunlight on metal high up above his head made him throw himself sideways. As he did the crash of an exploding musket echoed down the canyon and shot showered past him. A jezail? Was that an old-fashioned jezail? Who

15

the hell would be firing such a thing? The Afridi were all equipped – God knows how – with bolt-action rifles to match the Scouts' own. He'd been told that in these mountain passes thousands of British men, women and children fleeing from Afghanistan had been pinned down and massacred by just such guns. But that had been seventy years ago.

The silence and the darkness bore down on him and, the last of his courage ebbing fast, the terror of the hunted was taking its place. He ran, weaving and galloping like a hare, the sting of several ricochet wounds in his arms and shoulders urging him on.

At the Tit all was ready for the ordered retreat back to Fort Hamilton.

'Where's that new chap? Jock, is it? Anyone seen him? Someone tell him this is no time to sneak off for a pee! Wouldn't like to hear he'd got his cock shot off! He's what! When? Bloody hell! Why didn't someone . . .?'

'Sir! Sir! Look! Over there – three o'clock – that's Jock. He's coming in now! Running for it!'

Chapter Two

April 1922
Lily Coblenz was in a foul mood. She'd been in a foul mood for about a month. She could hardly remember the excitement with which she had embarked on her so long anticipated Indian vacation. She could only contrast her high expectations with the drab realities. Here she was where she had longed to be. India. Simla and the swirling glamour of a Viceregal Spring Ball. But really – she might as well have never left Chicago! Apart from the accents (and to her occasionally they still sounded cute enough) she could have been at any grand party at home on Lakeshore Drive. The men were the same, the clothes were the same; the same brilliantined hair, the same little moustaches. Even the food was scarcely different and the drink not different at all. But at least that was something to be grateful for! She took another appreciative sip of the perfectly chilled 1915 Krug and looked petulantly round the room.

Where were the turbaned men and veiled women, the exotic, unrecognizable instruments sketching an arabesque of sound unseen behind fretted shutters? She listened with resentment to the careful discourse of a refined string band playing another foxtrot and looked with disfavour at the white ties and white waistcoats, the long white gloves and pearl necklaces. 'It'll all be different when you get to Simla,' people had said. 'That's where the action is!' But where had that long, uncomfortable journey landed her? A change of address but a change of very little else. She had expected domes and minarets, mystery and romance, but Viceregal Lodge – built in the 1880s – was no more than some bygone architect's careful and ponderous essay in the Elizabethan manner and there was plenty of that to be seen back home.

Edward Dalrymple-Webster surreptitiously extracted his watch from his waistcoat pocket. Ten o'clock. At least two more hours to go. Two more hours making conversation to this sulky girl. Two more hours desperately trying to elicit a response. 'Get alongside, old boy!' Nick Carstairs had said. 'See what you can do! Tell you what – lure her out into the garden – I'll switch off the lights and switch on the nightingale, what! And the rest is up to you.'

'Beautiful girl,' someone else had said. 'Pots and pots of tin! Greatest heiress in the world bar three, they say.'

Well, rich, certainly. There was no denying that – but beautiful? Fair hair just a shade too far on the brown side to count as blonde, he would have thought. Thick and silky but cut fashionably short. And her eyes: large and lustrous but where one looked for an innocent shade of Anglo-Saxon blue one encountered an indeterminate green which could one moment rival the English Channel on a bad day and the next skewer a chap like a shard of green glass. Clever eyes that could express anything, apparently, with the exception of proper modesty.

He had done his best. He ran a finger round the inside of his collar which was damply collapsing. He had a spare collar, in fact he had two, but he wasn't quite sure if he could be bothered to change. Desperately he tried again. What other topics were there? Polo? The weather? The heat? The clothes? The quaint natives? The scenery? Polo? He had exhausted, he felt, all available topics.

'Where next?' he asked with a bright smile and a show of passionate interest. Dash it – who cared where this blasted girl went next so long as it was nothing to do with him! No reply. He tried again. 'Where next?'

She turned a cold eye on him. 'I beg your pardon?' she said.

How he wished she wouldn't say 'I beg your pardon?' to everything he offered.

'Where? he said. 'Where are you going next?'

She looked at him balefully. 'My plans haven't changed in the last ten minutes and as I told you ten minutes ago – Peshawar.'

He caught the eye of Nick Carstairs who passed by at that moment. 'Miss Coblenz,' he said, 'is off to Peshawar!' and to his relief and gratitude, Nick Carstairs sat down beside them.

'Off to Peshawar, eh?' he said vacuously. 'Can't think why. Terrible place! Only been there once in my life . . . never want to go again. Nasty dangerous place too if you ask me! Why don't you stay here? Season's only just started. Lots going on – race meeting at Annandale tomorrow, ragtime gymkhana the next day, jolly good little operetta the chaps have put together at the Gaiety. Stay here, Miss Coblenz, this is where the action is.'

'Action' – that word again! She took another sip of champagne and glowered.

Nick was burbling on. 'There's a topping treasure hunt on Tuesday and the Mysore Lancers have a Musical Ride on Thursday. Oh, no – you won't find anything like that in Peshawar! They'd hardly let you out of the house over there and there's nothing to see if they did. You mark my words!'

Charlie Carter, police superintendent, was eyeing her covertly. It had been his job to provide for her protection during her visit to Simla. An onerous task. But now, thank God, she was off to the frontier and would no longer be his responsibility. His opposite number in Peshawar could take over – and good luck to him! If they'd taken his advice (and they didn't) they would not have allowed a girl worth so very much money to be exposed to the dangers of frontier life. He had indeed said as much but behind that glamorous façade, behind those little girl good looks there was, he had discovered, a will of iron. 'I want,' she had said, 'to see the *real* India!' And, for her evidently, the real India was not in Simla.

She had seen elephants, she had seen bejewelled rajas, any of whom were inconveniently eager to make her acquaintance. She had seen the Indian Army in all its glamour and Viceregal and other balls had been laid out for her entertainment but this wasn't the India she had looked forward to. Where were the shots in the night? The murderous tribesmen sweeping down from the hills? The embattled garrisons of lonely forts? The lean, sunburnt, ruthless men with their devoted, native followers? She had understood that such things were to be found in abundance at Peshawar so to Peshawar she had determined to go.

Such was her determination that it came to the ear of Sir George Jardine. 'I'm under orders,' Sir George had said resignedly to Charlie. 'This comes down from on high and I mean as high as you can go.' He raised bushy grey eyebrows to introduce a flavour of intrigue. 'This damn girl is, I'm sorry to tell you, a sight more than a pretty face. Nothing to do with me, of course, but it's all very cloak and dagger. It all has to do with the motorization of the Indian Army. It seems the Coblenz Corporation has a mass of brand new military transport parked in depots all over the US and completely unused. It seems that the Royal Navy have half a dozen or more brand new destroyers and, with disarmament a lively topic, no conceivable use for them. There's a high level swap under negotiation and, believe it or not, the happiness of little Miss Coblenz is considered to be of some importance. Father Coblenz has come to Delhi to carry out negotiations personally and his daughter chose to accompany him. Someone told her it was the fashion to leave for the Hills when things started to get hot in the capital and her father agreed to her coming up here to grace Simla with her presence. She's nominally under the chaperonage of Lady Holland and it falls to us to make her happy. Fine state of affairs when the future of the British Empire is bound up with the holiday plans of a spoilt little halfwit. But times change. When

20

I was a lad "gunboat diplomacy" meant something rather different! But there must be something in it if the Viceroy *and* the Prime Minister . . .'

Meaningfully, his voice had died away and he had resumed, 'Someone is going to have to squire this girl into the North-West Frontier Province and, perhaps rather more importantly, safely back again!'

'For God's sake, sir,' Charlie had said in alarm, 'wherever else you look – don't look at me!'

'No?'

'No! Emphatically – no,' said Charlie. 'Whom have you in mind? Oh? What a shame! He would have been perfect but I suppose he's half-way home by now?'

Sly and plausible, Sir George took a moment or two before replying. 'Half-way home? Nothing of the sort – as well you know, Charlie! He's still got a month's leave – and, I will add, a month's richly deserved leave. In fact, it could hardly be more convenient when you consider where he has elected to spend the last few weeks.'

'Why? Where?'

'Well, you may not believe this and it's extraordinary how often these things fall into place but he is, in fact, currently in Peshawar. And why? Because a wartime friend of his, seconded to the Scouts, is commanding the fort at Gor Khatri!'

Not for the first time Charlie Carter felt a spurt of irritation at the way in which Fate played good cards into the hands of the manipulative Sir George. He had once said as much to his wife. Meg had looked at him pityingly and replied that in her opinion, if Sir George were ever to be so unwise as to play cards with Fate, you could be sure that he'd rigged the deck beforehand.

Dismissively Charlie said, 'Well, he may be perched up there in Peshawar but there's no reason to suppose he'd take this job on . . . I mean – poor old sod! – he's been trying to get home for nearly six months. He won't let you involve him *again*! Really, when all is said and done – why should he?' But even as he spoke he could hear himself

21

saying apologetically, 'Sorry, Joe! Did my best for you but – you know how it is with Sir G.'

Unaware of the plans that were being made for her future, Lily Coblenz sat amongst the debris of empty glasses, ashtrays and discarded buttonholes as the ball drew to its conclusion. An ADC appeared at her elbow. 'Sir George,' he said deferentially, 'would be delighted if he might have the next dance.'

Instantly Lily sparked up into complete wakefulness. 'Tell Sir George,' she said graciously, 'that I too would be delighted!'

She tried not to hear the sigh of relief with which Edward Dalrymple-Webster greeted this; she tried not to hear Nick Carstairs' 'Get me a brandy, Neddy. God knows I've earned it!' and with a courteous smile she allowed the ADC to escort her to Sir George's table.

Sir George watched the young woman weaving her way around the dance floor towards him. Damned little nuisance she might be but she certainly had style. He compared her confident carriage and elegant get-up with that of the other women present – mostly military and civil service wives. In her slender cream silk dress, its simplicity relieved only by a rope of black pearls (a gift, it was rumoured, from a susceptible nabob), she made the others in their pink satins, mauve tulles and raspberry chiffons look like a box of bonbons, he thought. 'Well coupled up, short back . . .' He appraised her for a moment and added, 'Nice mover!'

'Ah!' he said expansively, rising to his feet as she approached. 'You are the most elusive young woman, do you know that? I've been the whole evening trying to attract your attention – trying to hack my way through the throng of admirers. When you get to my age you don't expect preferential treatment.'

'Sir George,' said Lily firmly, 'you don't fool *me*! I've been trying to catch your eye the whole evening so it seems that we have at last both achieved our heart's limited desire!'

22

George had noticed that the girl's language veered between the two extremes of Edith Wharton heroine and Zane Grey ranch-hand. Tonight it seemed the Edith Wharton heroine was on parade and he was grateful for that.

The band moved smoothly from a foxtrot into the waltz from *The Merry Widow.* 'Just about my pace,' said Sir George comfortably, slipping a practised and surprisingly muscular arm around her shoulder. 'I can't tell you,' he said cheerfully, 'how much trouble this dotty idea of yours has landed me in! You can't imagine how close I have come to saying on more than one occasion, "Quite out of the question," because that's what everybody's been saying. But I'll cut a long story short – you leave for Peshawar tomorrow. By train. You'll be up there for a week and then you'll be back here again. I wouldn't go so far as to say I'll be *pleased* to see you but I will certainly be *relieved* to see you.'

Delighted, but not surprised to have got her own way, Lily favoured him with a flirty toss of the head and a knowing glance. 'My! Your sweet talk, Sir George, fairly makes my head spin!'

With dignity they stepped on to the floor together and Sir George resumed, 'There will be two companies of Scouts whose role is exclusively to look after you! And, further, I have arranged for you to come under the direct care and supervision of a policeman. A London policeman.'

Lily stopped in mid-swirl. 'Scouts? A London bobby? Sir George, what is this?' she said with suspicion. 'Are you going to add a London nanny and a Yeoman of the Guard too? I don't like the sound of this! Is it meant to put me off? Because I warn you – it won't!'

Sir George laughed. 'Don't get the wrong impression! When I say "Scouts", I'm not talking about little boys in knee pants doing their best to be prepared! I'm talking about the irregular forces which man the frontiers of Empire in this part of the world. Pathan other ranks, British officers . . . very tough men indeed! Best shots in the British Army, best horsemen too. They can run thirty miles under a hot sun, barrampta a village and be back in time for tiffin.'

'Carrying a mule on their back?' said Lily, unimpressed. 'If they were Texas Rangers they could!'

Sir George cleared his thoat and swept her into a tight reverse turn. 'At all events you'll find they're very businesslike. They won't stand any nonsense!'

'What do you mean by that?' asked Lily apprehensively.

'I mean what you're afraid I mean. They won't let *you* get away with anything and you'll have to do what you're told. Is that understood?'

'What I'm told? Who's going to tell me?'

'The man I just mentioned, the, er, the London bobby as you call him. The man I'm putting in charge of the whole security operation. He's an officer from Scotland Yard who just happens to be up in those parts.'

'Scotland Yard?' For a terrible moment a vision appeared before Lily of a helmeted, confidential, fatherly London Sergeant of Police, possibly with a restraining pair of handcuffs in his back pocket. 'What's the good of that? You folks have been lining up to tell me this frontier is wilder than the Wild West. What would I do with a bobby out there? I know about bobbies. He'll be armed with nothing more than his night stick! . . . This isn't going to be a stroll down Piccadilly, you know!' Lily was pleased to return in a starched English accent a phrase she had heard addressed to herself several times over the past few days.

'This chap is quite a – ah – quite what *you'd* call "a tough guy". He's Commander Joseph Sandilands, DSO, Royal Scots Fusiliers, ex-Military Intelligence.' Sir George smiled at a happy thought. 'Joe Sandilands halted the advance of the Prussian Guard for four hours. Single-handed. So – with the aforementioned companies of Scouts, of course – he should be a match for *you*!'

Chapter Three

Joe Sandilands sat at ease. The day had been spent in the company of a Scouts' patrol which he had learned to call a 'gasht'. He couldn't remember when he'd more enjoyed a day – a day spent happily in all-male company. He'd watched with admiration the meticulous precautions and the well-drilled routine. He'd admired the camaraderie between all ranks and now, at the end of the day, admired and appreciated the comforts of the fort. He was very glad to have a double gin, he was looking forward to a second. Shamefacedly he was glad to take off his boots and wished he was equipped with a pair of chaplis, the stout nailed sandals the Scouts and their officers wore. He rubbed his red-rimmed eyes and thought a pair of sun goggles would have been welcome.

Hungry, he wondered what was for dinner and if he had time for a swim in the large concrete tank which did duty for a swimming pool. His friend James Lindsay, having dismissed the gasht, came up to join him. 'Better slip along to the office, Joe, before you seize up – it seems there's a cable for you. Let me just finish here and then we'll meet for a swim. Dinner at half-past seven or thereabouts.'

And, unsuspecting, Joe went to read his cable. It was long. It ran to several pages. It was perhaps predictably from Sir George Jardine. It was friendly, it was colloquial, it was lengthy, it was unequivocal. It told him that he'd been awarded the job of looking after a demanding, irresponsible, independently minded, fabulously wealthy and totally infuriating American heiress. 'She's coming out

25

from Peshawar tomorrow and you're to welcome Miss Coblenz to the fort and show her something of the North-West Frontier, Joe. Bit of local colour and excitement, you know the sort of thing. She's looking for an experience I understand is no longer available to adventurers even in the wilder parts of her own largely now civilized country. She tells me she can "shoot like Wyatt Earp and ride like an Apache" – I wonder where she read that? – so I think it will be a sound idea to keep her well away from both guns and horses. As far as that's possible in a frontier fort, of course.'

Dumb with horror, Joe slumped on the edge of the tank, a towel round his shoulders and this terrible document in his hand, and here he was joined by James Lindsay who eyed him with curiosity.

'What's the matter, Joe? A further round of dizzying promotion? Knight Commander of the Star of the Indian Empire?'

It had been three years since they had last met but time had changed neither man and they had picked up their easy friendship without the slightest hesitation, a friendship based not only on shared memory and shared background but on something less overt, less explainable, amounting perhaps to an ability to catch each other's thoughts and moods with ease. It had not been a friendship either had expected or worked towards; it seemed to have announced itself from their first meeting.

They had met on the Western Front. James's mind went back to that pit of horror under the ridge at Passchendaele and his commanding officer's words: 'Royal Scots Fusiliers should be coming into the line on your right. Your first job is to get in touch with *them*. I can't give you any more men, you'll have to do the best you can with what you have. Don't know anything about these chaps . . . Borderers . . . Lowlanders . . . Sweepings of Glasgow . . . But they're probably all right. Look, lead this yourself. Leave Bill in command and work your way over to the right until you hit something solid. I can't say more than that but – good

26

luck! Here – before you go, have a swig of this!' And he passed across probably the most welcome drink in James's life. A silver flask in a leather case from – he noticed – Swaine, Adeney & Briggs of London but now filled with Glenfiddich, a touch of reassuring London elegance in the mud and stink.

Thus reinforced, at the head of a section, slipping, swearing and wading through the mud, he had set off into the darkness into the shower of mortar bombs and, leprously lit by flares, hoping as he turned each corner in the traverse to encounter the relieving Fusiliers, he saw at last the stolid figure of a sentry standing on the fire step. James greeted him as he turned the corner. 'Are you the Scots?' But there was no reply. He went forward and shook the man by the elbow. Faithful unto death, perhaps, but dead. James's torch illuminated a haggard face, dead for some time. But at this unpropitious moment there was at last the sound of fresh voices, there was the sticky tramp of muddy boots, and a man came into view.

James's torch caught a familiar cap badge and dwelt for a second on the identifying thistle and the swaggering motto – *Nemo me impune lacessit*. 'No one provokes me and gets away with it!' James translated and smiled as, below the cap, the light picked up black curling hair, dazzled dark eyes in a lean and smoke-blackened face, the flash of white teeth bared in a grimace against the glare of the torch. 'Can't say I haven't been warned!' James thought.

What do you say to a total stranger in a place like this? What James did say, extending a dirty hand was, 'You're a long way from the Borders?'

'Bugger the Borders!' came the reply. 'And put that bloody torch down!'

That was all they had time to say because at that moment a German mortar bomb came lumbering over the line, ricocheted from the parapet and fell straight into the trench some yards away. They dug each other out and spent the rest of that campaign fighting shoulder to shoulder and sometimes back to back, both amazed to have survived. James, the bolder of the two, came through the war unscathed. Joe, the more calculating and more careful of life whether his own or that of his men, did not. A head wound put Joe out of action for a while but not out of the war. His injury chanced to coincide with the virtual collapse of the Russian front. Bolshevik infiltration of Imperial Russian units was detected and people began to say, 'If it can happen to them it can happen to the Indian units on the Western Front. The Jerries are nothing if not skilled propagandists, you know.' And Joe found himself moved out of the shooting war and pushed in at the spearhead of the Military Intelligence operation to identify and counter the infiltration. His quick wits, his language skills and personal knowledge of the battle arena brought him success and esteem and his abilities had not gone unremarked when, after the war, he had decided to join the police force.

James had spoken lightly but, truly, he was curious to know the secret of his old friend's rapid promotion to his present eminence in the police force. He remembered the derision with which he and other friends had greeted Joe's decision to leave the army and become a policeman. ''ullo, 'ullo, 'ullo! Wot's all this 'ere, then?' they would say whenever they met Joe, and James had admired the patience with which Joe had received these sallies.

'Promotion?' said Joe, reading the cable again. 'Quite the reverse! It would appear I've been demoted to escort duties! Army Nanny? Military Gigolo? Not sure . . . What do you make of this?'

Silently Joe handed the cable to James. 'Just read this rubbish and use your wits. How the hell do I get out of this? Sir George! God Almighty! After the last round I thought he was my friend!'

'He is your friend. He's everybody's friend. Yours, mine, intimate friend of every scoundrel, eyes in the back of his head, a finger in every pie and a foot in both camps, shouldn't wonder. But he obviously has an especially high opinion of *you*. It's no secret, I think, that you were of considerable help to him down in Bengal. Cleared up that series of killings. Your reputation stretches to the limits of Empire, you see!'

Joe snorted.

'Got your man, didn't you?'

'The case was concluded successfully in the eyes of the establishment,' said Joe carefully. 'And that's as much as I can say, even to you, James. My hands were tied with red tape and I was gagged with a wad of moral blackmail. The Empire was served but not Justice.'

'Oh, I say! Less said, the better, eh? And then he sent you off up to the Simla hills to cool off?'

'Ostensibly. He shot me straight into a year-old unsolved murder that had been nagging at him and this was followed the minute I arrived by a second similar killing. Before you ask – yes, I solved that one too. Though "solved" is perhaps an overstatement. The killer is known to me and to Sir George but, the demands of diplomacy perpetually overriding those of justice in India, I'm afraid there's a murderer still at large in the country.'

'That wouldn't suit Honest Joe!'

'No. It's not white as the untrodden snow in England but at least I know what the rules are and so do the villains. George has a compulsion to find out the truth – oh, yes, he likes to know what's really gone on – but then, instead of letting the law take its due course, he diverts it, runs it down channels he's dug himself. It goes against everything I believe in! Cover-ups, pretence, turning a blind eye – it's not my style, James! I admire but I don't approve.'

'No, you never were much of a politician, Joe. But you're safe from his machinations out here at least. Plenty of shooting going on but it's all above board! But there can't be anything sinister in this request, can there? Dancing attendance on an American girl? Some would jump at the chance.'

'I don't like it. Look, James,' said Joe desperately, 'you command this blasted fort – or don't you? Can't you just say no? Isn't there a system of passes to travel west of Peshawar? There is, you know! I remember on mine it said in block capitals that no women were allowed into the war zone. And this is the war zone, dammit! We were shot at a dozen times this afternoon.'

'Believe me, Joe, I've been saying no for weeks! This place is filling up like a five star hotel. The Waldorf Astoria perhaps.'

'Why? How do you mean?'

James Lindsay rubbed his face morosely. 'Trouble is,' he said, 'the fort is something of a model. Football ground, hockey ditto. Squash court under construction. Tennis courts. Perhaps you'd care for a game of cricket? We can provide! Every conceivable modern convenience, every conceivable military convenience too for that matter. Security the like of which we've never seen on the frontier before so what's the result? Every wandering idiot in the bloody Empire with the slightest influence thinks he (and now *she*, it appears!) is entitled to a jolly weekend in the spearhead of British Imperial expansion! And on whom does the burden fall? On Sucker Lindsay to be sure! Do you realize this? – apart from ourselves and apart from those who actually do all the work, we have on board, or very shortly will have on board, a senior Indian civil servant from the Viceroy's office on a "fact-finding mission to evaluate the work of Scout forts and their significance in the overall defence of the Indian territories". Sir Edwin Burroughs, no less! Not the easiest man to have looking over one's shoulder.'

'Never heard of him. But, whoever he is, he'll never see a better run fort, James. No reason for concern there, surely?'

'Oh, but there is! Sir Edwin's views on the border forts are well known and very uncomplicated: "Shut the buggers down!" He's advising the government and anyone who will listen to him that the British should pull out, abandon the Durand Line and retreat back east to the Indus. And there are some days, believe me, Joe, when even I can see the sense of that! But for the duration of his visit I'm expected to put on a show of efficiency to make your eyes water. It's all a propaganda exercise to reassure HM Gov. that we're firmly in control. Or otherwise. What the hell am I supposed to *do* with him?'

Joe laughed. 'Take him out on a gasht and lose him! But, seriously, the chap's not military – he'll be cosseted Indian Civil Service from Calcutta or Delhi. All he'll be concerned about is that you offer him the right kind of marmalade for breakfast.'

'There's more, Joe! As if that weren't enough, even you will have heard of Dr Grace Holbrook? Pioneer of medical missionary zeal? She's much admired by His Excellency, she's quids in with Sir George and – unbelievably – quids in with the bloody Amir of Afghanistan! Our friend over the border. Ever since she successfully treated his piles or was it his worms? Anyway she's en route for Kabul, it's said to take up a post as the Amir's personal physician, and spending "a day or two in the fort" to rest and wait for her Afghani escort to take her on to Kabul. I tell you, Joe, this is going to be a shambles! At least it would be enough of a shambles if it weren't for Lord Rathmore who's also chosen this moment to drop in on us.'

'Lord Rathmore? Who's he, for God's sake?'

'Chairman of West India Trading, very eager to see British goods replace Russian goods in the Kabul bazaars and I don't only mean pretty leather boxes, tins of turtle soup and cakes of Pears soap – I'm speaking of military hardware as well. And, inevitably, there's a sheepdog to herd this mob, an RAF man, Fred Moore-Simpson (nice chap, I don't mind *him* staying). He's coming to consider the problems and advantages of aerial proscription and hoping to site a squadron of light fighter-bombers to patrol the frontier from the air. It's not a bad idea but I do just wish it could have cropped up at any other time.'

Joe had listened to this catalogue with a certain amount

of amusement as he saw James's anguished face. 'I think you're going to have to go over that cast list again for me! How many was that? Five including the Coblenz girl? And two of us – one more and we could have a dinner party! Or two tables of bridge! That's it then, is it?' he asked. 'Anyone else you've forgotten to tell me about?'

'Yes,' said James, his expression changing to one of happiness, 'there *is* one more. Betty!'

'Betty? She's not coming up here, is she? Surely it's against all the rules to have your wife on the station?'

'Well, since everybody else seems only too happy to break the rules I don't see why *I* shouldn't! And she's on her way. I shall be very happy to see her.'

'Me too,' said Joe who remembered Betty Lindsay very well. 'I shall be delighted to see her . . . always provided she hasn't got that wretched little dog with her! Did she bring it out to India? What was it called? Minto?'

James sighed. 'Minto yes. Can't promise you, Joe. I mean, after all, what would she do with him if she didn't bring him with her? Can't leave the little thug with anybody else. Bites like a baboon. Come on, Joe! Ten lengths – I'll race you!'

They both smiled, happy with their shared memories. When they had found themselves going home on leave on the same boat after their first campaign together Joe had asked James where he was bound. A stiffness had descended on the lively features and he had confided that he was going to spend his precious fortnight with the only family he had in England – two elderly uncles in Camberwell. It had been easy for Joe to say, 'Don't do that. Come and finish this game of chess at home with me. At least not *my* home but my sister's. She and her husband live in Surrey, place called Upfold House. There's not a lot to do – tea on the lawn, bridge, going to church. Pretty boring really, and I'm beginning to be sorry I asked you, but you'd be very welcome.'

'Heaven!' James had said. 'It sounds like heaven!'

And he had found his heaven, though not at Upfold

House. Joe discovered that James's constant visits to Upfold Rectory were prompted not by religious fervour but by a more particular interest (amounting perhaps to fervour) in the rector's pretty daughter, Elizabeth. All James's subsequent leaves, with or without Joe, were spent at Upfold and when the war ended he married Betty and took her back to India to resume his career. It had been decided that his military experience was exactly what was needed on the North-West Frontier, and Major and Mrs Lindsay were sent north to Peshawar.

To Joe's irritation James Lindsay won their race by a wide margin. 'I almost met myself coming back,' James said with satisfaction. As they emerged from the tank and wrapped themselves in towels, a Scout havildar came efficiently to attention at James's elbow with a written message in his hand. He spoke rapidly in Pushtu and James listened with close attention, interpolating a question or two from time to time. Finally he turned to Joe. 'Message,' he said, 'by helio. From one of our pickets. A cavalry force, thirty strong they say, is coming in down the Khyber road. This must be Grace Holbrook's Afghani escort. Typically twenty-four hours before I was expecting them! I think I'll send some chaps to meet them. I like to retain the initiative. But, on second thoughts, perhaps I'll go and meet them myself. Why don't you come with me? Just give me time to get dressed and hand over to Eddy Fraser and we'll go!'

He shouted down into the courtyard and at once horses were led out and mounted Scouts were forming up.

Twenty minutes later, Joe and James rode out through the main gate of the fort at the head of a small escorting group. 'We won't hurry,' said James. 'We'll just amble out to greet them, looking at the view and chatting of this and that as we go. Don't want to assume the character of an official delegation. This is just a private arrangement between Grace Holbrook and the Amir and we're doing what we can to help them. No more than that.'

33

Squinting into the sun dipping behind the forbidding khaki bleakness of the Khyber, Joe took out a pair of binoculars and focused on the riders coming on towards them. They presented an alluring blend of banditry and military precision. They advanced under a haze of fluttering battle standards. They seemed to be a regular army force down to the waist but irregular frontier raiders below that. Chestnut silk turbans, loose khaki tunics, patch pockets, cross belts and aiguelettes with, below them, baggy trousers and tall boots. Many were armed with spears which, taken in conjunction with the fluttering flags, managed to give an air of a medieval force. All, Joe noticed, were equipped with bolt-action rifles as good as anything carried by the Scouts. Their air of efficiency and menace was not lost on Joe. This was no carnival army.

'Friendly enemies, would you say? Or hostile allies?' he murmured to James. 'Are you sure we're not still at war with these gentlemen?'

'The third – but I suspect not the last – Afghan war was over three years ago and we signed a peace treaty with the Amir only last year.' James paused for a moment and added, 'But I'll remind you of an old Pathan proverb shall I? "When the peace treaty's signed – that's when the war starts." And I'll tell you something else – they're not coming into the fort! Plenty of them have got scores to settle with the Scouts and plenty of Scouts would welcome above all things an opportunity to have a go at them. They can camp on the football ground for tonight. We can board them but I'm damned if I'll lodge them as well. Far too volatile! Hell's bells! Shouldn't have let this happen! But then what could I do? Could you get me a job in London, do you think, Joe? This is all getting a bit delicate for me!'

They threaded their way through the irrigated, crop-green land beyond the walls which served both as a clear field of fire, vegetable garden and orchard for the fort and ambled on. The two troops closed until they were a hundred yards apart. The leading Afghan raised a hand and his men came to a halt. Escorted by one man riding at his side and a little behind, the leader came on at walking pace, mounted on a tall grey Khabuli stallion. To Joe he seemed a very impressive figure. Young and handsome with dark eyes and a heavy black moustache, he turned a direct and enquiring gaze on them. Over one hip was slung a Mauser pistol and over the other a jewel-encrusted Persian dagger.

James surveyed the newcomer through narrowed eyes.

'Who's this, James?' Joe whispered, curious and intrigued.

'Zeman Khan!' said James. 'Very prominent local citizen. Nephew – or is it cousin? – of the Amir. About twenty sons and brothers between him and the throne but that's not a formidable barrier in Afghanistan.'

'What – you mean . . ?'

'Oh, yes. The Afghan royal succession makes the last act of *Richard the Third* look like the Teddy Bears' Picnic! The present Amir owes his position to the fact that someone shot the top off the head of the previous one, his father, while he was asleep. Some say Amanullah knows more about that than he lets on and others say it was a nephew who killed him. We only care in so far as the present incumbent is not unfavourable to the British and discourages any Russian incursion from the north. Not sure where Zeman Khan stands though.'

He halted the escort and rode forward with Joe. 'Having said all that, I'll add that I wouldn't trust him one inch. He'll be staying with us tonight – guest of honour, you might say – and he won't have his eyes shut! He'll be looking; he'll be evaluating. He'll see what we're up to. He'll note the number of men we have, the quantity and quality of our armament. He'll count the pea-shooters and the catapults. Nothing I can do about it. I'll just have to make it plain that we know what he's up to and we're so confident we don't need to worry too much about a spy in the camp. I'd stick him down with the rest of his bandits on the football ground if I could but that would be a hideous social gaffe.'

He cupped his hands round his mouth and shouted in Pushtu and the oncoming horseman did likewise. Judging by the ribald laughter from both sides which greeted this exchange, it had been one of practised and amiable insult.

'God!' thought Joe. 'I wish I could do that!'

With outstretched hands the men advanced to each other. James spoke again in Pushtu then in English. 'Let me present Zeman Khan and this is my friend Joe Sandilands.'

The black eyes looked him up and down, resting briefly on Joe's scarred forehead and the row of medal ribbons on his jacket. They took in the unfamiliar police uniform, showing slight surprise that Joe was unarmed. Zeman Khan smiled and extended a hand. 'How do you do, Sandilands? I'm so pleased to make your acquaintance. I had heard that you were in Simla but never expected that I should have the pleasure of meeting you here. May I welcome you to this backward and flea-bitten annexe to the mighty British Empire?'

The voice was low and smooth, the accent pure British Public School. Joe mastered his astonishment and replied, 'I am flattered that the distinguished Zeman Khan, so close to his Highness the Amir, would condescend to know the name of so humble an individual as myself.'

They looked at each other for a moment and then began to laugh. 'Of course,' said Zeman, 'we should be speaking in Persian which is the language of elegant diplomacy but I will settle for the more comprehensible though less elegant language adopted from the conqueror.'

'Conqueror?' said James. 'Rubbish! You're wasting your time, Zeman! You won't fool Joe!'

Zeman flashed a slim silver cigarette case from his pocket and held it open to them. 'Russian cigarettes, I'm afraid,' he said, 'but supplies have been rather interrupted of late.'

'Relief is at hand, Zeman,' said James easily. 'I've arranged for two hundred Players Medium to be brought out for you. We are as aware of melmastia and the sacred ties of hospitality as you are.'

Joe had a clear impression that in these few brief exchanges between two practised duellists they had covered an agenda which politicians would have wrangled over for a week.

'Your charge, Dr Holbrook, is not expected until tomorrow, Zeman, so this will give you time to rest and recover from your journey and for us to enjoy your company. We hope that you and your aide,' he smiled towards the officer escorting Zeman, 'will consent to be our guests in the fort for the next two nights at least. We are expecting other guests to arrive with Dr Holbrook's party and I'm sure you will be happy to meet them.'

'My aide,' Zeman said, waving a hand at the young Pathan at his side, 'Muhammed Iskander Khan, and I will be delighted.'

Joe looked again at Iskander Khan. Watchful but not unfriendly green eyes looked back at him. He was a pale-skinned Pathan, one of the tribesmen who claim that their colouring comes from the ancient line of Alexander the Great whose Macedonian army had passed through these hills two thousand years before. His brown hair was bobbed and curled, wind-blown around his turban, his nose, like Zeman's, was magnificent, but he was clean-shaven and lacking the luxuriant moustache.

'Then come with us,' said James, turning his horse. 'Your men will be taken care of.'

He summoned a havildar who, though suspicious and wary, began with a formal bow to talk with the senior remaining Afghan.

Out of earshot, Joe leaned towards James and hissed, 'You might have warned me! What shall I guess? Wellington and Sandhurst?'

James grinned. 'No. As it happens – Rugby and Sandhurst. You'll have a chance to get better acquainted over supper. His mother is an Afghan princess, Durrani tribe, royal blood, and his father is a chief, a Malik, of a branch of the Afridis who live this side of the border. Now he's a nasty old brute! Hates the English but he's not above using

37

the large grants of English cash we give him to send his only son off to Europe for a military education. Nothing like learning how your enemy ticks from the inside, I suppose.'

'So when Zeman sticks his dagger in my throat I may expect him to say, "Sorry about this, old chap! Nothing personal you understand," in the best Sandhurst drawl?'

James considered for a moment. 'Yes,' he said, 'you've got it just about right. Don't forget to lock your door tonight!'

The next morning Joe and James stood together on the roof of the fort, already uncomfortably hot by ten o'clock, binoculars sweeping the road up from Peshawar. They were joined by Zeman Khan. 'When do we expect to see this so important delegation?' he asked easily, seating himself on the parapet.

'At any moment now,' said James, offering him the binoculars.

With a smile Zeman waved them away and looked towards the Peshawar road. 'At any moment now? Then unless I mistake, here they are.'

And a motorized convoy, an armoured car leading the way, began to appear, slowly making its way along the newly metalled road to the fort.

'Do you recognize anybody?' Joe asked.

'Well,' said James, 'one of the men in the first car is in RAF uniform so that can only be Moore-Simpson.'

'Moore-Simpson?' said Zeman, suddenly alert. 'I didn't realize he was coming. What's he coming for?' His tone was suspicious.

'Well, primarily,' said James pacifically, 'if he's done what I asked, he's got two hundred Players Medium Navy Cut fags on board for you. But, beyond that, it's not for me to expound the motives of my lords and masters. And with him in the car, I note, there's Sir Edwin Burroughs of the Indian Civil Service.'

'That's a funny pairing,' said Zeman. 'Moore-Simpson's well known to be in favour of bombing the wicked tribesmen into submission and Sir Edwin is in favour of anything, including a British retreat from the frontier, that might save money! Ha! I should think they had an interesting journey together!'

James evidently thought the same but didn't care to have British frontier policy explained to him from the other side of the tribal boundary.

'Next car? That's a Dodge, isn't it?'

'Buick, I think.'

'Delage,' said Zeman authoritatively.

'Well, whatever the car, it seems to contain none other than the formidable Grace Holbrook. Yes, undoubtedly – motoring veil! That's her all right.'

'Who's that in the car with her?'

'That must be the Lord Rathmore, I'd guess. And opposite him and turning towards us . . .' He spoke with studied calm. 'Yes. It's Betty. Do you see her, Joe?'

The first two cars were separated from the next two by a lorry full of Scouts infantry. A third car came in view.

'Luggage,' said Joe, staring. 'Nothing but luggage. Any more to come? What's the matter, James?'

'Well,' said James, 'I'm looking for the member of this party for whom I have the greatest anxiety and I do not see her. Where the hell's bloody little Miss Lily Coblenz got to, I'd like to know? Here comes another car . . . but there's no one in it but the driver. And there's the troop of Lancers bringing up the rear. That's it. Now what? My orders were absolutely specific! She was to travel in the second car with my wife and Dr Holbrook. Ah, dammit! I should have gone down myself!'

'Or maybe I should have gone down,' Joe said. 'Not sure when exactly my stewardship kicked in.'

Zeman eyed the two men in their manifest consternation with malicious amusement. 'Dropped your heiress by the roadside, have they?' he asked.

'Don't even mention such a thing!' said James, biting his

finger. 'If such an awful thing could possibly have happened, that's the end of *my* promising career! I'll kill that bloody Monty Melville!'

Joe looked a question.

'Monty Melville. Ninth Lancers. He was supposed to shepherd this convoy to us. There he is! Prancing about in front of the troop. What the hell have you done with her, Monty? I suppose the damned girl hasn't travelled with the Scouts?' he said, tracking back to the lorry-load of Scout infantry in the centre of the column.

All three men stared and said together, 'She's not there.'

'Perhaps she changed her mind?' said Joe hopefully. 'Perhaps she's stayed on to taste the delights of Peshawar?'

'The only explanation and what a relief that'll be!' said James. 'All the same, I'd have expected them to tell me that when they radioed they were about to set off, wouldn't you?'

'Probably changed her mind at the very last minute. Decided to go shopping or something. Didn't much like the look of the other travellers . . . anything . . .' suggested Joe.

Zeman had been sweeping the convoy with his hawk's eyes. Suddenly he laughed. 'This lady whose non-appearance causes you so much anxiety – would she be young and fair-haired, athletic, capricious? Yes? Then I fear I have bad news for you both!'

He pointed downwards to where the cavalry troop, partly obscured by a haze of dust, was coming more clearly into view. 'I had heard,' he said, 'that we were to be honoured by the presence of a British cavalry regiment. Rare but not unknown in this part of the world, and here they are. But that's not all! When I report back to the Amir do I tell him the red line is running so thin these days that the British are reduced to recruiting women?' He began to laugh. 'Hedged about in the centre of this martial array I think you'll find what you're looking for!'

James stared and stared. 'Bloody hell!' he said. 'Bloody girl! How the hell did she get there? I'll kill Melville when

I catch up with him! How on earth could he have let this happen?'

'I don't think you need worry,' said Joe. 'I think she's safe enough. I can't think of anywhere more safe within the bounds of the Indian Empire. Either way, I'm going down to meet the damn girl.'

'I think I'd better stay here with James,' said Zeman, 'though I must admit I am very curious to meet this paragon. She might be disconcerted to confront a hairy tribesman such as myself. I'm sure she must have been warned about "men like me".'

'If she has, she doesn't seem to have heeded the warning.'

Indignantly, Joe clattered down to the courtyard, mounted the horse being held ready for him and set off through the gates of the fort. Pausing briefly in the garden and leaning low he picked two choice roses and tucked them into his epaulette. He cantered down the road to meet the oncoming convoy, passing each car in turn with something between a wave and a salute, acknowledging the lorry-load of armed Scouts and finally confronting the troop of Ninth Lancers led by Monty Melville. Carefully sunk in the protection of this force, pink, dishevelled and wearing a borrowed Lancer's helmet, dark glasses pushed up on her damp forehead, riding firmly astride, his charge raised an excited face to him and he bore down upon her in wrath.

'Just what,' he said, hardly able to pick his words, 'the hell do you think *you're* doing?' He crooked an imperious police forefinger at her and indicated that she should withdraw from the crowd and present herself.

'Well, my!' The voice could not have been more cheerful and unconcerned and could not have been more incongruously American. 'I guess you must be my policeman, Commandant Sandilands!' she said, easing her horse out of the mêlée. 'Do you know – they tried to put me in a – what did they call it? – a staff car! I wasn't going to do that. I haven't come all the way from Chicago to drive about in

41

a Delage! Gee! This is just great! This is the proper way to travel in this country!' She beamed round her at the line of admiring British troopers.

'Young lady did well!' said the troop sergeant. 'Could have been doing it all her life.' And there was a murmuring of adoring agreement from the troop.

'I'm sorry, sir!' said Monty Melville. He turned a desperate face towards Joe and hissed, 'I know what the orders were and I did my best but you might as well explain King's regs to a langur monkey as get any sense into this blasted girl!' He shot a sweating and indignant glance at Lily. 'Especially as she seems to have got all my chaps on her side.'

'I see,' said Joe, turning a frosty glare on Lily, 'that I'm going to have to explain the facts of life – the facts of frontier life, that is – and, not to put too fine a point on it, you can count yourself lucky you're not put on the next "staff car" and sent back to Peshawar! If I had my way that's just what would happen. I'm getting too old to play hide and seek with little girls.'

'Aw!' said Lily. 'Don't be like that! This is what I came for.' She swept a complicitous glance around the troop and added, 'Sir George warned me about *him*. But they say his bark's worse than his bite! Is that right, Commandant?'

'Can I explain that this is a dangerous part of the world? You're not on a dude ranch here. You could get into serious trouble. I wouldn't mind that myself but some good men might find themselves put into danger pulling you out of it. I'm responsible for your safety – problem enough if you do what you're told, impossible if you don't. Is that clear, I wonder?'

Lily's reaction to this was to favour him with a cheeky salute copied, Joe supposed, from the convention of West Point.

Chapter Four

Dr Grace Holbrook was accustomed to come and go on the frontier protected only by her reputation and, accordingly, when she discovered that she was to form part of a well-armed and elaborately escorted convoy from Peshawar to the fort, she was not amused. She complained to her friend the High Commissioner. 'It's taken me nearly twenty years,' she said, 'to earn the trust of these people and I do so with difficulty all the time. It's going to do me nothing but harm to appear with a military convoy.'

Sir John Deane did his best to smooth her ruffled plumes. 'Nobody,' he said, 'is going to suspect you of all people of martial intent, Grace!' He smiled at the short, middle-aged figure leaning angrily over his desk. In her divided skirt, white shirt and brown silk tie held in place with a gold pin, Grace Holbrook presented an image of perfect decorum. 'They know you too well; they welcome you too warmly. Of course, it's up to you to wait until the present convoy has returned but I didn't imagine that would suit you either since it would involve holding up the Afghani end of this operation at the fort.'

'It certainly wouldn't suit me!' said Grace indignantly. 'I stick meticulously to any arrangements I may have made and I have arranged to be in Kabul in ten days' time. You might have warned me, John, that there was going to be some sort of awful jamboree going on at the fort! Not my sort of thing as well you know!'

'Well, you know how it is out here . . . nobody is told anything until the last second and that is an arrangement

43

I would be the first to defend. Imagine the consequences of this guest list becoming general knowledge before the event! Blood runs cold when I think of it! An heiress, a trading empire nabob, top civil servant and RAF top brass! And all gathered together in Peshawar – the kidnapping capital of the western frontier! But I'll tell you something, Grace – the only one of the party whose safety I really give a fig for is the one who's trying to shrug aside the protective measures on offer.'

Never an easy subject for flattery, Grace opened her mouth to give a sharp retort and he hurried on, 'Anyway, your professional services may well be called on during the journey.' Pleased that he had awakened her curiosity he went on, 'It's Betty Lindsay, James's wife. Yes, I hadn't told you that either! She is to be of the party. I know it's against all the rules but just this once I'm bending them! Fact is, Grace, she's in a delicate condition, er . . . um . . .'

'Oh, for God's sake, John!' Grace interrupted. 'Did you imagine I didn't know she was pregnant? I've been treating her for morning sickness for the past month! There's nothing delicate about Betty! She's a strong girl and doesn't need me or anyone else to sit beside her with the smelling salts but, oh, all right . . .' Grace gave him a surprisingly warm smile. 'I'll play chaperone. I'll go along on condition that I sit next to Betty and as far as possible from that little Miss Coblenz whose acquaintance I was unlucky enough to make at your soirée yesterday.'

Arriving at the fort, Grace watched in amusement blended with not a little satisfaction as a striking but grim-faced man rode determinedly down the column and hauled Miss Coblenz out of the troop. She threw back her motoring veil the better to watch the scene unfold. Good! Whoever this was, he seemed to be giving her a jolly good and well-deserved wigging. The American girl had delayed the whole column forming up outside Government House back in Peshawar for fifteen minutes while she objected,

44

argued and cajoled. At last she had got what she wanted which, perversely, appeared to be to ride twelve miles in the heat at the back of the column breathing exhaust fumes and dust and surrounded by twenty clattering and sweating Lancers.

'Did you see that, Betty?' Grace exclaimed excitedly. 'It looks as though she's met her match at last! I wonder who that authoritative young man is? What a face! I think he's going to shake her!'

'Oh, no!' Betty smiled. 'That's Joe! Joe Sandilands. He's the policeman I was telling you about. He may have the face of a killer – which is what I suppose he once was – but he'd never lay hands on a woman. There, you see, short and sharp and now she knows who's in charge!'

They watched as Joe reinserted Lily into the centre of the troop and began to trot back up the column. When he drew level with their car he stopped. He bowed to Grace, selected a white rose from his epaulette and handed it to her. 'Dr Holbrook, welcome to Gor Khatri.' Handing a red rose to Betty, his face alight with affection, 'Lovely Betty! How good to see you again!' And he rode on ahead of them to the gates.

Grace inhaled the strong fragrance of her rose with pleasure, intrigued by their new escort. She could admire a man who was capable of military firmness one moment and melting charm the next. A considerable man, was her fleeting first impression, a manly man, if that wasn't too old-fashioned an expression. His grey eyes were intelligent and humorous and his face must at some point in the past have been handsome. She wondered how the wreckage had occurred. Her professional eye diagnosed bad surgery on the battlefield.

Pity he hadn't fallen into her hands – she would have made a better job of it. Grace had acquired a reputation for restorative surgery over the years. The tribesmen were all too apt to slice each other up in their conflicts and would unhesitatingly come into Peshawar, often clutching the lopped-off ear or fingers, and ask her to make all good again. She had stifled her anger and disgust the first time a man of the Mahsud tribe had brought his wife to her. The husband had sliced off his wife's nose in a jealous rage and later regretted it. What could the good doctor do about it? Grace was proud of the technique she had evolved of cutting a Y-shaped flap of skin from the forehead and training it down to graft over the damaged area. She had lost count of the number of women she had treated. Behind their veils the women of the hills were as tough as their men, athletic and strong and well able to defend a fort or village if necessary, but some fell victim to gynaecological problems, cholera, typhus, stray bullets and mutilation at the hands of their husbands. And, since no male doctor would have been allowed to treat or even look at a woman, Grace was the only resort.

With the aid of her husband, also a doctor, she had established a clinic in Peshawar and to the astonished concern of the authorities had continued to run it, treating British citizens and Pathans alike even after the death, at native hands, of her husband. The tribesmen were more astonished than her compatriots. She was frequently asked by patients how she could bring herself to do this work, caring for the very people who were responsible for his death. Surely, they wondered, she must want to invoke the right of badal, to be avenged for her husband? Surely there was some young man of her family who would pick up and run with the tale? And she herself was well placed to take revenge, they would say, with a meaningful and nervous glance at her sharp instruments. She always reassured them that her only interest was in putting people together again. She usually managed to bring her God into the conversation too, explaining the theory of Christian forgiveness. They had come to trust her and she was a well-known and welcome guest in the tribal territories.

Frederick Moore-Simpson had acquired a pretty extensive knowledge of the frontier. He could ask sensible questions and he could give sensible answers. He knew his way round this Debatable Land. But this was the first time he had stood down on its earth. His knowledge had been acquired from a height of five thousand feet but the more he had looked and the more he had listened, the more he had become converted to the Forward Policy. To his calculating and pragmatic RAF mind it seemed that war on the ground must go in favour always of the native Pathan. Others had found this. The Moghul emperors had found it, as had the Sikh invaders and now the British, poised and ready to repeat the same mistakes.

When every corner of this land was overlooked by a defensible mountain crag, and every crag occupied by vigilant and highly trained riflemen, if there was to be any conclusion there had to be, as he put it, 'a change of bowling'. And the change of bowling could be supplied by the RAF. An adequacy of landing strips and the work once done by sweating infantrymen both British and Indian on the ground could be done by the modern cavalry – a squadron of light bombers. Fred knew a good deal about this. He had served on the Western Front. 'Aerial proscription' they called it and Fred was convinced that this was the way ahead. 'Trench strafing,' he would say, 'that's the stuff!'

He had expended much energy and much eloquence in pressing this point of view on the unreceptive Edwin Burroughs as they drove up together from Peshawar. Fred didn't like Edwin Burroughs. He didn't like his patronizing Indian Civil Service approach. He didn't much like his braying voice, his supercilious expression and his improbably shining silver hair. Least of all did he like his insistence that the way ahead was not to advance but to retreat. In effect, to pull back east of the Indus and leave the tribesmen to sort their problems out themselves, thereby saving the British Government a very great deal of money. Leaving the British Empire open on a thousand-mile-wide front to attack from Russia more like, Fred thought. Couldn't the man see that?

Fred understood his subject. He had cultivated an RAF

manner – casual and informal – but most people swiftly came to the realization that behind this there was an icy determination, by fair means or foul, to press and establish his view. James had at times been surprised at the vehemence into which Fred could so easily slip. So surprised, indeed, that he had applied for and obtained an intelligence report on Fred's background. Impeccable. Nothing suspicious there. Or was there? Among recent activities on the part of the RAF and in which Fred had been closely involved had been an early experiment in aerial proscription, successful within limits but revealing the surprising fact that the slow-moving bombers available to the RAF at the time were vulnerable targets to Afridi and Wazir snipers on the ground.

'Just like a covert shoot!' someone had said. 'Slow birds!'

Several young flying officers had been forced into crash landings in tribal territory. It was generally believed that a straight and lethal crash was to be preferred to a successful crash-landing. Pilots who in this way fell into Pathan hands in spite of handsome rewards for their return to the British did not last long and did not die easily. James had wondered if Fred's single-minded pursuit of his aggressive policy was fuelled in any way by hatred or even guilt.

Sir Edwin Burroughs was not in a receptive mood. His piles were killing him. The long journey by train to Peshawar had been bad enough, the accommodation in Peshawar had not been what he was accustomed to but the onward jolting, bumpy journey to the fort had of itself been a source of the sharpest anguish, intolerable at any level but brought beyond bearing by listening to that ignorant damn fool Moore-Simpson pressing the claims of the forward policy which in the mind of Burroughs and many others had long been abandoned by the sensible.

Burroughs had listened but had taken refuge behind the dry cough, the Olympian smile and the parade of saintly patience. He counted the days as best he could until he could be comfortably at home again in Delhi. He didn't want to spend time listening to Grace Holbrook explaining the views of the Amir. He didn't want to listen to the domestic preoccupations of the fort commander's wife (though he understood that James Lindsay was sound enough). He learned that a banquet – a Pathan banquet, if you please! – was being laid on for his benefit that evening. He detested native food. A lively curry always animated his ulcer. He feared that if there was anything at all to drink other than mineral water it would be beer of local manufacture. Aerated drinks did not suit him. He hoped – on the one hand – that he would find himself seated next to this American girl and, on the other hand, that she would be as far away from him as possible. He could do without the stirrings of senile lust which she provoked in him. And, if he were to believe all he heard, the modern American woman was better avoided. They were over-emancipated for many men's taste, bold and apt to have their own strong opinions. Trouble.

Dermot Rathmore was reputed to have done well out of the war. 'Something to do with army contracts' rumour had said and rumour, for once, was right. Seeing a gap in the market he had contracted widely to supply the American forces in France and, unusually, had beaten an American entrepreneur to the draw. And then there was his peerage. 'Lord' Rathmore! 'What was that about?' people asked. Blatantly – more blatantly even than most – his peerage had come from subscriptions to party funds but this was not widely known outside England, and the North-West Frontier of India was a lord-loving corner of the Empire. These events left him with a considerable sense of his own importance and an exaggerated sense of his own power to manipulate the situations in which he found himself to his further advantage. In the circumstances he was not pleased to find himself in his present company. He had expected a red carpet instead of which he found himself in something little better than a parish outing. He tuned for a moment back into the conversation of Betty and Grace Holbrook and decided it was worse – a Sunday School outing by charabanc was nearer the mark. And one of the wretched women had even brought her dog along for the ride. He looked with disfavour at the small white Jack Russell terrier lying at his feet, its eyes unwaveringly on his ankles. The commanding officer's wife appeared to be loosely in control of it.

And here was this missionary female, Grace something. He didn't associate with missionaries though he was told this one had the ear of the Amir of Afghanistan. She might be useful. If he was truly to establish trade relations between the Indian Empire and the Kingdom of Afghanistan a friend at court might come in handy, even a humble missionary. He wondered if he could offer her a retainer. Always worth a try.

Then there was that damn fool Moore-Simpson. DFC and Bar! Trench strafer! He didn't think much of him! But he was to be preferred to the officer commanding this fort. James Lindsay! He'd had the effrontery to write him a chit telling him how to behave; warning him that he wasn't to leave the fort without an escort; that he wasn't, it seemed, to do *anything* without an escort. He'd even had the nerve to give him a lecture on how to treat the local women! 'Do not meet their eye. Do not address them directly.' How childish and absurd! He could count the number of native females he'd seen since his arrival on the fingers of one hand and they had been so shrouded in veils from top to toe it was impossible to tell they were women anyway. He had a strong feeling that the natives in these parts – Pakhtuns or Pathans they called them, he believed – had been allowed to get a damn sight too big for their boots. Perhaps Moore-Simpson wasn't such a fool after all. People criticized General Dyer but certainly his action at Amritsar had nipped what could have have been a nasty bit of trouble in the bud. No – if they were going to trade in these parts it had to be on the basis of who's boss and who is not. And if that damn fool Burroughs had his way what could be a promising market could be flooded with cheap Russian goods. Dermot Rathmore was determined that this shouldn't happen. His confidence stemmed from the encouragement he had had at the very highest level. 'Why don't you go and have a look at the situation on the ground, old boy? Nothing like first-hand experience of the possibilities. Don't worry about security – we'll lay on a show for you. We'll expect your report on your return – just remember what we're interested in, what we're *all* interested in, is the feasibility of the project. Can we get British goods into Afghanistan and, assuming we can, what sort of goods should they be?'

Rathmore smiled to himself and took a small object from his pocket. His eyes lingered on the jewel-like painting of a saint. An icon, that's what these things were called. And since those Bolshies got into power in Russia and suddenly wealth and religion were frightfully unpatriotic they were finding their way over the border. He'd picked this one up in the bazaar in Peshawar for tuppence halfpenny. And there were other things too. Precious things, unusual things which would sell well in London or New York. Some of the works of the enterprising Monsieur Fabergé were filtering down to Afghanistan and onwards. His plan would be to get British goods into Afghanistan all right for the propaganda that was in it and to impress His Majesty's Government, but Dermot Rathmore's real profit would be in the goods his caravans brought back out again.

He stared ahead of the convoy, beyond the fort. His calculating blue eyes followed the newly tarmacked road that wound its way up into the dark jaws of the Khyber Pass. That would be the route his lorries would take. How far did the road surface extend? Was it safe? He supposed it all depended on the efficiency of this Lindsay in his tinpot little fort with his bugles and his handful of British officers. Dermot had heard that the vast majority of the thousands of enlisted men – Scouts they called them!

Scouts! – were tribesmen from these hills, brigands to a man probably. Dermot sighed. He'd come on a wild goose chase. But then he looked again at the icon in the palm of his hand and cheered up.

Betty Lindsay too was looking about her. She'd been cooped up with the other military wives within the walls of Peshawar for too long and was enjoying the wide horizons. She took off her heavy solar topee and shook out her thick brown curls, turning her head this way and that. There it was at last! So often imagined, so often described to her by James. Betty stared and stared again at the fort. James's fort – more or less James's creation. The centre of his world. 'No, perhaps not that. I know what's the centre of his world – me!' She was heartened by this thought in the midst of a landscape so hostile.

At first the fort was hard to see. Like so many things in this country it had a facility to disappear. A cloud would cross the sun, shadows would chase each other, the cloud would pass on and briefly the mud-coloured fort would reappear in the mud-coloured landscape. Long and low, the fort seemed sprawled across the foothills. She knew – because James had told her – that every possible use had been made of natural features to ensure interlocking fields of fire in the event of attack. Lookout posts and lookout positions ensured that no part of the surrounding landscape was ever in view from fewer than two separate outlooks.

'It's all very *male*,' she thought to herself. 'Nothing soft here. This is a world of nailed sandals, bugle calls, iron rations, binoculars and ceaseless watchfulness.'

They wound their way across the plain and Betty became aware of details as they approached the fort. She saw battlements, watchtowers loop-holed for rifle fire, perched like swallows' nests against the side of the fort, a signal station manned with a heliograph, but amongst the unrelenting military dispositions of stone and dried mud

52

there were the tentative beginnings of shy greenery. Very regimented greenery! Regimented but vulnerable in this harsh world. Recently planted fruit trees seemingly stood to attention where they had been put by a military hand. Vegetables stood likewise. An attempt had been made to establish a vineyard. The whole was efficient and promising 'but,' thought Betty with a lurch of the heart, 'totally without imagination.' Yes, this was James's work all right. 'If ever we live anywhere a civilized life is possible, I won't let him within a mile of the garden, that's for sure!'

She turned and said as much to Grace. 'All the same,' said Grace, 'persistence! That's what's needed. And that is certainly what James has.'

'It's what you're going to need over this next bit too, Grace,' said Betty, suddenly concerned and frowning. 'Look! If you look back the way we've come, what do you see? Civilization! Orchards, fields full of green crops, sparkling river, canals, the dome of Ismalia college and a froth of apple and almond blossom! It's quite heavenly! And then turn quickly and look to the west. Now what do you see? Hell! All shades of brown and not a tree or a blade of grass in sight. And as for that gate to Avernus,' she pointed at the black vertical fissure that marked the Khyber and shuddered, 'wild horses wouldn't drag me up there! I think you're awfully brave, Grace, going all that way. They say it's thirty miles from beginning to end. That's a long ride!'

'You kindly don't add, "At your age!" ' Grace eyed Betty calmly for a moment. 'I'm not exactly a tourist,' she said. 'I know these people and – at last – they know me. I'd go further and say they trust me, and that trust hasn't been easy to establish. Thirty miles! Yes, it's a long way but Afghanis say, "Halve the journey – travel with a friend!" and that's what I shall be doing.' Her calm was impressive. 'I've done it before,' she added placidly.

'I hope you won't think I'm overstepping the bounds of decorum, Grace –' Betty smiled, 'which of course means that I'm about to! – if I ask why *you* should go to dance attendance on the Amir? We need you in Peshawar! *I* need you in Peshawar! Surely there must be a supply of competent doctors in Kabul?'

Grace smiled. 'The Amir Amanullah has very particular requirements in a physician, the most important being that his doctor should not kill him! He doesn't trust the home-bred ones not to be in the pay of one of his aspirant relatives. Too easy to administer a fatal dose! For this reason he never allows himself to be anaesthetized – not even to have a tooth removed. But he trusts me. He's visited Peshawar several times to consult me and we get on well. He also appreciates my Western training. His country may still be in the Stone Age in many ways but Amanullah admires many aspects of Western culture. And so does his wife, Sourayah. Sourayah is a great beauty and her husband is very proud of her. She's even been photographed wearing Paris fashions without her veil – what a scandal! And, more importantly,' Grace leaned forward, her eyes shining with enthusiasm, 'the royal pair have a notion to overhaul education in Afghanistan and insist that it be provided for all girls as well as for boys. There has even been talk of enfranchisement for women.'

Betty began to understand Grace's reasons for taking on the dangerous employment. 'So, you'll get alongside Sourayah and encourage her to go in the right direction? But isn't that a bit dangerous, Grace? They're all firmly Muslim – you won't exactly be doing this with the good-will of most of the country, I'll bet,' said Betty shrewdly. 'The Mullahs, surely, won't be very happy with these schemes? You could run into some fearsome opposition.'

Betty looked again at the hills rising in jagged ranks, tier upon tier of rugged desolation until they reached the towering peaks of the snow-lined Hindu Kush, and she could no longer fight back a sense of foreboding. On an impulse, she reached forward and seized Grace's hands. 'Change your mind, Grace! It's not too late! Don't go up into that wilderness!'

54

Chapter Five

Glad to have a moment or two together, Betty and James Lindsay sat together on the roof of the fort.

'So glad you're here, Bets!' said James sentimentally, reaching out to hold her hand, having first made sure that no disapproving eye would observe this erotic proceeding.

'Well, at least I'll mastermind your dinner party,' said Betty comfortably, 'and I'll do place names if you like. Who would you like next to you, for a start?'

'It's not a question of who I'd like, it's who I should have and I suppose I should have that stupid old fool Burroughs on one side and Rathmore on the other. Put Zeman Khan next to little Miss what's 'er name . . .'

'Coblenz,' Betty supplied.

'Yes, that's right. Put Zeman next to Lily Coblenz and put Grace on his other side to keep an eye on him.'

'And where do you want me?'

'Oh, you can handle the dashing Group Captain and Zeman's mate. I wish this party was over! I'm quite hopeful that no one will kill anyone else but it'll be touch and go! That Lily is trouble on two legs if ever I saw it! I can't imagine how they ever allowed her to come up here! But there we are!'

They stepped out of the shade into the searing sunshine and looked down on the busy life of the fort.

'I must say, I could do with a swim!' said Betty.

'Don't even think of it! And don't let that blasted Lily think of it either!'

And they went their separate ways, Betty to oversee the

preparations for the evening – though oversee was hardly the word since it seemed unlikely that the Pathan cooks would take much notice of her – and James to conduct a tour of the fort. He had wondered very much whether Zeman and Iskander should be part of this. After all, potentially they were his enemies. He decided in the end that such was the excellence of his defensive arrangements, it could do no harm to show the tribesmen, through Zeman, what they were up against.

Accordingly the tourist party formed up on the parade ground. Lord Rathmore, continuing to resent finding himself one of a party, was acutely aware that his status was not being adequately recognized. Zeman was eloquent with a friendly babble of question and comment but Iskander hardly spoke. Though seemingly indifferent, he nevertheless had eyes everywhere and, while he did not exactly have a notebook open on his knee, he wasn't missing much and in particular he was noticing the high state of readiness of the Scouts' garrison. 'Good!' thought James. Fred Moore-Simpson was cheerful and tactless, his very English voice perpetually rising above the muttered responses of the other men. No problem there, thoroughly dependable and entertaining chap, James thought.

No, if there were going to be difficulties they would start with Lily Coblenz. She chattered and exclaimed, eyeing the men with unblushing appreciation, asking Zeman, to whom she seemed to have attached herself, indiscreet questions touching on the status of women in the tribal areas, perpetually pressing for a chance to leave the safety of the fort to try the alleged dangers of tribal territory. Her introduction to the two Afghan guests had been a warning. Strangely, it had been Iskander who had initially claimed her total attention. She hadn't been able to take her eyes off him and James could quite see why. The chap was a particularly handsome specimen. Iskander, outwardly at least, had not welcomed the attention and after an initial startled gaze, almost certainly his first close sight of an American woman, he had, in the polite Pathan way, avoided looking at her, not difficult when a good twelve inches higher than the object of one's scorn. James cringed as he remembered the first exchange between them. Looking boldly up at the tall Pathan she had said, 'Tell me, how did you come by those green eyes, Mr Khan?' And James remembered Iskander's level response, 'The same way you came by *your* green eyes, Miss Coblenz.'

It had been Zeman who came smoothly to the rescue. 'I always say he found them under a gooseberry bush!' he said and all were relieved to join in the laughter.

'Joe's supposed to be in charge of this girl, blast him!' thought James resentfully. 'I think he might have taken the trouble to explain that downcast eyes would not have been out of place. And that's the very least. If I had my way I'd put her in an all-enveloping, ankle-length burkha for the duration!' And he could have done without the hissing intake of appreciative breath when elements of Zeman's Afghani escort stalked by. 'Ah, well,' he thought with resignation, 'a few more hours, that's all we have to get through.'

James gathered his group around him and cleared his throat loudly to call them to order. 'Well, if the brass hats expect me to behave like a ruddy Cook's Tours guide, I'll give them their money's worth!' he had warned Joe and he began.

'Gor Khatri!' he announced. 'That's where you are but how many of you know what the name means? No one? I'll tell you. It means "The Warrior's Grave". Now we don't know what warrior or precisely where his grave is located but one day perhaps we will. I hope so. This has always been a strong place. You will have appreciated its geographical and strategic advantages: within an easy ride of Peshawar, covering the trade routes of the Khyber and the Bazar Valley, close to the river yet not dependent on it – we have three deep wells all safely within the confines of the walls. And as you see we are by no means the first to exploit the situation. Its origins are lost in antiquity; we know it was used by the Kushan kings of Gandhara over

57

two thousand years ago and I like to imagine Alexander the Great passing through and feeling safe here. Marco Polo visited the fort in 1275 or thereabouts.' James smiled. 'It's reported that he found this a place where "The people have a peculiar language, they worship idols and have an evil disposition." '

'But of course, nowadays we no longer worship idols,' Zeman said helpfully to Lily. She tried to stifle her laughter.

James continued, 'The Moghul Emperor Babur established a fortified caravanserai on this spot in the fifteen hundreds and Mountstuart Elphinstone found shelter here in the last century.'

'Say, James, weren't there ever any *women* here? I mean, we surely can't be the first to visit, can we?' Lily interrupted.

'As a matter of fact, there are evidences of a Hindu shrine which could well be the work of the daughter of Shah Jehan . . .' James went on.

'He's making this up!' thought Joe. 'Surely?'

'. . . and who knows? Perhaps I should expand my standard speech to mention that Lily Coblenz, the Calamity Jane of the twentieth century, left her mark.'

Lily very much appreciated this and was the first to burst out laughing. The company trailed after James in good humour as he led them around the fortifications.

'This,' said James, 'is one of the oldest parts of the fort. That tower is a hundred years old, maybe two hundred years old. You can't tell because the style didn't change for longer than that. And that alarm bell is about as old. We don't use it but there it is. When we first moved here it was there to summon help – to turn out the guard. I suppose if this was a ship you'd say to signal "All hands on deck". Even we have something a little more sophisticated now in the form of a siren if we need it but I've left the bell there. It's part of the history of the place.' And the inspection continued.

Apart from a close examination of the thickness, height

and strength of the crenellated and loop-holed walls, the Afghans' attention was caught by the sports facilities. Some of these (stage managed by James, Joe guessed) were being actively demonstrated by teams of Scouts who were obviously enjoying playing to an audience. 'This,' said James unnecessarily, 'is our cricket pitch. And that our hockey field. The Scouts play cricket but the Afghanis don't. We're hoping we can change that. All play hockey, of course, and basketball.'

Grace Holbrook, it seemed, was holding the whole party together. She was just as at home with the Afghani escort from Kabul as with the Pathan Scouts themselves; just as at home with the imperial establishment as with Lily Coblenz. Interested and competent, she was clearly enjoying her tour of the fort, asking sensible questions about the water supply and the irrigation system, admiring the dairy herd and making suggestions for the planting of a second orchard.

The inspection wound on its way until James was able to say, 'And this we're really proud of! This is our poultry yard. We've found that Leghorns seem to do best. This is Achmed, our head poultryman.' Joe turned to introduce to the party an appreciative Pathan and spoke to him at length in Pushtu, listening and translating his reply. 'We have problems,' he said. 'Wild pheasants raiding our poultry yard! For example – look at that thing!' He drew attention to a gaudy pheasant casually seated on a nearby roof. 'As soon as our backs are turned he'll come down like a wolf on the fold!'

'Why don't you just shoot him?' came Lily's eager voice. 'Why don't you let *me* shoot him? Go on, James! I wish you would!' And, turning to Zeman, 'Tell him to let me have a go!'

Zeman laughed. 'Go on, Lindsay! Let her have a go. See if she can do it. Every woman in my village could do it. Go on, Miss Coblenz – for the honour of the great American Republic! Slay and spare not!'

'This is not the OK Corral, Miss Coblenz,' said James,

59

smiling with difficulty, 'this is almost a war zone. Any rifle shot heard in the vicinity of the fort evokes a military response. As you can probably understand.'

Zeman looked around him with a wide gesture. 'But all the officers who could be expected to react are here present,' he said slyly. 'No harm, surely, in loosing off one round? Himalayan pheasant aren't built to withstand rifle fire. One shot should do it,' he added, cocking a conspiratorial eyebrow at Lily.

James nodded to Joe and, deeply reluctant but unable to dodge the challenge, Joe took a rifle from a nearby Scout and handed it to Lily. 'That's the safety catch,' he began. 'And remember once the bullet has left the rifle it travels for about a mile which is why, on the whole, we don't gun down marauding wild fowl with express rifles but I suppose it's safe enough while the condemned has its back to a rock face. Be careful now – that thing has a kick like a mule!'

Flushed and excited, Lily shrugged him aside, brought the rifle up to her shoulder and fired. In a cartwheel of feathers and squawks the pheasant virtually disintegrated. Amidst general applause, a Scout brought the battered body back and proffered it to Lily.

'Jeez!' said Lily, surreptitiously rubbing her shoulder. 'What am I supposed to do with this?'

'Put a tail feather in your hat,' suggested Lord Rathmore.

'Get yourself photographed with your quarry,' said Grace. 'That's what most shikari who come up here do.'

'I should send it down to the kitchen,' said Fred Moore-Simpson, laughing. 'Waste not, want not! Tell them to serve it up for dinner tonight.'

'Or what's left of it,' said Rathmore.

James took a look round, mentally calling the roll. 'Someone missing,' he said. And then, 'Where's Burroughs?'

'He had to leave us,' said Fred. 'He'll be flat on his back by now, drinking a little and thinking a lot and yearning for Delhi. Poor old sod.'

*　　*　　*

60

At the end of what had been a long day, a day in which Betty Lindsay had revised her seating plans at least half a dozen times, she surveyed her final arrangements. Not bad, she decided. Not perfect but the best that this incongruous mob could possibly supply. The men of course had done a splendid job and really the Pathan feast laid out in the durbar hall was very glamorous and impressive. Pathans were surprising. A warrior race indeed and, if she was to believe all she was told, treacherous, vengeful and ruthless, yet they could spend happy hours decorating a dinner table and to a standard that would put a Home Counties Women's Institute to shame. Thick rugs had been spread in the centre of the room and surrounded by tasselled cushions. A white cloth covered the rugs and this was decorated with candles and sprays of blossom and spring flowers. Dishes of Pathan and Persian food were to appear in procession to be set out down the length of the table so that the guests might help themselves. Nervously Betty wondered whether she had remembered to tell everyone to use only their right hand. Yes, she was sure she had.

She stood for a peaceful moment alone to calm herself before the guests arrived in the doorway of the durbar hall enjoying its unusual beauty. James had taken her on her own private reconnaissance tour that morning and she remembered his pleasure when she had gasped with delight on entering. 'Our pride and joy!' he had said. 'When I got here this was just a store room with the accumulated rubbish of two thousand years on the floor! About a foot thick, I'd guess. Dust, cigarette ends, goat shit, dead rats, fallen plaster – you can imagine! I set people to clear it up as a fatigue – a punishment, you know – shovelling muck off the floor, scrubbing it down, then we made the most remarkable discovery. Under the debris there was what you now see. I think it's a Buddhist stupa . . . second, third century AD? We cleaned it down and whitewashed it and left it to speak for itself.'

Betty looked again at the ancient tiled floor. How would

you describe it? Turquoise and gold? No – turquoise and chestnut. Polished, mysterious and serene, the floor reflected the encircling arcade. The last shafts of warm sunshine knifed down from the rim of the dome and seemed to set the floor ashiver. And how sensible, Betty thought, how typical of her husband that he would have left the room free of any Western frippery, content to allow the natural materials and the graceful proportions to make their own statement.

Betty moved aside as a procession of white-clad Pathans arrived carrying in the dinner dishes. Fragrant piles of fluffy rice spiced with saffron and spiked with almonds would surely appeal to everyone. The platters were accompanied by deep dishes of curried lamb, plates of roast chicken, mounds of mint-flavoured meatballs, heaps of flat Peshawar bread and, in pride of place, a roasted, clove-studded fat-tailed sheep. Her party looked good and promising. As the rest of the guests appeared and conversation built up Betty began to enjoy herself. Even her morning sickness had left her though, cautiously, she decided it would be sensible not to accept a glass of champagne from the steward who was handing out Bollinger and took a glass of iced fruit juice instead.

She looked around the table. How plain the British men looked in their white mess jackets, their white shirts, black ties and black trousers when seen alongside the two Pathans. Zeman and Iskander had obviously determined to make an impression, Betty thought gratefully. Already well over six feet, both men had increased their height by the addition of a tall, bright blue turban. They wore baggy blue trousers, white shirts and gold-embroidered waistcoats, red for Zeman and blue for Iskander. Both wore flat gold-embroidered slippers. They settled, cross-legged – obviously at ease – into their appointed places and each took a glass of sherbet.

As the light faded, pottery lamps were carried in and placed between each pair of guests. Flickering in the soft wind that blew through the open doors they reflected and deepened the colours in the tiled floor.

Betty decided that she had done her hostess's duty by setting herself between the two most unpromising social partners. On her right, Burroughs, white with anguish, hating everything that had happened or that he had seen during that day and his hatred compounded by the horror of his being required to sit cross-legged on the floor in evening dress contemplating a very long menu of food, none of which he could possibly digest.

Betty turned from him to Lord Rathmore on her left. Lord Rathmore was sulking. He had looked forward to this dinner party and had counted on sitting next to Lily Coblenz. He thought she had what he would have called a roving eye and might repay a little flattering attention. American girls, he had noticed, were impressed by a title. 'Just might be something doing there,' he thought. But now, to his annoyance, he found himself between Iskander Khan and Betty. 'What a waste,' he thought angrily. As his eye surveyed the dinner table he glanced up and caught his own reflection in a wall mirror. Automatically he smoothed his moustache which an Indian barber had given an almost Teutonic twist. 'Not bad,' he thought. 'Don't look a day over forty.' He flashed a conspiratorial smile at his reflection. A few weeks in the Himalayan sunshine had given his normally pink cheeks a ruddy depth. 'An improvement,' he decided as by chance his eye met Lily's for a second.

'Could do with a bit more height – like that conceited oaf, Sandilands. Perhaps look my best sitting down. Might impress on a horse perhaps? This little Lily Coblenz: not just a pretty face. Wielding quite a lot of influence, they say. Could be the makings of a commercial alliance there. "Coblenz-Rathmore Inc?" Must put that idea – among others, of course – into her head!'

'Ha! Ha!' thought Betty, reading his mind. 'He can't be bothered to make conversation with his hostess – other fish to fry. I've got a jolly good mind to take him boringly one by one through the twenty-five runs James made in Peshawar last month. That'd show him!'

She considered that Lily, seated between two seriously attractive men, had drawn the jackpot. Joe, on Lily's left, slightly battered, alluringly bemedalled, had, Betty decided, the sweetest smile she had ever seen. And, on Lily's right, the seductive Zeman. 'Two strong men stand face to face though they come from the ends of the earth,' Betty quoted vaguely from a Kipling poem. At least they were not face to face with Lily between them but near enough.

Betty had relaxed somewhat on welcoming the two women to the table. Both had taken up her suggestion that they should wear a long frock. She herself was setting the tone in a modestly cut Liberty lawn summer dress, not exactly evening wear but voluminous enough to sit in comfort at least. Lily was looking as demure as she could manage (which was not very), beautiful and animated, but entirely proper and unprovocative in a green chiffon dress and simple pearl necklace. She sat on her cushion, her heels tucked up tidily beneath her, her back straight, as though she dined like this every day of her life.

Grace was wearing the dress Grace always wore, a no-nonsense maroon silk with a necklace of jet beads. Thank God for Grace Holbrook! Completely at ease, socially competent, eating everything offered to her, changing effortlessly from Pushtu to Hindi and from Hindi to English and back again, completely aware of the approval of the whole dinner table and, thought Betty loyally, lucky to have James next to her on one side and perfectly able to make conversation with the chattering Fred Moore-Simpson on the other. 'I'll be like that when I'm a bit older,' she decided enviously.

The only incongruous note at the table was Iskander Khan. Betty eyed him critically. Yes, perhaps she had made a mistake with Iskander. It had been wrong to seat him next to the unattractive Rathmore whom she thought unlikely to make the slightest attempt to conceal his intentions which were simply to find a way into Afghanistan and, more or less, buy up everything of any possible value and replace it with shabby trade goods mixed in with a few obsolete rifles. The passionately nationalist Iskander would have little to say to him. Little indeed to say to his neighbour on the other side. As far as Betty understood it, Fred's general idea was that the proper way to keep peace on the frontier was to advance British interests deep into tribal territory and keep them there through the influence of rapid deployment of a squadron of light bombers. Perhaps she had made a bad mistake in seating him next to a potential target! But then, thought Betty, noticing the two deep in animated and not unfriendly conversation, effectively, strip aside the voice and the clothes and they were really very similar. With their positions reversed, Iskander would passionately welcome the opportunity of dropping bombs on Fred Moore-Simpson. And there they sat, each wrapped in his tribal habits and each perfectly understanding the other. And not dissimilar in appearance, Betty decided, comparing Fred's elegant figure, neat moustache and sleek fair hair not unfavourably with the exotic Iskander.

Her eye roamed to the head – or was it the foot? – of the table and rested on the lamp-lit red curls and humorous blue eyes of James Lindsay. 'My husband,' she thought. 'The best! Not the handsomest but certainly the best! There he sits. Well, I know who's the lucky girl at this table! He looks jolly tired though. I'll be glad when he's got rid of this crowd and can get back to his dangerous, responsible, hard-working, unresting life! Really! They ask too much of my poor man! Soldier, diplomat and now Mine Host!' Betty suspected that her protective instincts were wasted on the hardened and competent man she had married. At that moment James looked up. Their eyes met and she winked at him. He put his tongue out at her.

Before she could respond, a volley of shots rang out overhead. A pause and it was followed by another hail of bullets, accompanied by the scream of ricochets and somewhere in the distance the shattering of a pane of glass. For a moment everyone sat rigidly still, eyes wide, ears straining.

'Is that someone shooting at us?' Lily said.

'Yes, probably,' said James easily. 'Certainly sounds like it. More champagne, anyone?'

'Shouldn't you *do* something? Shouldn't you go out and *fight* them?'

For answer James crooked a finger at one of the jemadars who was standing by unmoving. 'Just go and see what all that was about,' he said. The jemadar bowed and left.

Lily didn't need to be told what it was all about. She knew. The fort was being attacked, though nobody seemed to be taking very much notice. She turned to Grace as another volley erupted. 'Shouldn't they do something?' she demanded excitedly. This was, after all, what she'd come for. Shots in the night! But where was the British reaction? 'I mean, I know you British go about balancing a straight bat on your stiff upper lips but isn't this going a bit too far?'

'I expect they know best,' said Grace placidly, dipping her fingers in a finger bowl as a burst of return fire rang out.

'Well, there you are, Lily, there's the armed response,' said Fred.

'I think you can leave this to the garrison,' said Zeman. 'If it's anything it'll just be a party of those hairy brigands the Zakka Khel Afridi raiding down from the hills for guns and women, firing from the hip as they come. They do it all the time! Tribesmen in these parts are disgracefully primitive in their reactions, you'll find.'

An uneasy thought occurred to Lily. She turned to Zeman. 'Hey! Zeman! You're an Afridi, aren't you? Which side are you on anyway?' Encountering a gleam of amusement in the eye of Iskander, Lily fell silent for a moment, thoughtful and indignant. At the next lull in the firing she spoke again. 'Okay, James! I said – okay! You can tell your guys to stand down now. Thanks, I'm sure, for the floor show! Well, gee willikins!' she drawled sarcastically. 'I'll certainly have something to tell the girls back home in Chicago now, won't I?'

Joe smiled at her cross face. He thought he might come to like Miss Coblenz after all.

Betty too was impressed. 'When I get you to myself, James Lindsay,' she thought, 'I shall tell you your little entertainment misfired!' All the same, she had admired the American girl's reaction. If Lily had had a rifle to hand, she'd have led the charge through the door to deal with the problem. 'If I were ever stuck on a covered wagon rolling across the prairie (and that's probably what the Coblenz family were doing a generation or two back!) I'd be jolly pleased to find Lily Coblenz at my elbow,' she decided.

She leaned forward and addressed the company. 'Well, I don't know about anyone else but my nerves could do with a bit of soothing!' (Not true – James had forewarned his pregnant wife of what was to come and sticking his tongue out had been the signal – but she felt that Lily had been made to feel foolish and this distressed her.) 'So shall we have the sweet things brought on? We have some candied fruits, some fresh fruit and even ice cream – there's quite a bit more to come.'

She was interrupted by a steward who came in gingerly carrying a small dish. He approached Betty and spoke diffidently to her. 'Oh, my!' Betty exclaimed. 'Humble apologies from the kitchens. The cook almost forgot the most important dish of the evening. Lily's golden pheasant! Apparently he's had a little difficulty with it but he's done his best and here it is. Not much of it, I'm afraid. Now who would like a helping? Does anyone have room to do justice to this delicacy?'

Betty asked eagerly but without much hope. The amounts of food consumed had been enormous and even that stuffed shirt Burroughs had unbent sufficiently to help himself to several of the dishes as soon as he had ascertained that, in fact, hardly any of them contained curry. Eyes slid away from hers and focused on plates, fingers fluttered in a dismissive way, even Lily shook her head. Pathan good manners came to the rescue and Zeman said cheerfully enough that he would be delighted to taste the pheasant. Gratefully Betty passed the dish and he managed to scrape up quite a convincing helping of pheasant fragments. Lily looked pleased. Betty, to keep her countenance and to flatter Lily, also took a helping, as small as she could decently contrive, and pronounced it delicious. It certainly was. She would commend the cook tomorrow on the inventive way he'd dealt with such unpromising material. The sauce was creamy – yoghurt? – and subtly spiced, the meat distinctly chewy but full of flavour. How wonderful it was to have recovered her appetite! She would actually welcome a dish of ice cream to round off the meal.

With the savoury dishes cleared away and the cloth bright with fresh and candied fruits and glass pitchers of pomegranate juice and a rank of champagne bottles, James announced the next diversion. A group of musicians were to play and sing folk songs. Five Khattaks entered with pipes and drum and stringed instruments. Wearing their native costume they strode lithely into the hall, black shining hair bobbing on their shoulders. They settled themselves on the dais at the end of the hall and began to play and sing in the soft, liquid accent of the southern hill tribes. Lily was enchanted. This, too, was what she'd come for. Eyes shining, she listened to every word, nodding her head gently in rhythm.

They became aware of one short song in particular – nothing more than a couplet – endlessly repeated. Lily's lips moved with the song. When the singers paused to take a glass of sherbet, she turned to Zeman and announced with some satisfaction, 'That last song – I've learned the words! Listen! I can sing in Pushtu!'

She began in a clear voice and with what sounded to Betty like a very convincing accent to repeat the two lines.

Before she was half-way through Grace leaned forward and spoke to her firmly. 'That'll do, Lily.'

'What do you mean?' Lily wanted to know. 'I was doing all right, wasn't I? Why can't I sing?'

James put his hand over his mouth. The musicians were barely suppressing laughter and Zeman had a problem too. The austere Iskander looked disapprovingly on.

'Because that song is frightfully rude and no woman should be heard repeating the words, especially when there are Pathan gentlemen present,' Grace hissed and at this point Zeman rose discreetly to his feet and went to talk to the musicians.

Lily persisted. 'Well, how tantalizing! Now you just have to tell me! You must – or I'll start singing it again!'

Grace eyed her with malicious amusement. 'You have to believe me, Lily.' She paused for a moment in thought and then said deliberately, 'Oh, very well. You did ask. But do wait until you're back in Chicago before you repeat it.' She moved around the table and slipped into Zeman's vacated place, moving his sherbet glass aside the better to lean over to Lily's ear. Speaking softly, her voice was only just audible. 'It's a very old song called *"Zakhme Dhil"* which means "The Wounded Heart". The singer is saying,

'Over the river lives a boy with a bottom like a peach,
But, alas, I cannot swim!'

Lily looked at her with incomprehension. At last she said, 'But the singer's a man.'

'You're very quick,' said Grace. 'And that, of course, is the whole point!'

Lily sank further into confusion. Betty Lindsay began to fear her party was about to implode but was too fascinated by the exchange to reach for the polite distraction etiquette demanded of a hostess.

'I don't get it,' Lily said finally.

'Then perhaps they don't *have* it in Chicago,' said Grace. 'I see I must explain. Amongst the Pathan, as with many

69

warrior races – Spartans, Zulus, British Public Schoolboys for example . . .' Her voice sank until it was inaudible to Betty but, much amused, she could guess the progress of the information being imparted by the deepening flush of crimson on Lily's face and the widening of her eyes.

The lesson over, Grace returned to her place and selected a candied peach, looking very pleased with herself. Lily gulped and began surreptitiously to examine the musicians under lowered eyelashes. When Zeman returned and took his seat next to her again, Lily's back became even more rigid and she turned in earnest conversation to Joe. Joe seemed to be having great difficulty in keeping his face in control but responded warmly in an effort to cover Lily's embarrassment.

After an interval the musicians began again, their songs, possibly at the suggestion of Zeman, taking on a plaintive and romantic mood. Cups of green tea were handed out and Betty watched, intrigued, as Iskander took a small silver box from his pocket and proceeded to sprinkle some of the contents on to his tea. Lily also was fascinated.

'What is that stuff, Iskander?' she wanted to know.

'Flakes of white cardamom, Miss Coblenz.'

'An excellent carminative,' said Grace. 'Frightfully good for the digestion. You should all try it.'

Lily held out her cup for a sprinkling of the spice from Iskander's hand and sniffed the fragrant brew, her eyes over the rim smiling her appreciation. Zeman watched her in some disquiet. He held out his cup and invited Iskander in florid language to favour him with the wherewithal to calm a stomach so full of good things after such a generous and delicious meal.

'Oh, Lord!' thought Betty. 'What comes next? Burps? Do Pathans do burps?'

Her thoughts were interrupted by, of all people, Edgar Burroughs. Almost silent until now, he had been steadily eating his way, Betty had noticed, through a good number of the dishes. At last he had a useful contribution to make to the general chatter. 'If it's stomach settling you're after, you fellows,' he said, addressing, rather uncomfortably, the two Pathans, 'you couldn't do better than these. Swear by them!' He produced a packet of bismuth tablets and passed them to Zeman. Politely concealing his surprise, Zeman took a pill and swallowed it with expressions of gratitude. Everyone else politely refused and handed them back to Burroughs who now felt free to avail himself of his favourite relief without the subterfuge of palming one into his mouth under the pretence of coughing.

Zeman, apparently determined to play the exotic and compelling mysterious man of the East, had reclaimed Lily's attention and was introducing her to Pushtu poetry. Lily listened, drawn in despite herself by the seductive sounds. The translations when they came had by all appearances nothing in them to give offence.

'I think that's just beautiful!' she exclaimed. 'Now tell me, who wrote that?'

Zeman smiled a secret smile and said, 'I think that is a Persian poet whom we sometimes refer to as Nisami. And he also wrote . . .' There followed a rush, a surge of soft Persian and then he murmured, hypnotic dark eyes on Lily,

'The silver fingers of the Moon
Explore the dark depths
Of the sleeping pool
And I wait to see your shadow fall
On the garden's midnight wall.'

Joe stirred uncomfortably. Should he intervene? Was Zeman playing his role with a little too much zest? Local colour was one thing but this was oversteering surely? She was just impressionable enough to want to be off with the wraggle-taggle gypsies-o, and he had no intention of shipping a heartbroken Lily Coblenz back to Simla. Better be safe than sorry. He cleared his throat. 'Shall you be racing at Saratoga this summer, Miss Coblenz?' he asked brightly.

He was not the only one to feel concern for Lily. Lord Rathmore had been keeping a watchful eye on her. And now the torrent of suggestive and sinuous verse poured into her innocent ear by this silk-clad tailor's dummy was more than he could stomach. If that police lout who was supposed to be squiring her was not prepared to do anything about the unpleasant situation that was developing, *he* would! He leaned forward and his voice boomed out above the general chatter.

'Are you aware, I wonder, Miss Coblenz, of our own English poets? Kipling perhaps? Ever heard of him? Excellent chap! Now he really knows how to put it together! Brings a tear to the eye every time! He has something very apt to say about this part of the world, in fact. Would you like to hear it?'

Stunned and annoyed, Lily could only nod dubiously.

'Here goes then! Now what was it? Ah, yes! Got it!' He prepared his voice for recitation with a disagreeable rasping noise, put one hand on his hip and the other over his heart and began.

> *'With home-bred hordes the hillsides teem,*
> *The troopships bring us one by one,*
> *At vast expense of time and steam,*
> *To slay Afridis where they run.*
> *The "captives of our bow and spear"*
> *Are cheap alas! as we are dear!'*

This was exactly what Betty had been afraid of. 'Men!' she thought angrily. 'If you take their guns and knives away, they'll fight with anything that comes to hand – even, apparently, lines of verse. Better than hurling bread rolls but not much. Rathmore! What a fool! Such a cheap shot! And now Zeman is insulted and will have to take his revenge!'

She decided to forestall this by closing down the dinner party and she began to rise to her feet, catching the eyes of the other two ladies, but too late, Zeman had rounded on

Rathmore. She could tell he was deeply angry by the sweetness of his smile and the softness of his tone as he addressed the red-faced lord.

'I see you know your *Barrack Room Ballads*, Rathmore! But you miss your chance to quote the best verse of that poem. "Arithmetic on the Frontier", wasn't it? May I?

> *'A scrimmage in a Border Station –*
> *A canter down some dark defile –*
> *Two thousand pounds of education*
> *Drops to a ten rupee jezail.*
> *The Crammer's boast, the Squadron's pride,*
> *Shot like a rabbit in a ride!'*

He clearly relished delivering the last line and asked smoothly, 'Have you calculated the worth of *your* expensive education, my lord, should some tribal owner of a ten rupee Afridi musket take you for a rabbit?'

The blue of Rathmore's small blue eyes intensified. All held their breath.

'Much the same as yours, I would estimate, old boy! Not a vast deal of difference between Rugby and Harrow, I should think. You tell me!' he replied, looking about him triumphantly for support for his thrust. 'And now, I can see that Betty is making a move to send us all off upstairs with our mugs of cocoa! Miss Coblenz, let me escort you to your room.' He put out an arm and, scowling and uncertain, Lily took it. They came over to Betty and thanked her in turn for their evening and left the room, Lily casting a speaking glance over her shoulder at Zeman.

The last they heard from Rathmore was a rumbling laugh and in a stage whisper to Lily, 'Rugby indeed! All paid for by the British, of course, if my information is correct.'

Chapter Six

Joe walked silently round the guest wing. 'Past eleven o'clock and all's well,' he was tempted for a moment to call out. But only just 'all well,' thanks to that bloody fool Rathmore! Blast him! He could have provoked a fourth Afghan war with his jingoistic rubbish. Just the kind of thing to raise the sensitive prickles of Zeman and, indeed, the even more sensitive prickles of Iskander. To insult a guest was against all the rules of Pathan hospitality – against all the rules of Joe's idea of hospitality too. Luckier than he deserved, than he even realized in fact, that Zeman had taken it so lightly.

Joe, James and Fred had stayed on with the two Afghans after the party broke up, James calling distractedly for brandy. Fred, bottle in hand, did the honours, pouring out with lavish hand glasses of a fine old cognac. Joe guessed that the generosity of Fred's measures reflected the relief of the five men that they had been left behind by the civilians. He could not deny that he felt more comfortable in the after-dinner company of Zeman and Iskander than that of Rathmore and Burroughs. To Joe's surprise both the Pathans accepted a glass of brandy. To Joe's further surprise they were quite prepared to settle down and do what Pathans enjoy after a good meal: they proceeded to swap news and scandal and tell stories and even to have a laugh at Rathmore's expense. Unexpectedly, Iskander gave an impassioned and hilarious imitation of Rathmore's declamatory style. This broke any remaining ice and they all relaxed gratefully into the familiar unbuttoned comfort of an after-dinner officers' mess.

So in the end, everyone had rolled away to bed in high good humour, beyond anything Joe and James could have expected. Accompanied by vigilant Scouts James patrolled the lower fort, Eddy Fraser the grounds, and it fell to Joe to check the guest wing. 'Remember,' James had said, 'the frontier never sleeps,' and, thankfully at last, his patrol complete, he had settled in for the night with Betty in the double-sized guest room on the first floor. Not much concession to marital comforts here! Two iron beds, two narrow mattresses, four coat hangers, two candlesticks, two candles, and two bedside tables. 'No concessions!' he had warned Betty. 'Not even for the memsahib! We don't want to get a reputation for having gone soft. This is a barracks not the Ritz!' But his wife's presence turned it into paradise. James had no yearnings for silk-clad houris reclining on damask cushions; Betty and an army issue blanket filled his world for the night.

Joe had seen that the defences were impeccable and he stood for a moment listening to the soft footsteps of sentries in their grass-soled chaplis on the walls above his head. Impeccable. Yes. As tightly controlled as one could wish. And yet the swift gleam of moonlight on a bayonet as a sentry turned awoke a sickening and well-remembered fear in Joe. For a dizzying moment he remembered that the fort was manned by over a thousand native troops, cousins of the very men against whom they were busily defending these walls. What held them and their loyalty in place? The handful of British officers? The King's shilling? Joe leaned his back against the wall as the vertigo took hold. What the hell was he doing here? What was James doing here? What business did they have in this unyielding wilderness? Had he elected to join a mad picnic party on the slopes of a volcano? All his senses were crying a warning.

He calmed himself by reaching in his pocket for a cigarette. The scrape of his match against the box was enough to bring a hissed warning down from the wall above. 'No, no, sahib! No smoking after dark!' Joe grinned, his tension evaporating. No problems with the security of the defences but he remained uneasy, however, as to the internal safety measures. The fort was not designed to cope with trouble from within. But what trouble could there be? Joe only knew that he felt uneasy. He had learned to trust his instinct and never to dismiss a prickle of anxiety however subconscious, however unfocused. He thought carefully about each occupant of the guest wing and came to the conclusion that his anxieties centred on Rathmore. Arrogant, eager to make an authoritative impression for Lily's benefit and even with a half-formed determination to put Zeman – 'and any other blasted tribesman' – in his place, Rathmore was troubling him. Had he learned a lesson? Joe wasn't sure but at least Lily, his primary charge, was safely tucked up in bed by now and alone. Joe had called to her to be sure to lock her door and she had briefly opened it with a derisive smile and had said impatiently, 'Don't you worry about *me*, Joe! I'm perfectly well equipped to defend myself but – if it'll make *you* feel easier . . .' And she had closed the door firmly. He heard her fumble with the lock and a last decisive click reassured him that in this at least she was prepared to take his advice.

'Now what did she mean by that?' he thought as he went along the corridor. 'Ought I to have checked her luggage for a secreted Colt revolver?' He remembered her remark about Wyatt Earp and the skill with which she'd shot the pheasant and he wondered again about Miss Coblenz. She was on the first floor also, between James's room and Joe's own. At the end of the corridor was Grace Holbrook. Well, for good or ill, there they lay in a row.

And, at least, all on the first floor were able to lock their doors. With the sudden influx of civilian visitors James had organized carpenters to fit locks to the guest wing rooms but supplies of ironmongery had run out when the first floor had been fitted and he'd decided to install the female guests – and Joe in his protective role – in the more secure accommodation upstairs. The gentlemen downstairs would just have to resort to the chair under the door handle routine if they were of nervous disposition, Joe thought with a smile.

He completed his patrol of the wing by checking on the ground floor rooms. Candles flickered under the doors of the first two rooms occupied by Zeman and Iskander. The next room was in darkness and silent apart from a stricken wuffle. Poor old Burroughs! Next to Burroughs an oil lamp was still alight and Fred Moore-Simpson was tunelessly whistling a selection from *The Mikado*. The room at the end of the corridor was Rathmore's. Dark and silent. Joe hesitated. To disturb or not to disturb? Well, he deserved it!

'Rathmore!' he said, tapping on the door. 'Is all well?'

'Perfectly well,' said Rathmore, adding impatiently, 'Tea at seven. And the papers, please.'

As he passed the stairs to the upper floor a low growl broke out. Somebody had thought it a good idea to house the appalling Minto here by the door in a hastily constructed box. Joe detected James's hand in this. He wouldn't want to spend his precious time alone with Betty fending off Minto and Joe guessed that the animal had been banished from the bedroom. And not happy with the arrangement either, Joe thought, judging by the noises he was making. Joe bent down and tapped on the kennel.

'Anyone at home?'

Minto swaggered out and made his annoyance clear.

'Hey, it's only me – Joe! Remember me? No, obviously not! There's no need to be unfriendly, mate.' Joe picked up Minto by the scruff as he spoke, scrubbed his furry chest and put him down again. 'Back in your kennel! Sit! Stay!' The dog looked at him malevolently. 'Wretched animal!' said Joe and he remembered that leopards in the hills were not uncommon and that they were known to fancy a snack of dog. 'Any hope, I wonder?' but he supposed the fort defences too strong.

Joe walked through the open archway and stepped into the garden for a few moments to clear his head before going to his own bed. It was a very private place enclosed on two sides by the guest wing and the now deserted entertaining rooms. A breath of cool air coming down from the mountains stirred the almond trees and blossom floated lazily down on to the dark pool. The only sound was the gentle gurgling of the piped river water constantly refreshing the swimming pool and for a moment Joe was tempted to throw off his clothes and plunge in. The icy touch of the water was just what he needed to wash away the anxieties and the uncertainties which were making his skin itch. Instead he breathed in the scents of jasmine and rose accompanied, as always in India, by a scent unknown to him. He wandered for a while amongst the roses and stopped to listen to the sudden song of a nightingale in the orchard beyond the wall, shot through by melancholy, aching to share this overpowering moment with someone close, his mind going back to just such an evening in a garden in Calcutta. 'Nancy! Be well, Nancy! I'm thinking of you. Wretched girl!'

He trailed sadly back upstairs to his room. Stifled laughter and the sharp click of a key turning in the lock as he passed James's door heightened Joe's feeling of loneliness. 'I shan't sleep tonight,' he thought. 'Mistake to have that second brandy. Always makes me maudlin!' But he was wrong and against all his expectations he fell straight into sleep. And into a series of disconnected dreams, dreams in which tribesmen jostled with London policemen and snatches of English rang out across the plaintive songs of the frontier. All at once, through this came a warning. Something had clicked him into instant wakefulness.

Dark night still outside and all quiet. All was quiet inside too. Or was it? A light shifted across the gap at the threshold and he slid out of bed and went to stand by the door. Carefully he opened it and peered through. Seeing two familiar figures moving quietly down the corridor, he stepped out. 'Anything I can do?' he called quietly.

James, holding a flickering candle, stopped dead and turned around. He did not smile or even speak, in fact he looked, Joe thought, distinctly put out to see him appearing in the doorway. James frowned, put his finger to his lips and hissed, 'Shh!' Grace Holbrook, following close behind, impressive in ancient plaid dressing gown and curlers and carrying a leather medical case, turned to Joe with a reassuring smile and said in a whisper, 'No need to worry, Joe! It's Betty. James came to fetch me but, you know – worried father-to-be! Her sickness has come back. Not surprising after that supper! Asking for trouble! Anyway I expect a little shot of Collis Browne's Chlorodyne will do the trick! Night-night! And don't worry! I'll fetch you if it's serious – James would want you close by, I think.'

Back in his room, Joe lit a candle and checked the time. Three o'clock. Poor old James! No wonder he looked so seedy! And poor old Betty. What bad luck to be struck down again just when she'd thought it was all over. Joe hoped it hadn't ruined their evening. Betty had steered a sure course through the hazards of that potentially disastrous party and Joe was well aware that her grace, humour and foresight had kept hands off daggers and smiles on lips. Perhaps he would find a vicar's daughter to complete his schemes when he got back to London. Yes, that's what he would look for – a girl who knew what the rules were and who had the spirit to break them. Yawning, he waited for a few more minutes in case Grace needed him and then fell back into sleep and back into dreams. 'Getting too old for the full Pathan Gastronomic Treatment,' was his last waking thought.

He woke as the first note of reveille sounded and at once the early morning hush was shattered. Running footsteps hurrying on the stairs, doors that opened and shut, Indian voices calling anxiously, a wave of distress rolled upwards. Other voices, English and Indian joined in. There was the clang of a water pot being set down and nailed sandals clattered up the stone steps. Joe scrambled hurriedly into his clothes and went to the door. The bearer was standing outside James's door banging loudly, wide-eyed and wailing desperately.

'What's going on?' Joe said.

The bearer turned to him with relief and a torrent of Pushtu as, shock-headed and bleary, James unlocked his door and appeared, shrugging into his jacket, and together they looked down the stairs and at the chattering and wildly gesticulating bearer. James stood seemingly paralysed and at last shook himself. 'Come on, Joe,' he said. 'Something fearful's happened.'

The door of Grace's room opened and she stepped out into the corridor, alert and ready for the day. 'James? Joe? What on earth's going on? Do you need me?'

'Too late if what the bearer has to tell me is right,' said James. 'But come with us, Grace, will you?'

They hurried to the top of the flight of steps and looked down. Sprawled diagonally across the stairs, half-way up there lay a body, apparently lifeless. A brown hand was extended upwards as though appealing for help, a chestnut turban had come unknotted and spilled like a waterfall down the white stone steps. Khaki uniform, shirt and breeches, shiny boots and an unmistakable face turned in profile identified the man.

'Zeman,' Joe said, aghast. 'It's Zeman Khan!'

James, fully awake and taking in the enormity of the event, was the first to react as the politician in the soldier took control and he began quietly to give orders. Joe caught the name of Iskander. 'We'll touch nothing for the moment.'

Stepping carefully they moved down the stairs and knelt beside the body.

'Somebody open the bloody shutter, for God's sake! I can't see a fucking thing! Oh, sorry, Grace! Forgot you were there. We've got a bit of bother here.'

'So it seems,' came the level voice of Grace Holbrook.

And the desperate voice of Iskander Khan: 'Zeman! Is he badly hurt? Did he fall? When did this happen?'

He came from his room buckling on his gun-belt,

already in uniform, and started up the stairs. Joe gripped him by the elbow. 'We've only just found him . . . but – I can't wrap this up – I think, and as I say it it sounds impossible – I think your friend is dead.'

Distraught and dangerous, Iskander looked from one to the other and back to Grace who broke the impasse. She took control at once. 'He may not be dead. Move aside. I must see what I can do! Iskander, will you please approach with me?'

Iskander looked over her shoulder and James and Joe knelt on the stairs. Something caught Grace's attention as she felt for his pulse at wrist and then neck. 'He's dead, I'm afraid, but – oh, good gracious! – look there – and there! Mind your feet and do be careful not to disturb anything, will you all?'

She was pointing to a trail of vomit which had oozed from underneath the body and dried on the stairs. Gently she turned the body over and a further gush of vomit flowed from his mouth. Iskander turned pale and looked aside to hide his distress. Silently Grace pointed to the trail which started at the door of Zeman's room, continued up the stairs and ponded under the body. She resumed her examination, bending limbs, examining eyes, gently feeling his skull.

'Why is he on the stairs? Where was he going?' Lily's voice, wavering and scared, came from above putting the question that had been in everyone's mind. 'And don't tell me to go to my room,' she added. Joe subconsciously noticed she was already dressed, wearing a brown divided riding skirt and a white blouse.

'Could he have been coming to see me?' said Grace. 'Obviously taken ill in the night and seeking assistance. Any opinion on that, Iskander?'

'I think you are right, Dr Holbrook.' Iskander spoke automatically and slowly, as one shocked. 'If he were taken ill he would have sought your help but only as a last resort. That is the Pathan way. He would not have come to look for me because I too am a man and a Pathan.'

Seeing incomprehension all around he elaborated. 'Sickness like this is despised amongst us.' He waved an impatient hand at the trail of vomit. 'It is a weak and womanly thing. If you were unlucky enough to suffer such a thing you would suffer it alone and never draw attention to it. He must have been in fear of his life if he attempted to reach the doctor.'

'That's true,' said James, and Grace nodded, her own opinion confirmed.

The poor, distressed body of Zeman and the sad evidence of a lonely and agonized death only filled the forefront of everyone's mind. All realized that the body before them was more dangerous dead than it had been in life. It needed but one Afghan to shout 'murder', Joe thought, and the fort would explode. And more than the fort. There were considerations here – badal, melmastia, a whole melting pot of barely controlled emotions and compulsions. It would be impossible to mourn the dead man until the facts of his death had been established.

James stood for a moment, unable to move.

'James, why don't you let me deal with this?' said Joe. 'Get some help and we'll take his body down to the hospital. Perhaps you would be willing to give it a proper examination, Grace? Would you agree to that, Iskander?'

Iskander thought for a moment and everyone was still, waiting for his reaction. 'Yes,' he said, 'certainly. I would, of course, much prefer simply to bury my friend but these are unusual circumstances, an unusual death. It is important for everyone to be clear as to how Zeman died. Dr Holbrook is the only one who can tell us this and she is trusted alike by you and by us. She is aware of our customs and religious observances and I am confident that she will honour them and show respect for the dead. But I would ask that three of my men be summoned to be present also. The Amir would expect it,' he added. He moved with an almost ceremoniously protective gesture to put himself between the body of his friend and the rest of the company. 'If you would kindly have a stretcher sent we

82

will carry our kinsman down to the hospital. Meanwhile, I will guard his body.'

The body of Zeman was laid out on a table in the morgue of the hospital. He lay soiled and lifeless but commanding even in death. 'What a bloody waste,' thought Joe. 'All his life before him. I liked and admired him. That man could have been my friend.' Three wide-eyed Afghan officers briefed by Iskander stood solemnly in the background, watchful and suspicious, and Grace began her post-mortem examination.

'Now you do all understand that I am not a pathologist,' said Grace, fixing on a pair of spectacles. 'But I do appreciate that Muslims bury their dead very swiftly and if we are going to get to the bottom of the cause of Zeman's death, I'll have to do my best. Sir Bernard Spilsbury would find much to fault in my performance, I'm sure.'

'Grace,' said James, 'he's in London, you are here. You're the best doctor in India and more importantly you're the only civilian doctor for three hundred miles so go ahead. Our own MO here is a jolly fine chap, as you know, you trained him after all – and none better when it comes to treating bullet wounds and sunstroke but he'd be the first to say, "Let Dr Holbrook do it." '

Grace stripped away Zeman's clothing with assistance from Iskander and began to work away patiently with a steady hand, giving a commentary on what she was doing in English and in Pushtu. She took the temperature of the body. She examined eyelids and lower jaw explaining that these areas would give the earliest and the clearest indication of the onset of rigor mortis but following this with the caveat that the relatively low temperature of the stone staircase would have delayed rigor. She asked her audience to mark the beginnings of hypostasis, pointing out the tell-tale pattern of staining which showed the points where his body had been in contact with the hard stone steps. They noted the livid bluish colour which had begun to gather at the waist and in the right buttock and thigh. Proof, as all witnessed, that his body had lain there where found for some hours and had not been moved from some other place and put on the stairs. She examined his limbs and torso finding no wounds, no puncture marks, nothing unusual.

Such an intimate examination of the body of their senior officer must have been unbearably stressful for the Afghans, Joe thought, but so extreme were the circumstances of the man's death and so acute the need to know the truth, they watched on, silent and wary. And the whole thing was only possible thanks to the impersonal, efficient and thoroughly scientific procedure Grace was demonstrating.

Finally, a gruelling hour later, she was ready to sum up. Pointing to a white china dish which held a sample of the vomit taken from the mouth and throat she said, 'Well, there you have it. The matter expelled consists, as you might expect, of semi-digested particles of the food Zeman ate at the banquet, poultry, rice, fruit and so on. I see no evidence of foreign matter but lacking the facilities of a chemistry laboratory that is as much as I am able to say. The state of digestion, as you see from the size of the particles, is not very advanced and this gives us an indication of the time of death. A time which is borne out, I may say, by the temperature of the body and the progress of rigor.'

'But why Zeman?' Iskander interrupted. 'We all ate the food. No one else has been affected!'

James and Grace looked at each other in horror and each said, 'Oh, my God!'

'What? What are you saying? Who . . .?' said Iskander.

'She's all right, Grace,' James burst out, grasping her hand. 'When I left her this morning she was sleeping like a baby and just as pink. She's all right!'

'I think you'd better tell us what happened in the night, Grace,' said Joe. Turning to Iskander he said, 'I think you should know. I heard a noise at three o'clock and woke.

When I looked into the corridor Grace was going along to attend to Mrs Lindsay.'

'James fetched me. And yes, it would have been at about three. I – we both – assumed it was a return of the sickness she's been suffering from lately, aggravated, no doubt, by the unaccustomed rich food. She told me she had a stomach pain, had vomited and she had a high temperature. I gave her some drops of Chlorodyne and she began to feel better. I sat with her for half an hour and she fell comfortably asleep so I went back to my room.'

Echoing everyone's alarm, James said, 'Look, I'm going to send a bearer to knock up everyone who was at dinner last evening and check whether they've been ill in the night. Who's left? That's Fred, Burroughs and Rathmore. Lily, as we saw for ourselves, is unscathed.'

He gave orders to a Scout standing in attendance.

'While we're waiting . . . is there any other aspect we haven't covered? Any other possible cause of this sickness? I'm trying to avoid saying the dreaded word . . .'

'It's not cholera. No,' said Grace firmly. 'Nor yet dysentery. But you're right. We've been concentrating on the internal workings. A poisonous bite perhaps from animal or reptile? As you all saw, there were no puncture marks on his body. A crack on the head will sometimes make you vomit, though perhaps not so . . . um . . . copiously. No sign of blood anywhere.' She had already taken off Zeman's turban and inspected his head but now she pushed her fingers gently into the thick black hair and palpated the skull inch by inch. With her fingers just beyond the right temple she stopped. She moved them slowly over the interesting patch again and sighed. 'There it is! Nearly missed it. There's an indentation. Three inches long and dead straight. Would you like to feel this, Iskander?'

He nodded and allowed her to guide his finger to the spot. He nodded again. 'As you say,' he confirmed.

The tension in the room was growing. The Afghan soldiers muttered to each other.

'A crack on the head! That's all we need!' Joe thought desperately. 'The Amir's bloody cousin, son of the local Afridi bad boy, killed in suspicious circumstances while he's under James's roof, protected by the shield of melmastia. Killed by one of us! We'll never get out of this alive! Grace, couldn't you have kept your mouth shut?'

But Grace now had the bit between her teeth, the complete professional, absorbed in her task and, watched intently, she was busily shaving away the hair from the suspected wound. 'There!' she announced with satisfaction. 'No wonder I didn't spot it. No bleeding, you see, and very little distortion.'

'It's very straight,' Iskander commented, his eyes watchful like a stalking cat.

'Yes, isn't it?' said Grace apparently unconcerned. 'As the skin has not been penetrated to any depth it was obviously not a blow from a talwar or sharp blade of any kind. The skull has not been crushed so it's not a rifle butt or any of the blunt offensive weapons I expect you come across every day in your work, Commander.'

Joe caught the edge of something in Grace's tone. She was appealing to him in some way. 'The poor old girl's probably feeling the strain of all this, though she hides it well,' he thought. 'It's been a one woman show so far and she's done it beautifully but she needs some help.'

'You're right, Doctor. Not the blow of someone attempting to kill him, you'd say. Just one blow and such an unlikely wound formation,' he said. 'In my experience of head wounds battering occurs. You find several blows on different parts of the skull delivered in uncontrollable rage or to make absolutely certain. And there are no defensive wounds visible, are there? I mean injuries to the hands and arms which a victim receives in his attempts to ward off the attack.' He looked again carefully at Zeman's hands and lower arms. 'No scratches. Not even a broken nail.' And then, 'Good Lord! I know what this is! Iskander – Zeman was lying slightly on one side when we found him, wasn't he? Which side? Do you remember?'

Iskander was ahead of him and broke in, 'It was the right side. Like this.' He demonstrated the position. 'And Zeman's head was resting across the step . . . like this. Are you saying, Sandilands, that he collapsed on the stairs and cracked his head on the straight edge? They are stone, those steps, are they not?'

'They are, and very sharp-edged! I barked my shin on one while we were carrying the body around earlier. There you are!' He rolled up his trouser leg and revealed a livid bruise across his shin. 'Same sort of injury.'

'Mmm . . . that has to be speculation though. Let's take a closer look, shall we?' said Grace.

Wretched woman! Did she never know when to stop? Joe wondered.

Taking a magnifying glass from her kit she peered over the wound, grunted, smiled with grim satisfaction, reached for a pair of tweezers and plucked out something invisible to everyone standing by.

Iskander knew what was required of him.

'They're doing a bloody double act,' Joe thought. 'What *is* going on?'

Iskander took the magnifying glass and held it over the end of the tweezers. He breathed out a gusty sigh. Of relief?

'A flake of white stone,' he announced solemnly.

The Afghanis queued up to examine it in turn, each sighing and nodding.

'So,' said Iskander with authority, 'we are evidently looking at a death by natural causes. Zeman eats something infected at supper, leaves it late before he attempts to seek help, dies on the stairs and hits his head as he falls.'

One of the other Afghanis said something hesitantly and Iskander nodded gravely. 'My friend is asking, Dr Holbrook, what are the possibilities that Zeman was poisoned? Poisoned deliberately?'

Again in two languages Grace began, 'It is certainly possible. Even likely. For this reason we must gather together all who were at the evening meal and find whether anyone else has been affected. We must establish the course of the meal, exactly what he ate and drank. James, could we meet at once in the library? No – back in the durbar hall – it may help people to remember more clearly. It would be a good idea to have last night's kitchen staff standing by in case we need to speak to them. And, Iskander, I would like your officers to be present at our deliberations.'

James gave instructions to his men, who hurried off. 'I've said – in the durbar hall in ten minutes. Hope that's all right?'

The hall when they assembled was clean and bright with no sign of the previous night's party. Joe and James dragged a rug into the middle of the floor and, as the other six people arrived, directed them to sit where they had been the night before.

News of the death of Zeman had spread. Fred Moore-Simpson slipped into his place next to Iskander, briefly placing a comforting arm around his shoulder and murmuring, 'Awfully sorry to hear what's happened. Dreadful, simply dreadful! He was a fine man. Let me know if there's anything – anything – I can do.'

Rathmore came in looking, Joe thought, shaken and apprehensive. Joe was automatically noting everyone's appearance, not quite certain himself what he was looking for but taking in details any of which might at some later point need to be dredged from his unconscious. And there was something different about Rathmore besides his loss of cockiness. He was walking unsteadily. Yes, definitely favouring his right foot. Hardly able to meet Iskander's eye, 'James, Iskander,' he said with a nod to each. 'Shocking bad news. Food poisoning is what I hear? Hasn't affected me, I'm pleased to say. Is that what you wanted to know?' He sat down when invited to do so on the right of Iskander as before.

Pale and exhausted, Edwin Burroughs was next to arrive. He merely nodded and took his seat. Lily, arm in arm with Betty, was the last to come down. With a cry of concern, James hurried to lower Betty on to her cushion. Betty looked miserable, white and pinched, and she twisted a handkerchief in her hands in agitation. The three Afghani officers ranged themselves around the room, an ominous presence.

'Well,' said Burroughs, finding his voice, 'is someone going to tell us why we're here? Isn't this where the chap from Scotland Yard tells us we're all under arrest?'

'Edwin,' said Grace patiently, 'no one is accusing anyone of anything. We think Zeman died of natural causes, probably food poisoning. We have gathered here to try to establish what exactly it was that killed him.'

'And we may as well start with you, Burroughs,' said Joe. 'You were ill in the night, I believe?'

'This is embarrassing,' snapped Burroughs, 'and I can't imagine how you know that or why you think it's any business of yours to question me in public about my health but, if you must know, I have an ulcer – an ulcer which responds badly to certain types of food. It was particularly lively last night and I slept badly. I had no unusual symptoms.'

'Can you tell us which of the dishes you ate? For elimination purposes.'

Burroughs looked a little put out and then replied. 'Every dish except the curries. And I drank three glasses of champagne and one of the pink stuff – what was it? Pomegranate? If you say so.'

'And the bismuth tablet,' said Lily sharply. 'Don't forget that! Zeman had one too. You gave it to him.'

'What was that? Madam! What can you possibly be implying?'

'Joe, please.' Betty's voice, subdued but firm, cut into a potential clash. 'I think we can cut this short. I've worked it out. It was the pheasant. The question remains, of course, as to how the pheasant was polluted – poisoned –

infected – call it what you will. But the pheasant, I think, is the villain. The very thought of it makes me feel sick again!'

She pressed her handkerchief to her lips as she finished and anxiously Lily scrambled up to fetch a glass of water. Betty took some sips and resumed. 'Zeman and I were the only ones to try Lily's pheasant. Do you remember it appeared late in the meal when most people had eaten quite enough? I think I remember Zeman ate quite a lot.' She looked to Iskander for confirmation. He nodded. 'And I ate only a little. I was ill in the night as Grace may have told you.' She raised huge eyes to Joe and said, 'Do you think the meat was infected or did someone deliberately set out to poison Zeman? Or me? Us? All of us or someone in particular?'

'No one,' said Joe with more firmness that he felt. 'It's my opinion that this was a tragic accident. Think about it – no one could have predicted which of us if anyone was going to eat the pheasant (if that is indeed the culprit). The dish was simply presented and offered to everyone around the table. It was pure chance that Zeman and you, Betty, tasted it. Far more likely, in fact, to have been *Lily* – she shot the thing after all and we all think of it as "Lily's pheasant". All the dishes were available to be chosen in any quantity by anyone. It would be impossible to select a particular victim at such a meal. A calculated attempt to kill any one or all of us would have led to all the dishes or a substantial number of them being poisoned. That did not happen. We'll proceed with the recording of each diner's choice of dishes for the sake of form and thoroughness but I agree with you, Betty – I expect we'll come down to the pheasant as the common denominator. And then, I think, it will be time to speak to the cooks.'

After ten minutes of queasy reminiscence all were agreed that the pheasant was at fault and the three Pathan cooks who were responsible for the feast were summoned. They came smartly in, Scouts uniform, stiff-backed, proud and not at all intimidated by the unusual assembly of guests and Afghanis. They agreed amongst themselves that the chief cook, Abdullah, would speak for all and James proceeded to interview him in Pushtu, translating as he went.

Abdullah pronounced himself overwhelmed with grief and rage to hear what had happened and hotly denied that there could be any abnormality of any kind in the food he had served. He demanded to know on what previous occasion anyone at the fort had suffered from eating dishes prepared by his staff. When James hurried to say, 'Never, Abdullah, never,' he continued. He asked to be allowed to send to the kitchens to seek for any remaining part of the pheasant so that he might eat it himself in front of them all to demonstrate that all was well with it. He had personally tasted the sauce.

'And very good it was too, Abdullah,' Betty interrupted. 'I meant to congratulate you on it.'

A messenger was sent to the kitchens to hunt for any vestige of the suspect bird while Abdullah treated them to a list of every ingredient in the pheasant dish and the manner of concocting the sauce.

'You say you tasted the sauce, Abdullah,' Joe confirmed, 'but I wonder if you actually ate any of the meat from the bird?'

'Ah, no, sir. The bird, wonderful specimen though it was,' said Abdullah with a polite bow to Lily, 'was very largely unusable. Such was the accuracy of the marksmanship which laid it low, there was little undamaged flesh on the carcass which I could put into my dish. You will understand, sirs, ladies, that with wild game birds such as the golden pheasant only the breast meat is usually cooked, the remainder being too tough to be pleasant eating. And even the breast meat requires long and careful cooking which is why it was later than the other dishes in being brought to table.'

News was brought from the kitchens that the pheasant dish and the carcass had both been disposed of. 'Thought as much,' said James. 'Abdullah keeps his staff up to the mark and their cleanliness and efficiency are legendary. Hot climate, you know – can't take chances.'

Grace, who had been listening intently to all that was said, now interrupted, her fluttering hands revealing her agitation. 'James! Iskander! This has nothing to do with kitchen management. I think I understand what's happened. It should have occurred to me earlier! How could I have missed this? Well, I know how I could have missed it – it's jolly unusual! Quite extraordinary! Fascinating in fact! I've known about it for years but I never thought I'd see a case! Oh, I'm sorry, Iskander – I'm letting my professional curiosity and surprise run away with me. Let me say again, I'm very conscious that we're discussing the tragic death of your friend but I think you – we all – will be gratified and relieved to hear that there is no mystery here. I think it very likely that Zeman died of andromedotoxin!'

Seeing puzzled faces all around, Grace went on eagerly, 'Andromedotoxin! It's very rare. I've never seen an example before though I've heard and read of it. Tell me, Iskander – you would know – does a plant called the mountain laurel grow in these parts?'

Iskander listened to her description of the mountain laurel and nodded, giving the Pushtu name for the plant. James also murmured in agreement.

'There! We have it then! The pheasant, partridge too, I believe, has the habit of feeding on mountain laurel which produces high levels of the poison andromedotoxin in its flesh. Anyone eating the pheasant will be, unawares, ingesting the poison.'

'What are the symptoms of this poison, Grace?' asked Joe.

'Nausea, vomiting, dizziness and loss of balance.'

There was silence as all absorbed the evidence and finally Joe spoke, catching the eye of everyone at the gathering. 'Would anyone, then, be inclined to disagree with the verdict, if this were a coroner's court, of accidental death due to food poisoning occasioned by the consumption of an infected bird?' Joe summed up.

Everyone looked at everyone else and all looked finally at Iskander. With dignity and taking his time, 'On the evidence we have,' he said carefully, 'I think that is the conclusion we would all reach. A desperately sad occurrence but in no way sinister, an occurrence which none of us could have foreseen or prevented which took the life of my dear kinsman Zeman and very nearly the life of the Commandant's wife.' He turned to Betty and bowed graciously. 'We must praise Allah that Mrs Lindsay survived and, indeed, that not more of us died.'

Everyone was nodding and murmuring in agreement and looking forward to escaping from the threatening atmosphere of the enquiry when there was a sudden commotion outside and a havildar stepped into the room. He addressed James who, puzzled and concerned, translated for the rest of the company. 'We have at the door the poultryman, Achmed. He insists on presenting himself to the Commandant to give information. Shall we . . .?'

'Oh, good Lord, whatever next?' spluttered Burroughs in exasperation. 'Does your laundryman have a view? Are we to hear the beekeeper's suspicions?'

'Send him in,' said James firmly.

An agitated Achmed, flushed and quivering with excitement and in his dirty working clothes, had obviously run straight in from the farm. On receiving a nod from James he started his story in a flood of Pushtu. Stopping him for a moment after the first few sentences to translate, James's face grew grim.

'What's he saying?' Lily spoke for them all.

'He's telling us that the pheasant was poisoned. Arsenic. He's saying it was arsenic.'

Chapter Seven

The Afghanis, who had followed every word, became even more alert at the mention of poison and began to exchange looks. Arsenic was well known to the Afghani aristocracy. 'Inheritance powder' was how they referred to it colloquially and its regular use kept a phalanx of food tasters in constant employ at the palace.

'Go on, Achmed, finish your story,' said James and the man, not at all overcome to find himself the centre of such concentrated attention, launched into the next part of his account. A dramatic raconteur, as with all his countrymen, he made the most of his evidence. James heard him all the way through to the end before translating.

'Well, that would seem to put the tin hat on it!' he said. 'Achmed and his assistant have been troubled for some weeks now by these blasted pheasants who have been attacking our prize Leghorns. There's a ban on shooting within the precincts of the fort and they came up with the idea of laying out doses of poison hidden in kitchen scraps. The poison comes in the form of rat poison: government supplies, control of rodents for the purpose of. Apparently their schemes have been unrewarded – plenty of dead rats but the pheasants appeared to flourish. Two days ago, determined to get the better of the pests, his assistant put out ten times the usual dose.'

Again there was silence as all took in the new information.

'I would guess that Lily got him minutes before the poison did.'

'If this has been going on for weeks without killing the bird (or birds),' said Grace, 'there will have been a build-up of arsenic in the bird's tissues, culminating in a massive last dose. Oh, dear! Andromedotoxin? Arsenic? Which one? Without the necessary laboratory facilities we may never be able to establish which poison killed him. But the effect would have been the same.'

The Afghanis were nodding their heads in understanding and acceptance of this last piece of evidence delivered with such emotion and regret by Achmed. Lily also was looking utterly distraught, turning her eyes constantly to Iskander who avoided her gaze.

'It's not Achmed's fault! Please don't blame anyone but me. I think I should apologize to everyone,' she said finally, unable to contain her grief and guilt a moment longer. 'If only I hadn't shot the wretched thing! Oh, why did I have to show off!'

Iskander was the only one in a position to offer any consolation and he hurried to do this, his voice grave and gentle. 'Never forget, Miss Coblenz,' he said, 'that it was Zeman himself who encouraged, indeed who challenged, you to make the shot. It is the will of Allah and that is all there is to be said.'

'And, indeed,' said Grace kindly, 'Zeman helped himself to the dish. As did Betty. He ate a larger portion than she did and this accounts for the faster onset of the attack and its greater severity, amounting to fatality.'

'You were about to tell us before we came to the durbar hall,' Iskander reminded her, 'at what time you estimate Zeman died.'

'Ah, yes, I was saying . . . the state of digestion of the food matter, the advance of bodily rigor, and the temperature of the corpse all point to the same time. I would say about one o'clock in the morning.'

Betty looked up sharply. 'Oh, no! You're saying that when you were attending me at three o'clock poor Zeman was lying there on the stairs? Dead or dying? It's too horrible to think of!'

'Already dead,' said Grace. 'Whatever else, we all saw that he did not linger for long once he embarked on the stairs.'

Iskander was looking at Grace keenly. 'At one o'clock?' he said. 'Are you quite certain of that, Dr Holbrook?'

Grace hesitated for a moment. She always weighed her statements carefully and was for a moment put out by having her decision questioned. 'Yes,' she said. 'At about one o'clock.' She added reluctantly, 'It *could* have been earlier, I suppose, but not much. Between half-past twelve and one. Why do you ask, Iskander? Is there perhaps something you want us to know? Any further evidence you can supply to throw light on this tragedy?'

Iskander shook his head and remained silent. Collecting himself, he gracefully thanked her for all she had done, made further kind comments to Betty and Lily and announced that he would now withdraw with his men to make arrangements for the burial of Zeman.

Distinctly subdued, the company dispersed to the officers' mess. As they trailed away, Fred Moore-Simpson was heard to say, 'Damn sad. And damn mysterious too! But I think I speak for all and would say – I need my breakfast!'

Joe, who was bringing up the rear, found himself face to face with Lily who shut the door quietly behind the last to leave and rounded on him.

'Commander,' she said, 'I have to talk to you where we may not be overheard by anyone. *Anyone*. I will come to your room in ten minutes' time. Can you be there?'

She entered silently in her soft riding boots, took a quick look around his room and settled down on the only chair. Joe sat on the bed close to her but not so close as to intimidate her. Perhaps she had come, needing a shoulder to cry on; perhaps she was to reiterate her guilt but he didn't think that was what she had in mind. There was something apprehensive and even furtive in her behaviour. It disturbed him.

She sat quietly for a few moments, chewing her bottom lip. She opened her mouth to say something, thought better of it and closed it again. She tried to meet his eye and could not. Her gaze constantly slid away from his and focused on her hands knotted with tension in her lap.

'Oh, Lord!' thought Joe. 'I recognize these signs! She's about to make a confession! We've got it all wrong and she's come to tell me she killed him! But how? Poison? In so short a time? Not possible. Not her style either – she'd have put a bullet in him perhaps or climbed on a stool and hit him in the nose, but I really can't see Lily – *didn't* see Lily salting his sherbet with a mysterious white powder. No, calm down, Sandilands! Too much imagination! She's decided that life on the frontier is a little too raw and she's come to ask you to take her back to the safety of Simla. That's it!'

'I have the most terrible confession to make, Commander,' she finally managed to say. 'I can't imagine what you're going to think of me!'

'Is this to do with Zeman's death?' he asked.

'Well, of course it is! What else would it have to do with?'

'Well, you could be owning up to putting that dead mouse in my bed yesterday,' said Joe, determined to keep the exchange light.

An unwilling smile broke out and she began to relax a little. 'Wish I'd thought of that. I say – did someone? Oh, no. Sorry. Just teasing, I suppose. No. It is about Zeman.'

Joe just smiled and listened and let her take her time.

'There's only you in the whole fort I can trust and I mean that – only you. Promise you won't reveal a word of what I'm going to tell you to anyone – not James, not Betty, not Grace, really not anyone.'

Joe nodded his agreement.

'It didn't happen like that at all,' she said rapidly.

97

'I mean Zeman's death. It couldn't have. You see, at that time – between half-past twelve and one o'clock – Zeman was alive and well and having a, oh, what shall I say? – a riotous time in the swimming pool in the officers' garden.'

'Can't have been a *very* riotous time!' said Joe gently. 'I heard no sounds from downstairs and I'm a champion light sleeper. A riotous time down there would have woken me up. Are you sure about this? And what do you mean by "riotous"?'

'You don't make it easy for a girl, do you? No, you're right. Bad choice of word because it wasn't noisy at all. Not at all. It was rather subdued but energetic, um, sexual congress.' She finished with a rush, blushing hotly.

Taken completely by surprise, Joe looked at her in horror and then said carefully, 'I think it might be better if you took me through this step by step from the ending of the dinner party, Lily.'

'Yes, it would. It'll be a lot easier to talk about now I've said those words. From now on I shall refer to the activity as s.c. Is that all right?'

'Quite all right,' said Joe.

'You saw the appalling Rathmore bundle me out of the room, lest I should fall victim to silken oriental seduction?'

Joe nodded and remained silent. 'Prescient old Rathmore!' he was thinking. 'More sense than the rest of us apparently!'

'Well, it was clearly his idea that I should fall victim to his own Western style of courtship. Not subtle! Oh, don't look concerned – I can handle unsubtle! He's suffering this morning from a dented ego and a bruised foot! Did you notice he was limping this morning?' she said, a flash of good humour returning. 'He marched me round the garden and pointed out that a nightingale was singing and the moon was shining. He reminded me that he was a lord, twirled his moustache and fell on me. Well, on where I would have been were I not such a fast mover! I escaped

98

and went to my room and he hobbled off back to his room, cursing me no doubt. Must have been at about half-past ten.'

'I made my rounds at eleven and everyone was in their own room. You locked your door when I asked you to.'

Lily gave him a scathing look. 'You were taken in by that old girls' boarding school trick? I locked and unlocked it again straight away.'

'But why didn't you complain about Rathmore's behaviour to you? I would have dealt with him. It would have given me quite a lot of pleasure in fact!'

She said what he knew she'd say. 'I can take care of myself. No need to involve anyone else. Everything went very quiet, Joe, when you finished padding about and I sat and waited.'

'Waited? Waited for what?'

'Do you remember the Persian poem Zeman said to me towards the end of dinner? About the moonlight on the pool and "I wait to see your shadow fall on the garden's midnight wall" – all that? I sort of, well, took it literally. I took it as an invitation to meet him by the pool at midnight.' She blushed but looked at Joe defiantly. 'Ridiculous, I know and I'm ashamed of myself but it was so romantic! Oh, I was imagining telling my friends! I thought at the very least he would try to kiss me and I'd decided that at the very least I would let him. No one I know has kissed a Pathan before! And this guy could out-smoulder Rudolph Valentino! If you know who *he* is?'

'I am aware of the gentleman and have even seen some of his moving pictures,' said Joe. 'And, yes, Lily, I can see what the attraction was! But, tell me – what time did you go out to the garden?'

'Just before midnight. I put on a dark dress and a pair of sandals and I crept out. I didn't disturb anyone. I got into the garden and decided to hide in the almond trees. Well, I didn't want to appear to be the first to get there – you mustn't seem to be overkeen, you know.' Lily fell silent again.

99

'And?' Joe prompted gently.

'He didn't turn up. I thought I must have misunderstood the meaning of the poem at first and then I thought he might be praying or giving orders to his men or doing something military so I hung on. I mean, how would *I* know how these guys pass their time? I guess I waited until, oh, it must have been half-past midnight at the earliest. And then I heard quiet laughter. Someone was coming into the garden. Someone who didn't want to be heard. I stayed where I was just in case it wasn't Zeman. But it was. It was Zeman but he was hand in hand with someone else. They went to the pool and they took their clothes off and slid into the water and then they, they, oh!'

'S.c. occurred?' Joe finished for her.

She nodded miserably and Joe felt desperately sorry for her. He felt a stab of anger too with Zeman for playing with the girl's fantasies. 'Good Lord! A scene like this could twist an impressionable girl's views of men for evermore,' he thought.

'Well, what was I to do?' she went on. 'Look, I was never taught to handle anything like this! I came through Miss Dana's Academy with flying colours. I can parse a sentence, I can quote the Lakeland poets, I know algebra, astronomy, and chemistry. I know how to flirt. I can pick up a handkerchief without showing my underwear. I thought I knew everything but – do you know? – if it hadn't been for Dr Holbrook explaining what went on in the military . . .'

'Who was with Zeman, Lily?' Joe asked.

It was no surprise to him when she replied, 'Iskander. It was Iskander.'

'Did you, er, watch the event unfold?' he asked carefully.

'Well, no! I should just think not! I shut my eyes of course. But I could hear. They were laughing and sort of . . . horsing around, you know? Grace was right. It does go on.'

100

'Look, Lily, I know I must be the thousandth person to tell you that the ways of the frontier are different from our own but in this case they really are,' said Joe, who had decided on the line he was going to take. 'It's easy when two good-looking young men like Zeman and Iskander speak our language fluently and have spent many years of their lives living in our society to think that they are of our culture. They are not. Their formative years were spent here in these hills living the life of their clan. And I believe that they are very dual. They know how we live and think, they find themselves reacting in Western ways to much of what goes on and I think they themselves are sometimes torn between the two demands on them. Pathan men do form close friendships. So do Englishmen. We express our friendship in different ways, that's all. Pathans often walk around hand in hand. It signifies nothing other than friendship. They probably think James and I are rather strange in that we *never* hold hands.'

Lily began to smile at the picture he was drawing.

'And they are young men. What would you say? – twenty-two? three? Not much older than you, Lily, but a good deal younger than me in age and experience. And boys horse about. Especially in swimming pools at midnight when they've both had a brandy or two they shouldn't have had! I think it all sounded much more sinister to you than it should have done because they were trying to splash about without drawing attention.'

Lily was looking at him with a good deal more brightness in her expression. 'I guess you could be right, Joe. But, well, whatever the truth of that, Zeman still broke his date with me!'

'And now you'll never kiss a Pathan!' Joe teased gently. 'But look, realistically, you were never going to. He would never seriously have expected you to meet him in the garden, Lily. In his world women go about veiled or even wearing a burkha. Their faces are seen only by other women or the men in their immediate family and their marriages are arranged for them by their parents. Zeman

101

knows that things are done differently in the West but he would never have thought that you would agree to a clandestine meeting with him unchaperoned in the garden.'

'I suppose you're right, Joe.'

'But, shocking though it was, I'm thinking your midnight encounter has an even more sinister significance.'

'Too right! You see it, don't you? Thought you would! If Zeman was alive – and he *was* – at the time Dr Holbrook says he was dead or dying, then she's either an incompetent doctor or she's telling a deliberate lie. Dr Holbrook? I can't believe it! And is James aware of this? And Betty? What's going on here?'

'You were aware of this inconsistency all the time we were deliberating and enquiring and you said nothing? Lily, that was a very, what shall I say? . . . mature decision.'

'Aw, thanks! You people keep telling me not to rock the boat, light any fuses and ruffle any feathers – "this is a delicate situation we have here on the frontier." I thought I'd better keep my mouth shut and go with what James and Grace were stitching up between them. I figure they must have a good reason. And anyway, I'd rather no one knew about my experience in the garden. But you do see the significance, don't you?'

Joe nodded thoughtfully. 'It's not only you who knows that the timing is all wrong . . .'

'Iskander! He knows! I had to wait in the trees until they'd finished whatever they were doing in the pool sometime between half-past twelve and one o'clock. But it wasn't over then. They sat on the marble bench drying off and talking for . . . it seemed ages but I guess it must have been about ten minutes – no more than a quarter of an hour.'

'Talking? What sort of talking were they doing?'

'Pushtu talking . . . couldn't figure out a word . . . but that doesn't mean I couldn't understand some things.'

Joe waited and she went on, 'It wasn't exactly a lovers' tiff but things did seem to turn a bit sour as they talked.'

Lily frowned in an effort to remember clearly her impressions. 'Zeman sounded kind of light-hearted whereas Iskander was threatening him . . . telling him off? He was certainly hissing at him a bit. I'd say they'd started off their evening adventure in high spirits but finished off not too happy with each other. No idea why. But anyway, by the time they drifted off to their rooms it must have been gone one o'clock.

'Iskander knows that his friend went to bed in perfectly good health just when the medical expert is saying that he died. He's going to draw conclusions, has already drawn conclusions and I'm not happy when I think about them.'

The gravity of the implications had been creeping up on Joe as she had revealed her story. 'Iskander seemed very prepared to accept Grace's version of events, even to the extent of smoothing her path and having all verified as above board by his officers. I thought he was as concerned as we were that there should be no charge of foul play.'

'He was,' Lily confirmed. 'I was watching him. He was happy with the decision and relieved, I think. But then, right at the end, he asked about the time of death and Grace's reply blew the top off the jam jar. He gave her a chance to change her mind or adjust her finding but she stuck to what she'd said and that's when his attitude changed.'

'You seem to have been keeping a close eye on him?'

'I spend a lot of time watching Iskander,' said Lily.

'So, where do we go from here? Shall I confide your evidence to James and question him on the stance he's taken?'

'You're the detective, you tell me!'

'Fine. Then this is what we'll do. We'd better sort this out ourselves, Lily, and we must be circumspect. I think Iskander has been alerted to some sort of underhand shenanigans and since he's not challenged James openly, I think he's gone away to work it out for himself and plan his next action. It looks bad, I'm afraid. If he concludes that there's been a lapse in the protection offered by the fort, if Zeman's death should prove to have been intentional, then it will be incumbent on him to seek revenge. I think he will try to avoid this if he can but once he's certain that an injustice has been done he'll act. He'll act swiftly, what's more. He's never likely to be offered such an opportunity again after all. He's a welcome guest, the subject of much sympathy, free to go wherever he likes in the fort . . . the Trojan Horse who could let in thirty Afghan warriors screaming for badal. Oh, I can tell you, Lily, I don't like to hear what I'm saying!'

'We can't do a thing until we find out what really happened. Come on, Joe, you say you're from Scotland Yard – would you have been happy with the combined investigation and coroner's court we've just been through?'

'Good Lord, no! I know we haven't got any of the facilities I would normally be able to call on but all the same there's quite a bit more we could do.'

'Where do we start?' asked Lily eagerly.

'I would have said with the body but they'll have taken it off for burial by now. Even if they haven't, a policeman poking about in the orifices wouldn't exactly calm any Afghan suspicions.' He considered for a moment and then asked, 'Do you think we could find our way into the hospital without being observed?'

'Sure. If we work around the wall instead of going straight down the main path we could do it. Together or separately?'

'I'm supposed to be riding herd on you so on the whole I think less suspicious if we're together.'

'Fine. If anyone sees us, you're bored out of your brains helping me look for that silver bracelet I dropped somewhere in the grounds this morning.'

A few minutes later they had slipped into the room where Zeman's body had been laid out. The table on which it had lain was empty but Joe was looking for something else. He found it in a neat pile set by the door awaiting collection by the orderly. Locking the door, he picked up Zeman's clothing and put it on the table.

'And this is a bit odd, don't you think so, Joe? He was wearing his uniform. When I saw him in the garden he was still wearing his evening dress – you know – the waistcoat, the blue turban, the whole outfit. Now why would he have put his uniform on to go to bed? Doesn't make a whole lot of sense to me! Don't these fellers wear pyjamas?'

'Well,' said Joe, trying to make sense of it, 'he might have changed from his evening dress into pyjamas and then back into his uniform if he wanted to make himself respectable to consult the lady doctor in the middle of the night.'

'Sheesh! That's more changes than one of Mademoiselle Chanel's mannequins could perform! But look, Joe – he's feeling so ill he thinks he may be dying and he takes time to pull on his top boots? Would he have bothered struggling into those?' Lily shook her head derisively. 'Such a lot we don't know about Pathans. Kinda hard to figure!'

'Well, file it away. It doesn't make sense now but if we dig a bit further something else may explain it later. Now, let's have a look at those . . . Right. Now, there may be nothing to see but if I were doing this properly this is where I'd start. I hope you're not squeamish. This may be rather disconcerting for someone untrained.'

'I don't faint easy. Carry on.'

Methodically Joe spread each garment out and inspected every inch. He gave a commentary as he went, becoming less sensitive to Lily's presence as she remained quiet and helpful. 'Waistcoat. Dried vomit, ponding around the right side of the neck. Pity we can't analyse this.'

Lily wrinkled her nose in disgust. 'Aw, jiminy! That smell!' she commented. 'Takes me back to children's parties!'

'Children's parties! Takes *me* back to closing time on any Saturday night in Seven Dials!' Joe broke off in sudden puzzlement. 'Or does it?'

'Urgh! There's bits in it!' said Lily.

'And you'd expect that if he did indeed die at the time Grace suggests,' said Joe in deeper puzzlement. 'You *are* perfectly sure of your timing, Lily?'

'Sure! Look, I've told you the exact truth with the exact timing and that's your base. That's where you start and everything else is hogwash!'

'Mm . . . Very well. Trousers . . . perfectly clean. And that's odd.'

'Odd? Why odd?'

'Arsenical poisoning is normally accompanied by diarrhoea. I've only encountered one case of arsenical poisoning.' Joe frowned. 'A wife had polished off her violent husband but it had taken her six months to do it. I'm afraid I just can't believe that anyone would die from eating a pheasant that's swallowed the stuff. But then, out here in the wilderness, how would we find out? Have to try other methods. I'm rather surprised Grace went along with the arsenic theory . . . And what was that other theory she had? The andro-what's-it poison? Does that sound likely? Anyway, let's have a look at his shirt. Same vomit staining though less copious.'

'Joe, look at this,' said Lily.

Gingerly she held up the cuff of the wide-sleeved cotton shirt that hung over the table on her side. The right sleeve. Joe took hold of it and looked. He slipped a magnifying glass from his pocket and looked again, then passed it to Lily.

'Rose thorns? This is what he was wearing when he went for his swim. Could he have torn it on the bushes?'

'I don't think these are the tears of rose thorns,' he went on. 'The holes are too big. And look at the shape. There are two of them and they're sort of . . . rounded at the puncture point and torn downwards. Look, if he held his arm like this,' Joe held the sleeve at an angle horizontal to the ground, 'then the tearing, the drag, would be vertical.'

'The holes are very small,' said Lily, 'and very close together. Puncture holes? Oh, my God!' She shuddered and dropped the cuff she had been holding. 'A snake! You're not going to tell me he's been attacked by a snake? Oh, why didn't anyone think of that? Cobras are always slithering in through the holes in the bathroom wall. He could have got back to his room, entered the bathroom and . . . I can't bear to think of it! Poor, poor Zeman! How long does it take you to die of a cobra bite?'

'Anything from fifteen minutes upwards, depending on the constitution of the victim. But, no, this wasn't a snake,' said Joe.

Lily looked again thoughtfully at the shirt, folded it carefully and replaced it on the pile. 'Were there any scratches on his arm? Did you get a close enough look at the body, Joe?'

'Yes, I did. There were no wounds of any kind except for the blow to the head he received when he fell against the stairs.' He explained the findings of the autopsy.

The remainder of the items including the turban were examined and produced nothing further of interest. Joe looked carefully at the dagger that Zeman had carried always in his belt. He held it in his hand for a moment, admiring the restrained jewelled decoration on the sheath, and then delicately slid out the blade. Lily could not hold back a shudder at the sight of the purposeful weapon revealed. Sumptuous and valuable, certainly, but this was no toy, no ornament. The stubby hilt was of carved black jade, encircled with rows of rubies which gleamed like drops of blood, the curved blade appeared black also, of damascened steel and decorated with a filigree pattern of gold in the shape of a tear drop. Joe took out his handkerchief and gently ran it along the midrib of the blade. He examined it carefully. There was no trace of blood, no

107

residue of any kind. The revolver also was innocent of recent use.

'Right,' said Joe. 'That's all we can achieve here, I think.' He grinned. 'Now let's go and lean on the villain who attacked Zeman last night, shall we?'

Chapter Eight

They approached the guest wing silently. They were anxious not to alert their suspect lest he should abscond before Joe had the chance to put him to the question.

Joe assumed a copper's voice. 'You cover the outer door, Lily, while I see if he's in there.'

He padded forward. ''ullo, 'ullo, 'ullo. Anyone at 'ome? You'd better come quietly. That way no one gets hurt.'

'We've got you surrounded!' added Lily excitedly.

Minto emerged from his kennel. His hackles were up. His teeth were bared.

'I think he's going to resist arrest!' said Lily.

Joe put his hands on his hips and looked menacingly down. 'Would you mind telling me, sir, exactly where you were at 1 a.m.? Or would you prefer to come down to the station and answer a few questions there?'

Minto unleashed a throaty growl.

'How rude!' said Lily. 'I can't believe he said that!'

'Just keep your teeth bared for a moment, would you, sir?' said Joe. 'Well, Lily, what do you think? Is this our man?'

'Well, we could send for his dental records or you could offer up your arm for testing purposes but I don't think there's any need. It's right there – one inch from canine to canine. Less than one and a half anyway.'

'Thank you, sir. That'll be all for the moment. We're releasing you on police bail. Don't leave town without notifying me.'

*　　*　　*

They stood for a moment looking at the bleak staircase where they pictured Zeman dying his lonely and agonizing death. 'Poison – the coward's weapon, they say,' Joe thought, and doubly despicable for Zeman, forbidden by tribal custom to declare his sickness or seek help before it was too late. He stood for a moment and traced the damp patches on the floor and stairs, cleaned now and smelling faintly of carbolic and marking Zeman's last desperate steps. And to be attacked, held back by the sleeve, in extremis, by that awful little dog was a note of near farce beyond contemplation.

Bleakly, Lily's thoughts had been echoing his. 'Dreadful, pointless death,' she said and then, after a pause, 'But there *is* something wrong here, Joe, isn't there? The dog – what's his name?'

'Minto. Named after the last Viceroy but three, I believe. Lord Minto.'

'Right. Well, does His Lordship only attack men?'

'No idea. Why do you ask?'

'When I came down at midnight I had to pass his kennel. He didn't come out. Oh, he was in there all right – I heard him growl but that's all and when I came back in at about one he didn't even bother to growl. Although, I was so upset I mightn't have noticed.'

'Perhaps he'd gone out for a midnight stroll too,' said Joe. 'He's not tied up after all and his kennel's right by the entrance.'

'But you heard just now the noise he makes when he's disturbed. It would have echoed up this stairwell. Now you'll have noticed – I certainly have because I was creeping about last night – that you can't hear a thing between rooms. The walls are thick adobe. But you can hear things happening on the stairs and corridor. I was still awake. It took me a while to sleep because I really was feeling hurt and angry. I *might* have heard the noise if he'd attacked Zeman but I'll tell you who would *certainly* have heard it!'

'Iskander was right next door and his door's pretty close

to Minto's kennel. Look, Lily, there's no one about, they're all still at breakfast and Iskander said he was going to talk with his men. I'll slip into his room if you keep watch. Oh, and stir up the beast again, would you?'

Joe went into Iskander's room, closing the door behind him. He took the opportunity of having a quick look around but there was nothing at all of note: the standard issue bed and furniture. There were no personal possessions other than his evening clothes hanging in a cupboard, and the damp floor and made-up bed told Joe that the staff had been busy and thorough in their daily cleaning. Almost at once he heard the din. Muted, thanks to the thickness of the door, but audible nevertheless. And certainly audible to a sharp pair of Pathan ears.

He emerged and ordered Minto back into his kennel. 'No doubt about that,' he said. 'If my war-ravaged ears could make it out I'm sure Iskander's keen senses could. And remember what the proverb says – "A Pathan never sleeps." They're famous for their vigilance – no one has ever taken a Pathan by surprise as far as I know. So, Lily, tell me – why didn't Iskander pop his head out to see what was going on? He ought to have taken a dog's growl as a message that something was not right and I would have expected him to investigate.'

'Unless he was already a part of what was going on,' said Lily. 'None of this makes sense, Joe. What are we saying? That Zeman didn't die at one o'clock, or he didn't die here, or Grace is deliberately lying, James is part of a cover-up and Iskander probably knows the truth and may even have killed Zeman himself. Is any of this likely?'

'Iskander would be my number one suspect, I think, if it weren't for the second victim. Keep an eye on Betty!' said Joe.

'Of course. The second victim. Was that unintentional, do you suppose? I mean I can't imagine that anyone, especially Iskander, would want to harm Betty.'

'No, you're right.' Joe sighed. 'It would be completely out of character. Pathans treat women with great care and respect, apart from their own adulterous wives, I understand. It would be contrary to their culture and their religion to attempt to murder even a British woman. As far as I know there's only been one case of an Englishwoman being killed deliberately out here on the frontier. It was two years ago. Colonel Foulkes and his wife were killed by a gang from the Bosti-Khel Valley. But they were outlaws and the local tribesmen were as outraged as the British authorities. And then again, thousands of English women and children were trapped in these passes on the road from Afghanistan seventy years ago. They all perished, shot with jezails or hacked to pieces with talwars. But that was war. How can you ever predict how men will behave in war or in peace?' he finished hopelessly. 'I wonder if Betty could just have been having a recurrence of the sickness she's been suffering for the last month? That was certainly what Grace supposed when she went off in the night to treat her.'

'And where does that leave us? This is a can of worms, Joe, isn't it? Can we get the lid back on, do you think?'

'Would you want to?'

She shook her head dubiously. 'No. We've got to follow this through. And I'll tell you something else – I don't think it's all over yet.'

'Well, I think there's one thing we can be relatively certain of and that's that *if* he was killed, he was most likely killed by one of seven people, if I exclude you and me, Lily. The people who were sitting around the dinner table and sleeping in this guest block. Look, they'll start straying back from the mess any moment now – let's go up on to the wall to discuss this further. It's about as quiet as you can get in a fort of a thousand men!'

To his surprise, in Lily he was finding a bright intelligence, an ingenious colleague, quick to understand what he was saying, asking the minimum of questions and quite prepared to put forward her own sensible suggestions. But, underlying the mask of efficient colleague, he sensed a paralysing uncertainty. Lily was struggling with an emotion he could not quite identify. She'd cheered up, however, when he'd staged his mock interview with Minto. 'I must keep it light,' he thought, 'to get the best out of Lily Coblenz.'

'Good back-up in there, Coblenz!' he said cheerfully as they climbed up and settled to look over the parapet. 'If ever you want a job with the Met. let me know!'

'You really are a policeman, aren't you?'

'Whatever else did you think I was?'

'I thought you were Military Intelligence, you know – one of Sir George's bright young men.'

Joe was very surprised. He'd been in India six months, working with Sir George, before he'd guessed at Sir George's ambivalent role in the government of India, a guess never articulated and certainly never confirmed.

'Are you suggesting that good old Sir George is a . . . what shall I say? . . . a grey eminence? An unseen mastermind?'

'Are you suggesting that you didn't know?'

'I'm not saying that,' said Joe with irritation. He could not resist asking, 'But tell me – who put such an idea into your head?'

'Oh, come off it, Joe! No one *puts ideas* into my head! I figure things out for myself. Wasn't difficult! "You want anything done," my father always says, "you go straight to the top." Well, in India, if you want anything done – forget the Governors, forget the Army Top Brass, even the guy in the feathered hat.'

'The Viceroy?'

'Yes, him. You go straight to the top of the pile and that's where you find Sir George. He huffs and puffs. He tried to make me see him as a woofly old sheep dog but us Yankee girls – we ain't so easy to fool! He pretends there's someone above him he has to consult but there isn't, you know. He's not that *easy* to handle but he's a straight arrow, I do believe. Good dancer too.'

In a flash Joe understood exactly why George had despatched Lily to the frontier. He could almost hear the

113

words – 'Ship the damn girl up to the Hills and set Sandilands to look after her!' Buying himself a week's peace and quiet in Simla. At Joe's expense!

It was ten o'clock and the guard was just changing. Joe borrowed a pair of binoculars from a Scout standing down and handed them to Lily. She turned the glasses to the Afghanis encamped below on the football field. 'They're having a pow-wow,' she reported. 'There's Iskander in the middle. He's doing all the talking. They seem to like what he's saying . . . there's an awful lot of agreeing going on.' She was silent for a moment then added, 'There's thirty men plus Iskander and they're all armed. They've got . . . thirty-five horses with them . . . good-looking animals . . . and a couple of pack mules. None of them are saddled up so I guess they're not thinking of going anywhere in a hurry.'

She handed the binoculars back to Joe and said thoughtfully, 'You know, Joe, there is a reason why Zeman was trying to get up those stairs. He could quite simply have been trying to put some distance between himself and Iskander. He was going up to James or Grace for help in the knowledge that his friend had poisoned him and all that stuff about vomiting being unmanly was just moonshine. Needn't have been arsenic. Could have been something quick to react that we in the West don't know about. I expect they all know about poisons.'

'It makes sense. And you say they were quarrelling in the garden. But what about a motive? Now there we're stuck, I'm afraid. Who knows what's going on in the ranks of the Afghani aristocracy? God knows what power struggles they're involved in! "Inheritance powder" – there might be a clue in that but it's a bit tenuous and how would we ever find out? I can hardly go down to the encampment and say, "I say, lads, what're the odds on the succession now? Iskander shortened a bit in the night, did he? Where's the stable money?"'

A more sinister thought occurred to him. Zeman was of the royal blood and, all would agree, a charismatic figure.

114

There might well be a faction at court who preferred Zeman's style to that of the Amir Amanullah. If Amanullah had found out it would have made good sense for him to engage a trusted lieutenant and someone close to Zeman to dispose of him discreetly, well away from the Amir's sphere of influence. If his rival were to die of natural causes under the unbiased eye of the Raj that would be nothing but good news for Amanullah. And doubtless Iskander would have his reward when he returned home. Joe knew he ought to be sharing these thoughts and theories, collecting information from James. But there was something in James's behaviour since the discovery of the body that Joe was not entirely comfortable with. His friend to whom he would entrust – and indeed in the past had entrusted – his life seemed, in some unseizable way, to have taken a step back from him. Joe decided to leave James out of his calculations and, meantime, Lily was filling the gap remarkably well. And pacing along with his unspoken thoughts apparently.

'And why wait do it here in the fort? Is that significant, Joe?' she asked him. to

'I think so. Yes. There are nine impeccable Western witnesses, some of them decidedly important and well-regarded people falling over themselves to prove he had nothing to do with it, that the death was entirely natural and unavoidable. Because the suspicion that Zeman had been killed by *anyone* while under the protection of James and through him the British Army could well lead to conflagration. We couldn't even accuse Iskander if we were certain he'd done it – it would be a frightful insult to the Amir.'

'What would he do about it?'

'At the worst, he would do what Amirs have done before. Declare a jehad – a holy war – against the British. They've done it on much slighter provocation. He would rouse the tribes on this side of the frontier to join his Afghani forces, he might even call on a little Russian support. They're already supplying him with bomber

115

planes. The Scouts you see manning this fort are all related to the tribesmen in the hills; they are Afridi, Khyberee, Mahsud, Wazir, Khattack, and though they are very loyal and very brave – best fighters in the world perhaps – they are also Muslim and the strength of their faith might well override any army loyalty. Every village has a Mullah holding the Koran in one hand and a drawn sword in the other! Every fort along the frontier could fall to a concerted attack from without and betrayal from within.'

'The frontier in flames?' said Lily, remembering a phrase she had heard on so many lips in Simla.

'The frontier?' Joe frowned. 'No, worse than that – the frontier today, the Punjab tomorrow and the rest of India would soon follow, Lily.'

'There's only one thing to do, Joe. Pull 'em in and give 'em all the treatment! Sweat 'em until someone coughs!'

'Lily, what have you been reading? Dime novels? No, I can't do that. So long as we can keep up the pretence of "natural causes" and all are content with that, the fuse remains unlit. If I start stirring about, expressing or imply-ing doubts, then we're lost. You too, Miss Coblenz! You must behave entirely naturally. Don't go around searching rooms and looking sideways at people.'

'Not even Iskander?' she asked innocently. 'Here, take a look! He's coming back in.'

'Right, let's go and meet him, shall we? Ask politely if there's anything we can do . . . see if we can establish what his plans are for the rest of the day.'

An extraordinary change had come over Iskander, Joe decided. He appeared to have taken over not only Zeman's commanding role but elements of his personality too. Grave, as befitted one who had just lost his friend and countryman, he was no longer a silent and menacing pres-ence but easy, responsive and prepared to answer ques-tions. Yes, there was something they could do, he said. He needed to write up a report on last night's unfortunate occurrence, perhaps Joe could point him towards a supply of writing paper? They walked with him to the library where Joe found and laid out sheets of the fort's headed writing paper, pens, blotters and all he could possibly need.

'The report will take some time,' said Iskander, 'probably the whole of the rest of the morning as I shall write it out in two languages. This afternoon I have arranged for my men to bury Zeman. There is, Commander Lindsay tells me, a small Muslim burial ground between here and the river, the remains, I understand, of the village which was razed to the ground to make way for the building of this fort. It will be entirely suitable to lay him to rest there. I think we must put off until tomorrow our return with Dr Holbrook to Kabul. Perhaps you would be so good, Sandilands, as to inform her of our change in plan and ask her to be ready to move off immediately after breakfast?'

Joe murmured his readiness to do this. Lily, obviously hunting for some way of establishing contact with him and finding nothing better said, 'Tea? I'll have some tea sent to you, Iskander.'

To Joe's surprise he turned to her and gave her a smile full of grace and humour. 'You are kindness itself, Miss Coblenz. I should be very grateful for tea.'

Iskander was grateful for tea three times in as many hours and all delivered personally to the library by Lily.

'*What* are you up to, Lily?' Joe asked impatiently, finding her coming for the third time from the library.

'Just keeping an eye on suspect number one,' she said. 'It's all right, Joe. He's just doing what he said he would do. It's taking a long time and there's a lot of pen chewing going on. But I think I was pretty helpful. You do spell "autopsy" with an "s", don't you?'

She continued to keep him under her eye during the

117

afternoon but from the distance of the wall of the fort. Joe joined her to watch the funeral unobtrusively. With distaste his eye took in the bleak Islamic cemetery, rocky and forbidding on a flat plain between two folds of unrelenting hillside, perpetually shaped and honed by the endless, searing wind. An empty plain covered with forgotten memorial stones on end. Memorial stones of all ages, some new, some hundreds of years old, some straight and true, others undermined by the wind and leaning drunkenly.

'What a place to await eternity!' thought Joe and his mind fled to England, to peaceful and ordered headstones, soft, dark earth, here and there a self-sown blossom tree, healing rain and caressive wind. To a Surrey churchyard: *'The Rev. Simon Graham, who departed this life . . .' 'Dora, beloved wife of the above, who fell asleep . . .' 'Benjamin Elliott, aged six months, asleep in the arms of Jesus . . .'* According to legend they waited in joyful hope for their resurrection but who, in this horrible place, would wait in joyful hope – or hope of any sort? He looked at the shallow grave prepared for Zeman and remembered the style of that subtle and perhaps even romantic figure and, for a moment, Joe grieved for him. 'I'd sooner be working with him than consigning him to this bleak and unforgiving stone yard!'

He cheered himself with the thought that warriors of Zeman's religion were guaranteed eternal felicity in the arms of timeless houris and hoped it might be true. He said a silent prayer to any god who was listening and noticed that Lily also, head bent, was lost in thought or prayer.

Following the funeral, a very brief affair, the Afghanis returned and to Joe's surprise Iskander approached James with the suggestion that some of his off-duty Scouts might be persuaded to teach the game of cricket to his men.

'Of course,' James replied. 'There is in fact a game scheduled for this afternoon for your entertainment but I had wondered whether to cancel it in view of the sad event of last night. Your men are very welcome to watch and get

118

the hang of the game and afterwards I'm sure the Scouts would be delighted to coach your chaps. That is if they are not too downcast by the death of their commander. I would quite understand if you thought they might prefer to spend the afternoon in quiet thought and contemplation.'

Iskander raised a quizzical eyebrow. 'These are hand-picked warriors as I'm sure you have noticed – a corps d'élite. They do not sit about quietly contemplating the sudden death of their commander. If they had some new activity, a competitive game to master, I think it would take their minds off the present sadness. And never forget, Major, that funeral games have a very long tradition! When our ancestor, Alexander the Great, passed through these hills two thousand years ago, his Greek soldiers would have done exactly the same to honour the dead.'

Joe was both impressed and amused by Iskander's practical approach to leadership and settled down on the walls with Lily to watch the entertainment. They were joined by Eddy Fraser.

'Not playing, Eddy?' Joe enquired and Eddy held up a bandaged hand.

'Stopped a lustful on-drive at short leg,' he replied. 'Are you interested in cricket, Miss Coblenz?'

'I don't know anything about it,' said Lily. 'Never watched it in my life, though I have a dim memory that it has to do with the winning of the Battle of Waterloo – or have I got it wrong?'

'It's taken very seriously in these parts,' said Eddy, not at all taken in by her sly humour. 'We recruit from the Afridi and the Mahsuds who do most things in friendly, well fairly friendly, rivalry and here they are confronting each other on the cricket field. I would have cancelled this but James's orders are "business as usual". It generates a great deal of heat between the two tribes.'

'Here we are,' said Joe, 'in the middle of nowhere and two cricket teams turn out who might be playing in England to all appearances!'

'Oh, yes,' said Eddy. 'This is serious stuff! Everybody in whites, everybody in cricket boots, stripy silk scarves round their waists! We have a little recreation fund which we milked to provide everybody with the appropriate kit. If you get into the eleven, you get the clothes to go with it. Bobby Carstairs – there he is – captains one side and Mike Burgoyne the other. I play when I can, so does James. I made forty last week but the men are developing at such a pace that I'm far from confident of my place in the side.'

'I'm shaking with excitement,' said Lily, drily. 'Can't you see? But you'll have to explain to me what's happening. It's kind of like baseball, I expect, but I don't know anything about baseball either.'

'No reason why you should,' said Eddy. 'Both English games.'

'My!' said Lily. 'Both English games! I don't believe anybody in the States knows that.'

'Probably wouldn't believe you if you told them,' said Eddy.

A Pathan and a Scouts officer tossed a coin together and took opposite ends as umpires. The opening pair made their way to the crease and the game began.

'If I shut my eyes,' Joe thought, 'this could almost be any English village green on a Sunday afternoon. If I open my eyes, on the other hand, what do I see? A pitiless blue sky, sun shining down that would fry an egg, the boundary line packed with vociferous turbaned figures, wild applause and even a blast on the bagpipes after every ball!'

With shrill applause in which Lily joined, the game wound its way onwards. The Afridis were all out for ninety-eight and Bobby Carstairs hit a winning six amid boos and hisses from half the spectators and cheers from the other half. The Afghanis invaded the pitch. They'd evidently decided amongst themselves to take a ball each and pass the bat from hand to hand with the applause and encouragement of the watching Scouts.

'They are damned odd,' said Eddy. 'Just watching them you'd say – natural cricketers. They've been doing this for all of ten minutes and they're showing more skill than your average county side!'

'Politically,' said Joe, 'it wouldn't be a bad idea if they carried this back to Kabul but I'm not sure that Afghans would qualify either by birth or residence to play for All India.'

'Oh, I expect we could fiddle our way round that. Fiddle your way round anything if you want to.' And Eddy shouted encouragement in Pushtu to the perspiring Afghan batsmen as they stood queuing to play. 'Of course, the game could have been invented for these chaps. Brilliant hand and eye co-ordination but something else as well – patience and planning. They'll wait for days, months, years even to get something right. Clever tacticians. I wonder what we've started?'

'There's Iskander lining up at the wicket. Obviously, he's played the game before,' said Joe as a mighty sweep of the bat sent the ball winging over the boundary to deafening applause from his men.

They went down together to welcome in the players. Lily, Joe noticed, went straight to Iskander to congratulate him on his men's showing and his own sparkling performance.

'Good Lord! The girl thinks she's at some awful American shindig! Handing out the rosettes and the silver cup.' The disapproving drawl came from Edwin Burroughs. 'Can't you keep that filly on a tighter rein, Sandilands? She's doing her kind no credit, you know. She's doing *us* no credit.'

Joe felt it would have taken up an hour of his time to challenge Burroughs' views. Instead he hurried forward to add his own warm comments on the game. Though Iskander and Lily were standing a good four feet away from each other Joe had, and not for the first time, the uncomfortable feeling that if he walked between them he would trip on some unseen connecting thread. Perhaps he ought to ask her to take her suspect surveillance a little less seriously? Iskander, Joe thought, was for the moment treating her interest as sympathetic concern and natural high spirits but if she were not more careful he might become suspicious.

'Hey! Why don't you all stay another day?' she was saying. 'Then your men could take on the Scouts and have a proper game. That would be good, Joe, wouldn't it?'

'Lily, I really don't think it's up to us to rearrange the Amir's timetable for him,' Joe started to say but to his surprise he was interrupted by Iskander.

'That is a very tempting suggestion, Miss Coblenz! Nothing would please my men more than to give a thrashing to the Scouts. If Major Lindsay were willing to extend his already generous hospitality for a further day it would delight us all. Our schedule is not so tight that we would be unable to stay for one more day. I will speak to Commander Lindsay.'

The blossoming of Iskander, as Joe thought of the change that had come over the young man since the loss of his commanding officer, continued through the day. Over the dinner table he entertained everyone with stories of the frontier and answered questions, however silly, on the Pathan way of life with patience and humour. Joe was intrigued to find that he had been educated not in England as had Zeman Khan but at the college in Peshawar. An orphan from an early age, he belonged to the same clan as Zeman and the two boys had been childhood friends. Joe could only begin to guess at the raw sorrow that he must be feeling at the loss of his friend. Unless, of course, he was himself responsible for Zeman's death. The thought would not go away. If James had died Joe wondered if he would have been able to face a dinner party and do more than hold his own in a foreign language. He found his respect for Iskander continued to grow.

But, equally, his concern for Lily, with her obvious interest in the man, grew. At the end of the meal when all got up to leave the table Joe saw Lord Rathmore hurry to

122

position himself by the door. As Lily passed in front of him he bent his head and whispered something to her which was evidently not to her liking. Before Lily had a chance to reply, Iskander had stepped between them and engaged Rathmore in conversation, allowing Lily to go on her way, evading Rathmore's detaining arm. Protective? Proprietorial? Or something more sinister? The gesture disturbed Joe.

As Joe caught up with his charge he asked, 'All well, Lily?'

She turned to him with shining eyes. 'All's very well, Joe. Apart from the appalling Rathmore. Did you see him just now? Some men just don't know when to give up!'

'What do you mean? What was he saying to you?'

'Some nonsense about meeting me later this evening. I couldn't make sense of what he was saying. Trying for another date, I suppose! Man's loco!'

'Lily, I don't want to have to bed down outside your room every night but if it comes to that you know I will! If I have the slightest suspicion that your, er, peace of mind is being threatened by anyone . . . *anyone* . . . I shall take steps.'

'Joe, thanks for the offer but my, er, peace of mind is quite robust enough to take care of itself,' she said and darted ahead in the direction of the guest wing.

Joe was overtaken by James and they walked along together, discussing the evening. As they went through the front door, Joe paused. Something had changed. Looking about he noticed that Minto's kennel had disappeared.

'What have you done with Minto?' he asked.

'I'm sorry to say I've had to remove him lock, stock and kennel up to our room. I had two complaints this morning, complaints on the grounds of hygiene and noise. The first was from Burroughs. He's convinced the dog is suffering from some sort of Indian dog disease – rabies or some such – and is afraid he'll pass it on to him. He's of the opinion that this is what killed Zeman and can't understand why Grace is not taking his opinion seriously.'

'And the second?'

'Lord Rathmore. Claims the dog rushes out and makes a noise every time he walks by his kennel and this is a serious restriction on Rathmore's freedom of movement. Freedom of movement! Why he wants to creep around unobserved I've no idea. Not the sort of chap who would make off with the regimental silver in the night, is he?'

'Just the sort of chap! Minto's a good judge of character.'

'Well, I'm not happy with the new arrangements I can tell you! What we've got up there now is a *ménage à trois* – in which I come a bad *troisième*.'

A light tap on his door woke Joe at dawn the next day. The orderly who stood there was obviously in the grip of a barely contained excitement. His message was that Joe should go down to the main gates at once where he would find James. 'There is trouble, sahib,' he added. 'Much, much trouble!'

Chapter Nine

James, in the light of flares, was calling out orders to a group of men. 'Trackers! Limited reconnaissance. Out for five minutes then return and report initial findings. Eddy – have them picketed, will you? This could be a trap and none of my men are walking into it unprotected. And, Eddy, prepare to take out a full gasht. Muster here in thirty minutes. Now where are the second watch sentries? Line them up. Picket gate sentries? Well, look harder and further! Joe!' He walked over to Joe, grim, alert, every inch the commanding officer.

'What the hell's going on, James?'

'The Afghanis have disappeared. Decamped in the night. No idea yet why, when or how. But we soon will have. Come and hear the sentries with me, will you?'

Translating for Joe he gave the gist of the men's story. 'No trouble in the night on any of the watches. The bloke on the 10 p.m. to 2 a.m. is the most interesting. Apparently the Afghanis were chattering and even singing round their fires until late in the night. All sounds ceased at 1 a.m. but the fires continued to burn. He didn't hear thirty-five horses clattering off in the night. We'll go out and have a look, shall we? But, just for once, arm yourself, will you?'

James and Joe walked, revolver in hand, through the gates and round the corner of the fort until they reached the football field encampment. Fires were collapsing into piles of white ash and embers in front of tents which looked as though they still housed sleeping soldiers. A glance up at the fortifications told Joe that they were being covered from every angle by watchful riflemen as they made their way around the encampment.

'I can't see how thirty-five horses and thirty-one men and two pack mules could have got away without someone being aware of it,' said Joe.

'You don't know Pathans,' said James. 'They can fade into the night without a sound. This is how I think they did it. Look.' He pointed to the beginnings of a trail of horses' hooves only just becoming visible in the strengthening light, heading towards the tarmacked road to the Khyber. 'See, it's one set of hooves overlying another, not spread out on a wide front. I think a few men made a racket to cover the departure of the rest of the troop who must have set off one at a time, let's say at one-minute intervals, so that all there ever was to hear was a single horse at any time and never a horde of thirty-five. They could have cleared the camp in under an hour. I've sent trackers to make a preliminary survey and we'll hear what they have to say in a minute or two.'

They wandered around looking into abandoned tents and finding no remains of the Afghans. Items borrowed from the fort had been meticulously cleaned and left behind.

'Why? Why, James? Iskander dropped no hint of this. He led us to believe he was intending to stay another day. What's gone wrong?'

'We don't know yet but you can be sure that there can be nothing reassuring about this way of leaving. It's against all the rules of hospitality. It's against all I'd come to think of Iskander in fact. I'm worried, Joe.'

The returning trackers reported as James had feared that the single line of hooves continued to move alongside the tarmacked road, taking the soft ground to one side of it, and, as far as they had been able to establish, it went on up towards the Khyber. Back to Afghanistan.

'Grace?' said Joe. 'Is Grace still aboard or have they taken her with them?'

'Still here. And as puzzled as we are. They told her nothing about this.'

'I don't suppose Iskander's been left behind by any chance?' said Joe uneasily. 'They haven't gone off without him as well, have they? I mean, how did he get out of the fort?'

'I checked his room quickly on the way down when the alarm was raised. Not there. Bed not been slept in. And it wouldn't be difficult for someone agile to shin over the wall and down when the sentry's back was turned. This damn fort's designed to keep people out, not necessarily in. But if my guess is right he used a much simpler method.'

'The picket gate?'

'That's right. The duty sentries have disappeared. Absconded, taking their rifles with them. They were both Afridis. Yes, Iskander's tribe.'

Joe kicked at a glowing log angrily. 'All that fraternization at the cricket match yesterday! Plenty of opportunity to get alongside long-lost kinsmen, ask a few questions, persuade the right pair to desert.'

'But why, Joe? Why?'

'Let's go back to his room. See if there's anything there in the way of a clue to this behaviour.'

The room showed no sign of occupation. The bed was unruffled, the rugs straight, the equipment in order.

'Look! There!' said Joe, pointing to the bedside table. There was an envelope addressed to Commander Lindsay in English and what he guessed to be Urdu. 'I know what this is going to say,' said Joe nervously as James opened it. 'It's going to say, "Dear Mother, Army's a bugger. Sell the pig and buy me out."' He peered anxiously over James's shoulder and they read the letter together.

To Major James Lindsay, Commandant, Fort Gor Khatri.
April 20 1922.
From Muhammed Iskander Khan, Captain, Service of HM the Amir of Afghanistan.

127

Enclosed please find copies of the report on the death of my kinsman and commanding officer, Major Zeman Khan, which occurred at the fort of Gor Khatri at a time uncertain in the early hours of the morning on the 20th instant.

It is with regret that I am unable to accept the finding of death by natural causes as established by the medical examination and subsequent deliberations, flawed, as it is, by inconsistencies. I believe my comrade to have been murdered by person or persons unknown.

Closely bound by ties of blood to my kinsman Zeman Khan, you will understand, Major Lindsay, that I am bound to avenge his death. If it were known who had killed Major Zeman Khan I would already have taken steps to avenge him. The British Army would then seek reprisals against me and my men and His Majesty the Amir would, in turn, become involved in an escalating spiral of bloody reprisal.

I believe you, Major Lindsay, to be, like me, a civilized man who would prefer to avoid senseless bloodshed and I offer you a solution to our problem. Firstly, the conclusion of the medical examination must be set aside and secondly, the identity of the person guilty of Major Zeman Khan's death must be discovered. The guilty man must be charged and judged by you. You have lived and worked and fought with our people; you understand melmastia; you will understand that my kinsman was a guest in the fort and under your protection. The murderer is thus doubly guilty. He must be executed and by a firing squad of British soldiers before the gates of the fort a week from now, at noon on the 27th of April. Badal will accordingly be satisfied. The chain of vengeance will be broken with the death at British hands of the man responsible.

The Amir will be satisfied as will Zeman's kin and they will not feel obliged to take further action. To ensure that you carry out the execution I have taken the precaution of removing one man from the fort as hostage. Lord Rathmore is accompanying us – unwillingly. He will be released to you when you have done your duty.

If you fail to do your duty Lord Rathmore's life becomes forfeit and his body will be delivered to the fort shortly after noon next Friday.

Joe and James read this hideous document through to its conclusion without a word and, having done so, turned back to the beginning and independently read their way through it once more. It was Joe who finally broke the silence between them. 'This,' he said, 'is absolute balls! Iskander's gone barmy! Don't you agree? Nobody in their right senses could act on this and he must be told so.'

James sank into a chair. 'You can't dismiss it just like that, you know, Joe.'

'I can and I do. The only problem is – how the hell do we communicate with bloody Iskander? We can't just send a man with a chit, can we? He – by which I mean they – are over there!' With a wide gesture he pointed to the circle of empty hills. 'Somewhere out there.'

'Well, as far as communications are concerned,' said James, 'it's not such a problem. We send someone out with a white flag and our reply. He puts it under a stone and plants the white flag next to it and in due course you may depend someone, and we don't have to know who, picks it up. It's not a problem.'

'Problem! said Joe. 'It's one bloody problem after another. Now look here, James – Iskander talks of inconsistencies. What inconsistencies? Have you any idea? You've got, if not an official autopsy, at least a sincere opinion expressed by a highly qualified source – Grace. I'm not prepared to just say, "Oh, dear," and forget it. And if, for some reason, we reject Grace's findings, we confront a more serious problem – "Who killed Cock Robin?" And how did they kill Cock Robin? "I, said the Sparrow, with my bow and arrow." How likely is it that we are going

129

to have a helpful sparrow step forward and tell us he did it?'

'The fact remains that if we reject the autopsy, an important citizen, Afghani subject, was done to death while in my care. Iskander is perfectly correct when he says that if this fact became generally known, a blood bath would ensue which would follow all of us to the grave and beyond. I couldn't be responsible for letting that loose. No,' James attempted a smile, 'in the circumstances, this is a pretty generous offer Iskander is making us. The solution he suggests would, in fact, defuse a nasty situation. There must be a victim.'

'A murderer found guilty?' asked Joe.

'Yes, of course. Just that.'

Joe looked at him in exasperation, 'Perhaps you could tell me whom you have in mind?'

James was silent. 'Just leave it to me, Joe,' he finally said.

'Not sure that I can, old mate,' said Joe, unhappy and fearful. 'As I see it, you have two alternatives: first – and this is probably what any other commander along the line would do – is to heave poor old Achmed into the firing line. Or Abdullah, whichever is the more dispensable. I wouldn't be surprised if that was what Iskander himself were expecting. No? Didn't think you would, so we're left with the second. You have a perfectly able Scotland Yard detective right here at your elbow. Make use of me! You're running me in blinkers, James! Give me your support to investigate this shambles properly and find out if it was murder and if so who is responsible. A week would be more than enough. I don't boast but it's what I do for a living.'

'No, Joe. Neither of your schemes is acceptable. And I refuse to discuss it any further. There is a third option and this is the only one available to me. Please take my word on that.'

'Third option?' Joe asked warily. 'What exactly do you have in mind, James?'

'There *will* be a victim offered up for execution at noon next Friday,' he said, unable to meet Joe's eye. 'It will be me.'

The two men contemplated each other. Joe, angry and puzzled, looked down at James, chill and haunted. 'This,' said Joe, 'is madness time. I can't for a second accept what you say and see no reason whatever to do so, for God's sake! Do you realize what you're doing? At the dramatic – I would even say hysterical – suggestion of Iskander Khan, you seem prepared to set all evidence that doesn't suit him on one side!'

He looked both anxiously and affectionately at his friend. 'I can't understand you, James! This isn't like *you*. Unless, of course,' he added lightly, 'you know something I don't . . .' and he resumed, 'What you should do is this – reply to Iskander Khan by whatever means recommends itself to you. A level and unflustered reply is what is called for. He speaks of "inconsistencies" – let him enumerate them. Say that if he's not satisfied with the findings – as far as they've gone – the authorities here are quite ready to pick the matter up. You can mention my name if you like. We've been friends for years and you probably haven't even noticed that I'm considered by some to be quite a star. Zeman had heard of me; Iskander may have heard of me. I'm sure that's the proper way to play it. It wouldn't be a good idea to ignore Iskander's letter but it's a bloody awful idea to accept this *Boys Own Paper* solution to the problem! See if you can get me some official status, James. Why not? Then I could deal with this as a proper police enquiry and we could, incidentally, drop the hint that as a preliminary to a measured police enquiry, we would expect the return of that damn fool Rathmore – and when you've got him in hand you can box his ears for having been so bloody inept as to get himself snatched! Be a man, James! You make me feel like Lady Macbeth! "Infirm of purpose, give me the dagger!"'

131

'Dagger? What dagger? Oh, yes,' said James miserably. 'But it's probably no use trying to send him a message. If he's gone off back over the border, he's out of earshot, so to speak. It's my guess he wants to avoid any parlaying. He's shot his arrow and wants no riposte. He'll sit up there in the mountains, out of our reach, and come down to witness the execution.' He sighed. 'He's got us sewn up! But I suppose we ought first to go and check on Rathmore. Iskander didn't write this letter in the middle of the night seconds before they set off. He wrote it – and this chills the blood, Joe – yesterday morning when he was closeted in the library for three hours. He'd had a talk with his men, they'd chosen their hostage, planned this action and they put it into smooth operation hours later. I wonder how the devil they managed to get him away?'

'And all that jovial bonhomie on the cricket ground was so much eyewash!' Joe said bitterly. 'All that chatter and joking was a blind. They were fixing the sentries using whatever pressure or inducements came to hand – I don't know what – family ties, favours called in, gratitude of the Amir . . . And the sentries turned a blind eye or even helped with bundling poor old Rathmore out of the fort through the back gate. They had horses enough. Four spares, was it?'

They hurried along to Rathmore's room on the ground floor of the guest wing and looked about them. 'Bed hasn't been slept in,' said James. 'Apart from that, nothing untoward, would you say, Joe?'

'All his personal effects are still here,' said Joe, checking the wardrobe and the shelves in the bathroom. 'Slippers under the bed so he was wearing his outdoor shoes. I don't have Rathmore's wardrobe by heart so I can't say for certain what he'd got on but I can't see here the outfit he was wearing when he arrived – wasn't it a sort of highly tailored colonial traveller's outfit? Khaki drill with lots of pockets and leather patches on the shoulders?'

'It was. So you're saying that after supper he comes along to his room and chooses to put on not his dressing

132

gown but a substantial suit and his walking shoes? Odd. Almost as though he knew he was going to be snatched!'

'Well, expecting to go out for a night-time walk, anyway. That's as far as we can go on the evidence,' said Joe carefully. He walked over to the dressing table and examined the effects laid neatly and innocently out on the top. A pair of ivory-backed hairbrushes, silver comb, a shoe horn, a flask of Trumper's 'Eucris' and a leather writing case. Joe opened the writing case and looked carefully at the contents. A few letters from England and copies of outgoing letters, a small diary with nothing of importance to Joe. An entry made for seven days hence told them that Rathmore was confidently expecting to be back in Simla. Unused envelopes, a writing pad, a fountain pen and two HB pencils made up the contents. Joe examined the pen. 'Out of ink,' he commented. Lastly, he took out the writing pad and held it at an angle to the light.

'Well, sometimes you have a bit of luck! Look, there's something here, James,' he said. 'Give me your torch.'

He shone the light at a narrow angle against the page.

'What does it say – "Dear John, Pig gone. Soldier on."?' James managed a weak smile. 'I see it. Indentations. Letters. From the page above. Must have been writing with one of those hard pencils for it to show through like this. Can't make it out though. I say, is this all right? I mean, peeking at a chap's correspondence? What's he going to say if he ever finds out?'

Joe ignored him and took out his magnifying glass. 'Got it! Well, one word at least and perhaps the most important. The first one, not surprisingly, while the pencil was at its sharpest. Look, you can just make out the heavier down strokes. And, if I've got it right, this word's nearly all down strokes. And Rathmore would appear to be heavy-handed in this as in everything! Looks like L I L Y. He's writing to Lily Coblenz! But why would he do that? He was sitting opposite her at supper, he could have said anything he wanted to say to her face.'

'Not if it were clandestine in any way,' said James.

'Something he wouldn't want any of us to overhear. Love letter? Oh, Lord, that's all we need!'

'Well, whatever it was, it must remain Rathmore's secret,' said Joe, 'I can't make out anything more. I wonder if the recipient of this billet doux will feel able to inform us? Let's go and have a word with the lucky lady, shall we?'

He was remembering the scene at the door of the dining room the previous evening, the last time he had set eyes on Rathmore. Joe tried urgently to conjure up the expression on Rathmore's face as he spoke to Lily. He had only had time to get out a few words before Iskander placed himself between them but his face had spoken volumes. Joe had not been able to interpret the emotion in that context but, looking back, he felt it had been one of triumphant complicity directed at Lily. Complicity. Joe, with a flash of insight, began to see how Iskander might have managed his conjuring trick – the disappearance of Rathmore. But did the conjuror have an assistant? Grimly, Joe decided he had a hundred hard questions to put to Miss Coblenz.

Their deliberations were cut short by the entry of Betty. Tense and pale, she stood for a moment, silent in the doorway. 'Lily,' she said. 'I'm looking for Lily. Anyone seen her this morning? Anyone know where she is?'

'Oh, she'll be around,' said James, 'somewhere. With Grace maybe? Having a bath? I don't know. You, Joe?'

'I don't know where she is,' said Joe suddenly alert, 'but I do know where she *isn't* and that's under my care. Oh, dammit! Bloody little nuisance! I'm getting a bad tremor out of this. Little earthquake about to happen? But – for a start – have you looked in her room?'

They ran upstairs to find Grace standing by the open door of Lily's room.

'She's gone, James! Lily's not there!'

Chapter Ten

With dreadful predictability a third pristine, unslept-in bed greeted them. James called for a havildar and ordered a complete search of the fort. Miss Coblenz was to be brought to him directly no matter where she was found or what she was doing. Betty and Grace went off to help in the search and, left alone in Lily's empty room, Joe and James looked at each other in silent despair. They could no longer do other than accept the truth – that Lily too had disappeared at some unknown hour the previous night.

Looking yet again at Iskander's letter although he knew every word by heart, James said, 'He mentions *one* hostage. Rathmore. He doesn't say he's taking Lily and, as you know, Joe, that's not the Pathan way. He wouldn't harm or inconvenience Lily or any woman. Oh, hell! The trackers are out. Eddy's gasht left ten minutes ago. I'll run another one in an hour and another an hour after that. I'll shake these hills until Iskander and his bandits fall out! For the moment, that's all we can do, I think.'

'Not quite all we can do, James, surely?' said a confident voice from the doorway behind them and Fred Moore-Simpson stepped into the room. 'I understand from Betty that our Afghan friends have bunked off in the night and you want them found? If there's some urgency about it I can probably help.'

Joe and James looked at each other and Joe nodded. Briefly James laid out the problem for Fred and handed him Iskander's letter, adding as Fred finished reading, 'And as well as Rathmore they seem to have carried off

Lily Coblenz, so all in all we have the makings of a situation with which these hills will still be resounding in a hundred years' time.'

'And, in the meantime, I expect you're planning to fall on your sword, James?' said Fred shrewdly. 'I can see why you would. But look, we've got some days to play with and it seems to me – oh, tell me to shut up if you like – that we can attack this problem on two fronts. Firstly, we have to try to contact these brigands and that means locating them. You're obviously doing all that you can on the ground but isn't it time you moved into the twentieth century? What about a little air support? There are some spotter planes based at Miram Shah down in Waziristan. We could telegraph them via Peshawar and have a plane sent up. One pair of eyes can cover many square miles from a thousand feet, see things you can't see at ground level. These planes are so small they could land on the football pitch here if you clear the goalposts – or the road, even the road would do.'

James turned an anguished face to them. 'Now why the hell didn't I think of that?'

'Medieval thinking, my boy,' said Fred. 'Not surprising in this bloody medieval country!'

'That would be a help indeed,' said James. 'Thank you, Fred! I'll get someone to take you over to the communications room. The lines are still working – they at least didn't cut the wires – and you can liaise straight away with Peshawar. Oh, by the way, I sent a signal to the fort at Landi Kotal – that's half-way down the Khyber, Joe – to watch out for and detain the Afghanis when they try to pass through. Nothing seen of them so far but they're going to wire us every hour on the hour with news or a nil return. But you mentioned two fronts, Fred?'

'Yes, the other solution would seem to be to do as Iskander insists. Find out who killed Zeman – if anybody did. And you'd better work fast, my boy, because your list of suspects appears to be shrinking at a quite alarming rate! Last night there were nine people here in the guest wing whose names might have been on any suspect list and now there are only six. And that's if Burroughs is still around. Anybody checked? At this rate Joe is going to find himself the only one remaining and he's going to have to top himself. But have you thought? – suppose that Rathmore is the villain. He's the chap *my* money's on. Hot-headed and jealous. Though I wouldn't have thought he was clever enough to have pulled off a stunt like this . . . Anyway, he's in custody and can't answer for himself but just suppose we find that he's guilty? What then?'

'In that case we take no action at all,' said Joe, 'and we wait for Iskander to do the dirty deed for us.'

'Sounds like the best solution all round,' said Fred cheerfully.

'Stop this!' said James. 'This is just silly speculation! I've told you what's going to happen!'

'And I told you what *isn't* going to happen! Let's get those planes up,' said Joe. 'Come on, Fred, we'll give those idle buggers in Peshawar something to do.'

Dermot Fitzmaurice Benson, First Baron Rathmore, was in anguish both social and physical. As the official precursor of an important trade mission, he was firmly and indig-nantly of the opinion that he had not been treated with the deference that he deserved. He blamed James for this. He blamed Joe to some extent. He didn't think Zeman – or for that matter Iskander – had paid him appropriate respect. He didn't after all expect the natives to presume to address him as equals. 'Bloody cheek! Quoting Kipling!'

So much for his social disquiet which was now com-pounded by a physical anguish even more acute. A note on a sheet of the fort's own writing paper had summoned him to an assignation with Lily. He had it in his pocket. He didn't need to look at it again. He knew it well by heart. 'Why don't we meet at eleven at the postern? L.C.' Lily Coblenz. There could be no doubt about that. But it had not been Lily who had kept this tryst but two Afghani

137

tribesmen. Untidy habiliments, long, dust-coloured shirts over baggy trousers, hawklike, wind-blackened faces and not much ceremony!

As he'd stepped up to the gate, strong hands had swept his legs from under him from behind, a cloth – through which it was difficult to breathe – was firmly tied over his mouth and another one put over his head and in spite of his solid twelve stones he was hauled out through the gate and on to the back of a waiting horse. A far from docile horse. A horse that skittered sideways and humped its back, a horse he just had time to see was grey with a wild white eye. He was at best an indifferent horseman and the thought came to him, 'I shan't be able to stay on that bloody thing! I could break my neck!' But, as he soon realized, among many dangers, falling from his horse was not one. His feet were tied firmly with leather straps under the horse's belly, the reins were thrust into his hand and with a slap across its quarters, the horse set off at a trot in the company of two – or was it three? – horsemen. From the noise, Rathmore deduced that they were at first walking then trotting and later cantering. For a while the hooves rang on a tarmacked surface and then broke off on to rocky ground and they appeared to be scrambling over loose stones and moving up a defile.

His captors muttered incessantly amongst themselves. A horseman drew up beside him and a soft voice spoke, just audible above the clatter of hooves and the rattle of falling stones. 'Good morning, Lord Rathmore – I suppose it is morning? I'm sorry to have to discommode you.' A hand came out and the cloth was taken from his head revealing the face of Iskander Khan. 'With home-bred hordes the hillsides teem, you see,' he said with a gesture to the gang of horsemen who'd gathered around, grinning at him.

Purple-faced, Rathmore recovered his breath and turned on Iskander. 'You won't get away with this!' he said. 'I don't know what the devil you're playing at but you won't get away with it!' He wished he could have thought

138

of something more original to say and added, 'Start from there and tell me what the hell's going on!'

'I think your normal good sense has deserted you, Lord Rathmore! I shouldn't need to explain. It must be obvious to the meanest intelligence – that you have been "kidnapped" and that you are now a hostage. A hostage to ensure the performance of an undertaking which I have laid on the good Major James Lindsay.'

'Where the hell are we going?' said Rathmore.

'The name would mean nothing to you. We are going to a place nearby. There are plenty of "places" in these hills, none of them frequented by the British. The comforts of these vary but we will do our best to make you feel at home. In any case your stay will not be a long one.'

Rathmore threw his head back. 'Help!!!' he shouted. To his bitter mortification this was greeted with a roar of laughter and remorselessly the clattering convoy went on its way. It was clear that Iskander was hurrying them all he could. As dawn broke, a rider offered a water bottle to Rathmore and another a handful of dried apricots. This apart, the journey proceeded in silence as the sun rose.

A way led them down a path in the hills, little more than a steep-sided cleft in the black rocks with a yeasty, brawling and rocky stream at its foot, a narrow ribbon of blue sky above, dotted with circling birds. Listening to the rattle of hooves, Rathmore became aware that a second group was following his but, straining and tied to his stirrups, he couldn't turn enough to see who or what this could be.

Ceaselessly, Iskander rode up and down the convoy, cheering and encouraging, and at last came to rest beside Rathmore. 'Five more miles,' he said, 'and then you can rest. I'm sorry this has been uncomfortable for you.'

'Who's that behind us?' asked Rathmore.

'Not, I'm afraid, Indian cavalry come to your rescue but someone whom I think you will be surprised to see. Let's get you untied. I don't think you could walk back to the fort from here. And, were you so foolish as to try, you would be picked off by a ten rupee jezail loaded with who

139

knows what, possibly a Lee-Enfield if you were lucky, before you had gone ten yards. You are in what we call and have always called "The Free Land". The warriors and the shepherds – and out here it's the same thing – who lurk behind every crag are not aware that they are "the captives of your bow and spear" and a barony is no breastplate out here, you'll find. And now we'll halt for a few minutes and get acquainted.'

With a rattle and a clatter the convoy drew to a halt where the track widened and descended to a surging stream. Rathmore's legs were untied and, stiff and sore, he turned in the saddle to watch the company bringing up the rear approach. Two Afghanis escorted a smaller figure who had been, unlike him, riding free. The small, fair-haired figure bundled up in an afghan poshteen was laughing with one of her attendant brigands. A terrible truth paralysed his mind and the only words he could summon up were a shocked exclamation.

'Miss Coblenz! Lily!'

He sat transfixed.

'Lord Rathmore! Dermot!'

'You little traitor! You little baggage! You've betrayed me to these, these bloody murdering wogs! This is all your doing! What the hell do you think you're playing at?'

Lily had enjoyed such high expectations of her visit to the frontier. It had seemed to her an area populated by free and dangerous men perhaps, dangerous situations certainly. It was here she would experience – and she tried to avoid the cliché – life in the raw. A long way from the conventions of American society, a long way from the restrictions of Simla, a long way from the straitjacket of the British Raj, its acceptances and expectations. It all seemed – as James himself might have expressed it – 'jolly good fun'. But there was no doubt about it, her enjoyment had faded in the face of the menacing reality of life on the frontier and after dinner, unable to sleep, she had wan-

140

dered from her room and climbed on to the wall. She sat quietly, feet dangling, looking inwards at the bulk of the old fort and out over the wall towards the gardens and the outer skirting wall of the lower fort. Peace, or what passed for peace, on the frontier seemed to reign. For the moment. Lily was uneasy and nervous. Something was going on which she did not understand, something in which she was involved but unknowingly involved and if there was anything Lily could not accept it was being in a state of not knowing.

In the centre of her vision was the rear postern gate with its watchful sentries. That old nuisance Rathmore! She identified him as the reason she could not sleep. What had he tried to tell her after dinner before Iskander had interceded? Some rubbish about meeting her at that gate at eleven. And that in itself would not have worried her but it was his manner – gloating, complicitous, out of key in someone who had been rebuffed in strong terms the night before. There was definitely something here that she did not understand. One thing was certain though: she was not going within twenty yards of the postern gate.

As she watched, the emphasis seemed to change. A dim figure had emerged and walked into the fragile lamplight that illuminated the gate. Straining her eyes, Lily was able to identify the heavy shoulders and the heavy walk of Rathmore. ('Call me Dermot,' he had said with heavy invitation.) 'Well, hi there, Dermot!' said Lily to herself. 'And what are *you* up to?' And with that thought the peaceful scene dissolved.

Two men, Afghanis, Lily thought, sprang from the shadows and without hesitation pounced on the strolling Rathmore, threw a cloth over his head, twisted his hands behind him and propelled him out through the gate. The sentries, the moonlight reflecting from their bayonets, held the gate open and then slipped through it themselves.

'Holy shit!' said Lily who did not often swear and for a paralysed moment she thought, 'What do I do now?' She opened her mouth to scream and alert the wall sentries

141

and then, remembering the behaviour of the two below, closed it again. For a further moment she hesitated. Nobody seemed to have noticed what was happening! Quite obviously the sentries were in on this, whatever it was!

'Joe! I must get Joe!'

She ran down the steps intending to make her way silently back to the guest wing but on reaching the ground was struck by a thought inspiring in its simplicity and immediacy. The alarm bell! Hadn't James shown them all a rope dangling somewhere around here? A rope attached to an old bell up there in the turret – a bell that would wake the whole fort and in much less time than it would take to get hold of Joe. She hunted about and encountered a hairy rope snaking its way down from on high. What had James said? 'Summon all hands on deck.'

But as she reached for the bellrope a slim, wiry and irresistible hand closed over her mouth and the voice of Iskander came in her ear: 'A good idea but, forgive me, Miss Coblenz, I'm planning to leave with His Lordship by the back door and I don't want you ringing the bell. Let the fort sleep.'

With an arm round her shoulders and under her arm, with a swift concentration of muscle he swung her out through the postern and on to a horse standing by. Lily tried to open her mouth to scream but the hand tightened about it. She changed her mind and sank her teeth into flesh, provoking, to her satisfaction, a muted cry.

'Good, Miss Coblenz – but not good enough!' said the voice. 'Now listen! Since you have chosen inconveniently to involve yourself in my affairs you must stay involved for a while longer. You will accompany us into the hills. You may do this in one of two ways. You may ride freely, untied, ungagged and silently, co-operating fully with us. No harm will come to you – I do not take women hostage. I place no such value on Rathmore who is decidedly a hostage. His welfare depends on your decision to agree to the first way. If you choose the second way and make a fuss Rathmore will suffer.' His voice, which had been calm and reasonable, took on a cold edge. 'And I will arrange for you to witness his suffering. Perhaps even his death – the man does not impress me with his physical fortitude. I would imagine that the mere sight of a skinning knife would bring on a fatal apoplexy.'

Lily's eyes grew huge as she peered helplessly over Iskander's large, muffling hand.

'Nod your head if you accept the first way,' he muttered.

Lily nodded.

'Good. I will have two men escort you and you will ride last in the file.'

He released her and handed her the reins. A moment's adjustment to the stirrups and a hissed word of command to his men and Lily was walking quietly forward towards the mouth of the Khyber Pass. Sandwiched in single file between her two warrior horsemen she trotted and cantered and then galloped, keeping pace with them. The moon had risen and Lily was glad to have the track illuminated. She wondered how on earth poor old Rathmore was managing with a bag on his head and his feet tied beneath him. The silly old fool certainly deserved something but not this, she thought. A cold gust of wind blew down from the mountains and she shivered. Sitting on the wall of the fort which still radiated warmth from the heat of the day she had been comfortable enough in her shirt but she knew they were headed for the mountains, most of which were still snow-covered, and however energetic the ride she would soon begin to feel the cold. She took stock of her circumstances. She was wearing her divided skirt and leather boots so riding was no problem. The horse was no problem either. A delight in fact. Lily almost grinned to feel the muscles surge at her commands, the sure-footed ease with which the big dark grey horse picked its way over the scree slope they were now embarking on. She looked about her, remembering the maps she had seen. The fort was well behind them now, in the east, and to the west the sinister Khyber stretched and wound on. Out of earshot of the fort they had followed the metalled surface of the caravan route up into the pass for a mile or two but then they had crossed the track and made off to the left down a defile which had not been visible to anyone riding up from the east. A horseman stood waiting for them on the track ahead. As they drew level, he threw a wrap of some kind to Lily and moved off ahead of them without a word.

A waistcoat. Judging by its retained warmth, a recently worn waistcoat. Wrinkling her nose at the smell of the hairy afghan poshteen, Lily gratefully slipped it on, holding the reins in her teeth as she manoeuvred.

Enveloped in the warmth of the garment and comforted by the thoughtfulness of the man who had handed it to her and whom she assumed to be Iskander, Lily began to relax and almost to enjoy her experience. But she wasn't going to be just an unwanted part of the baggage train – no sir! She looked up at the night sky and tried to find the Pole Star. She wished she had listened more carefully to her father when he had explained about navigating by the stars. Having no son, Carl Coblenz had taken his daughter with him and his hands when he patrolled the wide acres of his ranch and it was with senses trained and quickened in the wilderness of Dakota that Lily set about keeping a mental map of her journey into the foothills of the Hindu Kush.

After an hour's steady slog someone in the leading party lit up a flare. Two more were ignited and positioned half-way along the column in a formation that Lily guessed would have looked like the head of an arrow if observed from a crag overhead. At a signal from the hills and unseen by Lily, the head torch bearer appeared to swing his light around in a particular pattern and the convoy moved ahead. 'He's showing his passport,' Lily thought. The next time, she heard the signal – a high-pitched, short whistle – which precipitated the answering wave of the flare. 'We're being passed down the line! But what line? Going where?' She looked at the sky again and tried vainly to catch a

glance at her wristwatch. 'Sure as eggs, it's not Afghanistan we're headed for!'

Plodding along in the moonlight at an easier pace, Lily
had time to speculate on the reasons for abducting poor
old Rathmore. What on earth did Iskander want with *him*?
He obviously disliked the man and Rathmore qualified as
a credible hostage on account of his wealth and influence
but Lily was afraid there was more to it than simple
banditry. Iskander must have some dark reason for making
off with him. Iskander, she knew, had not been satisfied
with the official account of his kinsman's death. He must
have reasoned or got evidence that Rathmore was responsible. Lily thought back to the evening of the feast and to
Zeman's challenge to Rathmore's calculated rudeness.
Rathmore's self-esteem had been badly dented. He had
lost face before an audience of military men and the enemy
but also, and perhaps more importantly, he had come off
worst in her eyes and Lily was in no doubt that Rathmore
had set out to impress her. Had Rathmore taken it into his
head to punish Zeman? To kill him? She couldn't see how
this could have been managed but Iskander seemed to
have worked it out.

And now he was taking him off somewhere into the
wilderness to kill him. Probably to torture him to death.
Lily remembered with a shudder the appalling treatment
meted out to captured prisoners by these men of the hills.
In Simla Edward Dalrymple-Webster had embarked with
relish on a highly coloured account of the staking-out, the
emasculation, the eye-gouging and the skinning-alive suffered at the hands of the Pathan. Lily had assumed he had
exaggerated in his desperate attempt to make an impression but she had been chilled by something James had said
– 'We never leave a wounded man behind in Pathan
territory. Oh, no. The whole gasht will risk its life to carry
every last man – and his rifle – to safety.' And she had
pushed him further with a question. 'But suppose you
couldn't get back to him? What then?' And James had
replied with slow matter-of-factness, 'Then we'd shoot him

where he lay. Quick and clean. It's what we would all want. It's what we all expect.'

The troop ahead seemed to have called a halt at last. Dawn was breaking in the sky over her left shoulder and as she rode up to the main body she found she could make out familiar faces in the pale light. All looked weary and tense and the frequent glances up into the surrounding rocks did not go unremarked by Lily. They were not, apparently, riding into entirely friendly country. The horses steamed gently in the morning mist and made their way down to the stream to drink. She saw Rathmore being cut free and the cloth taken off his head. Was he aware of the danger he was in? Lily was consumed by a sudden rush of hot anger at the difficulties he had caused them by his arrogance and stupidity and now, she suspected, by his murderous guilt. And she would have to stand helplessly by and watch while these bandits tortured the truth out of him.

He turned and recognized her and, face crimson with rage, shouted her name. 'Traitor!' he added. And, 'Baggage!' The idiot appeared to be blaming *her* for the trouble they were in. When Lily got angry she didn't shout back. In any ruckus, she reckoned it was the one who kept his head that won. Sitting as tall as she could in the saddle she fixed him with a stare in which she hoped hauteur was blended with an equal amount of derision.

'Sir. You are the author not only of your own misfortune but of mine also! Your abduction cannot be laid at my door. For the fact that your hide is still in one piece, however, you may thank me.'

'In one piece? What the hell are you talking about, you Yankee bitch?'

'They threatened to skin you alive if I didn't come along quietly. They caught me as I was about to ring the alarm bell. Take your time to work it out and when you have I'll listen to your apology.'

She slithered from her horse and led it towards the stream.

Chapter Eleven

Threading his way neatly along the lines of communication linking the fort with Peshawar and Peshawar with the air base at Miram Shah, Fred, by being the only person in the fort who knew exactly what he wanted, had got his own way. Replacing the receiver he smiled with conspiratorial satisfaction at Joe and James and looked at his watch. '08.00 hours. There'll be a plane up in half an hour – I'd be happier with half a dozen but one'll have to do for now. It'll be landing here in . . . oh . . . just over an hour and then we'll tell the pilot what all this is about. I'll go and get a bit of a map together showing the search area and get the football field marked out for landing. All right if I take a squad of your blokes with me, James?' And he had bustled off, competent, purposeful, relishing the vindication of his views at last. But as he left the room some of his confidence left with him and James seemed sunk in gloom once again.

'You've done everything you could as a matter of urgency and first response,' said Joe, 'but let us note that we have a very serious situation here, one far beyond your immediate responsibility, James. Obviously, we've got to report back to Peshawar and seek their instructions.'

'How can I find the words to do that? said James despairingly. 'Tell me – how do I explain all this in a few words?'

'Here's the phone, James!' said Joe. 'This should come from you, not from me. I'm nobody. My only job is or has been to keep an eye on blasted Lily and a right balls I've

147

made of that! Now – make a few notes. Pick up the telephone. Ring up Sir John Deane in Peshawar and seek instructions. Tell him, in the first place, that Rathmore's disappeared. We may look on him as a bumbling halfwit in whose ultimate fate we have no personal concern but he's quite a prominent citizen. He has the ear of some brass hats in Delhi and Calcutta who will be interested to say the least in his fate. And the first thing you say to Peshawar is, "Your one-man trade delegation has been kidnapped. Sorry!" And the second thing you have to say is, "Zeman Khan, a prominent Afghani national, closely associated – indeed, closely related – to the Amir of Afghanistan, is dead in our care. The diagnosis from a reliable medical source speaks of food poisoning. Zeman's associate, kinsman, second-in-command and close friend rejects this diagnosis and has snatched Rathmore as a hostage it seems, threatening this or that unless the matter is reinvestigated or indeed investigated." And while the poor man is digesting this so welcome piece of information you should add that Lily Coblenz, American citizen, guest of the British Government, has also apparently been snatched. Unless, of course, she has run off to join the circus.

'And if all this mixed information doesn't stand his hair on end, I will be astonished. But what we need is instructions. You're not the Viceroy, still less am I. Throw the whole dismal heap into his lap and stand back – that would be my advice. And why don't you do it now, James? And while you're about it – why not send a tough reply to Iskander? Threaten him with the full weight of the entire Indian Army. Call Lord Roberts back from the grave – he'd know what to do!'

'Send a gunboat?' said James.

'Something of that sort. And when it comes to a gunboat, you've got some very good people here. It's not up to you to declare war on Afghanistan of course but get permission to rattle a sabre!'

'Hell, Joe!' said James desperately. 'I'm not often at a

loss but . . . I think this'll cost me my career,' he added miserably.

'Cost you your career? Nonsense! No such thing! Where, I'd like to know, is the old free-booting spirit of Clan Lindsay? Let's hear the skirl of the pipes . . . "Lochaber no more" and all that!'

Joe picked up the telephone and put it in James's hand. 'I'll leave you to it,' he said, patting him on the shoulder and pointing out of the window. 'I shall be there. Smoking a cigarette. The first of many, I dare say, before we've sorted this out. But just get on with it! I'll be composing a letter to Iskander if you don't mind.'

'Mind! I'd be very relieved!'

Joe had hardly lit the promised cigarette before James emerged, half amused, half exasperated. 'I don't believe this! The bastard! He's on the bloody golf course! On the golf course! The fate of nations hangs in the balance and the Commissioner is on the golf course! That's what's wrong with the Indian Empire! You've no idea how often this happens.'

'So how did you leave it?' said Joe.

'Well, just for once I took a strong line. I said, "This is a grade one emergency. I don't want to talk to anyone else about it. Get him back at the double." Was I right?'

'Right? Of course you were right!'

Joe took a sheet of foolscap paper and began to write.

To Muhammed Iskander Khan, Captain in the service of HM the Amir of Afghanistan.

Sir,

I have received and read with interest your communication of the 20th April 1922 and in respect of this seek confirmatory instructions from my superiors. In the meantime:–

1. I see no reason to reject the findings of the preliminary autopsy performed on the body of Major Zeman Khan here at the fort.

2. We are discussing an event which took place on Brit-

ish territory and as such the matter will be judged under the provisions of British law which must be upheld.

3. Obviously, I will be prepared to initiate a full investigation of the circumstances surrounding the death of Zeman Khan but would not be prepared to embark on this while the issue is clouded by the illegal apprehension and sequestration of Lord Rathmore.

4. No further steps will be taken in the matter until His Lordship has been returned to our care in good health. As a necessary preliminary to any investigation I must insist that you make arrangements accordingly forthwith.

5. The reaction of HMG to any failure on your part to meet this condition will be prompt, resolute and effective.

'"Prompt, resolute and effective", indeed!' said James. '*Sounds* good . . .'

'It's not very good,' said Joe, 'but if you're talking to the Commissioner it might be sensible to read it to him. I think you shouldn't utter a threat of tough stuff to come without his approval.'

'I very much agree,' said James. 'What do we do in the meantime?'

'Do what I'm about to do,' said Joe, 'have a whisky and soda. Steady the quaking nerves.'

At this moment the telephone rang. 'It's Peshawar,' said James, his hand over the receiver.

'I'll leave you to it,' said Joe. 'But be bloody, bold and resolute! Nothing to hide, after all.'

'You never know how he's going to take things,' said James nervously. 'Sometimes he can be all sweetness and reason and sometimes he can be an absolute sod!'

'Only one way to find out,' said Joe and, patting him on the shoulder, he stepped out into the sunshine and looked out on to the fort, puzzled to find his friend, usually so decisive, now apparently in retreat.

Faintly he could hear James speaking. Faintly he measured the intervals for reply. This went on for a long time. For a very long time in Joe's estimation. He fought off the temptation to stand at James's elbow and listen. He waited and waited until at last James appeared, flushed but, Joe was glad to notice, seemingly relieved and seemingly more cheerful.

'Well?' said Joe.

'Well!' said James. 'I think – well! The first thing I told him was that this was getting a bit beyond me . . .'

'Can't think why you said that,' said Joe, 'you're doing very well.'

'Not as well as all that. I explained to him that this had become a complicated police enquiry and that I'd got quite enough to do commanding the fort without going round on hands and knees with a magnifying glass. While I was there he put a call through to Simla. I don't know what's happened to the Posts and Telegraph Department of the Indian Empire but the speed with which these things are handled still surprises me – and the long and short of it is that I spoke to Sir George Jardine himself and – old boy – I hope you won't be too horrified – but you're still on attachment to the Bengal Police and, like it or lump it, you've been appointed to initiate, conduct and complete the enquiry! The return of Sherlock Sandilands in fact and – honestly – I simply can't tell you how relieved I am. Sorry, Joe! Didn't mean to drop you in the shit. But at least you've now got some official status. And, having cleared that out of the way – and I explained the whole plot to him – he said, "This is too important to be dealt with locally. It has to go up to the Council. And we need some political involvement."'

'Now what the hell does that mean?' said Joe.

'I think it means that the grand strategy should be put in the hands of one of the Heaven Born, not left in the hands of a humble cavalry major on attachment to the Scouts.'

'An Indian Civil Servant, you mean?'

James's face had cleared as he spoke and he almost

151

laughed as he replied. 'He said, "Now who can I think of? Who's available?" Oh, Joe! You're going to like this! An official with adequate powers is not only available but in situ! Know who he meant? None other than the Warren Hastings of the twentieth century – Edwin Burroughs!'

Joe was aghast. 'Good God! Didn't you explain to him that this is the same Edwin Burroughs whose name has risen several places to top the list of suspects? How can he possibly lead the mopping-up operation if he's under suspicion?'

James fixed Joe with a bleak but resolute stare. 'Look, Joe. None of us murdered Zeman if that's what you're implying. And I wish you'd stop harping on that. We have the opinion of Grace Holbrook on this – death by natural causes or misadventure at the worst if the theory about the arsenic is correct – and I'd be obliged if you'd leave it there. As you said yourself, we oughtn't to be stampeded into a barmy bit of theorizing just because Iskander wasn't happy with the official decision. And with this in mind, I think you should now go to Burroughs and explain what's happened.'

'Correction,' said Joe. '*You* can go and explain.'

'Further correction,' said James. 'We'll go together.'

They set off to bang on Burroughs' door.

'Come!' an irascible voice called.

They stepped inside to find Burroughs sitting up in bed, bottle of bismuth tablets in one hand and a glass of water in the other, gold-rimmed glasses on the end of his nose, pink with indigestion, girt in a pair of broad-striped pyjamas.

'I've been sitting here,' he said without preamble, 'like a damn fool, hoping that somebody would come and tell me what the hell's going on. So I could say in a manner of speaking I'm glad to see you. What have you to tell me?'

'Morning, Sir Edwin,' said Joe. 'Quite a lot to tell you one way and another.'

'Well, keep it short. There's only one thing in which I'm

152

seriously interested,' Sir Edwin interrupted, 'and that is – just how soon can it be arranged for me to leave? I have work to do in Delhi which really cannot be put on one side. I hadn't reckoned to be away from my desk for more than a day or two but I've now been away – thanks to the delay in Peshawar – for a week. I really need to get back. Now, you were saying?'

'There's been a bit of a change,' James Lindsay began tentatively.

'A change affecting your status in the affair,' Joe supplied. 'A change affecting my status too, for that matter.'

'What the devil's that supposed to mean?' said Burroughs. 'I've done what I came here to do which is to assess the present position in this part of the NWFP and all I have seen so far persuades me that the so-called Forward Policy has been a mistake and I shall continue to say so as soon as I can get back to Delhi.'

'It's not quite as simple as that,' said Joe and they explained.

Burroughs' face changed from pink to white and back again. He sat up in bed and gobbled. Disjointed words and phrases came across.

'Disgraceful . . . ridiculous . . . incompetent . . . no concern of mine . . . purely local difficulty . . . I've got better things to do . . .'

In a pause in his tirade James said, 'Sandilands has prepared this letter for Iskander Khan. The text has been checked and approved by Sir George Jardine. In the changed circumstances, we need your approval and your signature. With this I think I can get the letter into his hands although of course, as you will appreciate, his present whereabouts are still unknown.'

'My approval? I don't approve!'

'I'm ready to send this letter on its way – time is of the essence – and I do now need your authority to do so,' said James. He passed it to Burroughs with a pen and waited for him to countersign it.

Burroughs sank back among his pillows. 'This,' he said

153

petulantly, 'is precisely the situation I did not want. I hold you entirely responsible, Lindsay, for having let this arise. And I shall say so!'

As he spoke a drone began to grow in the sky above them.

'What the devil's that?' said Burroughs suspiciously.

'Aerial reconnaissance.'

'Aerial reconnaissance? On whose authority, I'd like to know? This is a sensitive situation! What fool authorized anyone to overfly tribal territory? If you're trying to explain to me that the situation is incandescent I can think of nothing more likely to precipitate serious trouble than a mob of aggressive flying corps subalterns galloping through the skies above a friendly neighbouring state! I suppose this is the doing of that damn fool Moore-Simpson! Where the devil's he? I need a few words of explanation from *him*! Where is he?'

'Preparing to take the next flight up again, I think. Er, would you like to accompany him, sir? I'm sure room could be found in the rear observer's seat for you,' said Joe kindly.

They left Burroughs spluttering with dismay and made their way to the football field in time to see a Bristol Fighter plane bouncing along to a halt feet from the boundary. The Scouts delegated to mark out the landing area doused the lighted flares they had set in each corner of the pitch and, chattering excitedly, hurried over to take a closer look at the aircraft. Fred was there to greet the two men as they climbed out and he introduced them to James and Joe.

The pilot pulled off flying helmet and goggles and held out a hand, smiling and cheerful. Hugh Blackett was very young, very blond and very blue-eyed. As yet untanned and unlined, he could not have been long in India. It must have been all of two minutes since he was captaining the first eleven, Joe thought with stabbing reminders of the hundreds of young sacrifices he had seen making their way over to the enemy lines in the war. The wings on his chest were very new. The second man, who saluted negligently and got straight to work on the plane, was introduced as 'Flight Sergeant Thomas Edwards, my ack emma.' The single Observer wing on his chest was very faded.

'Have to take your aircraft engineer with you in this country,' Fred explained. 'Now what I propose we do while Tommy does his stuff is retire to the ops room and have a look at this map I've got together. I'll take her up for the next tour while Hugh gets his breakfast and then he can relieve me. Joe? James? Either one of you want to come up in the observer's seat?'

They made their way to a whitewashed, mud brick building at the centre of the fort. Tidy and uncluttered with everything to hand, it was a scene they were all familiar with. A large table dominated the room, filing cabinets and bookcases lined it and in a corner the only unmilitary note: a gouty armchair, one of its legs propped up on a copy of *Whitaker's Almanack 1910*, a year-old copy of *Punch* lying open over one arm.

The four heads descended on the map Fred had taken from the maps room and James began to fill in the topographical details. 'Here's the fort and here's Afghanistan and somewhere between the two is what we're looking for,' he began.

To their relief the pilot took in the problem at once, asking shrewd questions and supplying useful information of his own. He noted distances from friendly forts, fuel supplies, possible landing areas and traced the known route of the escaping Afghanis to the last known point nearly half-way along the Khyber.

'Any word from Landi Kotal?' he asked.

'We heard nearly an hour ago that there has still been no sighting. They'll let us know the minute they have anything. The only thing moving in the Khyber has been a Powindah caravan. On its way down to us to overnight by

155

the river. They do this every year. They're coming from Samarkand and Bokhara and en route for Peshawar. I thought we might stop them and have a word. If our friends were in the Khyber then they'll know about it. The Powindah are a gypsy race. They're called the postmen of the province and nothing escapes their intelligence system. Their Malik owes me a favour. The local Afridi snatched two of their little boys who'd strayed behind the caravan to chase a wandering sheep last year. They reported it to me and I took out a gasht.'

'You took out a gasht?' said Joe. 'To chase up two boys and a stray sheep?'

'Fifty Scouts went out. Wasn't difficult. We found the mob, feasting on the missing sheep and one of them standing guard over the boys. We hauled in two of their sentries, held guns to their heads and didn't put them down until the boys had been released. But the Afridis complained that they had only snatched them in revenge for the two of theirs who were taken by the Powindah the year before. They sell the poor little buggers as slaves.'

James sighed. 'You can never get back to the beginning of these things,' he said wearily. 'Or the end. All you can do is make it clear we don't tolerate these goings-on.'

'Okay,' said Fred, anxious to draw their attention back to the map. 'So this is our area and we'll ignore the caravan on its way down. You'll question them when they get here, James.' He outlined with a finger the area of search. 'The Bristol can fly for three hours before refuelling so we'll count on – to be on the safe side – an hour out and an hour back. She can do a hundred and twenty-three miles per hour but we're aiming to take it slowly and steadily. Stooging about at a slow speed you can see an amazing amount in normal conditions but,' he sighed and swept a dismissive hand over the brown, crowded contours of the map, 'doesn't look very hopeful, I'm afraid. You could hide a division in this sort of terrain. And it's all rocks, overhangs and cover of some sort all the way up to the Afghan border. It's their own backyard. They have friends there who will hide them. They could be anywhere in fifty square miles by now.'

'And don't forget that they're camouflaged – their clothes are brown and floppy, even their horses blend into the terrain,' said James. 'Their hearing is acute. They'll hear you coming miles away and have plenty of time to hide themselves. It's a wild goose chase!'

'At least there won't be any opposition from the air,' said Joe, 'but what about sniping from the ground? Any fear of that?'

'There's always fear of that,' said Fred with a quick look at Hugh.

'Thought I was in for some trouble on the way over,' he said cheerfully. 'Came up over the Bazar Valley. Didn't realize it was miles out of your search area so I was keeping an eye peeled on the way. Twenty miles back over Afridi territory I thought I'd spotted a smudge of smoke in the sky. Here,' he pointed at the map. 'Rather high and no sign on the ground. Dispersing fire? I diverted to get a closer look but then I caught a flash of sunlight on metal. Looked like the start of a helio signal to me but then I remembered where I was and thought, "Rifle barrel. Bloody hell! Afridis are up!" I did a few acrobatics and went on my way. No shots.'

'Well, if that's all clear,' said Fred, rolling up the map, 'we'll be off. Coming, Joe? Hugh, old son, we'll relieve you of your hats and goggles and stuff.'

Ten minutes later Joe was sitting nervously in the rear seat of the plane, which had been turned on its axis, watching as Fred with total confidence, enthusiasm even, fiddled with the controls, interminably carrying out checks. At last he was satisfied. 'Switches off!' he called to the flight sergeant standing by the propeller. Tommy Edwards swung the big blade of the propeller.

'Contact, sir!' he shouted back.

'Contact!'

157

The twelve cylinder Rolls Royce engine, hardly cooled, fired up reassuringly at the first attempt. Fred waited, listening to the note and checking again the dials in front of him. He raised his hands above his head to signal for the chocks to be pulled away and two Scouts standing by obliged. He took a firm grip of the throttle and began to move slowly forward over the football pitch. Tommy saluted, rather unnecessarily Joe thought, to indicate that the sky was clear and the plane started forward, gathering speed. Fred pulled the joystick back and the machine swept gracefully up into the air.

Joe touched the folded sheet of paper tucked into his belt. Hugh had held it out to him the moment before he climbed into the plane. 'Better have this with you, sir,' he had said without emphasis. 'We all carry one. Just in case.'

Joe had run an eye over the short script. In English and in Urdu the document declared that a very large amount of money would be handed by His Majesty's Government to any person returning the bearer safe and sound. The better the condition of the airman, the larger the amount of money, it added. 'More arithmetic on the frontier!' Joe thought. He began to calculate the value of Fred's experience and training, to say nothing of his own, adding on the cost of the aircraft and converting the sum into rupees in an effort to distract his mind from the terror he always felt when he left the safety of the ground. He checked his revolver. He familiarized himself with the two Lewis machine guns mounted to hand in the rear cockpit. There might be men in these hills who could not read either English or Urdu. Another problem was that the scheme of rewarding the tribesmen for delivering chaps back to base instead of killing them had given them an unexpected source of revenue and now any plane that flew overhead was seen as a legitimate target, a cash bonanza for the village. The number of planes lost in the ensuing turkey shoot had actually increased. As James said – how could you ever disentangle cause and effect in this country?

He looked at the man who now held his life in his hands. The jaunty tilt of Fred's head told him that he, at least, was relishing the situation and Joe wondered again about the emotions, the compulsions even, that drove him. The skill and pleasure he showed in controlling this infernal flying machine were obviously high on the list and soon Fred's confident handling of the noisy, bucking brute began to soothe Joe's nerves. He thought perhaps he might relax so far as to release the two-handed grip on his seat with which he had unconsciously and futilely been attempting to keep the plane aloft.

Queasily, Joe looked over the side at the hills fought over so passionately for so many centuries. They had so little to offer and this was never more apparent than from a thousand feet up. Brown, barren, repellent, comfortless, he thought. In the distance green river valleys chequered with sugar cane fields and orchards only served to point up the desolation of the Tribal Territories. No wonder the inhabitants of this wilderness had made their living from raiding. Zan, zar, zamin – women, gold and land, and only available to those who were prepared to acquire a gun and use it to exact what they wanted.

Covering the port side, Joe swept the bare crags, all depth reduced from up here to ripples on a shingle-strewn sandy beach any one of which could be sheltering an invisible troop of thirty horsemen. In minutes they were overflying the Khyber Pass which snaked, dark and sinister, even from a height, making its tortuous way following the track of the rushing Khyber river for thirty miles. The only sign of life was a huge dust cloud beneath which nothing was discernible. The nomad Powindahs on the move towards the fort? Joe assumed so. The fort at Landi Kotal when they reached it was barely distinguishable from the surrounding khaki-coloured rocks but Joe was heartened to see a friendly signal flicker up at them from below as they flew over. They flew on right to the Durand Line marking the extent of British claimed territory and, having no wish to start an international incident, Fred turned before he reached Afghanistan but not before they had a chance to survey from an even greater height the routes into the country. Still no sign of a troop of horsemen. Fred gave a thumbs down and signalled that he was about to turn for home.

Chapter Twelve

Lily, a few feet upstream of her horse, eagerly scooped up the ice-cold water and drank. That was the first and perhaps the most urgent of her needs attended to and now her mind was filled with the remaining two. She looked around her. The men seemed to have decided to settle down by the stream for a while. Lily noticed with interest their order of priority. First each had taken a small mat from his luggage and, kneeling on it, said his morning prayer, then they had attended to their horses and now at last they were turning their attention to unpacking promising-looking bundles from the pack mules. Breakfast? She walked tentatively through the developing encampment, leading her horse to join the others tethered some yards away. She noticed that each man as she drew level with him averted his eyes. In their own territory again presumably native rules applied once more and being a woman she became virtually invisible. To look away so as not to embarrass a woman was Pathan politeness.

This just could have its advantages. Boldly, she walked to the far side of the encampment and kept on walking. No one watched her; no one followed her and with relief Lily found a large sheltering rock and spent some unsupervised minutes there. When she strolled casually back she found a fire had been lit and cooking pots had been set to boil up. Two men scrambled down from the hills carrying the carcass of a sheep and this they proceeded to butcher and prepare to roast, threading the chunks of meat on to long metal skewers which they held over the flat and now red-hot fire, fragrant with juniper and apricot twigs.

Lily, almost insane with hunger as the scents of the roasting meat and herbs drifted towards her, sat apart from the group, unremarked and apparently invisible. She found a sheltered spot in the sunshine with her back to a rock and stared ahead, trying to make out where on earth they had come to. She was puzzled. All her instincts and the geographical information before her eyes told her that they were now facing and travelling south and must have done a wide loop – a detour of at least thirty miles through the hills. The land fell dramatically below them into a lush green valley stretching from east to west. 'Wherever else we may be, that is definitely not Afghanistan,' she concluded.

She was quite certain that they were still west of the Durand Line that separated the North-West Frontier Province from its warlike neighbour to the east, still under, technically at least, the jurisdiction of the British Government, still the responsibility of Joe and James. Would they try to get her back? She couldn't believe that they wouldn't come for *her* at least. Her romantic imagination conjured up a picture of loyal Bengal Lancers riding knee to knee from the hills, sounding cavalry trumpets. And what about Rathmore, who only had himself to thank for his present perilous position? He was, after all, a Lord and Lords cut ice under the British flag. Hard to believe but she guessed he must be about as important as a US senator and certainly not dispensable, however stupid. The British would turn over every stone to find him. They'd send out the Mounted Infantry. They would muster every available soldier. Lily thought she knew about the British. Her original perception of 'egotistical bastards' had, thanks to her dramatic change in circumstances, mutated to 'chivalrous rescuers'. They wouldn't just let her be dragged off into the wilderness. They must know by now that she was missing. What were they doing about it? Her hopes of rescue, she found, always centred on Joe. It was Joe's grim face and

162

tall figure she expected to see around every twist in the trail. He would come.

But in rescue lay another problem. Iskander. She watched him as he moved amongst his men, sharing the menial tasks with them, talking easily, always alert. He appeared quite unfatigued by his night in the saddle, unlike Rathmore who sat miserably slumped, no longer tied up but still under guard on the other side of the fire. And there they had made their first mistake, she thought with a secret smile. To waste energy on guarding that barrel of hog's grease when they should have been keeping an eye on *her* showed a rigidity of attitude that could only work in her favour. Iskander, she was certain, knew more about the death of Zeman than he had declared so, by staying close to him, she ought to be able to find out what that knowledge was. He might come to regret taking her with him.

Even as the thought formed she was instantly cast into a dilemma. What would happen if it came to a confrontation between Iskander and Joe? Would Joe shoot Iskander? Could she let that happen? Lily checked herself. She'd heard the tales of white women who'd been captured by Indian tribes in the West and had grown so used to life with their abductors that they had refused to come home again. Briefly the thought was intriguing but – well – that wasn't going to happen to Lily Coblenz!

At last the meal seemed to be ready and the men were passing out small metal plates piled high with rice and gravy and little discs of grilled lamb. Iskander who, alone of all the men, seemed prepared to look her in the eye, strolled over to her sheltered place and handed her a plate. It was made of tin and it shone with impeccable cleanness. He had spooned rice which seemed to be studded with pistachios and sultanas on to it from a pot and topped it with meat.

'A small meal to keep you going,' he said, 'until we eat again properly at midday. We have not far to go now.'

Certainly the most delicious meal she had ever eaten,

163

Lily decided, scraping up the last bit of rice with her finger and licking it. Custom still pricked her to give a quick look around to make sure no one had seen her poor table manners but, of course, all eyes were averted and for that matter, all were licking their fingers. Basking in the sunshine with a full stomach and weary from her night's ride Lily was almost asleep. A few seconds more and she would have missed it. As it was, her sharp ears picked up the sound even before the men were aware of it. A low buzzing sound was approaching along the valley from the south-east, a sound which she knew instantly to be the engine of a plane. Iskander rapped out a single word of command and the men froze, their khaki tunics and flowing baggy breeches melting into the rocks and earth. The fire had been doused, the horses were under the overhanging cliff. Lily realized that they were invisible to the plane even if it had been flying directly overhead.

Iskander gave her a narrow-eyed glare which quite clearly told her to stay still. She nodded briefly back in understanding and, reassured, he turned his head, as had all, to look up into the sky, fascinated by the strange sight. Lily looked too. RAF roundels told her it was British and therefore, she estimated, flying from the base at . . . she couldn't remember the name but she knew there was such a base about seventy miles south-west of the fort. Joyfully, she figured that this plane must be on its way to Gor Khatri and that her reasoning had been correct: the fort lay to her left. She fingered the shining tin plate which still lay on her lap and looked up at the sun. Helios. James had explained the signalling system to her. A tin plate was no substitute for the complex arrangement of mirrors and reflectors the army used but it would have to do. Swiftly calculating the angles, she waited for exactly the right moment. There would only be a split second available to her.

As she watched, the plane veered from its course and came slightly over towards their position. Had it spotted them? Now! She tipped the plate, catching the rays and bouncing them back at a shallow angle. She held the angle as long as she dared and then flattened the plate again, slipping a fold of her waistcoat over it.

The plane buzzed and hiccuped towards them watched intently by the men. But then, a second later, for no apparent reason, it jinked abruptly, rising and twisting, bridling like a spooked horse and then sliding back on to its original course. Iskander's head turned and he shot a look of intense enquiry at Lily. Lily didn't appear to be aware of his scrutiny. Like everyone else she was staring, open-mouthed and hypnotized by the aerial spectacle, her arms hugging her knees.

When the plane was out of earshot once more Iskander gave the order to move off. Rising to her knees, Lily managed to slip the plate between two rocks and strolled, unconcerned, to her horse. Once again she was allowed to ride free and almost unnoticed at the rear of the column. She was tempted but for no more than a second to wonder what would happen if she lagged behind and then turned her horse and rode like the wind to the east. She was sure now that she would get back to the fort and in much less than the thirty miles it had taken them to get this far but the picture of herself galloping down a series of dark defiles, topping a series of razor-backed passes, no clear idea of where she was going and probably shot at by pursuing tribesmen – to say nothing of the threat of the sinister fate that might await Rathmore – kept her riding once more demurely in convoy. She would do her best to get back to civilization, pull every trick in the book – that was every captive's duty – but only if she could be sure she wouldn't bring down the scalping knife on Rathmore.

They were entering more heavily populated country, she decided, as time after time they were challenged by unseen men from the hills. Always Iskander called back the same response and Lily guessed that passwords were being exchanged. Certainly the repeatedly called name of Iskander seemed to open all barriers. Usually, after a satis-

165

factorily answered challenge, the challenger would show himself, waving his rifle in greeting. And a terrifying bunch they were too, Lily thought. All young, wild-eyed, grinning, with the general facial attributes of an eagle and heavy black beards. The troop moved smartly on, working their way through the hills and keeping the distant valley always to their left.

Iskander ranged up alongside and said, 'Five miles more and we shall arrive at our destination,' and rode off again.

When Lily had calculated they must be just about there they rounded a bend and came across a herd of sheep crossing under the care of their shepherd. This was a lad, small and still unbearded. He was wearing a tattered tunic and trousers and a felt hat decorated with two pink roses. He carried slung over his shoulder a gun so ancient it looked desperately dangerous but his reaction to finding the track blocked by a troop of warriors was instant. In one smooth movement the child had swung his rifle forward, sunk to his knees in the middle of the path and covered the front riders with an unwavering barrel. He rapped out a challenge, a challenge incongruous in his unbroken voice. The troop halted at once and Iskander answered the challenge. The boy was not satisfied and asked, apparently, for further information. Patiently and seriously Iskander replied and, after a moment's consideration, the boy stood and lowered his rifle. Lily noticed that not one of the men laughed or said anything patronizing or even complimentary. The boy had done his job – he had behaved as they expected he would behave. She began to wonder what other surprises awaited her at her destination amongst these surprising people.

The little convoy wound on and the way grew narrower and the enclosing hills higher until the sky appeared only as a ribbon of blue, a ribbon of blue in which eagles ceaselessly circled above them. Fancifully, Lily thought that however efficient Fred Moore-Simpson might be a

166

flight of eagles would be a good deal more effective than his little biplane.

Sometimes trotting but more often picking their way over stones they rode on. Dizzy from her sleepless night and choked with dust, Lily began to appraise her situation. 'Well, I know for sure how I got here but I do wonder what I'm *doing* here in this moon landscape. This is . . . er . . . Saturday morning. To think – I could be partnering Edward Dalrymple-Webster at badminton if I'd stayed in Simla! Past – imperfect, present very far from indicative and future not simple, whatever else! I wonder what lies round the next corner?'

What lay around the next corner was predictable: a further narrowing of the gorge until they could only ride in single file, the thunder of a waterfall crashing down, it seemed, from the sky, the perpetual rattle of falling stones and the click of advancing hooves. The creak of saddlery and jingle of bits blended into a symphony of sound which to Lily's dulled senses acquired a quality that was almost soothing and she hardly noticed that their way grew abruptly steeper as it led towards a saddle amongst the rocks.

Iskander came riding back towards her. 'Miss Coblenz! Lily!' he said with concern. 'You're nearly asleep! I'm sorry you've had this arduous journey. I've said it before and now I'll say it again – a few more paces and you will see our journey's end.'

He shouted to the men ahead of them and at his command they separated, leaving the way clear for Lily to ride to the head of the convoy and over the saddle. Here he waited for her and with a smile and a proud gesture pointed towards the land below. 'Behold,' he said, 'Mahdan Khotal! The fort and the lands of my people welcome you.'

Lily sat back in her saddle with her hands on her hips. 'What's this you're showing me? El Dorado?' she said but, in truth, she was impressed, she was allured, she was even charmed by the landscape before her which was of orchards and cornfields, of peacefully grazing sheep and hastening streams, terraced cultivation and the tinkle of water blending with the tinkle of sheep bells.

Iskander was eyeing her intently. 'Yes?' he said.

'Yes indeed! It's perfectly lovely!' said Lily, anxious to give nothing away, but all the same she saw this as a land worth fighting for and if necessary worth dying for. The hillsides were dotted with houses large and small, many with watchtowers enclosed within defensive walls. Folded with such skill into the hills that Lily was not at first aware of it was a considerable village, itself within a defensive wall, surrounding an interior fortress, large and forbidding, the home of Iskander and the home of Zeman.

'We will ride in,' said Iskander. 'You have to meet the tribal chieftain. His wife died last year so you will be received by his new wife, Halima Begum. Don't be alarmed.'

'Why should I be alarmed?' said Lily automatically.

'You would be forgiven if you were,' said Iskander smiling. 'It must be very strange to you.'

They rode through the guarded gates in the outer enceinte and across a stretch of open ground the size of a parade ground to reach the central fortress. Everywhere crowds of people stopped to smile and shout and wave at them. The business of a thriving village was being conducted here – market stalls lined the shaded part of the walls, animals were being led about, water jugs carried, and the enticing and unmistakable smell of a bakery wafted towards her. Metallic clashing and a blast of scorching air as they passed might have announced a blacksmith's forge but the shining new rifles and gun parts stacked outside hinted at a more sinister activity. Small children, boys and girls, ran about barefoot in the dust dashing dangerously close to the horses' hooves in their eagerness to get a close look at the visitors.

As they approached, the fortress itself presented a truly forbidding appearance. The encircling mud brick wall appeared to be about six feet thick and about thirty feet high. It was crenellated and without windows. Lily became aware of square watchtowers on the battlements and massive corner towers. The defences were manned and the sun picked up from time to time the reflection of a rifle barrel. The massive iron-studded gate was closed and Lily began to feel very small as they advanced towards it. It creaked gently open to reveal a courtyard where, flanked by armed tribesmen, a bearded man sat waiting for them, as one carved from the surrounding hills in silence and immobile, controlling with a sinewy hand a white-eyed black stallion.

'That,' said Iskander superfluously, 'is our chief, Ramazad Khan.'

Without a word of command being spoken her horse and that of Rathmore were taken in hand and held back to the rear of the troop. The men dismounted. The Khan dismounted. Lily and Rathmore did the same and small boys ran forward to gather up the reins and lead the horses away. With his men formed up behind him Iskander Khan sank to his knees and kissed the hands of his chief. They spoke to each other in what Lily judged to be a formal greeting. She looked closely at the impressive figure who was Zeman's father and wondered whether the news of his son's death had reached him or whether it was going to be Iskander's duty to reveal it now.

For the first time in her enforced flight Lily felt true fear. She realized that until this moment she had been placing faith in Iskander's reassurances that women were not harmed by the Pathan. She had been cushioned from reality also by the sense of her own status. Her father was unimaginably rich. Rich enough to buy up this whole territory, she estimated. Rich enough to buy his daughter out of any scrape she got herself into. And suddenly, here, in the middle of this wild country which obeyed no laws that she had ever heard of, her fate depended on the whims of this chieftain. Iskander, she felt certain, would never harm her but here he was before her eyes making obeisance to this formidable man. And, quite clearly,

169

Iskander's continued protection must be dependent on the chief's decisions. What had James said about him? She thought she had overheard him telling Joe that he was a malicious old brute who hated the British. Would he know the difference between British and American? Would he care? Lily thought that they were probably all ferenghi to him.

She looked at him again and decided that James was probably not exaggerating. The Khan was quite obviously the father of Zeman, the likeness was striking, but where Zeman had simply worn a moustache this man had a full and long black beard streaked with grey. The hook-nosed profile was as handsome but where Zeman's eyes had been full of merriment and cynicism his father's eye was cold. He was as tall as Iskander; his back was straight, his movements lithe. In fact, he was every last inch a chieftain, thought Lily. And when he found out who she was and, even more pertinently, who Rathmore was, she guessed there was going to be trouble. Lily began to wish Iskander had taken them off to Afghanistan. She thought they would have had a better chance of survival with the Amir who sounded really rather a jolly little feller if Grace was to be believed.

Now what was happening? The men, apart from two who remained one on either side of Rathmore, were dismissed at a signal from Iskander and went off into the village. She dreaded that Rathmore would try to assert himself and put the Khan in his place and tried to give him a warning look. Iskander spoke for a long time to his chief, answering questions put to him in a stiff voice from time to time. Such was the chief's control of his emotions that Lily could not make out the exact moment when Iskander revealed to him that his son was dead. Finally, the old man turned a baleful glare on Rathmore who opened his mouth to speak and even managed a few words of the 'I say, are you aware of who I am? . . . His Majesty's Government . . . Certain reprisals . . .' type and then, under the spell of the old man's scorn, thought better of it and fell silent. The

170

chief called forward one of his aides – an interpreter, Lily guessed – who gave him the gist of Rathmore's pronouncements. Ramazad put a few questions to Rathmore, again pointedly not involving Iskander in the exchange, and then sent Rathmore off with an escort. He turned his attention to Lily and she stared straight back at him unabashed. Summoning up the little Pushtu she had persuaded Zeman to teach her, she greeted him in his own language. He looked at her in astonishment and snapped out a command to Iskander.

At once Iskander took charge of Lily. 'Follow me, Miss Coblenz. I will take you to your quarters.'

He strode off across the central square and Lily trotted after him.

'Where are you taking me?' she asked.

'Over there.'

He pointed to the far side of the square to a long two-storeyed building with a series of tall narrow windows running along it. Made of baked mud like the rest of the fort, it would have been ugly had its starkness not been relieved by a pretty balcony which ran the length of it and by the delicate tracery of the wooden screens which filled each window. Iskander waited at the closed door and very soon it was opened to them by a veiled woman. She greeted Iskander with great warmth, taking his hands in hers and drawing him inside. She slipped the gauzy rose-coloured veil from her face and looked at him with affection. A tall, light-skinned Pathan with green eyes and rich brown hair, she was beautiful and young and Lily, feeling travel-stained, small and awkward, wondered who she could possibly be.

The girl listened to Iskander explaining the appearance of the dusty little sparrow at his side, looking from one to the other in astonishment. Finally, 'This is Halima Begum, the wife of our chief,' he said. 'Go with her, she will see to your needs.' He turned on his heel and walked away, closing the heavy door behind him.

Halima Begum took Lily's hand and spoke to her in a

171

low, sweet voice and, to Lily's surprise, in English. 'How do you do, Lily? Please enter.'

Lily was relieved to be out of the sun and the dust but uneasy at the abrupt disappearance of Iskander who had been her lifeline for the past hours. Nervously she greeted Halima Begum and asked, 'Is this the chief's house?'

Halima hesitated for a moment and replied slowly, 'All house here is chief's house. This is harem house. You are in harem.'

Chapter Thirteen

James Lindsay set his binoculars down on the wall beside him and rubbed his red-rimmed eyes. 'Can't see a bloody thing,' he grumbled. 'Blasted Powindah! Always glad to see them of course but I'd rather they hadn't chosen this moment to build an impenetrable dust screen across the Khyber! God knows what's happening behind it!'

'What might be happening behind it?' said Joe, staring northward.

'Anything!' said James. 'Anything in the world. Anything or nothing. Let's go out and meet them, Joe. Whatever else they operate – and sometimes it's better not to enquire too closely – they operate a damn good news service. Not much happens,' he pointed, 'not much happens over there without their knowing about it. If Iskander and his mates are on the caravan road to Afghanistan – and that's the *only* road to Afghanistan – they'll know where they are and what they're up to. Care to come? I'm turning out a Mounted Infantry detachment anyway and they can escort us. Probably quite unnecessary but, as I say, you never know what's happening behind the dust. Come on, Joe! A breath of far from fresh air won't do us any harm. I'll just tell Eddy what we're up to. Betty too. Not feeling too good, poor old thing. This bloody country! Knocks you to bits in the end, even the stoutest.'

At the head of an MI detachment of thirty Scouts James and Joe clattered out of the fort together and made their way into the gut of the Khyber Pass and here they drew aside, halted amongst the rocks and settled down to watch.

As the haze of dust blowing ahead of the caravan grew thicker, the noises also began to reach them: a weird dissonance of shouting men, braying donkeys, tinkling camel bells, the whole pierced by an occasional peal of wild girlish laughter and all underpinned by the dull, ear-numbing, earth-drumming pounding of thousands of hooves and hundreds of feet. Overwhelmed, Joe stared and stared again.

'Not quite what you were expecting?' said James.

'I'll say not! I was expecting – oh, a single file of camels and a few gypsy tribesmen. Not this . . .' His voice trailed away as his eyes took in the ancient and barbaric splendour of the advancing caravan.

'It's a whole people on the move. They're thousands strong and they've been nomadic since history began. They're tough too. They follow the Silk Route, coming down from Samarkand and Bokhara and Kabul, trading all the way. Everyone they pass knows the caravan is full of goods they want for themselves. Some try to take them by force not by haggling in the prescribed manner and usually they end up dead. The Powindah men are hard bargainers but they're harder on anyone who tries to steal from them or defraud them. You never know quite who you're going to meet as you emerge from that mountain hellhole – could be Alexander the Great and a squad of Macedonians in a bad temper, a band of Moghul warriors on the rampage or – like today – just a couple of admiring chaps bringing gifts.' He held up a gilt-wrapped package of Gold Flake cigarettes. 'The mounted fighting men come first, you'll see, followed by the young men of the tribe, all armed to the teeth, on foot, then the main caravan with protective outriders and a final rearguard. Oh, and you'll see dogs. They roam everywhere and are trained to tear bits off anyone who so much as looks at them, so don't engage their attention. Ah – here they come!'

They waited to the side of the trail as the advance guard emerged from the dust cloud. First there came perhaps a hundred strong, well-dressed and well-mounted

Powindahs. Tall, warlike, watchful, competent and completely unabashed: this was the series of Joe's impressions of the colourful mob. But no – 'mob' was not quite right. Colourful army? 'Yes,' Joe decided. 'More like an army.'

Their leader paused as he caught sight of James and escorted by three others drew aside to greet him. As far as Joe could tell the greeting was a formal one but by no means without humour and James replied in kind.

'What's he saying?' said Joe, irritated as always not to understand.

The next part of the exchange was easier to follow as James with a smile and a bow handed over the package of cigarettes. With an exclamation of delight the chief was obviously thanking James and handing over, in turn, a small gift. Not such a small gift though, Joe thought, admiring the silver snuff box which made its way into James's pocket. The formalities over, James then embarked on a long speech which included gestures towards himself, the MI troop and many gestures pointing towards the Khyber.

Joe watched the Powindah's face carefully. The leathery features to be observed between grizzled beard and voluminous white turban were by no means inscrutable. Joe looked on, fascinated, as one expression melted into another, accompanied at times by deep sighs or hissing intake of breath as James's story progressed. Finally when James fell silent on a question, the old man's face grew grave and still. He thought deeply for a moment then called out a question to one of his lieutenants. Considering the response, he nodded and then began to speak. He spoke for quite a while, clearly and openly with gestures which conveyed to all around and to Joe the message that he could not be of any help. He had no answer to James's questions. Joe was certain that he was lying.

With expressions of mutual regard, the meeting broke up and the four riders made their way back to the head of the column. As the contingent of young warriors on foot drew level with them, on a word from James the Scouts closed in and established themselves on either side of the track. A bearded Rissaldar began to address the advancing horde.

'He's saying,' said James, 'that they have to leave their arms at the little checkpoint we've set up at the next stream crossing. They're not allowed to carry arms through into British India. They know this perfectly well. It happens every year. I never think it's tactful to mention it in the presence of their leaders since they must find it somewhat galling and our convention is that they and we pretend it isn't happening and leave it to the lower orders to sort it out amongst themselves. "Diplomacy Lindsay" they call me!'

'No joy with the Malik, I gathered?' said Joe.

'Afraid not. No sighting or report of them anywhere along their route and they've come, as we expected, straight down the caravan way from Kabul.'

'You know he was lying?'

'Of course. Nothing we can do about it though.'

'I don't believe this!' Joe said with a desperate look around him at the tumbling rocks and crevices. 'They're up there somewhere! Watching our every movement through field glasses at this very moment!'

'Could well be,' said James. 'And if not them, there'll be others up there, one behind each crag keeping an eye on things. We'll hang on for a while if you don't mind, Joe. There's someone in the caravan I always stay to greet.'

It seemed to Joe, looking up the track, as though the whole bottom of the pass had worked loose and was moving slowly towards them. Amidst the dust storm he saw the caravan separated into its component parts, sheep in hundreds – no thousands, camels, families on the march, three and four generations loaded on to the same camel. They stayed in place as the caravan rolled by almost overwhelming them with the noise and the stench of the goats and sheep and camels. Joe was amazed by the sight of so many camels each piled high with tottering heaps of trading goods, of tents and equipment and children. He laughed and waved as three children, each clutching a puppy, went by, small heads bobbing in rhythm with the camel's stalking stride. From time to time they were the subject of inspection by the herd dogs, mastiffs, some as big as ponies, who approached with warning snarls, vicious eyes gleaming under matted black fringes. He cast interested sideways looks at the young Powindah girls who leapt from rock to rock herding the sheep, each with a rifle slung across her back. They went unveiled, tall, brown and beautiful, striding freely in their long brightly coloured dresses.

After an hour's assault on the senses Joe thought he could see the end of the caravan coming into view. One or two camels brought up the rear in the company of a number of armed riders. These appeared to be mainly middle-aged men. 'The veterans,' Joe thought, admiring the careful deployment of protective measures throughout the caravan. As the last camel swayed by James moved closer and looked up expectantly at the rider.

'Watch'er cobber!' sang out a shrill voice.

'Watch'er Maggie!' James yelled back. 'All well with you, Sweetheart?'

The figure on the camel, Joe now saw, had dusty grey hair which might once have been blonde. She turned a laughing face to them, as brown and folded as the hills, and shouted back, 'All dinkie doo! Can't complain, ducks! Can't complain!'

'James! Have I gone mad?' said Joe. 'Is this the Khyber or Koolgardie?'

'That was Maggie,' said James. 'Strange place to find an Australian woman you might think until you know her story. When they discovered gold in Australia they also found they had a problem – the mines were in desert areas and the only transport that worked effectively was camels. Trouble is – camel driving is a very particular skill. They recruited dozens of young camel-handlers from this part of the world to do the job. As you've seen from this cavalcade, the average Powindah youth is a staggeringly good-looking chap and our Maggie fell for one . . . and she wasn't the only one! She was a miner's daughter and she fled the Australian outback for the Indian outback. She's happy with them and they're very happy with her. She's become quite a matriarch – must be grandmother to half the tribe by now! Every year the British Government in the shape of the fort commander makes a point of checking on her welfare. Hey! What the hell! What's this?'

He stopped in alarm as a young boy loitering behind the caravan emerged from behind a rock and with a cheeky yell of 'Watch'er cobber!' hurled a stone at Joe.

Joe felt the stone whiz by his left ear and land in the sand a few feet away.

Tensely James said, 'Pick it up. Pretend to throw it back at him. He'll slip back behind the rock and disappear. Shout something rude and put the stone in your pocket.'

Smoothly Joe slid from his horse, executing what he thought was a pretty convincing pantomime of an enraged British officer failing to get a shot at target. As they started back for the fort, Joe asked, 'Are you going to tell me what that was all about?'

'Think about it, Joe! If a Pathan boy wants to hit you with a stone, he most certainly will! You've seen a sample of their throwing skills on the cricket field! He was aiming to miss and he was obviously one of Maggie's brood because he announced himself in Australian. Don't touch the stone yet – eyes everywhere and I don't want to get Maggie into trouble – but I'll bet there's more to it than you might think. We'll have a closer look when we get back to the fort.'

Puzzled, intrigued and with the stone bumping tantalizingly against his hip he rode back and waited patiently while James dismissed the Mounted Infantry then walked with him to the ops room. There they found Fred Moore-Simpson and Hugh poring over the map.

'There you are! Glad you didn't go off with the gypsies too – we were beginning to get a bit anxious,' Fred said cheerfully. 'Hope you fellows have had better luck than we have. We've had to tuck the Bristol up for the night but we'll fly off a dawn patrol first thing tomorrow morning. I have to say, today we've drawn a complete blank. We've marked the territory we've overflown if you'd care to take a look. Just a nil return, I'm afraid.'

'Sounds as though you could all do with a reviving cup of tea,' said Grace Holbrook entering with a large brass tray. She busied herself pouring out tea and handing round cups and, taking one for herself, she settled down in the armchair to turn the pages of *Punch* and listen.

'We had no luck either,' said James. 'The Powindahs declared they hadn't seen or heard any news of our target. The only thing of note was that a nomad boy threw a stone at Joe and missed. May be nothing but my imagination of course but let's have a look, shall we, Joe?'

Feeling that an anticlimax was about to overtake them Joe fished the stone from his pocket and laid it on the map table. Hugh looked, mystified, from one to the other and said uncertainly, 'Ah. The very stone, I take it?'

James peered closely at the triangular-shaped, unremarkable piece of shale, reached out and turned it over. The underside was flat and across it was scrawled, just distinguishable, a word in badly formed capital letters in heavy indelible pencil.

MARDANCOTAL.

'Thank you, Maggie!' said James fervently. 'There! I told you – if he'd wanted to hit Joe, he would have done!'

Fred looked at him in puzzlement. 'I say, do you mind telling us what's going on?'

James explained who Maggie was and the trick she had played to give them this information. 'Normally the old dear would just bellow out any information we needed and quite a lot we didn't need but today she was silent and eager to hurry on. Friendly as ever but silent. The whole tribe must have been put under some pressure not to tell us what they knew! And it doesn't take much wit to work out what the pressure was! The Powindah have to travel for hundreds of miles through Amanullah's country. If

179

they crossed him – or one of his lieutenants, let's say Iskander – he could make their lives very unpleasant. I thought the old Malik was making quite a show of not telling us anything. Someone was watching him and us. Maybe one of our own Mounted Infantry, maybe someone up in the crags, most likely one of the three men of his escort. Now he's squared with the Amir and his bully boys as far as appearances are concerned but Maggie – Maggie must have found out something she didn't quite like the sound or sight of and found her own way of letting us know.'

'I've known Maggie for years,' said Grace from her armchair. 'It would be my guess that she knows there's a girl involved. I don't think she'd risk the well-being of the tribe for any old chap – I mean, I can't see Rathmore's plight tugging at her heartstrings – but, bless her, she's always stood up for her sex. If it came to her ears – and there's not much that doesn't – that a young girl had been carried off against her will, she'd go out of her way to make sure the right people knew about it.'

James pointed to the map. 'Mahdan Khotal. I'll bet anything that's where the buggers are!'

Hugh stirred excitedly and peered more closely at the map. 'I say! There! But that's near where I saw the flash of light on my way over here! Look! Can't be more than five miles east of . . . what do you call it? Mahdan Khotal, did you say? What is that anyway?'

'It's the village, the fortified village of Ramazad Khan. The father of Zeman Khan,' said James. He looked carefully again at the map and, smiling, shook his head. 'Clever Iskander! Can you see what he's done?' His finger traced the route the Afghanis had taken from the fort up towards the Khyber. 'He leads us off in this direction – the direction we expected him to take, straight back to Kabul – but then he disappears before he gets half-way through the pass. He must have gone down one of these defiles. There are plenty we've never explored. And then he slogs it over these ridges and down more defiles, thirty miles or

more of tough riding, I'd say, but all through Afridi country, and approaches Mahdan Khotal from the back. He's
done a huge loop, put us right off the track and now he's
sitting up there in that eyrie above the Bazar Valley watching us! He can't be more than fifteen miles away as the
crow flies!'

'Hooting with laughter every time he sees the plane take
off towards Afghanistan!' said Fred admiringly. 'But look,
James, if that's where he is it's an afternoon's stroll down
the valley to get at him, isn't it? What do we do now?
Gather the troops? Get reinforcements from Peshawar?
Attack in force? Not yet! First we get a flight of bombers
up from Miram Shah and give the buggers a surprise.
Soften them up a bit. It worked for us last year in Mahsud
territory. I'll just go and check how many we could muster
– if we got the go-ahead, of course.' And he hurried off to
the communications room.

He left Joe, James and Hugh looking at each other in
consternation.

'Hadn't realized Fred was such a fire-eater,' said James,
with a speculative look at Hugh.

'Who would blame him?' said Hugh awkwardly. 'I mean
. . . after what happened to his nephew last year.'

'What *did* happen to his nephew?' said James. 'Can't say
it's generally known up here in army circles.'

'Philip . . . I think he was called Philip . . . came out from
England a fully trained pilot, eighteen years old, eager to
see some action, regretful to have missed the war . . . you
know the sort of thing . . . and his first sortie was a recce
over Waziristan.'

James sighed. The Wazirs were the most fierce and least
tractable of all the surrounding Pathan tribes. He didn't
want to hear the rest of the story.

'He never came back.' Hugh spoke reluctantly. 'No sign
of the plane and his body was never recovered. The whole
op was being run by Fred.' He fell silent, uncomfortable
with the information he had just imparted.

In silence they continued to study the map.

181

'Nothing comes to mind yet, I'm afraid,' said James slowly. 'But if we're going to see Lily and Rathmore alive again, I think we'd better come up with something a bit more subtle than the scheme Fred has in mind. In fact, the more I think about it, the more concerned I become.' He traced the short route from the fort and down the Bazar Valley with his finger and up into the hill country above. 'Oh, I know it looks a doddle on the map but on the ground, and believe me, I've been on that ground, it's not so easy. In fact, I'll tell you – it's impossible.'

'What do you mean – impossible?'

'I don't think anyone's even seen the fort at Mahdan Khotal. There's a good five miles of rugged ground, stream beds, ravines, overhangs, between the valley bottom and the stronghold. Think of the Persian army trying to take the narrows at Thermopylae. A million invaders were held up for days by a tiny army of three hundred determined Spartans. Ramazad Khan's men fight like Spartans and there's a sight more of them! You could send the whole of the Indian Army against him and he'd laugh at you. Perhaps we'll all fall back on Fred's strategy after all?'

'But it's only one small tribe! James, you're forever taking gashts out and organizing barramptas to teach small tribes a lesson. What's so special about this one?'

'It's been tried.'

He passed a hand wearily over his forehead before continuing. 'Before the war – 1910, I think it was – Ramazad Khan had a reputation for being a firebrand and he did something that really got up the noses of the military. One thing led to another and it all ended in disaster. Many mistakes made, dead on both sides and no lessons learned. Thoroughly bad show.'

'And the British found another way of taming Ramazad Khan, I understand?' said Joe tentatively.

'Oh, yes. Not proud! The government tried to buy him off. Offered the old bugger a few sackfuls of cash, technically "in reparation for the lives of his valued clansmen" lost in the fight. Not a usual device but these were special

182

circumstances – the manipulative old sod had had two sons killed and did he ever make the most of that!'

'And Zeman it was who benefited from all this? Didn't you say he was sent off for his expensive English education on the proceeds?'

'That's right. And where has all this landed us? Two thousand pounds of English education and a Sandhurst training and where is it all? Under four foot of earth in an abandoned cemetery! What a waste of a man!' He turned from the table in disgust. 'And now it's all happening again! We'll never break the bloody circle!'

'Another cup, anyone?'

Grace's comfortable voice was more appropriate to the calm order of the drawing room than to the tense atmosphere of the ops room. 'Milk, James? Joe? No use brooding on the past, you know. No use at all. Now, there *is* a way through this. Oh, yes, a very simple way. I'm surprised that it hasn't occurred to either of you!'

Chapter Fourteen

While Joe and James listened to Grace's suggestion, Sir George Jardine in distant Simla lit a cigar – a thing he did not often do and to those who knew him well it was a sign of agitation. He had been more disturbed than he would have admitted by James's news of the death of Zeman. He had had his eye on Zeman for some years, an eye blending suspicion and admiration. He had often been heard to say, 'I believe I could make something of that young man!' He had seen him as an unreliable friend, as a dangerous ally but, nevertheless, a force to be exploited. And now that promising young man was dead and, as far as Sir George could understand, in circumstances unlikely to reflect credit on the British administration.

'The situation in those parts is always dangerous,' he thought. 'I don't want this! Dammit! I think I'm getting too old.' He addressed himself to the task in hand which was to finish and enjoy an expensive cigar. This ritual complete, he set in train the complicated process by which he might put a telephone call through to Joe on the ground and set himself down to wait.

Startled, agitated and finally convinced by Grace's outrageous solution to their problem, his cup of tea, now cold, still clutched in his hand, Joe turned to listen to the Scouts officer who came to find him. 'Hurry, Joe, if you can to the communications room – we've got Sir George on the telephone!'

Through the usual swishing and gargling sounds inseparable from the Indian telephone system, Joe heard the voice of Sir George.

'Good afternoon, Commander! I count myself fortunate to be able to engage a few moments of your valuable time. God knows where you've been! It's taken them long enough to find you. By the time they'd searched the football field, the polo ground, the bazaar and apparently Lily Coblenz's bedroom, the best part of half an hour had passed. My time is valuable. But now perhaps you'll tell me if I've got this right? The Afghanis have snatched my old friend Dermot Rathmore. Correct so far?'

'Yes,' said Joe, determined not to be caught on the back foot by Sir George. 'In a nutshell, that is one of our problems.'

'And fast becoming one of *my* problems,' continued Sir George. 'And at the same time, Miss Coblenz has allowed herself to drift into the hands of a particularly inscrutable and shadowy young man of Afridi blood and her present whereabouts is precisely unknown. Correct? And as though that were not enough, we also have the Amir of Afghanistan who is sitting in Kabul moaning, I'm told, and awaiting medical treatment which it is beginning to look as though he will not be receiving in the foreseeable future since the doctor he has ordered up is detained for who knows how much longer at the fort with you. So, Joe, I'm asking you this question – what are you going to do about it?'

Sir George seemed, for the first time since Joe had known him, to lose confidence momentarily. He heard the hollow flourish of his own last question and hurried to answer it himself. 'In fact I know what your answer would be – "Nothing." Nor could I blame you. There are always people ready to exploit an awkward situation and the death of Zeman is a damned awkward situation, I can tell you. The American Embassy don't know that Miss Lily has, as the Australians would say, "gone walkabout" nor does her father but when they find out there will be a mild – not such a mild – diplomatic explosion to say nothing of

185

an outburst of paternal rage. His Excellency is not too pleased and is indeed sabre-rattling to an alarming degree about the sequestration of Rathmore. Now in my book the more often Rathmore disappears into the trackless Himalayas and the longer he stays there the happier I shall be but not everybody sees it that way. I am told to mobilize all the force I can, and that includes the Peshawar garrison, and set off into the altogether unexplored interior and – cost what it may – bring these birds back to hand. I pause for your reply.'

'I think,' said Joe, 'before you hear my reply you should hear James's. He's here with me now and has heard your comments.'

'Ah! You've got Jock Lindsay at your elbow, have you? I'd have expected that berserking old moss-trooper to be out there skirmishing already! Put him on!'

'Lindsay!' Sir George's merry voice came cheerfully over the air. 'Sorry you should have got landed with this. Should have explained that wherever Sandilands goes trouble follows! I'm sorry all this should be going on in your back garden. Now, I'm here to ask you – will you be prepared to climb on to a horse, gather up a division of lusty Scouts and gallop across the intervening countryside firing from the hip, shooting down the opposition and bring these two safely back again? Rather your style I think, Jock? Would you be prepared to do that?'

'No,' said James Lindsay. 'I need hardly tell you, sir, that this one calls for velvet glove not mailed fist. It's our opinion that a mass assault on the enemy position would result in unacceptable carnage and the first of the casualties would in all likelihood be the two hostages. We would ask you to do all that you can to persuade the military to keep their sabres firmly sheathed until we've had time to put our own plan into operation.'

'Ah! You have a *plan*?'

'We have made some progress regarding the location of our quarry, sir. We believe them to have sought refuge with the Afridi Malik, Ramazad Khan – yes, the father of Zeman, sir – in his fort at Mahdan Khotal.'

Joe thought he heard a groan and a splutter at the other end but James persevered. 'It's one thing,' he said, 'to have located our wandering charges but it's going to be quite another to extricate them from the situation they've got themselves into.'

'I'm not stupid, Lindsay,' said Sir George testily. 'And of all the places within many hundreds of miles that I would rather they didn't end up – Mahdan Khotal! – and of all the people I would rather they didn't end up with – Ramazad Khan! If I was writing his end-of-term report I would say, "Ramazad Khan is incapable of distinguishing truth from falsehood." He is archetypally a tricky bastard, two-faced, an eye to the main chance, in fact an eye to nothing else, so don't make the mistake of believing anything he says and don't be deceived by the seeming sincerity. But realize that Mahdan Khotal isn't a mud brick pill-box perched on a hillside. It's more in the nature of a medieval castle, or I might say, a strong medieval fortified palace covering a considerable acreage. Not the sort of place you stroll into having rung the doorbell! Now – as to the extrication of the wanderers, what precisely do you have in mind?'

'We are advised,' said James carefully, 'by Grace Holbrook.'

'Ah!' said Sir George. 'Wondered when you'd get round to consulting her. What had Grace to say?'

'Well, we agreed there are three possible lines of approach: first, if we are to follow the advice of Moore-Simpson – send in an aerial barrampta which Fred insists on calling "trench strafing", and when the air strike has softened up the opposition in the fort, by which I mean has destroyed their defences, we follow it up with a land attack by, shall we say, a force of five hundred Scouts with Mounted Infantry attachment.'

'Doesn't appeal to *me* very strongly,' said Sir George.

'Doesn't appeal to me very strongly either. We could also turn to Edgar Burroughs and see what he's got to say.'

'Don't bother,' said Sir George. 'I know what he'd say! "About turn! At the double! March!" Am I right?'

'Substantially, yes,' said James. 'But as so often there is a third way.'

'Glad to hear it,' said Sir George. '"Third Way Jardine" they call me.'

'Well, the fact is that the only person who can walk into Mahdan Khotal safely is Grace herself, as she has pointed out. They know her. They trust her. She looks innocent because she *is* innocent. I'm not sending her in there alone but any other European would last all of two seconds if he were seen to approach Mahdan Khotal. No one as far as I know has ever been there.'

'I've never been there,' said Sir George. 'Seen it from a distance. Strong place! Couldn't beat the door down with less than a division but in case you were thinking otherwise, Jock, I'll just tell you firmly that *you're* not going in there either! As far as the Afridi are concerned, and unless I misremember, you have what Joe Sandilands would call "quite a lot of previous" and, incidentally, what does Joe say about all this?'

'You'd better speak to him.'

Joe came on the line and spoke rapidly. 'Can't let Grace go in there all by herself . . . can't send in any uniformed British support . . . must send *somebody* with her . . . not really a problem . . . will go myself and before you say anything else – I shan't be going in police uniform, I'll be going in Scouts' uniform with perhaps a couple of Scouts in support. Just as long as I look reasonably convincing from a distance I should be in a position, with Grace's support of course, to open up a dialogue with Ramazad Khan. Dialogue . . . dealing . . . these are the only tools we can use in this situation; feats of arms are quite out of the question. But let's not forget that Iskander knows me. I think if we can only sit down and talk about this sensibly we will make progress.'

188

'Mm, yes,' said Sir George, 'Iskander. Mustn't forget *him*. And I'll tell you something and you must bear this in mind. It could just give you an edge.' He paused for a moment for emphasis. 'You will find that Iskander is far from popular with Ramazad Khan. We hold a balance – Ramazad holds a balance. He doesn't want anybody to upset it. It's my guess that he doesn't want Rathmore in his fort, still less does he want Lily! What are they to him? Hostages? Guests? No, they're damn nuisances! And yet Iskander has thrown down a glove and he's not going to let him down by repudiating the tough stance Iskander has adopted. Oh, yes, there are angles to this you may be able to exploit. In a funny sort of way you may find that you and Ramazad are saying the same thing. But with a blood-stained question mark hanging over the ultimate fate of Zeman you may find him a little reluctant to admit it. Never forget that Zeman was his only remaining son, apple of his eye. And never underestimate the importance of a son to a Pathan father.'

He sighed and then added, 'It looks bad, Joe, I can't deny it.'

There was a further silence at the other end and for a moment Joe thought the line had been cut. After a while the clickings and mutters resolved themselves and the raucous interference on the line Joe was able to identify as Sir George clearing his throat. '. . . and look here, my boy, if you're going to disguise yourself as a Scout be sure to have a photograph taken. I shall want to put one on top of my piano. When are you thinking of leaving?'

'At dawn,' said Joe.

189

Chapter Fifteen

Lily gasped, turned and fled mindlessly down the corridor with a half-formed notion of reaching the door and calling to Iskander for help. In four long strides Halima had caught her and, hands on both her shoulders, had spun her round and seized her firmly by the upper arms.

'Lily! Lily! What's the matter?' Her voice was gentle and amused.

With dire memories of a dozen seething romances each centred round the fate of innocent European girls lured into harems, Lily's voice was shrill and apprehensive. 'No one's putting *me* in a harem! How dare you! Let go! Iskander can sort this out. If that bearded old barbarian – oh, my God, I'm sorry – he's your husband, isn't he?'

Halima looked puzzled. 'Ramazad Khan? Yes, he is my husband. And you are his guest. As his guest you stay here.'

'If he thinks he can shut me up with all the rest of his women, well, he can just think again! Any finger he lays on me gets broken! They can kill Rathmore if they like – I don't care! Tell Iskander the deal's off! I have rights! I'm an American citizen! You're not to forget that!'

Halima laughed, saying patiently and slowly, seeking her words, 'I have said this is harem, Lily. I explain. The word "harem" in our language means "sacred". Women are sacred and in this place they live in safety. For you there is no safer place even among your own people. Here live all Ramazad's female relations – his mother, his aunts, his sisters, cousins, nieces. And, of course, his wife. Me.'

'Wife? Just the one?'

'Of course! Now will you not come and have a bath and some food? I think you are very tired after your journey.'

To some degree reassured by the concern in the girl's voice and allured by the idea of a bath, Lily decided to trust her and followed her up a staircase and into a long, airy room whose arcaded windows looked out on to the blossom-laden trees of an orchard. Lily stopped in the doorway and blinked. After the bleak strength of the exterior of the building the opulence of the interior was unexpected. The walls were hung with tapestries, the floor thickly carpeted and strewn with silken, tasselled cushions. The room was furnished with tables and chests of dark wood, intricately carved.

The six women who had been sitting by the window chatting and laughing turned, large-eyed, to look at her. Halima explained in Pushtu who Lily was and what she was doing in the fort. 'I tell them that you are American princess,' said Halima firmly, 'and that you are honoured guest of Iskander and my husband.' One by one the women, who ranged in age from very old to about sixteen, came forward, friendly and curious, to greet her and, though Lily was sure she would never remember them, Halima gave her each woman's name and position in the family. The formalities at an end, Halima clapped her hands and two maidservants came hurrying into the room.

'I will tell them to prepare your bath and then bring you back here to us where we will have food,' said Halima.

With much cheerful giggling and chattering, the girls led Lily to an apartment at the end of the first floor corridor, part of which she was delighted to see was a bathroom. Nothing like a home-style bathroom but to travel-weary Lily it looked perfect. A large sunken, shallow stone tub lay ready for her. The maids went off and returned some minutes later with brass cans of hot water, mixed this with cold from stone jars standing by and poured a sweet-scented liquid into it from a tiny phial. A scatter of rose petals over the surface and all was ready.

Lily peeled off her dusty clothes to the fascinated comments of the girls who, she guessed, had never seen a Western girl or Western clothes before. They did not seem impressed. Lily tried to explain by mime that she wanted her things washed and returned to her. It took a tug of war to hang on to her boots but there was no way that the escape she had always in the forefront of her mind could be effected in the pair of backless gold-embroidered slippers she was being offered. In a puzzling world she thought her pioneering ancestors would applaud her forethought. At least she would allow herself to be put into one of the fancy costumes on offer until her own clothes were returned, she thought and looked in astonishment at the piles of colourful silks the girls had fetched. They seemed keen for her to choose a bright pink outfit shot through with gold thread but, with a vision of herself escaping through the hills looking like a stick of candyfloss, she turned it down, insisting on a green three-quarter length tunic over a pair of baggy trousers in the same fabric caught up at the ankle, and accepted, though she did not put it on, a gauzy yellow face-covering veil.

Her companions looked her up and down doubtfully and suggested alternatives and improvements. They brushed her hair for her and turned with great seriousness to make up her face with sticks of kohl and little palettes of this and that, ignoring her protests and holding up a silver mirror for her to admire herself, which – after a moment of shock to see herself transformed – she duly and sincerely did.

'Goodbye Chicago!' said Lily. 'What *have* I become?' An errant thought came to her. 'I suppose these guys don't *sell* people? But if they do – why! – I'd make a good price!'

She was escorted back to the durbar room where she found assembled a much larger group of women and several small children all preparing to eat a midday meal which had been laid out on a cloth in the centre of the room. Halima beckoned her to join her at the head of the table and all sank down on cushions to eat. For the first time Lily noticed as Halima lowered herself with a slight awkwardness on to her cushion that under her flowing tunic the chief's wife was heavily pregnant.

'Good Lord!' Lily thought. 'How could I have missed *that*! Under all that drapery she's enormous!' Lily tried to remember the few details Iskander had given her about the set-up at the fort. This Halima who really couldn't be much older than herself – quite possibly younger – was, improbable though it might seem, married to the fearsome old Malik whose first wife, Zeman's mother, the Afghan princess, had died last year. Had she got that right? There was no way she could find out. Lily had a hundred questions she wanted to ask Halima Begum but, apart from the barrier of Halima's uncertain hold on the English language, the customary meal-time silence had descended. As she worked her way through a sequence of dishes Lily began to think the lack of conversation was in fact quite relaxing and certainly had the edge on exchanging mindless chit-chat with Nick Carstairs and Edward Dalrymple-Webster.

She eyed Halima Begum covertly from time to time, wondering how it had come about that such a young person had not been married off to a young man of the tribe – Zeman, Iskander or any one of the handsome faces that had risen up from behind rocks to shout a greeting to them as they drew near the fort. Surely her preference must have been for such a one? Lily had tried to engage Zeman in a conversation about arranged marriages but, smooth and courteous, he had neatly avoided being drawn by her questions so she could only speculate as to their customs. But Halima, smiling and confident, giving out brisk orders to the servants, playing happily with the children, didn't seem to call for any romantic Western sympathy. 'Now suppose President Harding did me the honour of making me the First Lady,' Lily considered, 'how would I feel?' She decided her fantasy was getting somewhat out of hand.

From the other women's manner towards the Malik's wife, Lily judged that Halima was, regardless of age, top of the pile, reflecting her husband's status in the tribe. Even a middle-aged, dark-haired woman with the same hatchet features as the Malik and whom Lily assumed to be his sister appeared to defer to her. But all, judging by the smiles and laughter which abounded, liked her. As Halima stopped in mid-sentence to lay a protective hand on her stomach, women scurried to fetch water and extra cushions, hands were extended in support and, judging by the giggles, racy remarks were made. Lily knew nothing about pregnancy but, having once got Halima's bulge in focus, she decided two things: firstly that the birth must be imminent and secondly that it was a physical impossibility. She compared the ante-natal treatment Halima was enjoying – the jokes and the cosseting – with what she speculated would have been the hand-out in Chicago: a stiff doctor in morning coat, striped trousers and a butterfly collar dispensing calomel. Lily had shaken hands with a gynaecologist once and the memory of his bony fingers still made her shudder.

A swift calculation told her that, following his first wife's death, the Malik must have made Halima the happiest of women with indecent speed. 'In American culture, anyway. Keep a hold on that, Lily Coblenz,' she told herself. Perhaps the Malik had always had an eye on this girl and had deliberately neglected to arrange a marriage for her, putting her in cold storage so to speak until his elderly princess dropped off the twig. A seriously cold thought pushed the more frivolous ones from her mind. Zeman! The Malik's last remaining son was now dead. Oh, Lord! There was more riding on this than they knew.

Once the meal was cleared away and hands – and faces in the case of the children – had been washed, excited chattering broke out again. Lily knew most of it had to do with her but she sensed also from the women's gestures

194

and the way they hurried at the slightest sound from the courtyard below to stand by the window looking down that there were more earth-shaking events to be witnessed and discussed than the arrival among them of an 'American princess'. Something was about to happen. Was, indeed, happening.

Left to herself in Halima's company Lily shyly began to congratulate her on her forthcoming child. Halima's initial broad smile and returned thanks faded and turned to a look of anxiety. Afraid that she might have broken some unknown convention Lily could only grasp her hands and begin to stammer out an apology.

'No. No,' said Halima hurriedly. 'I am pleased that child come. But now since news this morning . . . since Zeman dead . . . most important that son – another son come!'

'You know that Zeman is dead?' said Lily in surprise. 'Did Iskander tell you? I didn't hear him mention Zeman's name?'

'Letter come from fort. Gor Khatri. Since three hours. Letter for Iskander. Ramazad read it. He tell me but no one else. It say Zeman his son is dead. Ramazad say fort commander with red hair kill Zeman. Ramazad say he put head of soldier with red hair on gate of Mahdan Khotal!' Halima gave a vivid mime of the impaling of a head on a spike.

Lily was silent for a moment working out the significance of the information. If James had sent a letter to Iskander care of the fort that meant he knew where she was, didn't it? Clever old James! Or was it clever old Joe? They'd thought their way around all Iskander's meanderings in the hills! A spurt of hope was soon extinguished as she recalled the impregnable position and defences of Mahdan Khotal. No, the only way out of here was by diplomacy or trickery, she decided. Either way she was going to need help.

'The red-haired soldier,' she said, 'is called James Lindsay and he didn't kill Zeman. I'll tell you what happened . . .'

195

Lily stuck closely to the official Grace Holbrook version of the death and to her relief Halima seemed to follow what she was saying with ease. '. . . so you see, if Iskander hadn't taken it into his head to run off into the wilderness with Lord Rathmore – and me incidentally – there wouldn't be a problem.'

She had obviously said the wrong thing. Halima frowned and stuck her chin out in disagreement. 'Iskander very clever man! Very good man. He always Zeman's friend. He take badal for Zeman. If he take this Rathmore, then this Rathmore kill Zeman! Rathmore die,' said Halima flatly.

Lily remembered the warmth of the greeting between these two and wondered if she had stumbled on a Queen Guinevere-Sir Lancelot situation. 'I think you are very fond of Iskander?' she asked tentatively.

The reply was decisive. 'Of course! My brother is the best man of the tribe after Ramazad. He teach me English. He learn English at school in Peshawar. Strong man. Never tell lies.'

A fluttering and an intensification of noise at the fretted window above the courtyard drew their attention. 'Jirga start,' Halima announced. 'Jirga is village meeting.' Women made way at the window for them and they stood to look down at the men gathering below. With excited squeals the older children pulled cushions to the window, piling them up to stand on for a better view.

Lily saw about two hundred men, talking and gesticulating, arrive and settle themselves on the ground around the spreading tree in the centre of the square. Iskander approached and stationed himself, standing, arms folded, on one side of the gathering. With a pang, Lily saw Rathmore escorted on to the scene and told to sit, exhibit A, at centre stage. Someone seemed to have tidied him up a bit. His clothes were brushed, his hair likewise and he walked with his usual jaunty step. 'Good old Rathmore!' she couldn't help thinking. 'He's keeping his pecker up at least!' She found herself admiring the way he settled to scan the assembly as though he were taking a board meeting, nodding and smiling and confident. 'That's the style, Dermot old boy! You show 'em!' she muttered.

The Malik then entered to a roar of greeting and stood opposite Iskander. Imposing and noble, he dominated the crowd merely by his presence. He held his hand up and, taking a letter from his bosom, began slowly to read. All listened with breathless and unwavering attention, Halima amongst them.

'What's he saying?' said Lily but she was waved to silence and the account wore on accompanied by sharp exclamations and intakes of breath from the listeners until at last Ramazad closed the letter, folded it and put it away. At once there was a howl of dismay, of horror, of anger. He had obviously just announced the death of Zeman to the crowd and Halima confirmed this. The howls from below turned to raucous and angry shouts. Men stood up and waved their fists, some brandished their rifles. Lily needed no translation. This was a call for revenge, for badal.

Iskander waved his arms to silence the crowd but it was not until the Malik had intervened that he could make himself heard. In a voice free of emotion Iskander appeared to be telling it as it was, Lily thought, and again Halima's translation bore this out. 'He is saying that soldier from fort kill Zeman. Red-haired soldier. Iskander has demanded this man's death and if this is not granted then the hostage Rathmore die instead. In five days' time.'

There were mutterings from the floor and one or two men stood up, pointing at Rathmore and calling out with savage gestures what appeared to be suggestions for making his death more interesting. As Halima did not translate these, Lily assumed her guess was right. The Malik began to speak again and all fell silent. He spoke for a very long time. The children standing around them began to get bored and drifted away but the women were riveted by the speech. Halima's face was tense and she began to bite her lip, her gaze running constantly from Ramazad to her brother. Her commentary had dried up and Lily was going

197

mad with suspense. The old devil, she was convinced, was up to something. His tone conveyed a blend of blatant honesty, charm and conviction. Lily had heard much the same delivery from a snake-oil salesman in Sioux City.

She looked closely at Iskander. He too appeared to be uneasy with the Malik's delivery and attempted to interrupt. He was at once called to order in very cold tones by Ramazad. Lily began to recognize that what she was witnessing was a power struggle within the tribe. She'd sat in on board meetings where her father had set out to fillet the opposition but this time she suspected she was rooting for the losing side. The old stag, heavy with antlers, was lowering them to ward off the challenge from the younger blood. And with the death of Zeman perhaps the way had become clear for Iskander. And perhaps this was resented by Ramazad?

The Malik began to gesture to the sky and his voice took on an edge of barely suppressed rage. 'Ramazad say ferenghi have planes to bomb us. No soldier can take Mahdan Khotal – no soldier on the ground – but the soldiers who fly can destroy our fort. He say that Iskander bring the bombs on our heads. Rathmore who is Iskander's hostage is big Khan in his country . . .' The Malik indicated Rathmore with a courteous gesture at which Rathmore rose and presented himself to the crowd with a small bow and the modest smile of an Englishman who has just hit a six.

Unconsciously, Lily seized Halima's hand and the two women shared their anxiety and powerlessness in the clutch of cold, tense fingers. 'Iskander wrong to bring death on the tribe. Ferenghi soldiers know hostages are here and attack from sky then, when walls are dust, attack from ground and finish us off. Remember what ferenghi do against Mahsud villages last year. And one of these hostages is a memsahib. This brings great shame on the tribe and great danger. Ferenghi fight more strong to get her back.'

A derisive shout went up from the crowd. 'Our Malik is getting old! These are the fears of an old woman!'

'Who's afraid of the ferenghi? We're not!'

'How many sons must Ramazad lose before he takes badal?'

With a face of thunder Ramazad called for silence. 'Whose sons are killed by ferenghi devil? Whose sons? Yours, Mahmood? Yours, Asnil? No! The sons of Ramazad!' He beat his breast for emphasis. 'My son Zeman is dead and I, Ramazad Khan, will avenge him. I know who kill him. Soldier with red hair who kill my two eldest sons now kill my third and last son. I will nail his . . . skin? . . .' Halima hesitated.

'Hide,' Lily whispered.

'. . . to the gate of Mahdan Khotal. Red hair soldier and all ferenghi soldier from fort. But this is *my* badal and I do not bring it on the tribe. Leave Ramazad's badal to Ramazad! Iskander does not think. He has done great wrong to the tribe. We are all now in danger.'

This last pronouncement of the Malik's was accompanied by the casting upwards to the sky of a fearful eye. 'Jeez!' thought Lily. 'Can this guy ever ham it up! And now he's got them eating out of his hand. By promising to take the load of retribution on his own shoulders – spiking poor old James, I guess I mean – he leaves the tribe free to look after their own concerns without losing face and avoid a showdown with the British Army and Air Force. But this isn't looking good for Iskander. The orphan with no close relation to speak up for him. No one but his sister and she can say nothing! He's going to make *him* carry the can!'

Halima seemed to have come to the same conclusion. When Iskander attempted to speak he was hooted down and fists were shaken. Icily proud, he fell silent and shrugged a shoulder. An outbreak of shouting and argument followed and finally the Malik intervened, the respected chairman bringing the meeting to order. He appeared to propose a motion and Lily looked enquiringly at Halima.

'Jirga decide,' she said, hardly able to get the words out, 'if Iskander be sent away.'

'What? Sent away? Outlawed, you mean?' Lily was incredulous.

She was never quite clear as to how the voting was conducted but after a very short time loud cries and yells broke out again and Iskander, with a face to freeze the blood, turned on his heel and stalked away. Lily didn't quite like the congratulatory pat on the back Rathmore delivered to the Malik as he swaggered off.

Halima gasped, murmuring her brother's name, and turned from the window to run from the room. As she turned she caught her foot in a pile of cushions abandoned by the children and fell with a crash to the floor. The women gathered round her at once, making sounds of concern and encouragement. They tried to raise her but she cried out in pain. At once the woman Lily had decided was the Malik's sister took charge. Servants were summoned and Halima, moaning pitifully and gasping out terse orders, was carried from the room and placed in a smaller room next door.

For the rest of the day, Lily, unnoticed, could only sit anxiously in a corner of the common room watching the bustle as women hurried in and out with basins of hot and cold water, little chafing dishes in which burned strangely scented spices, piles of white linen cloths and trays of tea from which someone always remembered to hand her a cup. She tried once to sneak into the room where Halima was lying but was turned away in a polite but firm manner and she didn't try again.

Her own situation was not looking very healthy either, she thought. In a surprisingly short time the only two people in the fort she felt any affinity with had both been put out of action. Iskander outlawed. Had he left already? Did the sentence have immediate effect and was there something she could do about that? And Halima in the throes of what exactly she wasn't sure but it could be anything from sprained ankle to childbirth. So she was left to the mercies of that manipulative old Malik. 'If I ever get out of this,' she thought, 'the first thing I'll do is warn James Lindsay that the Malik has got his number. And that he's gunning for any English soldier who puts his head above the parapet. And what was all that about the red-haired soldier killing the old brute's two older sons? James? Does that sound likely? Well, that's what soldiers do, I suppose. Bad luck though to lose three sons to the British.'

She flinched as Halima groaned again.

The cries and moans went on at intervals for the rest of the day and seemed to be growing in intensity. Lily watched as the Malik's sister took a piece of paper from a pile on a table and wrote a note. This was handed to one of the children, the largest boy, and he ran off outside carrying it in his hand. 'Notifying the boss,' thought Lily. 'So that's their system.' She was intrigued to see a few minutes later the lone figure of the Malik appear below the window. He began to pace about in the square and after one or two circuits he settled under the tree, looking up from time to time at the shadows that passed in front of the fretted window.

Lily eyed the pile of papers and the pencil on the table speculatively. It seemed this was the way the women communicated with the outside world. Not so very different from those little 'chits' the English women annoyed each other with in Simla. In the bustle no one noticed Lily sidle up to the table and help herself to a sheet of paper. She wrote a short note, folded it carefully and settled down to wait for the right moment. As two women attending Halima left – change of shift, Lily calculated – she went into Halima's room. One girl still present and holding the hand of Halima who, eyes closed in agony, was sweating and writhing waved to her to go away. Lily played dumb for as long as she could and then slowly made her way back to the door. In the doorway she paused and called to the boy who was standing by and acting as messenger. She crooked a finger at him and, wide-eyed he approached.

'Iskander,' she said, tapping the folded letter. 'Halima Begum . . . Iskander.'

The boy nodded in understanding, took the letter and scurried off. Lily settled by the window on watch.

Chapter Sixteen

'At dawn.'

The phrase has its melodramatic ring and, as he delivered it, Joe had been aware of this and wished he could take back the words. Confronted now with the reality of dawn in a forbidding landscape drained of colour and with a sharp wind blowing off the hills, he felt many things and gallantry and confidence were not among them.

He looked at the two Scouts who had been told off to accompany this lunatic foray. Aslam and Yussuf were already standing by at the chiga gate, eager to start out.

'How did you select them?' Joe had asked James.

'Not easy,' had been the reply. 'Every bloody man in the unit volunteered. No surprise to me! That always happens. And you're faced with the alternatives of offending everybody you don't select and inflating the consequence beyond measure of the two you do select. But still, they're good men these two, you'll find. Very reliable, very experienced. And they are not of the same tribe – don't want any tribal combining, thanks! They'd serve you well even without the bonus of six months' extra pay I've offered them to bring you both back out again safely. Six months' pay! Enough to buy them a rifle or a bride. They'll take good care of you!' He paused. 'And I had another reason for choosing this pair. They both have brothers in the unit.'

'Hostages, do you mean to say?' Joe had asked.

'Yes,' said James. 'More or less. More or less. That's how they'll see it anyway!'

Joe looked the Scouts up and down. They wore nailed sandals, woollen hose-tops, baggy shorts and long shirts crossed by bandoliers each carrying fifty rounds. Their beaming faces were surmounted by a Pathan pagri, a length of khaki cloth wound around a dome-shaped, padded kullah, and the loose end of the pagri trailed behind in a shamleh, protecting the back of the neck from the sun. Joe thought they looked pretty good; they looked businesslike, spare and effective.

He couldn't, he thought, quite say the same of the third member of the party as Grace joined them. She looked swiftly round. 'I was expecting two Scouts,' she said. 'Why do I see three?' She stared and started. 'Well, I'm damned! Not bad, Joe! Not bad at all! Nearly fooled me and that takes some doing.'

Joe was not taken in but he was amused by Grace's cheerful by-play. He thought he did look pretty convincing; a little kohl rubbed into his eyebrows and around his eyes and quite a lot of dirt massaged into his face had worked wonders. His tall athletic frame was very like that of the other two Scouts and the company barber had carefully given the three the same short regimental haircut the night before. He had wondered whether to pull his turban down slightly over one eye to cover his war wound but the Scouts had advised against this, pointing with pride to their own wounds, and he gathered it gave him authenticity and even prestige. They had scrutinized him carefully, made a few adjustments to his gear and finally were satisfied – 'The sahib will pass as Pukhtun so long as he does not get off his horse,' said Aslam mysteriously and explained further that 'Ferenghi walk with ram-rod up their arse but Pukhtun walk like leopard.' Joe's not entirely serious practice attempts to walk like a leopard were greeted with stifled laughter. 'Not *camel*, sahib – leopard!'

'The question is, Grace,' said Joe, 'will it fool anybody else?'

'Oh, yes, certainly. If you keep your mouth shut, stay in the background and don't take your trousers off.'

'I wasn't thinking of doing so,' said Joe,' but why particularly?'

'I have to ask the question – circumcised? Uncircumcised?'

'The latter,' said Joe, 'but I reckon that given time you could fix that as well!'

'Certainly I could,' said Grace. 'But perhaps we haven't got time today. You'd have to make an appointment and my book gets full! But, anyway, you've been warned. Be careful.'

Her practical good humour lightened the grey morning and eased the tension coiling in his stomach. He looked with a smile at her outfit. She was wearing voluminous red trousers, a hat and a veil and a man's loose white shirt belted at the waist.

'It's all right,' she said. 'I know I look ridiculous but this is my campaign gear. Pathan women wear red trousers when they're out and about – it's a signal to gunmen that they're not a target. Like this I can be seen from far off. I take nobody by surprise and,' she looked down at her billowing trousers, 'I confess, I think they look extremely becoming! Don't you?'

Her horse was led out for her and a Scout – was it Aslam or Yussuf? – it was hard to tell them apart – came forward and cupped his hands for Grace's foot and swung her into the saddle. The other Scout attached Grace's medical case to the crupper and they were ready. Their exit from the fort was deliberately discreet and in minutes they had slipped through the chiga gate and headed west at a trot down the broad valley along the banks of the Bazar river. Joe noted the easy way Grace sat in the saddle, moving with all the economy of a cavalryman.

'I suppose,' he thought, 'that, to the Pathan, Grace is a sort of honorary man and as such transcends all the normal rules. But then, I can't think of any place where Grace wouldn't feel at home from Viceregal Lodge through lecturing to medical students to worming children in the market place. And I wouldn't be surprised if she'd brought half the hairy scoundrels who lie in wait ahead of us into this world! Such a reputation must be worth something!'

Grace tuned into his thought, turning to him as they rode and saying seriously, 'Being in my company is a sort of good conduct pass but it won't carry you all the way. Remember, Joe, that as far as is known and with the exception of actual prisoners (like Rathmore) no ferenghi – no European, that is – has ever made his way into Mahdan Khotal. Sacred ground, you understand. It's very important therefore that you should be as invisible as possible and when we get a bit closer I'll ride ahead with Aslam who is Afridi and you can ride behind with Yussuf who is Khattack. Should anyone ask, we'll tell them you're a Chitrali from the north. That'll explain any awkwardness with language.They'll notice the leading hand but won't pay so much attention to the matched pair behind. In any case, three armed Scouts are not likely to be perceived as much of a threat, particularly since they have no idea that we're on to them.'

She paused and looked back over her shoulder as a Bristol fighter roared its way into the sky behind them and made its patient and pointless way north-west over the Khyber. 'Good old Fred! That'll keep them guessing!' Her tone changed. 'Once we've been admitted to the fort the nature of the game changes. You, I and the two boys will have become their guests and thereby under their protection. It ought to work but I'd be more comfortable if – just in case it doesn't and, as the saying goes, "the worst came to the worst" – you had one of these.' She reached across as he rode beside her and put a red glass capsule in his hand. 'Cyanide,' she said and continued, 'I expect I'm being histrionic but there is just a chance – more than a chance – that this could go wrong.' She gave him a level glance and resumed, 'Put it where you can easily get at it.'

'It's glass,' said Joe, momentarily puzzled.

'Should you be in a position where you need to use it, a mouth full of glass will be the least of your problems!'

Joe pondered the implication, saying at last, 'Believe me, Grace, I don't want to be there when it goes wrong but if it does I'll just carry on taking the tablets and see you in a fortnight. Correct?'

'Yes, that's about it.'

The easy way in which Grace handed out a lethal poison reawakened all Joe's suspicions. The scene might have changed into a desperate rescue dash into the hills to bring out Rathmore and Lily but his main objective remained to find out who had killed Zeman. He was sure that much would flow from that solution. He had never accepted the theory of andromedotoxin poisoning that Grace had put forward and was even less happy with the idea of a fatal dose of arsenic delivered through the medium of the unfortunate pheasant and, what was more, he knew Grace could never have subscribed to these theories either. Achmed's so fortuitously timed confession had played innocently into her hands but he found he was left with the inevitable conclusion that Grace was involved in a cover-up, a cover-up in which she had been caught out by Iskander. But for the midnight swim, all would have been happy or at least accepting of the arsenic theory. But for whom was she covering? Herself? James? Iskander? Someone else?

He imagined the pressure on Grace as she had performed her autopsy with a Scotland Yard detective present and all too literally sticking his nose in. Her sangfroid was amazing and, surely, could only, in a woman of such high principles, stem from a perfectly clear conscience? He decided to take advantage of their present circumstances to put further pressure on her. Out here she could not evade his questioning.

'There's a lot riding on this expedition,' Grace was saying. 'I don't put these things in any order of priority but we have to extricate that damn fool Rathmore and we have to winkle out Lily.'

'How easy you make it sound,' said Joe, 'but have you paused to consider that, whereas Rathmore undoubtedly was kidnapped, Lily may well have gone off with Iskander of her own accord? Lord knows why! A yearning for adventure? Spoilt little madam whose head's been turned by too many moving pictures? An admirer of Rudolph Valentino perhaps? Perhaps she's simply inherited her father's enterprising spirit? I gather Coblenz senior is a financial pirate of the first water who, in his time, has gobbled up half the resources of the West.'

'And perhaps his daughter is now making a play for the East?' said Grace. 'No. She has her faults but treachery and stupidity are not among them. She's clever and, I do believe, good-hearted. No. I'm sure she was forced or tricked in some way into going with them. If she went at all willingly – and this I don't believe – it would be on account of her feelings for Iskander.'

Joe reined in his horse in surprise. 'Feelings for Iskander? Grace, what are you saying? Lily was flirting with both young men and – goodness! – one sees why! But, if anything, she showed more interest in Zeman!' Joe carefully kept back the revelation that Lily had attempted to meet him in the garden. Once again he had the strong impression that he was fencing with Grace, always feinting and falling back, hoping to lure her into making a false step.

'Oh, Joe! You don't know much about girls, do you? Look – girls of Lily's age regularly take an indirect route to claim the attention of the one they're really interested in. This is why "best friends" are so useful! By scintillating – I think Lily would call it "sparking" – with Zeman she was actually showing herself off to Iskander who was always there, as I'm sure you noticed, a ready audience.'

'But he appeared to take little notice of her.'

Grace sighed. 'That's part of the game, the ritual. Look, Joe, I'm rather a prosaic old countrywoman at heart

208

but even I couldn't help catching the ripples, the backwash, from some of their encounters. Disturbing. Very disturbing.'

'But they only set eyes on each other four days ago! Nothing of any serious emotional significance could have occurred in that short time?'

Grace was laughing at him. 'Joe, when you meet the right girl, I know what you'll say to her – after a decent interval of course – "I say, old thing, I'm afraid something of serious emotional significance appears to have occurred!" You were standing right next to Lily when it happened, as was I, as were eight other people. They looked at each other and that was that. Instant recognition. It happens. The French call it a *"coup de foudre"*. A thunderbolt.'

'Grace, you're a scientist, a doctor, you surely don't believe such things happen?'

'I *know* they happen!' she said sharply. 'I wasn't always fat, forlorn and forty-five, you know!' she added quietly.

Joe was embarrassed for a moment. 'Ah!' he said. 'A *coup de Grace*?'

'Bad joke, Joe!'

Joe fell silent. He was again being led, gently and with humour, down a path he had no particular intention of following and he was determined to get Grace back on the track he had chosen. 'You don't mention what I consider to be the main problem in all this – the death of Zeman. Enough of the girls' gossip – don't forget, Grace, I am a policeman, inquisitive and suspicious by nature. Are there things about that mysterious episode that you'd be prepared to tell me?'

The road narrowed and for two hundred yards or so Joe and Grace were constrained to ride in line ahead and Joe's question was left floating in the air. As the track widened once more, Aslam led them down to a stony ford across a hurrying stream, a tributary of the meandering Bazar river.

'As good a place as any,' said Grace, 'to water the horses and form up. Gather our strength before we take on the difficult part of this expedition into the hills.'

'It wouldn't be a bad place,' said Joe, 'for you to answer my question. I know *how* you killed Zeman, but I can't imagine *why*.'

Chapter Seventeen

'Then your policeman's imagination does not deceive you, Joe,' Grace said lightly. 'I'm glad about that. You say you "can't imagine why". Well, that could be because there is no reason why. I did not kill Zeman.'

Unabashed, she met his level gaze, rendered all the more penetrating by the sooty emphasis of his eyes, and said again, 'I did not kill Zeman. But I'd really like to hear what you mean by "knowing *how*" I could have killed him.'

For the sake of peace on the frontier Joe would have kept silent – *had*, until now, kept silent, unsettling images from the dinner party still with him. He had a picture of Grace moving around the table to talk to Lily and occupying for a minute or two Zeman's vacated place, setting his sherbet glass negligently to one side as she settled. She could easily have palmed a pill and Grace, so experienced in all practical matters pertaining to Life and Death, with a working knowledge of poisons, could easily have dropped it into the glass. It hadn't been cyanide. In manhandling the body on the stairs Joe had come close enough to check that there was no bitter almond smell about the man's mouth. The vomit also had been innocent of any betraying smell of poison known to Joe. And cyanide was an instant killer. Whatever else, it wasn't cyanide.

With a start of horror Joe wondered what would have been the Amir's reaction when it was revealed that his personal physician designate – both female and foreign – had done away with his kinsman, a trusted serving officer? If, as many thought, he was searching for the trigger for a holy war against the British, surely none better than this would ever offer? But Joe hadn't dismissed the theory of a palace coup and he remembered flakes of what Iskander described as white cardamom being liberally sprinkled into Zeman's tea and Grace's voice, casual and authoritative, 'Why don't you all try it? It's an excellent carminative.' A cover for Iskander? So easy to put something besides the cardamom into his superior officer's cup. Were Grace and Iskander conspiring? The only thing the unlikely pair would work towards together would be the preservation of the fragile status quo, he thought. Joe had liked Iskander. He thought him clever and reasonable with a sense of humour which appealed to him. Perhaps that had put Joe off his guard.

In a heavy police voice he took Grace through his suspicions and train of thought, feeling rather foolish in the face of her quizzical and only slightly exasperated reception of his account.

'Good, Joe. Very impressive,' she said finally. 'But I can't imagine why you didn't tell me all this earlier. You shouldn't have kept it to yourself. I could have helped you with it. I could have pointed out that there were a hundred ways of getting poison into Zeman at that party if anyone seriously wanted to. Lily, for example, drew everyone's attention to the fact that Edwin Burroughs gave Zeman a bismuth tablet. Was it a bismuth tablet? How will we ever know? I didn't examine it. Did you? And if you think about it, Burroughs has much more valid reasons for wanting to stir up trouble on the frontier. A full-blown incident with the Afridi at everyone's throats would suit him, *does* suit him very well. He may puff and bluster and give you and James a hard time but when your backs are turned, believe me, there's a nasty calculating gleam in his eye. Don't be deceived – he's delighted by the turn of events. And who's to say he hasn't had a hand in turning them! It's no secret, I think, that Britain sank all its resources into that carnage in France. We're stretched, Joe, for men and for cash. The administrators, like Burroughs, who hold the

212

purse strings are quite desperate to retrench and this little corner of Empire is dashed expensive to maintain in a state of battle readiness. There are those who say that this sideshow is no more than a self-indulgent training ground for young army bloods who are determined to see a bit of action in the one remaining part of Empire where there is actually blood still being spilled.'

'And it would be your suggestion that Burroughs eliminated Zeman to set in train a series of events so threatening as to allow the government to decide that a policy of retreat beyond the Indus would be the prudent step to take in the circumstances?' Joe was aiming for a lightly quizzical tone but what he heard was heavy derision.

Grace turned a serious face to him. 'Never forget that the third war with Afghanistan was a trumped-up affair involving a quarrel over the ownership of a garden, if you please! Your war began with the assassination of an Austrian Archduke in an obscure Balkans town. Peripheral to the main event you might say, the occasion and not the cause?'

Joe was silent, unable to challenge her.

She went on, now openly teasing him. 'But I can see that you are not seduced by the idea of Burroughs as our killer. To be honest – nor am I! We were all passing plates around the table, helping each other to dishes that were just out of reach. Have you considered Betty? I saw her spooning out food for Zeman. Has it occurred to you that she could have faked her own sickness to throw suspicion on that wretched bird!'

'*Faked* her sickness? Betty? Could she?'

'Oh, come on, Joe! Every schoolgirl knows the trick of sticking a finger down her throat to bring on a vomitation. It can get you out of all sorts of situations you'd rather not be in – hockey lesson in January, tea with great-aunt Mildred . . .'

Joe stirred in irritation. 'But *why* . . .?' he began.

'Exactly! *Why*? Betty has the same motive as myself, which is to say – no motive! But while we're at it, let's

consider Fred Moore-Simpson. Clever chap. Good strat-
egist and quite ruthless. If he wanted to poison Zeman
I think we wouldn't be aware of the *how*. I certainly didn't
see him approach Zeman's food or drink during the course
of the meal. Did *you*?' She looked up at him sharply. 'But
afterwards . . . after the ladies withdrew, I mean. What
happened then, Joe?'

'We all had a brandy or two – those of us who stayed on.
That was me, James, the two Pathans and Fred . . .' His
voice trailed away and Grace was after his thoughts like a
greyhound.

'And who dispensed the drinks?' she asked.

'We dismissed the staff – said we'd wait on ourselves
and Fred took charge of the glasses and filled them.'

'From a new bottle?'

'No. It was about two-thirds full. It was in the cabinet in
the durbar room.'

'Did Fred know where it was?'

'Yes. He went straight to it. Oh, all right! Yes, he certainly had the opportunity, but, no, Grace. Not Fred.'

'I would seriously like to know, Joe, why you say with
such decision "Not Fred" when you are perfectly ready to
accuse *me* of this insanity?'

From some this would have sounded petulant. But not
Grace, Joe thought. She sounded genuinely intrigued with
– as always – an undertone of cynical amusement.

'Well, again we come down to *why*, don't we?' Joe
persisted.

'You barely know Fred. Don't be taken in by all that
bonhomie! He's ambitious and ruthlessly efficient. Perhaps
I don't need to tell *you* that any flyer who survived the war
must have survival instincts coupled with a degree of luck
to make the mind reel! There's been talk of reducing the
RAF drastically, axing the senior ranks of whom Fred is
one. League of Nations-driven disarmament is the fashion-
able preoccupation; a stance that leaves Fred and his like,
as advocates of gunboat diplomacy, finding themselves
part of history. Now Fred is in the prime of life and has no

214

intention of becoming surplus to requirements! An incident of this nature on the frontier to demonstrate in earnest how badly needed aerial reconnaissance or, even better, aerial proscription is, would play right into his hands. Instead of being sent back to a desk job in London for the rest of his air force life (which is on the cards) he now finds himself in an actively warlike situation requiring his special abilities and an extra squadron of bombers on the frontier. You saw as I did how he was relishing the developing situation. He's already reaping the benefit of Zeman's untimely demise.'

She paused and then added, 'And it's not only the Pathan for whom revenge is a compulsion. You remember what Hugh had to say about Fred's nephew?'

'Grace, this is barmy! You don't think Fred killed Zeman!'

'Of course not! Just letting my imagination run away with me. Now – there's James. He was sitting right next to Zeman throughout the meal, he had access to the brandy . . .'

'All right! Enough! Too many suspects! Too many with motive and all with opportunity! We'll have Fifteen Men On A Dead Man's Chest before we're much older!'

'Yo, ho, ho! And a bottle of rum!' said Grace.

They turned from the easy riding of the Bazar Valley, cutting off to the right, and began to climb into the hills. From now on all speech was to be in Pushtu. The Afridi have ears as keen as their eyes, Grace reminded him, and Joe was increasingly aware of scrutiny. Scrutiny from above and from either side as the track narrowed and began to rise steeply.

His spine began to trickle with sweat and he tried to subdue a shudder as he became aware of the eyes and possibly the gun barrels trained on his back. Which was the worse fate, he speculated – to be sniped at crossing a desolate Flanders field, his body never to be recovered

215

from the enveloping mud, or to be blasted to bits by a jezail and left to desiccate on the hot stones of the Frontier?

Riding a few paces behind and knee to knee with Yussuf, Joe eyed Grace who was chatting easily with Aslam. A clever woman. A brave woman. What had he expected from his outrageous challenge? A confession? Probably not. The best he had hoped for was a sharing of the knowledge he was certain she had of the circumstances of Zeman's death. Her answer had been evasive if not deliberately misleading. He had been half minded to share with her his evidence of faulty diagnosis to further unsettle her. He weighed the satisfaction of demonstrating to this confident woman that he was not the plodding policeman she had obviously marked him down as against the disadvantage of disturbing her when she was about to try to carry off the most enormous bluff. The next hour would test her resolve and her cunning to their extreme and Joe decided he could not pile on any greater pressure. Later. If there was to be any 'later'.

The covert scrutiny abruptly turned to overt challenge. Two tribesmen appeared, blocking their track, and Joe was aware of riflemen on either side of the defile. Aslam shouted a response and two men emerged from behind rocks to return the greeting but Joe noticed they did not relax their vigilance. Grace added a pithy comment in Pushtu, apparently recognizing one of the Afridi as she called out his name. For once Joe could follow what was being said. It had been well rehearsed at the fort and the Pathan love of gesture, drama and joking repartee made all very clear.

Aslam began by exchanging brief but friendly greetings. He paused, waiting, relaxed and confident, to be waved on. He did not state their business but affected to assume the challenging guards were aware of it. Back came the questions as expected and with a touch of impatience Aslam told them to stop prevaricating and let them through. Time was short. There was a perceptible stiffening in the guards' attitude and they again questioned Aslam. Eyes rolling with exasperation, he said, enunciating clearly, that the lady doctor had been summoned to attend the Malik and how come they didn't know that?

The guards consulted amongst themselves and all declared that no message had gone out. A runner had come through yesterday morning with a message from the ferenghi fort but that was all. Were they sure they'd been summoned? Aslam, half in anger, half in joke, shouted at them. 'You silly sods! You've been sitting up in those rocks so long you're growing moss on your arses! The message came through to the fort at Gor Khatri. The Memsahib's staying at the fort for a day or two before going on to attend the Amir Amanullah. She could do without this detour but as a favour to the Malik and because it sounded so urgent she agreed to come. The message came in the night. You buggers were all asleep – come on, admit it! Well, no skin off our nose – we can just turn round and go back. Just explain to old Ramazad why his medical assistance didn't get through, will you?'

With a show of bad temper, Aslam began to turn his horse around. This was an uneasy moment. Joe could hardly breathe. If they failed now they would all be shot dead in seconds. At his side, Yussuf yawned negligently, spat in the sand and leaned over to pass a comment to Joe in Pushtu. Joe nodded, grimaced and idly began to pick his nose.

'No! Wait a minute!' The cry went up just as Aslam had predicted. But then something unexpected: one of the Afridi, apparently with a rush of insight, shouted at the others, his pronouncement accompanied by a loud guffaw. The others, understanding dawning, joined in his laughter, one of them counting ostentatiously on his fingers. It was evident to Joe that ribald jokes were being exchanged.

Yussuf leaned towards him and whispered, 'Laugh with me, sahib,' and, digging him in the ribs, they too appeared to be joining in a joke which was a total mystery to Joe. With a new sense of urgency and all smiles, the leading

217

Afridi waved the two gunmen to come down from their cliffs.

While they were conferring together Grace moved her horse close to Joe and hissed an explanation. 'What a piece of luck! I'd been thinking it was about time Allah, the All Merciful, took a hand and now they assume I've been sent for to attend the Malik's new wife. (I hadn't heard the old one was dead!) She's due to give birth any day now they reckon. They're actually fixing up an escort for us to get us through to Mahdan Khotal with all speed! God knows what we'll say when we get there. I'll have to play it by ear when the time comes!'

Lily had finally reached the end of what had been the longest day in her memory. Gently and firmly – with kindness even – she was escorted to the room that had been made ready for her and it was clearly explained that she should stay there and keep quiet.

'What's the good of that?' Lily thought. 'There's no way in this world I'm going to sleep tonight. Everything's happening all around me and I take no part. I don't want to be here any more. I want to be back in Gor Khatri with people I understand. There's a drama unfolding in this horrible place. Drama? A tragedy, more like!' Her dismal thoughts were punctuated by the sound of lamentation from Halima's room. Her cries had grown fainter and further apart and yet there was no one to whom Lily could turn to ask what was happening. Silently she made her way back to the main room and settled down on a heap of cushions by the window. She closed her eyes and fell instantly asleep.

She woke as swift-moving dawn broke once more, lighting the barren hills and sliding across the courtyard below, rolling back the shadows of the night. Lily jerked into full wakefulness as though she had never slept. She looked down on pacing figures in the courtyard and remembered why she was there at the window. She listened intently for noises from the next room and was relieved to hear a faint groan from Halima. At least she was still alive. Nothing then had changed in that long night.

She rolled over on her elbow and looked down on the rigid figure of the Malik who, it seemed, had not abandoned his silent vigil throughout the night. 'What now?' thought Lily. 'Is there nothing they can do? Surely primitive women in a primitive tribal area know more about childbirth than anyone in the world and yet they seem helpless.'

The morning wore on. Women went in and out, their expressions increasingly sad and desperate. Down below a holy man joined the Malik and the two prayed together repetitively and with repeated gestures. The words were formal but the Malik's anguish was manifest and Lily's heart went out to that vengeful and violent man. Silently she added her own prayers to theirs. The children, she noticed, had all been sent away to play at the far end of the courtyard and Lily remained alone, anxious and frustrated as the hours crawled by. Finally, 'I'm not going to waste another second,' she decided. 'I'm going to see what's going on! At least I can sit with Halima for a bit. She may be surprised to see me. She may not even remember who I am but I think she might be glad to have me by her. It's worth a try. I'm not going to spend another second in this room.'

She jumped to her feet but her attention was instantly diverted to a rattle and tumult from below. To Lily's surprise, amidst shouts, the gate of the fort was creaking open as four men pushing the heavy timbers before them worked to admit a small cortège. Two Afridi tribesmen preceded a strange group of riders. Lily's heart leapt as she saw that three of them were in Scouts' uniform. She observed their approach with a spurt of hope. Perhaps they'd come to rescue her, to escort her back to the fort at Gor Khatri. Perhaps they would get her out of this alarming place. Perhaps a deal had been done. At least they represented something familiar. 'Now I'm not alone,' she thought.

The fourth member of the party was, on the other hand, completely incongruous and completely unfamiliar. A female figure. A female figure astride a horse. Surely that was unusual? She was dressed in red, veiled and in native clothes though she didn't look like any of the native women Lily had seen since her arrival. This woman was short and stout and carried herself with some authority. She flung a leg over her horse's head, jumped with surprising agility to the ground and began to fluff out her baggy trousers, calling out commands to her accompanying Scouts. Accustomed as she now was to the deferential attitudes of women in the presence of men, it was a surprise to hear and see a woman prepared to speak and speak loudly; a woman, moreover, to whom it seemed the Afridi were prepared to listen. Who could this be?

And at once Lily saw who it was. Grace! Grace Holbrook. Solid, uncompromising, organizing and efficient Grace! Grace who now turned and fixed her gaze on the Malik. The Malik, standing with the Imam by his side, looked from Grace to the Scouts and to the pair of his Afridi warriors who had escorted the small group into the square. He was speechless for just long enough. Grace hurried to greet him heartily and spoke to him in Pushtu. Such was his astonishment or his fatigue he could only reply in a hesitant voice, pausing to exchange dazed looks with the holy man. The exchange was very brief and Lily, with unspeakable relief, saw the Malik with a sweeping gesture invite Grace to accompany him to the harem. Grace took her medical case from the horse and followed him. Lily heard Grace begin to climb the stairs and ran to the door to greet her.

'Oh, hullo, Lily,' said Grace, ridding herself of her veil. 'There you are! Talk to you in a minute. I think I'd better find out what's happening here first. Just for the moment – be a good girl and get out of my way!'

She turned to address the assembled women crisply,

220

firmly, unsentimentally. They all reacted in their different ways to welcome her. She went into Halima's room where she remained for about ten minutes before emerging to say briefly to Lily, 'Pencil and paper!' before hurrying back inside.

This was Lily's chance. She took a sheet of paper and a pencil from the table and at last was admitted to the sick room. The wax-like figure on the bed was hardly recognizable as Halima. Lily just managed to stifle a cry of alarm as she came to the awful conclusion that Halima was dead. But she must be mistaken – two women were gently smoothing her forehead and holding her by the hand. Lily tried to avert her eyes from the slopes of the enormous abdomen over which Grace was now working and wondered what to do next. Grace snatched the paper from her hand and started to scribble a message, talking to Lily in English as she wrote.

'Lily, you're to get this to the Malik right away! We've got a potentially lethal situation here. One more hour and we'd have lost them both. I have to operate.'

'Do you mean . . .' Lily began, searching for the right word, 'do you mean a caesarean? Is this a case for a caesarean operation?' Such procedures were rarely talked of in Lily's world and always in tones of horror.

'Yes,' said Grace, 'it certainly is. But more than that – it's serious enough for me to need the Malik to tell me whether, if it comes to the point, he wants the child or his wife to survive. In a few more minutes it may be too late to choose.'

Lily took the paper from her hand and, in what she could only imagine to be an acute breach of protocol, ran down the stairs in a swirl of drapery pulling on her veil as she ran, rounding the corners, racing down the second flight and out into the sunshine to the surprise of the watchman at the door, looking neither to left nor right, to the waiting Malik who turned on her with a searching look of blazing enquiry. Lily remembered at the last minute to look down and fold her hands in a gesture of humility

221

while he read the note. The Malik held it and read. He read it again. He turned and gazed up at the sky. He looked up at the fretted window and sighed. For a moment he put a hand over his eyes and then turned to Lily and spoke almost apologetically.

'Halima,' he said.

Lily ran, taking the stairs two at a time and back into the room where Grace was working and the women were waiting. Grace looked at her steadily.

'"Halima". He said, "Halima."'

'Hmm,' said Grace. 'These blasted people! I'll never understand them! Now buzz off, Lily! This is where it all starts to get very messy and I can't be doing with . . .'

But Lily had already disappeared.

Chapter Eighteen

Half an hour after she had fled from the room, Lily, back at her station by the window, was electrified to hear a sharp squawking. She had never heard a newborn baby yelling but the sound, as old as time itself, was unmistakable. She leapt to her feet and ran, afraid to enter, to hover by the door of Halima's room. Minutes later the senior Afridi woman emerged and for the first time Lily saw her smile. She beckoned her to come and inspect the bundle she held in her arms. In awe Lily approached and stared and stared at the little round head with its thatch of black hair. Proudly, the Afridi twitched back the wrappings and presented the rest of the baby to Lily, inviting her to share in the pleasure and relief that another boy had been born to the tribe. All Lily could think of to do was plant a kiss in the middle of the smooth brown forehead and wonder.

'Halima?' she asked.

Smiles, nods and a torrent of Pushtu conveyed a joyful message before she slipped back into the room. But it was another hour before Grace Holbrook appeared, looking white, exhausted and ten years older. Her white blouse was spattered with blood and her arms were stained to the elbows.

'Halima?' Lily asked again.

'Yes! Come and see her now,' she said. 'She's asleep. Still under anaesthetic and quite worn out of course but I think she'll be all right. Strong girl and very young. Very resilient. Most would not have come through but she's as tough

223

as whipcord! And her baby just the same no doubt. But it wasn't easy.' She wiped the back of her hand across her forehead and looked round, groping for support, and took Lily's steadying hand.

'It was the fall that did it,' she said, suddenly garrulous. 'The baby must have been turning itself round, taking up its head-first diving position for birth . . .' Lily realized that Grace was taking the trouble to choose terms she would understand. She'd probably said exactly the same to the assembled Afridi women in Pushtu. '. . . when it was interrupted by Halima crashing to the ground. So we got not just a breech presentation which the women had no doubt seen before and could just about have coped with but a lateral, sideways presentation which was quite outside their experience. One shoulderblade was completely blocking the exit. All that pushing getting nowhere I'm afraid. Total impasse. Lucky we got here when we did. Now. I'll take a few minutes to smarten myself up . . . I'm determined to break the news to Ramazad Khan myself. That can be my reward. Even at my age you can enjoy a bit of a flourish! Besides,' she added thoughtfully, 'Ramazad and I have some unfinished business to conclude.'

Behind Grace's usual calm detachment, there seemed a resolution and a grim intent which Lily had not heard before and which seemed out of key with the news she had to impart. 'It's time,' she said, more to herself than to Lily. 'It's high time to close the circle.'

Holding the baby to her breast, Grace went to the head of the stairs. Alone, she made her way carefully down and out into the courtyard. The space was deserted, people having been kept well away from the harem, but watchful faces followed her from every doorway. Only the three Scouts remained at the far end cross-legged and silent. They looked up sharply as Grace appeared. Grace caught sight of the Malik seated under the tree. He rose to his feet and went slowly forward to meet her, his eyes on the

224

bundle in her arms. Lily watched as Grace spoke to him quietly. With the gesture the Afridi woman had used, she presented his son to him. More exchanges followed and the Malik raised his eyes to heaven and appeared to be giving thanks for his good fortune. But Grace had not finished. Indicating the seat in the shade of the tree, she led the Malik over to it and sat down. He sat down next to her, his eyes following his child. Lily reckoned that if Grace had chosen at that moment to lead him over the edge of the world he would have followed.

A long conversation ensued in which Grace played the major part. Incredibly, it looked to Lily as though Grace was telling him a story, a long, complicated and dramatic story. When she finished she put her head on one side and waited for his reply. He thought for a long time and then asked a question. Grace answered and he made an impatient and violent gesture. Grace spoke again calmly and again he listened intently. Finally, he spoke again, at first hesitantly then more firmly. Grace nodded her head. They were both silent for long moments and then began to talk more easily. They talked for a very long time and as the sun began to decline the shadow of the tower crept across the square. None too soon for Lily, the baby began to squeak and fret and Grace drew the conversation to a close.

She left the Malik and turned to retrace her steps to the harem and as she came on, she looked up at Lily's window and Lily could have sworn, just for a moment, that Grace winked.

She handed the child to one of Halima's attendants and spoke to another who promptly ran off. 'I've asked for your things to be returned to you, Lily,' said Grace. 'No time to change; I want to leave at once. Let me look at you . . . yes, you can ride in those trousers. And have you got a veil somewhere? Good. Put it on. The Malik has agreed to lend us an escort to see us and the Scouts off his territory. It's generally believed that I was brought here by miracle. The Imam and the strength of his prayers is the talk of the village apparently. I'm not telling them otherwise!'

'There is no "otherwise", said Lily fervently. 'Me and Ramazad – that's just about the only thing we'd agree on! You're a miracle, Grace!'

'Well, our thanks are largely due to Halima's little boy,' said Grace. 'He's our ticket out of here! But I'm not hanging about. In the excitement of the new arrival it may be forgotten that you shouldn't be here. You may be safe enough for the moment at least. But all hell is about to break loose! The news of the birth – the birth of an heir – is running like wildfire already. Soon every man with a rifle in his hand and a horse between his knees will ride in and – there! – listen! Can you hear? Drums! This is only a beginning and thank God for it! We can sneak out in the racket. I don't usually go out by the back door but the circumstances are unusual, I do believe. This'll go on for days! Just what I wouldn't prescribe for my patient. Nothing we can do about it though,' she added as the drums grew louder and, in a fusillade of shots, one party after another galloped into the fort, bending their horses through the crowd, barely visible through the thickening dust.

By the time Lily had slipped in to whisper an unheard goodbye and drop a kiss on the cheek of the heavily sedated Halima, a little party had formed up in the square. Their horses had been cared for and seemed ready for the return ride. Two of the Afghan stallions had been brought round, one for Lily and one for Rathmore. Rathmore! In the excitement of the birth his fate had completely slipped her mind. He was looking annoyingly jaunty and totally pleased with himself, and she tried to avoid his eye.

'Ah, Miss Coblenz, good to see you again and I . . .'

'*You* will remain silent until we get out of here,' Grace said curtly. 'Aslam will ride ahead with our two escorts, Lily will ride next to me and I want you, Rathmore, to

226

bring up the rear with the other two Scouts.' She spoke in Pushtu and the two grinning Scouts fell in, one on each side of Rathmore.

'Well, he won't get up to any nonsense with those two villains watching him,' Lily thought with satisfaction, 'and the rest of us won't have to listen to his braying voice telling us how he impressed the Malik.'

She leaned over and spoke to Grace urgently. 'Something missing, Grace? I mean your Afghani escort. Somewhere about this place there's thirty fellers who must be wondering just where they're meant to be headed. Surely the Malik isn't holding *them* hostage?'

'He's planning a phased release. They're being allowed to leave tomorrow so we've a chance to get back to the fort and warn James not to blow them to perdition when they arrive and ring the bell.'

Lily scanned the mêlée of men and horses in the courtyard one last time as their small procession picked its way carefully around the edge and made for the great gate but still there was no sign of Iskander. Was this good or bad? He didn't even know about his sister's child. But in these parts it seemed everybody heard everything before it happened so he would surely be told.

Aslam set off at a good pace and soon they were saying a friendly goodbye to the two Afridi escorts who handed over their guns and went back on sentry duty in the rocks. Lily saw Grace's back stiffen as they rode on as though she could sense rifle barrels trained on her spine and she did not appear to relax until they had rounded one or two bends and begun to descend to a broad valley. After an hour's riding Grace called a halt in the shade of a clump of twisted apricot trees near an ancient bridge over the Bazar river. Apprehension at last seemed to melt away. They were no longer playing mouse to the Malik's cat. Lily was glad nevertheless to be back under the watchful eye of the Scouts and comforted to mark their continued state of readiness. Eyes were always moving, surveying the land

227

ahead as well as behind them, hands were never far from rifles.

Two of them tethered the horses and melted silently away – scouting ahead, Lily supposed. To them the whole expedition was a gasht with its usual precautions being taken. This was no picnic by the river. But this thought was instantly belied by the third Scout, who began to take tea-making equipment from his saddle bag. Idly Lily's mind drifted away to the memory of so many lake-shore picnics with starched table cloths and cascades of napkins. Attendant and obliging young men in blue blazers and straw boaters standing by: 'Let me pass you an anchovy sand-wich, Miss Coblenz.' Lily supposed it was all still going on on the other side of the world.

She looked about her – pitiless sun in a pitiless land-scape. 'Pitiless people too. Still, *he* looks peaceful enough,' she thought, her eye on the third Scout. She watched as he lit a fire and admired his deft and economical movements as he picked an old bird's nest from a cleft in a tree, made a little teepee of broken rushes, added some driftwood from the river bed and applied a match. No straw boater here, just a mud-coloured cloth twisted carelessly into a loose turban.

Lily looked at Grace expectantly, waiting to hear her story. Negligently Rathmore accepted a tin mug of tea from the Scout and sat down a little apart from the women.

'Wouldn't it be great if someone emerged from those rocks and shot him – just shot him!' Lily thought viciously.

'We can't stay here long if we're to be back at the fort before sunset,' said Grace with an anxious glance at the sky. 'Sunset! What a day! It seems to be an eternity since I set off at dawn.'

'Won't they be thrilled to see us back again, all in one piece!' said Lily with satisfaction.

'Especially Joe?' said Grace, slyly.

'Joe! Fat lot of use *he* was!' said Lily. 'Funny – all along

228

it was Joe I was expecting to come to my rescue. For a while back there I really thought he cared about me! But when it came to the point, well! – where was he? Probably playing squash!' Pink with indignation, Lily looked from one to another. As she spoke the third Scout, the silent, enigmatic third Scout looked up.

'Jor ye?' he said. 'Jor ye, missy baba?'

Grace began to laugh. 'Very good,' she said. 'Very good, Joe! And speaking Pushtu, it seems?'

'Can't spend a day in the exclusive company of these boys without picking up a bit. Anyway – I enjoyed the "hallagullah"! I think I've got that right – it seems to mean "uproar". Useful word.'

Lily stared and stared again. She reached out a hand to touch Joe's shoulder to make sure he was real. 'Why!' she sputtered. 'You old devil! There you were all along! You fooled them all!' And more soberly, 'You darned well fooled me! You *did* come for me! And,' she added seriously, 'I'm not going to forget that. And when I'm a little old lady in mittens in a rocking-chair I'll tell my grandchildren about you and all the hairy bandits who didn't spot you! But Joe! That was a dangerous thing to do! Those men would have killed you if they'd known!'

'Well, I'm damned,' drawled Rathmore, not pleased by this turn of events. 'So the forces of law and order make a belated appearance!'

'I don't know what you mean by "belated"!' Suddenly angry, Grace turned on him. 'It was Joe who worked out where you were being held and it was Joe who risked his skin coming into enemy territory to get you out of the spot you'd blundered into, smug, self-satisfied and supremely unaware. I think a little more gratitude wouldn't come amiss.'

Undismayed, he opened his mouth to speak but was interrupted by an excited shout from the Scouts patrolling the area. All turned to look and look again as they took in the sight of the two Scouts. Between them was a third man, a man in Afridi dress. He was being encouraged along

229

with a pistol in his side towards the group by the fire. At the sight of him, Lily and Joe leapt to their feet calling out his name, Joe in puzzlement, Lily with recognition and relief.

'Iskander!'

'Joe, you're not to shoot him!' said Lily urgently. 'He's an outlaw now, did you know? And we've got an arrangement. At least I think we've got an arrangement,' she hissed mysteriously.

'I think I'll wait to hear what he has to say for himself before I shoot him,' said Joe easily. 'Tea, Iskander? I think I can squeeze another one out.'

Aslam handed Iskander's weapons, a pistol and a dagger, to Joe.

'Well, this is very jolly!' said Grace. 'Anyone else lurking in the rocks you'd like to invite?'

'No, no,' said Iskander, completely unabashed. 'Be reassured! We are alone. I waited here, knowing you must pass this way. This is the place everyone stops on their way to Peshawar or the fort and there is adequate cover for brigands or outlaws as many less careful than yourselves have found to their cost.'

He settled down between Grace and Joe, confident of his welcome. 'I was hoping to hear your news.' His eyes flicked to Lily and she was quick to reassure him.

'Your sister is fine, Iskander. And, thanks to Grace, so is the child. It's a boy. They both looked very healthy when we left them.'

Joe noticed again the instant understanding between these two and wondered with trepidation what exactly was the nature of the arrangement Lily had mentioned. He began to fear that his career as chaperone might have been compromised. 'I think we all have many questions but the main one must surely be addressed to Dr Holbrook. What magic did you use, Grace, to prevail on the Malik to release us? Are you able to tell us now?'

Grace looked consideringly at each questioning face raised to hers – Iskander, Lily, Joe and Rathmore – and replied slowly, 'Yes. In fact there are things I would like to clear up before we get back to the fort. I have things to tell you – a story going well back into the past, a story that starts in a ravine not far from here . . .' Grace looked around her and shivered, '. . . that encompasses the death of Zeman and ends with the birth of that small Afridi boy. But I can see only half the picture and we must look to Iskander to fill in the details that have been hidden from me.'

Iskander nodded. No one interrupted and she resumed, a supreme raconteuse, apparently telling a story by a camp fire but Joe sensed that she was taking no pleasure in the telling. Her eyes were full of pain and fixed on a distant past.

'Before the war, about four years before the war, a section of the First Peshawar Scouts, based at Fort Hamilton as Gor Khatri was called before it was refurbished, was in the throes of a more than usually bloody struggle with the local Afridi. They'd been having problems for some months – the Afridi had somehow or other got their hands on large numbers of first-class bolt-action rifles and were keen to show their prowess. A barrampta – a punishment squad I believe they called it – was sent out to teach them a lesson but they got into difficulties and had to make a run for it. The whole thing was botched I must think – the patrol was under strength for the job it had to do and the Afridi had been underestimated. They were cock-a-hoop and tails up and giving our chaps a thorough pasting. Several wounded, some dead.

'They were making their way back, over rough ground, retreating to the shelter of a back-up force that came out belatedly to cover them with Lewis gun fire when an awful thing happened. One of the men – he was their medical officer – fell from a cliff he was climbing with others and was very badly injured. Not walking, not even crawling wounded. Well, I don't need to spell out the implications. His own men wanted to go in and fetch him out in spite of the thick enemy fire and the difficulties of the terrain.

231

Harry – the MO was called Harry – was lying in an impossible situation at the bottom of a ravine with Afridi lined up overhead ready to pick off anyone attempting a rescue.

'It would have been a suicide mission had it taken place but it was never attempted. The Colonel commanding ordered the men to stand down and who shall say he was wrong?' Grace paused, thoughtful.

'Couldn't they have shot him?' asked Lily anxiously. 'I mean, I think that's what they would normally do, isn't it?'

'Yes, it is. But he was at the bottom of the defile and they couldn't get him in their sights. Well, there was one man in the company who wasn't prepared to leave it like that. He was a subaltern, only twenty years old at the time and he'd only just joined the unit but he knew what was bound to happen to Harry if no one acted. His name was Jock – his nickname I should say – inevitable, because he was a Scotsman.'

Joe stirred uneasily but made no attempt to interrupt.

'And, as many Scotsmen do, he carried one of those little daggers they have in the Highlands . . .'

'A skian dhu,' Joe supplied.

'Yes, that's it. It means a black knife, I believe. He also had his pistol and armed with these he set off by himself, disobeying orders, into the gathering gloom. As he crept along he noticed that the Afridi had melted away in their Pathan way and left the ravine apparently clear for him. But when he got to the place where Harry had fallen he found he was too late – others had got there before him. Two Afridi lagging behind the rest had found Harry and were robbing him. They'd taken his gun and were searching through his pockets. They were so occupied with this they didn't hear Jock approach and he killed them both silently. When he turned his attention to Harry he realized there was little he could do for him. The man was a doctor and knew perfectly well the gravity of his own injuries. He told Jock that his back was broken and he could not possibly survive and he asked him to do what was expected of him.'

'Poor man! And poor kid! What a god-awful thing to have to do,' Lily murmured.

'Yes. Bad enough for Harry but he was a seasoned soldier and medical man. He knew what was what and what had to be done. I can't imagine what it must have felt like for that young subaltern to have to pull the trigger. The first time he'd killed in action and he had to put a bullet in his friend. He'd become very fond of Harry . . . everyone was fond of Harry.' Her voice was becoming more indistinct. She rallied and said more brightly, 'But, at the end, I thank God he met his death looking into a friendly face! If Jock hadn't made that brave but suicidal dash into the ravine, much, very much, worse would have occurred.'

'And Jock made it back safely?' Lily hardly dared ask.

'Oh yes. He was much applauded, of course, and nobody bothered to remind him that he'd disobeyed an order. They were very relaxed about such things in those pre-war days. He only just made it back though. He was shot at as he ran and was slightly wounded. Shot at by someone firing an old-fashioned musket, a jezail.'

'And you're telling us that all this is linked in some way to Zeman?' asked Lily, trying to understand.

'I think it must be,' said Grace. 'You see, the two Afridi who had discovered Harry's broken body were young boys no older than Jock, but not just any boys, they were the two older sons of Ramazad Khan.'

'So it would have fallen on the youngest of all, Zeman, to do this badal thing? To be avenged on the British for his older brothers?' Lily frowned, working her way through to a conclusion Joe had come to some time ago. 'But, hang on – what you're saying is – not just *any* old Briton – you're saying *the* Briton, the one who knifed the Afridi? You're saying this Jock?' She fell silent for a moment and then breathed, 'Grace, this Jock, we wouldn't all know him by

233

some other name, would we? Like it might be James? James Lindsay?'

'Yes,' said Grace, 'James Lindsay. Bless the man!'

With a lurch of the heart and a sudden insight, Joe cursed himself for his blindness. He looked at Grace with anguish and asked quietly, 'Why do you say that, Grace? Why do you say, "Bless the man!" with such emotion?'

Tears had begun at last to shimmer in Grace's eyes and she dashed the sleeve of her blouse hurriedly across her face before replying slowly, 'Because at the risk of his own life, James Lindsay saved my husband from suffering an unspeakable death. Harry, my husband, Harry.'

Chapter Nineteen

There was a deep silence as Grace's story ended. They listened to the song of a bird hidden amongst the apricots, a thrush perhaps, Joe thought, adding its own sad coda to the tale. At last Iskander stirred and began to speak diffidently. 'Dr Holbrook, would you mind if I . . .?' His voice trailed away.

She smiled at him. 'I was hoping you'd be able to fill in the gaps in my tale, Iskander.'

'We speak of a time long ago. Twelve years but the memories are very clear for you and for me. I was only a boy of nine at the time of which you speak and Zeman was a year older. He was always much more the warrior than I was and used to trail about behind his older brothers begging them to take him with them on raids. At last when he was ten years old they agreed to take him and they supplied him with the only weapon that came to hand, an old jezail that had long done no more than decorate a wall of their home. He watched the battle from the safety of the crags, delighting in the British discomfiture. Finally, when the Lewis guns were brought up the Afridi decided to call it a day and retreat. Zeman's brothers were in the rear, angry at their orders, unwilling to withdraw when they were doing so well and, bringing up the rearguard, they came upon an injured British officer. He'd fallen from a cliff face and was unable to move. Zeman was told to keep watch for them up in the rocks while they . . .' Iskander paused briefly then resumed, 'robbed him and considered their next move.

'Before even Zeman was aware of what was happening a figure had leapt from the shadows and stabbed his brothers to death. The man, a man with red hair, then pulled up the shirt of one of them and slashed his flesh with the point of his dagger.'

Lily gasped and shuddered.

As though speaking only to her, Iskander said, 'This would not be the surprising and sickening deed you might think. It is the custom among the tribes to carve their tribal symbol on the backs of their enemies.'

'And sometimes they even wait until they're dead,' said Rathmore waspishly.

As though he had not even heard the interruption Iskander went on, 'Zeman remained calm. He did not cry out but aimed his jezail and fired. But the hammer stuck and the British soldier began to run. Zeman tracked him as he ran and pulled the trigger again. This time it freed itself and he was certain he had hit him. He climbed down to attend to his brothers. With a burning anger against the man who had done this he copied the letters which he could not understand on to his arm with a piece of burned wood and later copied them on to paper so that he might one day identify what he assumed to be a tribal symbol.'

'What did it say?' asked Lily. 'Do you know, Iskander?'

'No one could work it out, not even the ones among us who knew English. I showed the word to my English teacher one day in Peshawar and he could not understand either. Look!' He took a stick and wrote in a few brisk strokes in the sand: EENDO!

'Can't figure it out,' said Lily, considering.

'Nor could Zeman until some years later. At school in England he was idly writing out the letters which he regularly did to keep it fresh in his mind and his anger glowing when the boy at the next desk looked over and said, "I say, Khan, never would have taken you for a Scotsman!" Zeman asked him to explain. His neighbour was a McGregor and had recognized the motto of an enemy tribe – the Lindsays. "E'en do and spare not!"'

'Look, I'm awful sorry to be slow here but I still don't know what it means,' Lily complained.

'"Even do . . ."' said Joe. 'In other words, "Go right ahead and take no prisoners!"'

'So when, after many years, Zeman encountered in Peshawar a certain red-haired Major Lindsay who had served on the frontier before the war he resolved to be avenged for his brothers.'

'And Grace's escort duty provided the perfect opportunity,' said Joe.

'Yes, indeed. I was supposed to be in charge of the troop but Zeman insisted on coming with us as senior officer. He counted on being invited into the fort where he could get close enough to Lindsay to kill him.'

'Zeman? I'm finding this a bit hard to swallow,' said Lily. 'He was charming, he was amusing – he got on so well with James!' She gasped and then said slowly, 'Oh, Lord! Do you remember? I think I recall . . . when I was about to shoot that darned pheasant Zeman said, "Slay and spare not, Miss Coblenz!" Was he needling James? Saying, "I'm here. I know who you are." Taunting him?'

'Yes, all that. I'm sure, Lily,' said Joe. 'But look, Iskander, you must have seen this situation developing, have been aware of the awful consequences of such a rash act? I didn't see you as a bloodthirsty warmonger!'

Iskander replied a little stiffly, 'I am Afridi. I too live by the laws of pukhtunwali. I understand badal and I understand Zeman's compulsion. In his place I would have felt the same urge to avenge my brothers. Nevertheless, the time was not an opportune one. I was uneasy because we were the guests of Major Lindsay. He had welcomed us as friends within the gates of Gor Khatri. That evening after the feast I tried to talk Zeman out of his plans, to persuade him to pursue them at a later day.'

Joe wondered whether Iskander was trying to convey a message to Lily by this little speech – 'Once an Afridi,

237

always an Afridi. Untameable. *Untransplantable.*' Grace at any rate seemed to have understood and she flashed at Joe a look of unfathomable intensity.

'And what were his plans?' asked Joe, feeling he already knew the answer.

'We were both to change into our uniforms and be ready to leave the fort by the chiga gate that night. Our men had been warned and we had bribed the guards. Zeman was to go up to Lindsay's room in the middle of the night – he had found out from the sweeper which was Lindsay's room – and stab him in the throat with his dagger just as Lindsay had killed his brother. I waited all night for Zeman's signal but it never came. With some relief I assumed he'd changed his mind and I fell asleep until the noise on the stairs awoke me the next morning.'

Joe flicked a glance at Grace who was staring at the ground, determinedly silent.

'But there were two people in James's room,' said Lily. 'There was Betty. What about Betty?'

'If she had wakened he would have killed her too. Two brothers, two lives in reparation. It would not have been *my* way but I do believe Zeman was corrupted by his contact with the West where it is nothing to kill a woman. An everyday occurrence you might say. I am sure Sandilands can confirm this,' Iskander said with a touch of defiance. 'I was unable to dissuade him.'

'But he didn't succeed in his attempt,' said Joe. 'I heard James lock his door on retiring at eleven o'clock. The downstairs rooms including yours and Zeman's do not have locks and there was no reason to suppose that those on the first floor would have. But they do. Zeman would not have known that. If he had reached James's room that night he would not have been able to get in without banging the door down and that didn't happen.' He looked again at Grace but she avoided his eye. 'And Zeman died of poisoning. Now I know what you're all thinking – we've got an easy equation here. At last we have a motive and it's all beginning to add up. But is it?

Zeman is about to attempt to kill James so James, the target, finds out somehow and forestalls the attempt by killing Zeman first in a sort of premeditated self-defence. Mmm. That makes no sense to me. I know my friend. He's got a hell of a temper – I've seen him kill with a gun, a knife and even his bare hands. He wouldn't go sneaking around popping poison in his sherbet. What have you to add, Grace?'

At last she responded to his direct challenge and her eyes narrowed for a moment. A signal? A warning?

'I know your interpretation is the correct one, Joe. I am equally certain that James did not kill Zeman and I will swear to that on a Bible if you have one. But it doesn't matter, I'm afraid, what *I* think or what *you* think, because in the minds of the Afridi – and for this *you* must take the blame, Iskander – James did away with Ramazad's third son whilst his guest at the fort and also his two older sons and that's quite an overdraft on goodwill!'

'How heavily did that weigh with Ramazad when you were bargaining with him, Grace?' asked Lily.

'Ramazad! I think I caught him, just for once in his life, at an emotional moment! I told him clearly that I'd just presented him with the lives of his wife and son – he knew quite well that they would both certainly have died if I hadn't intervened. And I slipped into the balance the death of my husband fighting the Afridi.'

'Three all?' said Lily.

'Three all. As you say. It was a gamble and I was far from sure I'd be able to talk him into giving up the need to demand badal with all that tribal pride at stake, but I think he was moved by the story of my husband's death and he said to me what the Afridi always say – "But your husband died at Afridi hands!" (Not quite true but near enough.) "How can you bring yourself to save Afridi lives?" I think the euphoria of having his wife restored to him turned things in our favour and after a bit of bluster and some very uncomplimentary epithets linked with James's name, he agreed to wipe the slate clean!' She sighed. 'I think . . . I hope this marks a significant turning in our dealings with the Afridi. But what an effort!'

'And all so unnecessary!' drawled Rathmore.

They all turned to look at Rathmore who had been sitting silently with a derisive smirk on his face. 'For an intelligent woman, Dr Holbrook, you show surprising lack of insight! All this talk of weighing in the balance, bargaining lives for deaths, tribal pride, is so much sentimental claptrap!' He looked triumphantly round at the astonished faces turned to him. 'Tribal pride, indeed! I can tell you what tribal pride is worth! Oh, yes! I am in a position to tell you down to the last farthing precisely what it takes to buy off tribal pride!

'And as for *you*!' He turned his scorn on Joe. 'I suppose it makes a welcome change from routine police work haring about the desert dressed in that gawd 'elp us get-up but – really! – when it comes to being a Khan – I suppose some Khan and some just Khan't!' He greeted his own joke with a bark of laughter but no one joined him.

'Do you know what your mistake was?' he plunged on. 'Well, I'll tell you! You made the mistake of underestimating the Afridi. You assume they're just a bunch of medieval savages locked into their centuries-old traditions and you think you can get the better of them by playing them at their own tribal customs game. Nonsense! They would always beat you at that! Oh, no, that's not the way. I, on the other hand, saw straight to the heart of our problem and solved it! We were always going to be released today. Oh, yes! I had negotiated it before ever the circus came to town!' He cast a derisive look at Grace and Joe and Lily, still wearing their native dress. 'Would you like to hear how I did it?'

'Nobody's going to step out of the rocks and shoot him,' Lily thought. 'I'm going to have to do it myself!' She touched for reassurance the bulge of the small pistol she kept in her boot and calmed her irritation by deciding which part of his bloated body to aim at first.

Not waiting for a reply, Rathmore pounded on. 'It's

240

obvious to me that a man who can run a tribe of such size efficiently must be a fair sort of businessman. And that's how I dealt with him. He recognized me for what I was . . .'

'And what were you, Dermot?' Lily drawled.

'A businessman like himself and one empowered to deal with him in the name of the British Government. Money, Miss Coblenz. I'm sure I don't need to tell you of all people how the power of money transcends all languages, all little local difficulties. I explained my plans for opening up a trade route over the frontier and into Afghanistan. He understood at once what was involved and made some positive and very helpful suggestions. Roads. That's what it all comes down to. He pointed out (I had already noticed) that the road system is not good. Patchy and unsuitable in most places for the lorry transport I have in mind. Did you know that the contracts for road building in this country are hotly sought after? No? It's the local tribes who undertake the work and there is strong competition between them to be awarded the contracts by the govern-ment. The Afridi lost out last time to the Mohmands and they've never forgiven them. I was able to say, "This time it'll all be different, Ramazad, because I will be the one advising on the distribution of contracts. But of course I can only do that if I am free to deal in Simla." He took my point at once, of course. He offered, very sensibly, to extend the terms of reference to include an Afridi protec-tion squad of Khassadars, I think he called them, who will guard the road workers initially and stay on as road patrols for the convoys when they start coming through. Excellent man! He has quite an eye for detail and is a tough negotiator. Just the kind of man I like to do business with!'

'In Chicago, we call this a "shake-down",' Lily muttered. 'He didn't try to sell you tickets to a ward ball too, did he?'

Rathmore ignored her and his tone hardened. 'He was quite distressed that I should have been put to such incon-

241

venience by that man.' Rathmore pointed an accusing finger at Iskander. 'And agreed to make amends by outlawing him. Quite right too. Least he could have done. Known troublemaker, everyone agrees. And now an outlaw. I wonder if you're aware that under Afridi law I could shoot him where he sits, no questions asked?'

The shaft of hatred Iskander directed at Rathmore was more disturbing to Joe than the unsheathing of a dagger but Rathmore seemed comfortably unconcerned.

'I'd arranged for an armed escort for myself and Miss Coblenz back to Gor Khatri and I have to say I was afraid you might have wrecked my careful arrangements when your rag tag and bobtail outfit rolled into the fort!'

The deep silence that followed this flourish was finally broken by Lily. She looked lazily at Rathmore and addressed the company in her thickest western drawl. 'Gee! If this were Daddy's ranch I'd ask Slim and the boys to string this feller up by his balls from the nearest cottonwood tree.'

'Don't think those wizened old apricots would take the strain,' said Grace ambiguously. 'The river? We could dunk him in the river?'

'No, an anthill's what we want,' said Joe looking round. 'Isn't that one over there? If you peg a chap out over one . . .'

'That takes too long,' said Iskander. 'Three days at least. But the sun's still high. We could slit his eyelids and tie him to a tree facing west. He'd be blind and mad before sunset.'

'Oh, very funny!' snarled Rathmore. 'Sticks and stones may break my bones . . .'

'Okay, then,' said Joe, 'sticks and stones it is!'

He jumped to his feet and Rathmore ran for his horse, screaming abuse over his shoulder as he ran. '. . . ungrateful! . . . police clod! . . . when I get back to Simla! . . . Johnny Simpkins in the Home Office . . . cut you down to size! . . . pounding the beat in Seven Dials!'

He set off at a gallop heading west for Gor Khatri.

'All the same,' said Joe, laughing but rather ashamed of their display, 'I'd rather he didn't get too far ahead of us. Lord knows what rubbish he'd put into James's head if he arrived before us.'

'Okay. Mount up, folks,' said Lily and she made her way at Joe's side over to the horses now tethered in the shade of the thickest tree. She paused, her hand on the bridle, to look up into the branches. 'Look at that, Joe,' she said. 'The bird. You kind of forget in this wilderness that creatures can thrive in the nooks and crannies. What is that?'

Joe looked. A parent bird was balancing precariously on the edge of a nest, thrusting something unspeakable into the throat of its young. He stared and was quiet for a moment. 'It's a bloody marvel, that's what it is! It's the answer to everything! Oh, sorry, Lily. The bird. Yes, it's an, er, a lesser-spotted Himalayan mountain thrush. Yes, that's what it is.'

'Oh yeah? And you're a greater-spotted liar bird! What's up, Joe?'

A second later, she answered her own question. 'Jeez! I see it too! Oh, but they couldn't have! Could they? No! Bet they did though! Oh, Joe, we've got a few questions to put to certain parties who've been pulling our legs and jerking our chain when we get back to the fort!'

Chapter Twenty

James Lindsay reviewed the chaos into which his life, both private and official, had descended with considerable misgiving. From the lookout post above the gates he scanned the distant hills. Joe, his dearest friend, was out there, probably in danger of his life if not already dead. And this was not his problem! Honest Joe! Working so desperately towards doing the wrong thing! Should he have confided in him? James considered for a moment and then decided, in his soldier's calculating way, that it had probably been worth the risk. But where had it left them? It had left them with Joe running the risk. Thinly – very thinly disguised as a Scout, he was in a situation where, if he was discovered, he would be instantly executed as a ferenghi. And all in an effort to extricate Lily. Unreliable Lily! Lily on whom the only reliance that could be placed was that she would say or do the wrong thing, be in the wrong place and, if she could find a way to do so, enter the wrong room in the wrong clothes at the wrong time. He contemplated Lily and shuddered.

And as if that weren't enough, James acknowledged that he had an abiding problem with Iskander! Enigmatic, a subtle plotter and – whatever else – a major player in the unravelling of the cat's-cradle into which local politics seemed to have descended.

Once more, binoculars pressed to his eyes, he swept the approaches to the fort. What was this? He squinted again into the late afternoon sun. A solitary rider was coming in. A rider on a large Afghani grey. James stared and stared.

'Rathmore? Rathmore, by God! Now what?' Rathmore coming in alone? The lone survivor of some awful catastrophe? With a shudder James remembered the desperate ride of Dr Brydon who was spotted by the garrison at Jelalabad, struggling in half dead on an exhausted horse across the plain only to whisper that he was the only man of a force of sixteen thousand to make it back from Kabul. The rest had been shot and slashed to pieces by Afghani tribesmen, the women with them killed or taken hostage. Eighty years ago and now it was happening again.

In agony, James wiped the sweat from his eyes and squinted through his field glasses. No – the rider was not quite alone. He seemed to be the one-man advance guard of a party of five or six. Was he being pursued? James thought not. The group following in his wake were not attempting to catch up with him but riding at more or less the same pace, keeping their distance. Through the dust rising round the party it was hard to tell who they were. But it was undoubtedly Rathmore in front and going at quite a pace.

'I'm not in the mood for Rathmore,' James thought. 'Do I go and meet him? Do I have him sent to me? That might give me a moral edge. No, I'll go down.' He picked up his cap, set it on his head and reluctantly descended the stairs so that when Rathmore arrived at the fort, he was standing ready to receive him with an insouciance he did not feel.

Stiff and indignant, Rathmore slid from his horse.

'Lord Rathmore! An unexpected pleasure! I had hardly hoped to see you. And now what can I offer you? Not too late for tea, I hope?'

Rathmore eyed him sourly. 'That's enough, Lindsay!' he said. 'The sooner you realize that you're in considerable trouble the sooner we can start talking sense! I am here in an official capacity . . .'

James interrupted him. 'I would have said a semi-official capacity but do please continue.'

'. . . in an official capacity,' Rathmore repeated, 'and

245

under your very nose, almost I would say with your connivance, I have been incarcerated!'

'Would you say "incarcerated"?' James enquired mildly. 'I would have said "kidnapped". But go on.'

'I have been seized upon, made off with, exposed to every sort of indignity and I want to know what you're going to do about it! There!' he pointed. 'There's the scoundrel responsible and I want to know what you're going to do with him!'

The small party wound its way towards the fort and James stared and stared again. He identified three Scouts, one of whom might be Joe; he identified, bobbing with excitement, the fair hair and slender figure of Lily dressed in green native tunic and trousers; he saw the comfortable figure of Grace taking as always the day's problems one by one. Finally he saw the figure of Iskander, calm, debonair and unruffled, sure of himself, apparently sure of his welcome and very ready to greet James as an old friend and valued colleague.

'There he is!' said Rathmore. 'There's the rogue! He kept me prisoner and threatened to slit my eyelids. I insist on his immediate arrest!'

'One moment, Rathmore,' said James and he stepped forward to greet the party. 'First things first. Aslam! Yussuf!' he called out in greeting to the Scouts. Smiles, laughter and exclamation followed and the Scouts were dismissed, both men pleased to be setting off for barracks with the keen anticipation of telling their story to the rest of the unit.

'Grace, Lily, Joe, Iskander,' James nodded to each in turn. 'Delighted to have you all back again safe and sound. If you'd like to come with me to the durbar hall I can offer you some refreshment. Now where have you got to? Tea? Or would a glass of sherry be more welcome?'

Rathmore was dancing with rage. 'You're not going to invite that black-avised fiend back inside the fort! Think, man! Think what happened last time! Don't you ever learn?'

246

'I haven't made up my mind quite yet,' said James, 'whether to offer Iskander the hospitality of the fort or the guardhouse. I will let you know when I have made further enquiries. Now, perhaps you would all like to return to your rooms which are standing ready – I'm sure you'll all want to freshen up and, er, change – and we'll meet in the durbar hall in, let's say an hour. That suit everyone?'

Rathmore turned with a splutter of disgust and stamped off through the gate. The others followed, entering with varying degrees of eagerness the confines of the fort. Joe lagged behind in the hope of exchanging a few words with James but his friend was avoiding his eye and, it seemed, anxious not to hear Joe's story for the moment. There was something about his manner that puzzled Joe. His old confidence and decisiveness had returned, though, knowing what Joe now knew, this was inexplicable. Oh, well, Joe would go along with it for the time being. His moment to unravel all this would come.

'By the way, Joe,' James was saying, 'hope you won't mind but I've had your things moved down to Zeman's old room. Had to accommodate yet another VIP who arrived this afternoon and I thought it more appropriate to put him upstairs.' He waved a hand to the far side of the square where there stood an open-topped tourer, grey with dust, the flag of the High Commissioner of the North-West Frontier Province drooping wearily on the bonnet.

'See you in an hour then.' He put a hand on Joe's shoulder and his voice lost its briskness. 'Damned glad you're back! I'll go and tell Betty – she's been worried sick. Now, where's Grace?' And he went back to help Grace who was struggling to take her medical case from her horse.

In a few quick strides Joe caught up with Lily Coblenz and neatly placed himself in front of her before she could go through the archway into the guest wing. She looked up at him, resigned and truculent.

247

'Into the garden. Now,' said Joe pointing an imperious finger.

When he was sure they were not being observed he said carefully, 'I was wondering if you had anything to say before this all gets a bit public? That, you can't have failed to notice, was the Commissioner's car in the courtyard. When we appear in front of him with our stories I'd like to think we were saying the same thing.'

'What were you expecting me to say?'

'Well, to start with, something on the lines of "Sorry," "I apologize for the trouble I've caused," or even "Aw, shucks!" and, to go on with, an explanation of the precise nature of your "arrangement" with your abductor. And before you tell me it's none of my business – it certainly *is* my business! I've been placed in the unenviable position of answering for your safety for the duration of your stay. If I feel I am no longer able to fulfil this obligation I shall put you – hog-tied if necessary – in the back seat of Sir John Deane's motor car ready for delivery back to Peshawar.'

'I've nothing to apologize for! All this and worse would have happened if I'd not been here. Why, you wouldn't even have known where we were, I'll bet, if I hadn't signalled to that plane!'

'That was *you*? Ah. That was well done, Lily,' said Joe, relenting. 'The pilot noticed your flash and it confirmed other information we had concerning your whereabouts. But Iskander? What have you to reveal?'

'Nothing. I've had no chance to speak to the guy! You know he was sent away from the village!'

'Not good enough, Lily! Something's been going on.'

'Oh, okay then, I suppose you'll have to know. There was this jirga meeting of the whole tribe – men, that is – and I saw it all. Halima told me what was going on. She's the Malik's wife but she's also Iskander's sister, bet you didn't know that! Iskander set himself up against Ramazad. Big mistake! He was outranked, out-talked and then outlawed by Big Chief Serpent Tongue. Well, I felt kind of sorry for the feller. He's no family apart from

Halima and now he hasn't even a tribe. He doesn't deserve that, Joe! Now I know these Pathans love their native land but they do travel. It's not unknown. In fact, they're all over India and some have even gone to Australia. I sent him a note before he disappeared telling him to meet me back at the fort and discuss . . . coming back to the States with me,' she finished defiantly. 'That's no mean offer, Joe!'

'I'm sure it's not but, tell me, Lily, and I intend to press you on this – on what terms exactly did you envisage Iskander would be accompanying you?'

'I've given that quite a lot of thought,' she said. 'And I'm open to suggestions. Bodyguard, companion, adviser on Indian affairs? How does that sound? He could be based in Delhi or even come back to the States with us. Who knows? He's just the kind of man my father would get along with. He'll find him a job. Iskander speaks English better than your average American, he's smart and he's charming.' Her eyes narrowed for a second and she added, 'Besides which, things going as they are – the company expanding into India – it wouldn't be bad to have someone on the ground who knows how things work. Someone we can be sure will look out for our side because the other side has rejected him. That's the best kinda loyalty you can get, Joe – the one-way pull kind.'

'Yes, I see what you mean and I agree, but Lily – this man is no one's poodle. And we all heard what he had to say about his Pathan nature back there at the river. I think he was trying to warn you, prepare you for his rejection of your offer. And, anyway, there's probably little we could do to help him in the circumstances. He must be under considerable scrutiny by the powers that operate in this land – after all, he's guilty of kidnap and abduction times two and though *you* may be prepared to forgive and forget, Lord Rathmore will be demanding retribution.'

'Retribution? What kind of retribution?'

'Very serious, I'm afraid. In fact, if I'd been Iskander, I would have avoided coming back here. He could easily have done that. He is, under British law, guilty of abduction, kidnap, threatening to kill. I think Rathmore could talk this up into a capital charge if he sets his mind to it.'

Lily's face darkened. 'Rathmore! He'll set his mind to it all right! Joe, you've got to find a way of fixing him! Can't you think of something?'

'I'll try. It would give me considerable personal satisfaction to nail the man but I'm not hopeful. Men like Rathmore are protected by often unseen and undeclared forces. They do favours for those high up in government and one day they call in those favours. He struts around and behaves as though he were impregnable and I'm sad to say that's because he very probably is. I think it certain that he has it in his power not only to wreck my career but that of James as well and certainly to see to it that Iskander is either hanged or, at best, put into the deepest dungeon in Peshawar and left there for many years. We'll find, I think, that in all this he will be supported by Edwin Burroughs. I must say, Lily, I'm not looking forward to this meeting.'

To Joe's surprise Lily put out a hand and rubbed solicitously at his eyebrow. 'You'll think of something, Joe! But no one's going to pay a whole lot of attention to you if you don't smarten yourself up a bit and wash off that eye paint or whatever it is. Come on! Let's hear that Lindsay war cry again – what was it? – "E'en do and spare not!" That's not bad!'

An hour later, washed and confident in a fresh uniform, Joe ran upstairs and tapped on Lily's door. She joined him looking cool in a short blue silk dress and a simple sapphire-studded necklace.

'Not sure what sort of entertainment James has lined up for us – could be anything from court martial to beauty parade,' she said. 'But if the Commissioner's going to be there I thought it couldn't hurt to go for the angelic look.'

'You missed by about a mile,' said Joe, looking at her appreciatively, 'but don't worry – he'll like the result.' He peered at her face more closely and she swept a concealing hand over her nose.

'I know! I look simply awful! Ride two days without a sun helmet and see if your nose looks any better!'

'Before we go down, Lily, there's something I'd like you to look at with me. What do you say to a little breaking and entering?'

He paused outside James's room and listened, ear to the door. 'No sound.'

'There won't be. I left my door open because I wanted to hear Betty if she came upstairs. Just to say hullo . . . They never came up. I guess they stayed down there in the durbar hall. Grace didn't come up until about half an hour ago – now I wonder what can have detained her downstairs, don't *you*, Joe? Telling tales out of school? She went back down five minutes ago. We're alone up here,' she finished quietly. 'How about the ground floor rooms?'

'They've all gone over apart from Rathmore. I heard him still crashing about. I listened shamelessly at the door.'

Joe smiled. Lily knew exactly what he was up to. He pointed in silence to the door of James's room.

'I had already noticed that,' she said, eyes dancing.

Joe knocked on the door and called, 'James? Betty?' Hearing no answer he opened the door and stepped inside followed by Lily. A perfectly ordinary scene met their eye. Neat, clean and utilitarian, there was nothing apparently to attract attention but Joe methodically gave every item of furniture an assessing look. Of the two narrow beds, the one nearer the door was obviously that of James. Tucked underneath the brass candlestick on the bedside table there was a War Office pamphlet. Lily could not resist moving closer to read the title.

'"Victualling On The March"' she read out, rolling her

eyes in disbelief. 'Jeez! Do you suppose he's reading it aloud a chapter a night to Betty?'

On Betty's matching table between the two beds was a Bible and a copy of *Home Chat* wedged under her candlestick and open at a story by P.G. Wodehouse. At the foot of Betty's bed was Minto's box. Peering inside, Joe grunted. 'No one at home. Our furry friend has apparently gone to the meeting as well. I think I've seen all I need to see. How about you, Lily?'

'One more thing, Joe.' She moved to the small cubicle which passed for a bathroom and opened the door. 'Same as the other rooms, I guess,' she said. 'Water jug, washing bowl, washing things. Yup! That's it! We can go now.'

They left the room, closing the door behind them, and stood together at the head of the stairs before descending. 'Almost impossible,' thought Joe, 'to come downstairs from a bedroom floor and not look guilty! Perhaps we should come down hand in hand? That would baffle and enrage Rathmore! Baffle and enrage Burroughs too. Leave them all with the impression that Lily and I have spent the last hour in bed together!' And with a sudden stab to the heart, he thought, 'How I wish it were true!' In a moment of mutual solidarity and bravado, they linked arms and went downstairs.

As they walked across the square towards the durbar hall, the insistent notes of a bugle call floated over the fort and, to amuse and distract Lily, Joe sang the words the soldiery had long ago fitted to the Officers' Mess Call:

> *'Officers' wives have puddings and pies*
> *But sergeants' wives have skilly,*
> *And the private's wife has nothing at all*
> *To fill her poor little belly.'*

'I know how she feels! Do you realize, Joe, I've had nothing to eat for over a day? What I wouldn't give for a bowlful of skilly – *whatever* that is!'

'It's grits – I think you'd call it grits,' said Joe. 'But didn't they give you food at Mahdan Khotal? The Scouts and I were only there for about three hours but they sent us three lots of refreshment in that time. Surely . . .?'

'Oh, they kept sending me plates of this and that but I couldn't eat. When someone you like's screaming in agony and probably dying in the next room it sort of shuts down your appetite.'

'We may find the next hour has much the same effect,' said Joe lugubriously as they arrived at the open door of the durbar hall.

They stood for a moment in the doorway allowing their eyes to adjust to the darker interior. Already seated around a table which had been set out in the centre of the room, James and Betty waited side by side, ready to defy the world. A small white face peered out from Betty's lap and snarled. Minto, too, was ready as always to defy the world. Edwin Burroughs, bored and bleak, was giving nothing away; Iskander sat with blank face and expressionless eyes; Fred, as ever cheerful, smiled his pleasure at seeing them. Grace, looking exhausted and wary, just managed a wan smile of welcome. At the head of the table with his back to them was a grey-haired and solid figure. All turned to greet them as they stepped into the room.

'Well, there you are!' came an amiable and gravelly voice and the figure at the head of the table turned. Not the Commissioner. Much, much worse! Inevitably perhaps: Sir George.

'There now,' he said, his face wreathed in avuncular smiles. 'There now! The two people above all whom I wanted to see! Sandilands, the Harbinger of Doom and Miss Coblenz, the Sower of Discord. The fact they should both be under restraint can hardly have escaped anybody but we will first see what they have to say. Now, come and sit by me, Miss Coblenz, and may I say how well it suits you to have been out in the sun? Sandilands, why don't you sit next to your charge? And now we only await Lord Rathmore.'

He turned again to Lily and said conversationally, 'I had a telephone call from your esteemed father yesterday morning. How on earth he got through I can't imagine but there you are – that's Americans for you. And didn't they after all invent the electric telephone? Or have I got that wrong? He asked how you were. I didn't know how you were! So I said, "Fine!" He then asked *where* you were. I didn't know that either so I said you'd gone to spend the weekend with friends. That's rather a loose description of your recent excursion into the inaccessible interior but I didn't think the time was ripe for a larger account. I'll just pause there and ask you the question – "How are you?"'

'Starving!' said Lily with spirit. 'Haven't had anything to eat for twenty-four hours and not much to drink.'

'Help yourself, Lily,' said Betty, suddenly contrite. 'There are sandwiches. Not very exotic, I'm afraid. I cut them myself. I didn't know how many to cut for.' And a very English-looking plate of hard-boiled egg and cress, cucumber and corned beef, lamb and pickle sandwiches was hurried down the table to Lily.

'Aw! Wow! It's not puddings and pies but it shore beats skilly,' said Lily, helping herself.

'In a manner of speaking, Sir George,' said Joe with a helpful smile, 'you could well say that Lily had spent the weekend in the country with friends. She was never for a moment out of the sight of Iskander or Iskander's sister and later Grace and myself. Lord Rathmore too, of course, was of the party.'

Joe was momentarily taken aback by his own suppleness. George's ability to manipulate the truth was evidently catching. A fleeting narrowing of the clever old eyes in satisfaction made Joe want to kick himself. Was he already following in the direction George had decided they would all go? He looked critically at the man Lily had concluded was the chief, though unacknowledged, authority in India.

To recognize the fact that it was Sunday and not, therefore, a working day, he was suavely but casually dressed in a dark blue blazer bearing on its pocket the insignia of an obscure but distinguished and long-defunct Cambridge cricket club, white flannel trousers and a club tie. George Jardine looked as though his Bentley had just dropped him off at Hurlingham to watch a chukka or two with friends. There was no indication in his bearing that he must have set out on his journey immediately after putting down the telephone on speaking to Joe at nine o'clock on Saturday morning. Joe knew just enough about the workings of India to guess that he had been driven to Umballa to get a train – probably a special summoned up at a moment's notice for official use – and travelled the four hundred miles west to Peshawar. Sir John Deane would have sent a car to pick him up at the station somewhere round about midnight.

After a night's sleep at the Commissioner's residence and an unhurried opportunity over breakfast to fill himself in on the situation to date and to decide with Sir John what the official line was going to be, Joe calculated, he would have set off for Gor Khatri. Sir George's jocular charm did not disguise from Joe the realization that his very presence here at the heart of things testified to the extreme seriousness of their predicament. Joe might be the Harbinger of Doom but George was, to his mind, the Deus ex Machina, the Big Gun wheeled out to level the opposition. His anxiety increased. This spoke of a formidable opposition.

Lily, however, seemed unaffected. 'That's right! I was with friends the whole time and if any nosy parker wants to know, that's what they'll hear from me!' she said stoutly.

Edwin Burroughs tapped his finger ends on the table with exasperation but remained silent. Fred wrestled with a smile.

'Family occasion, you might say,' Lily went on, enjoying

her invention. 'Iskander took me to stay with his sister, the Malik's wife, and I was lucky enough to be there for the birth of her child.'

It was Grace's turn to look thoughtful.

'Ah, yes! Alexander! The convenor of this jolly expedition, the Afridi Robin Hood!' said Sir George. And then, turning to the company at large, 'I always call him Alexander. It's what Iskander means – did you all know that? Alexander the Great! He rose to the occasion, you know, conquered the civilized world, and the interesting thing to see will be if Iskander can do the same. For various reasons this would seem to be a time of opportunity.' He smiled benevolently around the table.

On cue but with her mouth full, Lily cut in, '*We* have an opportunity – that is to say the Coblenz Corporation have an opportunity, an opportunity in which we may be so lucky as to involve Iskander.'

The room looked at her with astonishment. All, that is, except Iskander himself who looked thoughtfully down at the table in front of him.

'It's obviously no secret,' she went on, 'but just so's everyone's got it straight – I've offered Iskander a position with the Coblenz Corporation. Either in Delhi or in the States, it hasn't been decided yet. And I should say he's still considering the offer – it's still on the table, you might say.'

'Well,' said Sir George genially, 'I may be old but I'm not too old to experience surprise occasionally and there aren't many people around in this part of the world who can surprise me but, Lily, it would seem you are one of them! Perhaps you can surprise me too, Alexander?' he said.

'We are in a discussion,' said Iskander. 'These things do not depend on me. There are many people to be consulted. Perhaps some of them are round this table. It would not be right to say more than that the proposition is under discussion.'

'Politics,' said Sir George, 'are like unto running an infants' school. Did you know that? Put the infants

256

together and they will either play together or kill each other. I've seen it time and again. And the question is – and the reason for my being here at all is – which is it to be?' He turned to James. 'Anything in that bottle, James?' he enquired, pointing. 'It's been a long day. I wouldn't refuse a whisky. Others may feel the same . . .'

'Yes, of course,' said James, hurriedly passing out glasses and jugs of water. 'There's whisky and sherry and fruit juice of some kind. Please help yourselves. Oh, and I should say that I've arranged for a meal to be laid on for all of us in the officers' mess as soon as we're finished here.'

'The reason for *my* being here,' said Iskander carefully and quietly, 'one of the reasons, is to ensure that the proper enquiry is made into the death of my cousin Zeman. It seems to me that there is still a mystery hanging over this event, a mystery which more than one present would like to see resolved.'

Edwin Burroughs helped himself to a glass of water. 'So far as I have any function round this table,' he said peevishly, 'it is to evaluate the relevance of what seems to be laughingly called the "Forward Policy" in the light of recent events. I make no secret of it – I recommend withdrawal from this cockpit of war. Our presence here is an incitement to military response. By withdrawing to a sustainable frontier we will cut down dramatically on expense – of lives and materials.' He sat back in his chair and looked round the room.

'It perhaps goes without saying,' interpolated Fred, 'that I am here to consider the extension of the Forward Policy. I believe, unlike Burroughs, that the only way to assure peace is to patrol the frontier from the air. But the issue is an extremely complicated one and I'm not prepared to say more than that at this moment. I reserve my position.'

'Good old Fred!' thought Joe. 'He's learning!'

'And now,' said Sir George, 'since we're all showing our shopping lists, I turn to Grace. Grace who has so often "stilled the seething cup of discord with a cool breath of

257

wisdom". Your move, Grace,' he said, cocking a lively grey eyebrow.

'My concerns,' she said almost angrily, 'do not vary from year to year or month to month, certainly not from day to day. They are, as they have always been, to create a situation where "every man can sit under his fig tree or under his vine and no man shall make him afraid." Little enough to ask, you'd think. Unfortunately, in this part of the world, anyone sitting under a fig tree for ten seconds together is likely to get shot and his figs stolen. It is my purpose in life always to save lives not squander them and I have no respect or sympathy for those of any race who would endanger others whatever their motives. As far as I have any purpose here I suppose it would be to urge that this corner of the frontier be left in peace.'

'And I – we – share Grace's aspiration,' said James, 'as we always have. Whether we're any nearer to achieving it remains to be seen.'

'Thank you, James. Thank you too, Betty. I always know where *you* stand.' Sir George sat back in his chair, evidently pleased with what he had heard. 'So, it appears that, although we approach from different angles, we are all aiming for the same thing – peace.'

The door at the end of the hall banged open to admit Rathmore. He was – and to those present it seemed his habitual state – purple in the face with rage. Lily looked at him critically. 'He's a sort of not very successful mass-produced copy of Sir George,' she thought. It was almost as though he had waited to see what Sir George was wearing and had dressed himself likewise. The blazer: large golden insignia on the pocket. The tie: widely striped and accompanied by a matching silk scarf supporting flawlessly creased white trousers. The cuff-links: where Sir George was wearing a battered gold pair, Rathmore wore large amethysts.

Rathmore exploded indignantly, 'Sir George? Good Lord! Wasn't expecting to see you here! I'm hoping we've met here to bring certain people to justice! And I'm pleased to see, by your presence, that at last the powers that be are taking this seriously!'

George got up and walked over to seize Rathmore by the hand and shake it with what Joe considered to be undue warmth and for an undue length of time. 'Indeed!' he said. 'And the purpose of this meeting, my dear Rathmore, is to determine exactly what has passed over the last few days and make any recommendations that seem appropriate to my lords and masters in Simla. But I don't need to explain the inner workings of government to a fellow statesman and diplomat . . . enough, perhaps, to say that it is my aim to see that "every brother has his due". Eh? What? We've kept you a seat at the foot of the table.' An unctuous smile and a languid hand ushered Rathmore into the last remaining place, facing Sir George.

Rathmore was looking surprised and a little deflated but, Joe would have sworn, was beginning to recover something of his accustomed air of smug arrogance. 'Ah. Yes,' he said. 'Pleased to see that someone in this sorry mess is on the square!'

'"On the square?" . . . "Every brother?" . . . George! The old weasel!' thought Joe. 'I know where he's going with this! Perhaps I'll help him along!'

In a spirit of mischief Joe rose quietly to his feet, poured out a large whisky and deferentially offered it to Rathmore. 'You're one behind us, sir,' he murmured, patting him lightly on the shoulder. 'I think you take it neat?'

Puzzled and wary, Rathmore grunted but seemed happy to take a large swallow followed by another. Joe, hovering solicitously, topped up the glass and, leaving the bottle by Rathmore's elbow, resumed his seat. Sir George raised his own glass, admiring the delicate amber of the Glenlivet against the soft lamplight. 'Only the best for the officers of Gor Khatri, what! It's not champagne but I can't think of a more suitable tipple with which to charge my glass and toast the hero of the hour! Lord Rathmore! I understand that congratulations are due. Single-handedly, you have

259

pulled off a coup which has eluded the combined efforts of His Majesty's Government and armed forces for decades. You have brought us peace and a trading agreement with the Afridi.'

Rathmore gobbled in astonishment.

'I see you're surprised that I know already? Grace and Iskander were both eager to fill in the details before the meeting started. I make a point of finding out what's going on from the horse's mouth, you'll find. The only way, I think you'll agree?'

Grace and Iskander were both fixing George with suspicious eyes but he carried on oblivious, 'When the authorities in Simla hear about your exploits – your mad dash into enemy territory . . . running the gauntlet of the Afridi forces . . . (by the way, old chap, if you take my advice you'll say you "took safe conduct" – that's the phrase – don't want to appear *too* hot-headed, no one trusts a hothead!) and when they hear about your bargaining with the old rascal Ramazad, you'll find yourself fêted. (He's been known to get the better of many a wily old negotiator including, I have to admit, yours truly!) You'll be a hero! You must be prepared to be consulted as to how to deal with the Pathan – prepared to reveal how you managed it – prepared to be an *authority*. I have to warn you that after a time you may find it begins to weigh a little heavily though – let us learn the sad lesson of notoriety from Lawrence of Arabia!'

'"Rathmore of the Frontier",' hissed Lily. 'Doesn't quite have the same ring.'

Joe looked around the table. For the first time ever, Burroughs and Fred Moore-Simpson were united in their expression which was a blend of outrage and unwilling admiration. James and Betty were tight-lipped and staring at the table. Grace, uncharacteristically, was concentrating on sipping her whisky. Iskander was staring mutinously into the opposite wall.

'Watch it, George!' Joe thought. 'I see what you're doing but any moment now you're going to *overdo* it and Rathmore will catch the edge of your scorn and all your masonic advantage will be lost. And two promising careers will be lost too, to say nothing of Iskander's life!'

He stood up and raised his glass. 'A toast!' he announced. 'To peace on the frontier!'

Everyone, including Lord Rathmore, including Iskander, raised a glass and echoed his words.

Lily leaned to Joe and whispered, 'That was quite a performance! And like a good shepherd George has got all the sheep herded into the right pen! With a little help from his faithful dog, of course! But do you suppose, Joe, he hasn't noticed that one of 'em's a *black* sheep?'

Chapter Twenty-One

'That there's a killer still at large, you mean? Nothing escapes his notice. What we've just heard is the first barrel of the shotgun. Wait for the second!'

After the strained silence of the occasion, a general hubbub broke out as relief washed through the company and they began to talk amongst themselves. Fred was anxious to question Rathmore on the strength of the defences and the layout of Mahdan Khotal, Edwin Burroughs to establish the strength of the Malik as a diplomatist and as a leader of armed men. He wished to know if the Malik would conform to the Tammany definition of an honest man, that is, 'one who would stay bought'. Grace, serious and concerned, engaged Iskander in conversation about the state of health of his sister when last seen and offered her congratulations on the birth of a healthy nephew. Rathmore downed his third whisky and launched himself into his first public account of his adventures behind enemy lines. To the shared amusement of Joe and Lily, it was noticed that already his role was becoming more dashing in retrospect and they had no doubt that by the time he got back to Simla he would be presenting himself as a blend of Curzon and Kitchener with a dash of T.E. Lawrence.

Genially, Sir George broke in, calling his flock to order. 'I know James has organized supper for us all in the mess . . . something special, James? Shepherd's pie? Wonderful! My favourite! Especially with a good burgundy. And a jam roly-poly to follow? Perfection! Perhaps we shouldn't keep the staff waiting then? Dermot, Edwin, Fred, if you'd like to start off, the rest of us will join you in a minute. I believe there's just one more i to dot and one more t to cross before I can write up my report. The matter of Iskander's query. Easily resolved, I think, if we can just hear what Grace has to say but no need to detain everyone . . . . Fred, I can see, is ready for his nose-bag.'

Fred, indeed, was eager for his supper but quick also to understand the dismissal and co-operatively led the way from the durbar room. The rest of the party seated themselves again and looked at each other. James and Betty were sitting close together, Betty's hand protectively over James's. Grace and Iskander were giving nothing away. Sir George's smile faded as the others left the room.

'Here comes the second barrel,' said Lily.

They all looked expectantly at Sir George.

'Had a boil on my neck once,' he said. 'Nasty great red thing. Used to call it a "Delhi sore", I believe. Swelled and swelled and the medico said there was only one thing for it – lance it. He did. Messy business, pus and gore all over the place, but he was right. The minute the pressure was relieved and all the nastiness expelled it started to get better. I have a feeling we have the same sort of situation here with this business of the death of Zeman and I'm going to prescribe the same sort of treatment. Short and sharp but I'm afraid none of us is going to escape uncontaminated. And I'm handing the scalpel – not to *you*, Grace – you're part of the problem – but to Joe. Carry on, Joe!'

'Iskander's persistence in questioning the official account of Zeman's death, it must be admitted, was entirely justified,' Joe began without hesitation. George had no time for hesitators. 'Zeman did not die an accidental death due to food or any other kind of poisoning. He was killed that night but not in the circumstances described, not in the place in which his body was found and not by the method all had assumed.'

'Well, that'll do for the first cut,' said Sir George. 'Now squeeze the rest out inch by inch and don't forget *I* was not a party to this little charade so you'll have to fill in the details to *my* satisfaction. So, continue, Joe!'

'I'll start with the testimony of two witnesses who, I am certain, have been telling me the apparently inconsistent truth right from the start. Lily. And Minto.'

The terrier looked up on hearing his name and bared his teeth with a rumbling growl.

'That horrid little dog?' said Sir George, unbelieving.

'No other! And while he's showing his teeth, I'd like everyone to note the size of the gap between his canines.'

Everyone peered at Minto's mouth. Although pleased by the attention, he turned his growl up a few points.

'It was a hot night and we had all eaten far too much; some of us had, indeed, drunk more than we should have done.' He moved smoothly into the next part of his story – Lily's account of her agonized hour in the garden – deciding shamelessly to edit it to spare her blushes. 'Lily could not sleep, she has told us, and went down to the garden to get a breath of air at – oh, what did you tell me, Lily? – sometime before one o'clock?'

Lily nodded. Iskander looked up, surprised and anxious.

'When she went into the garden she heard Minto growl as she passed his box which at that time was at the bottom of the stairs. But she saw that the garden was already occupied by others who could not sleep. There were two figures seated on the marble bench. Could you tell us what you saw, Lily?'

'It was Zeman and Iskander. They seemed to be arguing. Or at least Iskander was angry with Zeman – Zeman was just laughing. I guessed it was a private moment and I didn't want to interrupt – I mean, it was hardly the time for a sociable chat – so I hid behind a tree and went back into the guest wing after they did. Oh, and this time, Minto didn't growl at me.'

'This tells us two important things,' Joe went on. 'That at the time Grace gave us for his death Zeman was alive and well, and this must cast doubt on the whole of Grace's testimony. It was this false timing that alerted Iskander to the possibility of dirty work at the crossroads and inspired him to pick up a hostage and flee with him until we British had begun to acknowledge the obvious facts.'

Iskander nodded.

'And secondly, that Minto was no longer in his box when Lily returned to her room. So, where was he? Where more likely than where we see him now? Tucked up with his mistress. Can you confirm this, Betty?'

Betty cleared her throat and spoke carefully. 'Yes, Joe, that's true. At home in Peshawar he sleeps on my bed and I suppose he couldn't understand why he was suddenly being banished, and in this strange place. James and I locked our door at about eleven, I think.'

'Yes, I heard you while I was on my beat,' Joe confirmed.

'Well, we talked about our evening for a bit and James fell asleep at about midnight, I should guess. I stayed awake because I wasn't well. In fact I was sick. At about one o'clock. Not sure if it was so-called "morning" sickness striking again – it can happen any time of day or night, did you know that? – it doesn't have to be in the morning. James was so fast asleep I didn't want to disturb him so I crept about and used the washing bowl in the gulskhana. I decided to leave it there till morning. It was very late and, well, I didn't know what else to do. When I was getting back into bed there was a scratching at the door. Minto. He wouldn't go away and started whining and making a noise. I unlocked the door and let him in. He leapt at me and was so fussy I forgot to lock the door again. He settled down on my bed and I think we both fell asleep.' She paused, unwilling to go on to the next chapter.

Joe continued while she put her recollections in order. 'Iskander has told us that what appeared to Lily to be an argument in the garden was most certainly at least a difference of opinion. Iskander was trying to dissuade Zeman from carrying out his long-held plan of assassinating James.'

Joe paused to allow everyone to react to this in their own way. For once Sir George seemed to show the greatest surprise. He went on, 'Badal. This was revenge for the deaths at James's hand of his two older brothers twelve years ago. The ideal moment had come and Zeman was not going to let it pass. He had made his plans for escaping from the fort with his men, Iskander was unwillingly standing by and Zeman had changed into uniform ready for the long ride back to Afghanistan. At three o'clock he left his room and set off up the stairs to James's room.'

Betty began to shake and James put an arm around her. 'I'll tell you what happened next,' he said sharply, 'because this part concerns me and, quite honestly, I wish for Betty's sake it could have been left to lie!' He gave George a sour look and continued in the clear-cut, unemphatic tones of a soldier. 'I woke at whatever time you say it was with a knife at my throat. Zeman had a hand over my mouth and the point of his dagger pricking my jugular vein. He didn't want to kill me while I was unconscious – he woke me deliberately because he wanted me to understand *why* I was about to die. He hissed the names of his brothers and said he'd been there in the hills watching when I killed them all those years ago.' He paused for a moment and shook his head. 'He could only have been a child of ten. He was the one who fired a jezail at me. A jezail! Must have been as big as he was! He'd tracked me down and made a point of getting to know me when we met in Peshawar. I thought he liked me. As a matter of perverse fact, I think he did. But whether he liked me or not would be neither here nor there against the compulsion of badal: the dismal *danse macabre* of vengeance and counter vengeance. I've seen it before and I know how implacable, how destructive, it can be,' said James slowly. 'But that's the Pathan way. How we forget! They'll plot and plan and take years if necessary to get something right.

'But there was something even Zeman couldn't have calculated for! Frightful little Minto! He woke up and just went for him! Launched himself across the space between

266

the beds and went for his arm. The arm holding the dagger. Took Zeman completely by surprise. He started to pull his arm away but not fast enough and the dog got his teeth into Zeman's sleeve. He missed his flesh but it was enough. He swung his weight on Zeman's sleeve and fell between the beds, hanging on. That was deflection enough for me! While Zeman was trying to shake him off I picked up the candlestick by my bed – it's Benares brass, heavy and with a square base as I'm sure you've already checked, Joe – and I hit him on the head with it. A lucky blow, I think, because he slumped down without a murmur and I'm pretty sure he died very quickly after that.'

This was the account Joe had expected from James. He waited a moment to see if James had anything to add but his friend remained silent and, as it seemed to Joe, weary.

'Three o'clock and you and Betty were left with quite a problem!' said Joe. 'A guest, a military guest of some standing and influence, lying dead from a blow to the skull in the bedroom of the commanding officer of Gor Khatri. I wouldn't like to have to unravel all the implications of the code of melmastia! But you saw that it was a situation which could so readily be exploited by anyone with a fancy to do so, and they are thick on the ground in this part of the world! Afghan and Afridi would both have been at your throat next. As Grace pointed out to me, wars have started with much, much more trivial pretexts.'

'For the good of everybody, we had to pass it off as a death from natural causes,' Betty said. 'But we couldn't do that without Grace's help.'

'So I went along to Grace's room and asked her to attend Betty who'd been sick and that's what she thought she was being called to do when *you* opened your door and saw us in the corridor,' said James.

'Yes,' said Joe. 'The last person you would want to find sticking an oar in – Sandilands of the Yard!'

'Honest Joe who can't be doing with cover-ups and the diversion of the truth!' James said, remembering. 'Bit awkward that, I have to admit! But we did what we had to do. Grace came into the room and checked Zeman. He was dead by then . . .'

'Yes, nothing anyone could have done for him,' said Grace. 'And, while I'm in the witness box, so to speak, I'll just say that the real cause of death, the one I should have given at the autopsy was – a blow to the head resulting in subdural haemorrhage. The sharp edge of the candlestick had been to some extent blunted by a fold of Zeman's turban but the blow had been delivered with force enough to crack the skull and rupture blood vessels under the bone and bleeding had occurred internally into the space between the skull and the brain membrane. His thick hair also to a large extent concealed the wound which was not in itself very dramatic in appearance. You can imagine for yourselves the imperatives which led me to decide there and then to conceal the violent nature of this death.'

She paused and looked round, saying at last, 'Look here! I've worked for peace on the frontier all my grown-up life. I've worked to bring what James so truly called a *danse macabre* to an end at last. I'd have done or said anything to cut the cycle of death and revenge!'

'It was my idea to pass it off as poisoning, Joe,' Betty said. 'We thought first we'd just carry his body to the stairs and position the straight line of the wound along the edge of one of the stone steps to make it look as though he'd fallen but then we thought, "That's not going to deceive anybody!" Pathans move like cats – they don't go falling over their feet, not even in the dark. And, anyway, what would he have been doing on the stairs in the night? Too many questions raised! We had to think of some more natural reason for his death and then I remembered that, by chance, Zeman and I had both eaten the pheasant dish – no one else. If we could say that he and I alone of the group had been taken ill – food poisoning or something – that might be convincing. I told Grace I had actually been sick earlier that night and that gave her the idea . . .'

'We had to work fast,' Grace interrupted, sensing that

Betty had some qualms about recounting the next step of the deception. 'There was the question of hypostasis, of course. We would have to deal with Joe and we weren't quite sure how much knowledge of post-mortem procedure and the physical aspects of death go with being a London policeman these days, so I had to assume the very best information and evidence would be required. The body had to be placed without delay where eventually it would be discovered so that the blood and other fluids could settle into a convincing pattern. I took a flake of white stone from the steps and inserted it into the wound and then addressed the problem of the vomit.'

She looked round the pale faces at the table with a slight touch of malicious humour and said, 'In deference to everyone's sensibilities – and none more sensitive here than Iskander and Betty herself, I imagine – I will simply say in answer to your unvoiced questions – syringe! From porcelain washing bowl to the throat of the corpse was the work of a minute.'

'And then you artistically placed a trail from Zeman's room to the body and left a pond under his chin,' Joe confirmed.

'Yes. But this is where we hit a problem during the autopsy. I don't think it escaped your eagle eye, Joe, that the, um, solid material contained therein was relatively fresh. I had to assume that every London-trained policeman is familiar to some extent with vomit . . .'

Joe nodded. 'Ruined many a pair of copper's boots!'

'So I decided to tell the truth about the time of the expulsion of the part-digested matter rather than the actual time of the death. I skewed the estimate of rigor mortis and I don't think anyone was aware of that. It can vary quite a bit anyway. If I'd given 3 a.m. as the time of death Joe would have guessed at once that the pantomime in the corridor was not unconnected.'

'There was an alternative course of action,' said Joe.

'Yes, of course. We could have told you there and then. Tried to enlist your help. Don't think it didn't occur to me!

But James was adamant. He refused to confide in you.' She looked at Joe, head on one side. 'And now I know you better, Commander, I understand his reservations.'

'But there was something about the sick that gave it all away!' Lily said. 'I remember, Joe, when we went back to look at Zeman's clothes you said, "The smell – it takes me back to any Saturday night in Seven Dials." And then you went quiet for a bit and said, "Or does it?" I know what you were thinking! No alcohol!'

'That's right,' said Joe. 'George, you for one won't know that, unusually – and I have to ascribe this to stress brought on by association with the infuriating Rathmore for the space of an evening – Zeman and Iskander both indulged themselves in a brandy or two at the end of the meal. There was no olfactory trace of alcohol in the vomit ascribed to Zeman. "Children's party" rather than "Seven Dials gutter", you might say! Sorry, Betty! This isn't easy for any of us and particularly hard on you. So, incredibly, if the eleven o'clock vomit sample didn't belong to Zeman, no matter how intimate its association with the corpse, then it had to be someone else's eleven o'clock vomit. Betty had been sick at the appropriate time and – she was the only person at the party who did not drink any alcohol.'

'So if Betty was involved, James was involved too and Grace was helping in the cover-up,' Lily concluded.

'But I can't see,' said Grace, 'how you guessed about Minto's part in all this.'

'The tooth marks!' Lily said. 'Joe and I went back to the infirmary and checked over his clothes. There were holes in the sleeve of Zeman's shirt. And the distance between the holes was what you've all just seen between the teeth of that little mutt over there. And we knew he'd been trying to get into Betty's room because there are scratch marks in the paintwork on the door.'

'A formidable pair of investigators, you and Lily, it would seem,' said Grace. 'But tell me – if you had worked it out with such ease what stopped you from revealing all this?'

'I think it must have been the curlers!' Joe allowed himself a smile. 'I was unwilling to believe that a lady in curlers and dressing gown could possibly be on her way to a murder or the cover-up of a murder. I was completely taken in by you, Grace. And as for Betty – she should be treading the boards at the Old Vic!'

'We had a certain amount of luck too,' Grace admitted. 'The poultryman's revelation that the pheasant had been poisoned with arsenic was a bonus.'

'Yes! Innocent old Achmed! Played right into your hands. Rather superfluous, though, coming after your colourful account of death by androthingamajig!' Joe smiled. 'What imagination!'

Grace shook her head. 'Andromedotoxin! And I didn't make that up! There *is* such a condition – though I'm still waiting to see a real case of it.'

'This is all getting a bit self-congratulatory,' said Sir George reprovingly. 'May I remind you that we're accounting for a most regrettable death? What a devious crew I have to deal with! I don't wonder Iskander decided to hold a pistol to your heads! But where, politically speaking, do we stand now?'

'*I* would ask where, in the eyes of the Law, do we stand now?' said Joe firmly.

'I expect you're ready to answer your own question?' said Sir George.

'The death, being occasioned by an attempted murder on the part of the deceased, must be viewed as justifiable homicide,' said Joe. 'A clear case of self-defence. James had no alternative . . . anyone would have done the same. He was a man with, literally, a dagger at his throat and the thought that his wife also was likely to be similarly done to death as she slept at his side. No court in the land, military or civil, would convict James of murder or even manslaughter in the circumstances, but for the sake of order and clarity and honouring the legal process he should be arrested and charged and the case brought to court.'

Grace and James exchanged a look but remained silent.

'Well, there speaks the voice of Scotland Yard and the British Judicial System,' said Sir George, 'and, indeed, if James were so foolish as to crack someone on the head with a candlestick in a bedroom in Berkeley Square, I would agree that a trip to the Old Bailey was distinctly on the cards. But we are here on the North-West Frontier, practically a battle zone, not a court of law for hundreds of miles and a fort to run while James is languishing in chains. Hmm.'

Joe waited. He had grown used to hearing George rehearse an apparently insuperable problem which he would promptly solve by a quick change of direction. George turned suddenly to Iskander. 'This is your land, Iskander, the loss was your loss, an Afridi loss. What have you to say?'

'Dr Holbrook has spoken of the arrangements she made with Ramazad Khan. She bartered three lives for three lives and Ramazad agreed to cancel the debt. Before the whole tribe, he had taken upon himself the duty of badal for Zeman. As far as the Afridi are concerned the trail of revenge ends there.' He shrugged his shoulders and stared at the wall. 'What the British official response is does not concern me any longer. I wanted to know the truth. Now I have an admission of the truth. What *you* now do with it is your affair. Bury it if you wish.'

There was a long pause as everyone pondered his words. Yes, they had the truth but who had any use for it any longer? Apart from the intellectual satisfaction of knowing the answer to a puzzle there was solace for no one in it. Joe suddenly realized that he was the focus of everyone's attention. Iskander had reminded him that the Afridi were no longer in pursuit of revenge or justice and had passed the initiative back; Sir George would do and say anything which would smooth over the situation and Grace would support him in that. Betty looked at Joe, stricken and appealing, but James, expressionless, refused

272

to meet his eye. They were all waiting for him to speak, sensing his struggle with the uncompromising puritan side of his nature. Joe felt a flash of resentment. He was not a judge and jury – his role was to find out the details of a crime, ascertain who was responsible and deliver the accused up to the proper authorities. It was no part of his job to decide whether to pursue or abandon an enquiry. He knew exactly where his duty lay.

He considered the worst that could happen if he did that duty. An unpleasant few months for James and Betty while James was suspended from active service. He would be acquitted, of course, but in the meantime there would be gossip, speculation and probably exaggeration. He had seen Indian drawing rooms at work. And Grace, what of Grace? She would have to give testimony, a testimony which would do her great discredit as a doctor. The Amir would have no use for a physician whose name had been linked, in however misleading a context, with the mention of a poison. The Pathan who became aware of the story would no longer seek her help. Grace knew better than anyone the fragile nature of trust in these parts.

Joe held his friends', if not lives, at least careers and hopes, in his hands. It was easy to make a case for demanding the due process of the law; the official phrases formed unbidden on his lips. He looked at Sir George, whose expressive features were for once enigmatic.

Lily broke the silence. She seemed to be quoting from a poem that was unfamiliar to Joe.

> 'So many gods, so many creeds,
> So many paths that wind and wind,
> While just the art of being kind
> Is all this sad world needs.'

Lily added, 'Ella Wheeler Wilcox. Something to be said – after all – for an American education?'

Joe smiled at her. This darned girl, for whose safety he'd once condescendingly assumed responsibility, had the knack of reading his thoughts, pricking the balloon of his pomposity, of pushing him in the direction he knew he ought to be taking. 'I'm not aware of your Miss Wilcox, Lily, but I applaud her sentiments . . . though I prefer the more lyrical approach of Portia perhaps.'

Sir George interrupted. 'No need to go into all that "quality of mercy" business. We're all familiar with it. But how many people bother to quote a later line from Bassanio in support? Just one line. Says it all really. "To do a great right, do a little wrong." Often say that to myself. What about it, Joe?'

'Would there be any objectors if, after all, I proposed that the original findings of the autopsy carried out by Grace be adopted as the true record of what passed here at the fort on the evening of Thursday and the early morning of Friday?' Joe asked.

All shook their heads or murmured, 'No.'

'Carried unanimously,' said Sir George. 'And now I think we can all be away to our supper.'

As Joe walked along to the mess Lily took his arm and asked, 'Joe, can you tell me whether I'm left or right-handed?'

Joe was puzzled, thought for a moment and then said, 'Right-handed, but I couldn't swear to it.'

'Yes. You say that because you've watched me eating with my right hand but, actually, I'm *left*-handed. There aren't so many of us lefties around and I always notice when I come across another.'

'I see where you're going with this, Lily and – yes, you're right! But in view of what was said just now in the durbar room I think – better left alone, don't you? No good and quite a lot of harm might result if we went about stirring things up again. Time to practise "the art of being kind", wouldn't you say?'

'Okay by me,' said Lily cheerfully. 'Let's just think of it as "doing another little wrong", shall we? I understand now how Sir George can sleep at night!'

Chapter Twenty-Two

Grace stood on the wall looking down on the courtyard where her escort was assembling, feeling, for perhaps the first time in her life, the giddiness of self-doubt. She reminded herself briskly that cantonment life didn't really suit her. She wasn't cut out for intrigue (though she had done her best!). It suited her better to be in tribal territory. Issues were clearer there. She smiled. What nonsense! That's what she would have said a week ago. But now if she were honest she would admit to discovering in herself a quite reprehensible natural ability for deception! And *that* was a skill which might well come in very handy for survival in amongst the palace intrigue she was heading for! She brought her thoughts up short. Harry! What *would* Harry say if he could hear her?

As she watched, a troop of Afghani horsemen was forming up. The escort to Kabul, and the sort of people she could deal with. But they must be a bit puzzled by all their comings and goings over the last week! Perhaps it was just routine for them? And at least they were heading for home now. And Iskander? Grace acknowledged there were fences to mend there. How could you ever be sure with Iskander? On the whole, Grace thought he had probably forgiven her. And, after all, they were always, both of them, on the side of peace. It would even be a consolation to have him close by in Kabul – but that wouldn't please poor Lily.

Her thoughts were interrupted by a high-pitched, raucous wailing which made her flinch. Filing out into the courtyard, beaming with pride and preceding the escort through the gates, came the Scouts' pipe band. Hill men themselves, the Scouts were accustomed to bagpipes though not perhaps the authentic Scottish article. They were, nonetheless, practised in Scottish airs acquired from long-forgotten Victorian pipe-majors. Acquired also were the pipe banners, bright tartans, the pride of long-gone Scottish officers, making, as they fluttered in the wind, a gay contrast to the mud-coloured buildings, the mud-coloured hills and the khaki uniforms.

As Grace watched, James came and stood beside her. 'Come on, Grace!' he said as the pipe band struck up. 'This is all in your honour! "Bonnie Charlie's noo awa . . . Will ye no come back again?" Hope you don't mind? They're putting on quite a show to see you off!'

The band, playing lustily, skirled its way through the gates and fell in outside. The Afghani horses kicked and fretted, each restrained by a lean and rock-like bridle hand as they too lined up, baggage horses at the rear, Grace's horse and that of Iskander standing ready at the head of the double file. Joe, Lily and Betty made up a farewell party. All goodbyes and farewell speeches, Sir George officiating, had been said an hour earlier and there was nothing to prevent a smart take-off into the hills. Betty silently watched the departure of Grace, her friend and refuge. Reserved and watchful, Joe and Lily looked about them. Joe followed the direction of Lily's gaze and found, with no surprise, her attention concentrated on Iskander.

Calm and authoritative, Iskander said a few words to James and stepped forward to lead Grace to her horse. He handed her up on to the tall grey and took the reins of his own horse while Grace waved goodbye to the line of civilians and turned her head resolutely to the Khyber. The cortège started on its way. With the pipe band still playing enthusiastically, Joe, Lily and Betty began to make their way back into the fort.

'Let's go up on to the wall to watch them go,' said Lily. 'Anywhere so long as it's out of earshot of this mob!'

But once inside the fort Betty hurried to her room in

distress. Walking slowly, Lily took Joe's arm. It was an emotionally charged moment and clearly she was wrestling with indecision, wondering perhaps whether to confide in him until, 'Go ahead – ask me, Joe!' she said finally. And when, tactfully, he just looked a question, 'Nothing to tell, I'm afraid. He hasn't said a word about his intentions! He had chance enough but I suppose he has to get back to Kabul to find out what his position is there. Who knows – he may turn up in Simla or Delhi and then we'll think again. But I'm not counting on it! I think he's gone for good, Joe.'

Joe looked at her carefully. What was he looking for? Signs of a broken heart? There were none. No tears. A level tone. Could Grace have misinterpreted Lily's interest? She seemed thoughtful but there was something overriding this. Relief? Yes, he thought – relief. Perhaps Lily Coblenz had, after all, regretted her rash offer of a golden cage to a man of the hills. She would take back to Chicago the romantic and desperately sad tale of a handsome Pathan who broke her heart and whose heart she broke when she left him behind, in the comfortable knowledge that the man himself was not there to spoil her story with his awkward, untameable nature.

Joe wondered whether he was close enough to Lily to risk asking her directly about her feelings for Iskander. What the hell! He decided he was. 'Look, Lily,' he said. 'They made me responsible for your welfare and your safe return to Simla. Not a job I wanted but it's turned into more than just a responsibility. I care very much that you should return in good heart as well as sound in limb. What I'm trying to say is – well – I'd be very distressed if I thought you'd given your affections to a man who is incapable of returning them, a man who, as we speak, is riding away over the frontier, perhaps for ever. It might sound like the last reel of a moving picture, cinema organ playing in the background, but in real life it can be miserable! So – can you tell me? I'm your friend, remember!'

Lily took his hand in hers and smiled up at him, a smile

full of kindness and humour. 'I didn't "give my affections", Joe. They were snatched! I fell for the man! And it hurts, it certainly hurts that he didn't feel the same way. But I'll tell you something – when I was little, ten years old I think, Father took me to the mountains one summer. One of the hands brought in a black bear cub, an orphan I guess. Have you ever seen a black bear cub, Joe?'

He shook his head. 'No, but I can imagine the effect one would have on a ten-year-old girl!'

'Yes. Well, this was a particularly lovable animal and I was a very susceptible little girl. I was allowed to keep him for the whole summer. But it came time to go back to Chicago and I had to send him back into the forest to take his chances. Nearly broke my heart. I cried for a week and made everyone's life a misery. And perhaps that was a sort of . . . what do you call it? . . . an inoculation? It's happened again but I'll get over it. Strong heart, Joe!'

They trailed slowly on, each wrapped in thought, but suddenly Lily turned an anxious face to Joe. 'Listen! The band!'

Joe grimaced. '"Bonnie Dundee"! Again! Must be the third time they've been through that tune! Surely they could stop now?'

Lily was pale and tense. She gripped his hand. 'Not if no one told them to! They're awaiting orders. They're waiting for James to tell them to pack it in and fall out.' And then, 'Where *is* James? He's not come in!'

For an agonizing moment Joe was fixed to the spot, cursing himself for having ignored his instincts. He turned and started to run back towards the gate.

'Joe! Wait!'

He turned, angry at being delayed.

'No gun! Here! Catch!'

In one swift movement Lily threw a small gun to him.

He reached the gate and looked about. The Afghan troopers were well on their way to the Khyber but James had disappeared and only the pipe band remained, sweating and puffing. He seized a Scout by the arm. 'Major Lindsay?' he yelled above the din. 'Where is he?'

'Gone to cemetery with Iskander Khan,' he said pointing. 'Say one last prayer for Zeman Khan, sahib.'

Two hundred yards away James was walking briskly with Iskander, their backs to Joe. Iskander was leading his horse. Desperately Joe shouted a warning but it was drowned by the opening chords of the fourth rendition of 'Bonnie Dundee'. He set off to run, remembering at last the gun in his hand. He looked at it with dismay. Christ! What was this? Somebody must have put this in Lily's Christmas stocking! Would it repeat or was it single shot? Was it even loaded? Would it stop a man? A determined man? Joe had his doubts. But still it might make a warning noise. He fired it into the air. The two figures walked on oblivious.

Joe ran faster, thoughts pounding in his head as the energy coursed through his body. Iskander had even warned them. 'Always an Afridi,' he had said. He had reminded them that he also lived by the Pathan code of pukhtunwali. It had no significance for him that Ramazad and the tribe had washed away their right to badal – Iskander never had! He wouldn't be bought off. He had stayed true to his customs and to his friend. He loved Zeman and had taken it upon himself to exact retribution from whoever had killed him. Alexander and Hephaestion? That's what poor Lily had run into, all unknowingly. And he had returned to the fort as he had told them clearly himself to identify the killer and had sat opposite James when he confessed to the killing. He wouldn't kill James while he was under the shield of his hospitality but now, outside the walls of the fort in the Muslim cemetery, he was free to do so. And what better place than at Zeman's grave?

Yes, that's what he was planning to do! Leave James's body on top of Zeman's grave. The symbolism was obvious. A grave for two warriors! Joe could hardly breathe. The hot air was scorching his lungs and through cracked lips he gasped and heaved as he ran. Sweat ran down his

280

face blinding him. He swept his eyes clear to see that the two men walking companionably together had arrived at the grave-side and Iskander had tethered his horse and taken up a position facing the fort. James, across the grave from him, still had his back to Joe and his head was bent in prayer. Joe screamed again and fired the gun. James almost turned around but Iskander spoke to him and reclaimed his attention. Iskander had spotted Joe.

He put his left hand into his tunic, drew something out and extended his right hand to James. James leaned nearer. The old Pathan trick! Grasping their target warmly by one hand they would use the other to stick a knife in his ribs.

'James! No! The knife! James! Watch for the knife!' Joe could hardly raise the breath to shout. Too late, Joe saw James turn towards him, hearing him at last but now, by the very act of turning, exposed and fatally distracted. Joe had played into Iskander's hands. The deflection of James's attention left him wide open to the inevitable quick lunge.

The crack of a rifle shot threw Joe automatically to the ground. He crashed down, raising a cloud of dust and sand that clogged his mouth and filled his eyes. Unbelieving, he raised his head and rubbed the grit from his eyes to see the body of James lying over the grave. Iskander, weaving from side to side, his left arm shattered and bloody, had been sent spinning back several yards by the force of the shot. As Joe watched he staggered back to the grave, stood for a moment and collapsed across James's body.

Careless of further rifle fire, Joe surged to his feet and hurled himself forward, arriving, lungs bursting, to stand groaning helplessly over the two blood-drenched bodies.

'Shit! God Almighty! Fucking hell!'

Joe sobbed with joy to hear a stream of curses such as he had not heard since he and James had shared a trench.

'Course I'm all right! When a bloody .303 bullet whizzes past your ear, you hit the ground! See you did too! How

281

did you know, Joe? My God! Get this murderous bugger off me, will you? And who the hell fired that shot? Wasn't you with that little pop gun!'

They looked back to the fort where for a second a blonde head bobbed between the battlements and disappeared.

'Oh, my God! Annie Oakley!' said James.

Together they raised Iskander's body, from which the blood was pumping at an alarming rate. The left arm was a shredded mass of flesh and ribbons of khaki sleeve. But, 'He's alive!' said Joe. 'James, he's still alive! Give me your lanyard and I'll try to get a tourniquet on this.'

With practised hand, Joe worked swiftly to stop the blood flow. 'Grace! Where are you?' he groaned. 'Half-way to bloody Kabul by now! Here, put a finger on this, James.'

As they worked on him a knife slipped from the shattered left sleeve and fell on to the blood-soaked earth. Rubies winked in the black jade hilt and Joe recoiled from it as from a rearing cobra. Iskander's eyes flickered open for a moment and Joe caught a familiar green gleam of amusement.

'God! That was meant for me!' said James. And with relief of tension came a flood, a rush of confused words. 'He asked me to come out here with him. To discuss the siting and wording of a headstone for Zeman . . . said he wanted to say one last prayer for him . . . thought it would be a good idea if I joined him. Least I could do, I thought. He was going to kill me,' said James. 'Wasn't he, Joe? For Zeman. He was finishing the job for him. Look.' He reached over, shuddering, and took something from Iskander's right hand.

Joe peered at it. 'It's a crucifix,' he said in puzzlement.

'It's *my* crucifix,' said James. 'I put it into the hand of Harry Holbrook seconds before I shot him. He was a good man. A man of God. I thought it might bring him some comfort at the last. He firmly believed that God was with him in these hills. Though the behaviour of those two bloodthirsty tormentors must have tested his faith to the

282

limit . . . They were torturing him, Joe. The very worst they could think of . . . He could never have survived such treatment. He couldn't ask me not to give Grace all the dreadful details – they'd torn out his tongue – but I knew what he wanted me to say when I got back and I said it. I've never told anyone the truth until now. But Zeman must have found the crucifix on the body and kept it all those years. A talisman? A reminder? A clue to the identity of the man who killed his brothers?'

'All those, I expect,' said Joe, putting a calming arm around his friend's shoulder. 'And he must have vowed to return it one day. I think he had it with him to press into your hand as he killed you. Iskander removed it from Zeman's body – there was a moment on the stairs when he and his men had sole access to the corpse. He must have taken it then and put it away intending always to use it himself. To complete the circle.'

'Well, it seems to have taken a rifle shot to get their attention! Here comes Eddy Fraser sprinting ten yards ahead and the whole pipe band at the double!'

As the sun dipped behind the line of the Hindu Kush a bugle sounded the haunting notes of the Last Post and the small party by the second fresh grave in the Muslim cemetery turned and began to make its way slowly back to the fort.

Betty left James to escort Lily and hurried to take Joe's arm. 'There's no good time, Joe,' she said, 'to thank you for what you've done. This is a bad time and I'm having trouble with my thoughts and my words . . . but if I've learned anything from this awful country it's to do and say things at once however badly because it doesn't often give you a second chance. If you hadn't noticed that James was missing it's his grave we'd be standing by now.'

'And Iskander would be well on his way to Afghanistan, his duty done.'

'Not happy, though,' said Betty. 'I will do him the justice

283

of saying that he would not have been happy.' She paused for a moment, looking at the two warriors' graves side by side. 'His men didn't come back for him. Why, do you think? They must have heard the shot?'

'Obeying orders. I think it was simpler for Iskander to just say, "Ride! Don't look back, don't come back. Take Dr Holbrook and I'll join you if all goes well." It's what I would have done.'

Betty sighed. 'So Grace is a hostage up there with those barbarians?'

Joe laughed. 'Grace is *never* a hostage! She is up there with friends. Friends who understand her, who value her and who will make sure she gets to the Amir in safety.'

'And there'll be no reprisals? About Iskander, I mean.'

'No. I don't think so. You heard Sir George on this. What he had to say was brutal perhaps but the truth. Iskander was an outlaw. There will be no follow-up from the Afridi. The Amir? Iskander wasn't directly related to him and there's no shortage of eager young officers to take his place. That end of things should be all right, I think, especially since there'll be Grace in position to keep the lid on.' Joe was being determinedly cheerful. Betty had twice in the past week had to deal with murderous attacks on her husband and, if he had it right, was carrying a sad burden. He wondered if she would ever be ready to share it with him.

'How do you think Lily's taking it, Joe? I mean, I have a feeling she thought Iskander rather special . . . not so special as Zeman perhaps but she seemed to get on well with him. What do you think a woman feels when she's killed a man? Lily had to do it, I know, but even so . . . taking a life, Joe, that's something women should never have to do. It's something completely against our nature. We save life . . . we give life. Will she ever . . . do you think there's a chance she will ever be reconciled with what she's done? With what she had to do?'

'Devastating. It was devastating and it will take her a long time to recover from it but she's a resilient girl and very intelligent. She knows she did what had to be done.' He smiled. 'Do you know what she said when James asked her why she hadn't simply ordered the sentry to fire at Iskander from the wall? She said, "I didn't know the feller – how was I to know how good a shot he was? This was a job that had to be done right. First time. I knew I could do it so I grabbed his rifle." She had the time to think about what she was doing and made, in my estimation, the right decision. Bless her, she tried for a wounding shot – went for his left arm – darned near impossible at that range – and she very nearly pulled it off. But it's not only women whose natural impulse it is to thwart an aggressor. It's a very basic human reaction. We're born with it and so I suppose you could argue that it's God-given. But women have one great advantage over men. We can take lives but we can't create them. It may seem an odd thought but it's my idea that when Lily has a child of her own, when she has created life, that's when I think she'll start to forgive herself for taking one. I shall pray for Lily. No reason why God should listen to *me*, I've been off the air so to speak for quite a while, but I'll have a go.'

Betty stopped walking, turned to him and looked up at him earnestly. 'Joe?' she said quietly. 'When communications are restored – would you mention my name too?'

Joe squeezed her arm. 'I already have.'

Lily was glad of the support of James Lindsay's strong right arm. Pale, with red-rimmed eyes, she was avoiding contact with everyone except for James and Joe. They had found her, a shaking heap behind the battlements, wild-eyed and speechless, the .303 rifle by her side, and it had taken Joe a long time to persuade her to let him take her back to her room. He recognized shock when he saw it and stayed with her for hours, his arm around her shoulders, talking quietly. If she'd been a man he'd have known exactly what to do. What the hell! He'd summoned a havildar and sent him off to find half a pint of rum.

285

'I've arranged with Sir George that he will take you back to Simla tomorrow if that's still what you want, Lily,' James said. 'Joe will be going with you too. Couldn't have a more perfect pair of knights to escort you.'

Lily managed a smile. 'Joe is more like Sir George than he would ever want to admit, I think. In fact, give him a few more years and you won't be able to distinguish the one from the other.'

'Lily,' said James. 'Will you forgive me for ever thinking . . .'

'James!' said Lily, interrupting. 'I think we've both had to do a little reassessing. I was a lot smarter than you gave me credit for and you were a lot dumber than I thought. Forget it.'

'Well, at least let me thank you for what you did this morning. I can't believe it but I haven't until now had a chance to . . .'

Again she broke in. 'Thank me for saving your life? Any woman would have done the same. Ask Betty.'

James stood still and looked about him. They were out of earshot of the rest of the group. 'You know?'

Lily nodded.

'But how? What . . .?'

'Joe and I looked into your room. We knew what we were looking for and we found it. Candlesticks on each bedside table. You and Betty are both right-handed. I notice these things. If you, James, had really hit Zeman you would automatically have picked up your own candlestick from the table on the right of your bed – that's on the side away from Zeman's knife hand, and hit him . . .' She aimed the side of her hand at James's head. 'Allowing for the fact that he was hovering over you . . . somewhere about there. On the left side of his head. You'd need to be a contortionist to have hit him where he was hit – over the other side. But for Betty, reaching for her own candlestick . . .'

'Does Joe know this?'

'We haven't talked about it but he's pretty smart so

I shouldn't wonder. He seems to catch on to things a minute or two after I've worked it out.' Again a faint smile. 'But we're neither of us the kind to go shooting off our mouths where it's not necessary. I think it would be a very bad idea if anyone else were to find out. For Betty's peace of mind. And that's what you have to hold on to, James. Not much else matters in this ghastly affair. Don't be concerned for me. I'm tough and I guess I don't have Betty's Christian conscience to wrestle me down. Don't get me wrong – I have a relationship with God but it's not the regular kind.'

They stood to watch the last blood-red segment of the sun slide out of view and Lily shivered. 'Sundown. Bad time of day for humankind, my pa always says.'

James ran his eyes over the horizon and the gloomy shadows of the Khyber. 'Bad country for humankind. Brings out the best but it brings out the worst as well. Look at that uncompromising ugliness! What are we all doing here? It isn't a country worth fighting for. It's not worth the bones of either of those gallant men in that cemetery. Leave it to bury its dead, Lily.'